ESPRESSO

A ZION SAWYER COZY MYSTERY

Volume 3

ML Hamilton

www.authormlhamilton.net

ESPRESSO

First print

Writing started as a hobby when I was very young. I never would have dreamed it would become something that gives me such joy. I hope it gives my readers even a fraction of the joy it gives me.

Thank you, as always, for your undying support and may there be a truly excellent cup of coffee in your day.

Writing started as a hobby when I was very young. I never would have dreamed it would become something that gives me such joy.
I hope it gives my readers even a fraction of the joy it gives me.
Thank you, as always, for your undying support and may there be a truly excellent cup of coffee in your day.

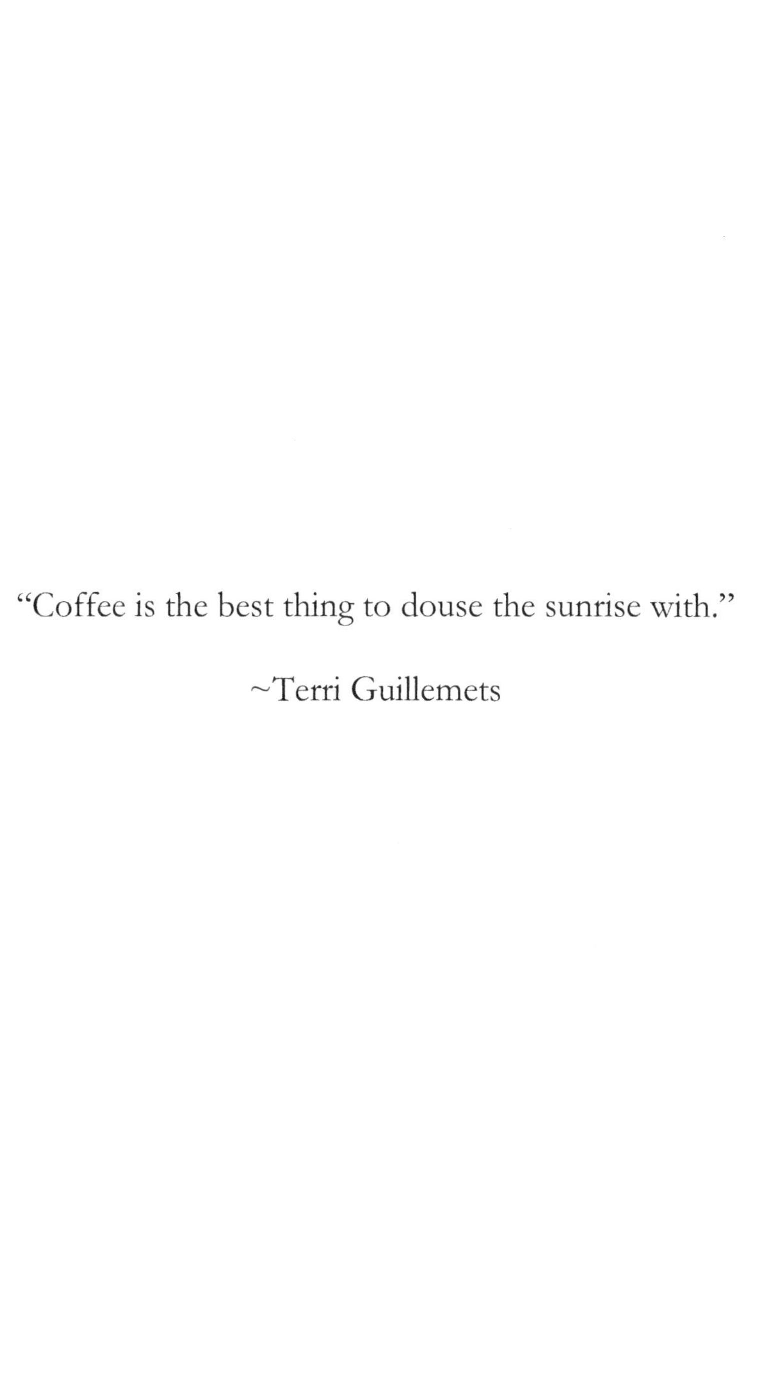

"Coffee is the best thing to douse the sunrise with."

~Terri Guillemets

CHAPTER 1

"Zion!"

Tate.

She quickened her pace and moved through the kitchen to the counter. What was wrong now?

"I'm here," she said, crossing around the counter to meet him in the middle of the floor.

His eyes darted around the room and Zion became aware of everyone staring at them – Tallah behind the register, Dottie at her kneading board, her mother at the table before the window. A young couple sat on the couches to their right.

Focusing back on her, he drew a deep breath.

"What's up?" she asked him.

He opened his mouth to speak, then before she could react, he stepped forward, catching her face in his hands. Zion didn't move as he lowered his mouth and kissed her. And what a kiss! Her hands fluttered as he deepened the kiss, then finally they came to rest on his shoulders, pulling him toward her, rather than away.

After a moment, he broke off and braced his forehead against hers. "Don't go away with David," he said in a husky voice.

* * *

Zion looked out the window of her little cottage and noticed the leaves had started to fall. It was early October and she'd been in Sequoia the last six months. In that time, she'd inherited a cottage and a coffee shop, got and lost a boyfriend, and recently become a social hermit. She eased back behind the curtains as Tate Mercer pushed a lawnmower out of his garage and onto the lawn.

Last July, she'd been seeing her lawyer, David Bennett, but Tate had ruined that for her.

She sighed. She wasn't being fair. She'd been thinking that things weren't right with David before Tate had forced her into a decision.

She replayed the scene over in her mind as she watched him pull the cord to get the lawnmower going, the muscles in his forearms flexing.

She hadn't gone away with David, but then she hadn't exactly started anything with Tate either. His kiss had taken her off-guard. She'd liked it. She liked him, but she felt like she was betraying David when she found herself returning the kiss.

A difficult talk with David had ensued. He'd been so hurt, so upset, he'd even agreed to forgive her for kissing another man. That made her feel horrible about herself. What sort of person went around kissing other men when she was supposed to be going away on a romantic weekend with her boyfriend?

Her best friend, Rebekah, hadn't understood her dilemma. To Rebekah, kissing Tate was just Zion's inner soul telling her the relationship with David was over. But Zion wasn't Rebekah and kissing meant something. Going away for a weekend meant something, so naturally, she'd broken things off with David as a result. She hated it when Rebekah was right, even when she was wrong.

Her mother hadn't scolded her, and both Tallah and Dottie thought Tate's gesture was romantic, but he hadn't let her come to her own decision about David and that made her mad. She braced her forehead against the window molding and closed her eyes.

She wasn't being fair again. She'd known the relationship with David had a shelf-life. Going away for that weekend had been a really bad idea. It was a desperate attempt to hang on to something that was already dead. David was the man she would have gone for when she lived in San Francisco. Educated, polished, fashionable, gainfully employed. He was perfect in every way, but when he kissed her…when he kissed her there weren't any sparks.

There were with Tate and that made Zion angry and confused. Tate had a past that scared her. Tate was an ex-cop and something had happened to him that put shadows in his eyes and ruined his marriage. Zion didn't need that. She didn't need someone with darkness lurking in their soul. But God, when he'd kissed her, she'd responded like she'd never responded before. He ignited something in her and she couldn't get him off her mind.

For three months, she hadn't been able *to get him off her mind*, which is why she avoided him. Thankfully, he also avoided her. He hadn't come into the *Caffeinator* and she hadn't gone to the hardware store. It was better this way. Any man who elicited a riot of emotions in her had to be all bad. When they were forced into contact with each other, they spoke politely and distantly. No one would guess what lay between them, except most people knew. Gossip in a town like Sequoia was rampant.

The last social function they'd both had to attend had been the funeral of their mutual friend Jaguar's mother. Jerome Jarvis, aka Jaguar, had returned home after a successful career as a rock god. His mother had suffered from Alzheimer's and she'd died tragically just a few months ago. Nothing was going to keep Zion from going to her funeral and being there for her friend, not even Tate.

Although she had to admit, seeing him in a collared shirt and slacks had made her heart flutter a little in excitement. He'd treated her politely, as if he hadn't had his mouth on hers in her own store. She'd acted the same way. She didn't need a man. The fiasco with David proved that. She needed to keep working on herself.

Cleo, her kitten, rubbed against Zion's legs. She was getting so big, all long legs and whip thin body. Zion picked her up and nuzzled her dark head, sighing in pleasure when Cleo started to purr. She was going through her awkward teenage stage, but she was Zion's little princess and Zion told her so every chance she got.

She let the curtain fall closed and blocked the sight of Tate pushing the lawnmower over his lawn, his brown hair covered by a baseball cap, the sexy panther tattoo visible on his forearm, his muscular calves on display in his board shorts. She missed him. She missed their friendship and she missed…

No, she wasn't going to let herself think it. She didn't miss anything else. She was working on herself and that was enough for now. The problem wasn't Tate; the problem was having days off. They gave her too much time to think and to want things she had no business wanting. Dottie was making her take at least one day off a week. That day off had never coincided with Tate's day off before. That was why she couldn't get him off her mind today.

Her cell phone rang distracting her and she set Cleo down, hurrying over to the coffee table and snatching it up. Her mother's name flashed across the display, asking to video chat. She climbed onto the couch, folding her legs under her, and thumbed it on. Cleo jumped up in her lap, turned a few circles and settled.

A moment later, Gabrielle Sawyer's face appeared on the screen. She had dark blue eyes, framed by glasses, and a shag haircut that had gone mostly grey. She wasn't as tall as Zion and had a pear-shaped figure, but Zion smiled seeing her. She missed her parents so very much now that she'd broken things off with David and had put her friendship with Tate on hold. *It was lonely working on yourself,* she thought.

"Hey, Mom," she said brightly, hoping she didn't sound manic.

"Hey, sweet girl, how are you doing?"

"Great. How are you and Daddy?"

"We're great. Your father took the day off to go golfing. He's starting to do that more and more. I think he's planning to retire."

Zion squinted at the screen. She could just see something in the background, behind Gabi's head, but she couldn't make it out. "How do you feel about him retiring?"

"If that's what he wants to do, I'm all for it. We each have to make our own journey, darlin," she said.

A few months ago, Gabi had discovered yoga. That had caused a transformation in all their lives from kale smoothies to talk of Zen mastery to yoga in Zion's front yard in yoga pants. Before that it had been piano playing, but the neighbors had complained so much, Gabi had given it up just to keep the peace.

"How's Rascal?"

Gabi bent over, giving Zion a view of the image behind her. Zion leaned closer again, blinking. She still wasn't sure what she was seeing behind her mother, but she forgot it a moment later as Rascal's scruffy face filled the screen.

"Here's our widdle, precious man," Gabi said, kissing the terrier's head.

Rascal licked her in return.

"Hey, buddy," Zion called, waving at him.

Gabi set him down again and Zion squinted a third time. Suddenly, it coalesced in her mind and her eyes widened. When Gabi again filled the screen, Zion realized her mouth was hanging open. "Um, Mom, what's that behind you?"

Gabi looked over her shoulder, then turned back to Zion, beaming. "The studio."

"The studio? What studio?"

"My art studio. Your father designed it in the atrium."

Zion pressed a hand to her forehead. This conversation was about to take a weird turn and she felt it as sure as she sat here. "What atrium?"

"Oh, we had an atrium added to the back of the house. The natural light coming in there is divine."

"Hold on. You built an atrium why?"

"For my painting. I need natural light for painting."

"Painting?" Zion blew out air and winced as Cleo began to knead her legs through her sweats. "Since when do you paint?"

Gabi thought for a moment. "Um, September 4th. Yeah, it was September 4th. I woke up in the morning and I thought, you know what I've always wanted to do, I've always wanted to paint."

"What about yoga? And kale smoothies?"

"Well, I think yoga is for people who can reach an inner calm. I tried to reach my inner calm, but for the most part, I think I reached inner country road, which was better than my usual inner interstate highway, but not nirvana." Gabi's eyes widened. "Oh, did I tell you? I'm into *Nirvana* now. Their music inspires my painting, but I have to make sure I use my headphones. The neighbors are some old fuddy duddies."

Zion blinked a few times. There was a lot in that conversation that needed unpacking. "Okay, can we just back this train up a few feet?"

"Sure."

"You built an atrium?"

"Yes."

"And you've started painting?"

"Right."

"And you've given up yoga and kale smoothies, but you're into *Nirvana*?"

"On the nose."

Zion had reached the part of the conversation that she hadn't really wanted to have. "Is that one of your paintings behind you?"

"It is."

"Mom," said Zion in her calmest voice. "It looks like a nude."

"Oh, it is. I'm taking a nude painting class at the community college."

"You're what now?" Zion could feel a headache hammering in her temples. "Is that a nude man from the class?"

"No," said Gabi, glancing over her shoulder. "That's your father."

Oh, hell no! Zion slapped the phone down on her thigh. You couldn't unsee that. There wasn't enough bleach in the world to wipe this image out of her mind.

"Zion? What happened? Where did you go?"

"Mom," she moaned, "why?"

"Why did I paint your father? Well, we've been married for a long time, Zion, and sometimes you need to reignite…"

"Nope, no, don't say it!"

"Oh, stop it. I didn't raise you to be a prude. There's nothing wrong with the human body."

"There is when it's your father." Although, to be fair, Zion would never have guessed that swirl of peach colored paint was her father. Gabi was more of an abstract artist, if Zion were being charitable.

"Oh, you're being so silly. Turn the phone back over."

"Move away from the painting first," Zion said, covering her eyes as if she could still see it.

"Oh for goodness sakes!" huffed Gabi. "Fine. I've turned around."

Zion cautiously lifted the phone, peeking at the screen. She saw Gabi and the green wall behind her…wait, green? The walls in the house had always been a pleasant taupe. What the hell was wrong with her mother?

"The walls are green?"

Gabi looked over her shoulder. "Are you going to tell me you have a problem with this too?"

"No, but what's going on, Mom?"

"What do you mean?"

"Is this a midlife crisis?" she asked worriedly.

"I'm a little beyond midlife, Zion. No, this isn't a midlife crisis, this is a woman who is finally free to be her best self. I'm exploring new and exciting things. Your father's onboard."

He hadn't been onboard with kale smoothies, but apparently, he'd agreed to pose in the nude for her mother.

Maybe he was onboard. She shuddered at the visual image that popped into her head.

"You get to this point in your life, sweetheart, where you say what the hell, why not? What have I got to lose? And you just go for it."

Zion sighed, a frown knitting her brow. *What the hell? Why not?* She eased Cleo onto the couch and climbed to her feet, going to the window and pulling back the curtains to look out. Tate was using a hedge clipper to trim the hedge before his windows, the muscles in his back flexing. She'd replayed their kiss in her mind so many times. It had been hot and wild and full of potential. But he scared her. She knew there was something in his past, something dark and tragic, something that she didn't need to get entangled in. However, if her mother could take risks at her age, so could she, right?

"Zion?" called Gabi.

Zion lifted the phone and smiled at her. "You're right, Mom. Why the hell not?" she said.

* * *

After wandering around the cottage for most of the day, Zion decided to drive into Sequoia and get dinner at the *Bourbon Brothers' BBQ*. Her closest friend in Sequoia, Cheryl Ford, owned it with her husband and his brother. Of all the places in Sequoia, the barbecue was hopping all hours of the day.

She parked in the municipal parking lot and walked down to the restaurant, passing Jaguar's music store. It hadn't opened yet, but he was planning a Grand Opening in a few weeks. She was looking forward to it. His past bandmates were coming and there was going to be food and music and dancing.

The windows of the store were covered with butcher paper, so she couldn't see inside. She tried the door, but it was locked. She hadn't seen him in a few days and she was wondering how everything was coming along. Jaguar had rubbed her the wrong way when he first came back into town, but she'd soon realized that the arrogance was all part of his act.

She crossed the street and hurried to the barbecue. When she opened the door, the sound of classic rock and the smell of roasting meats struck her. The younger brother, Daryl Ford, manned the register. Daryl was clean shaven, handsome with warm brown skin and deep chocolate colored eyes. Daryl always had an interesting pattern shaved into his hair.

He waved at Zion when he spotted her and called into the kitchen. Zion walked up to the counter next to him, noting that most of the booths were filled with customers. No matter what time of the year, the barbecue was always busy.

"Hey, girl," he said, flashing his white-toothed smile at her.

"Hey, Daryl, break any hearts since breakfast?"

"All of them," he said, laughing.

She could see his brother Dwayne through the order window. Dwayne had a full black beard, speckled with silver, and short cropped black hair that was also threaded with silver. His arms were the size of small trees and he was a few inches taller than Daryl. He spotted her through the window.

"You know you can just come on back," he said, jerking his chin toward the door.

Zion went around the end of the counter, but stepped back as Pedro, the busboy, came through the swinging door, carrying a bucket for dishes. "Sorry, Pedro," she said, easing around him.

"No worries," he said, smiling at her as he went out to clear off a table in the restaurant.

She pushed open the door and stepped inside. Alfred, Dwayne's short-order cook, came out of the walk-in refrigerator. Alfred always buzzed around like a busy bee, and he and Dwayne had worked out a sort of ballet between them, moving from the grill to the prep counter without running into each other.

"Out of the way," Alfred said.

Zion moved back against the wall to avoid him. She didn't think she'd ever heard Alfred say anything else to her. He was always scolding her that she was in his way. She didn't even know if he had a family or where he'd come from. Alfred was not a man concerned about making new friends.

"Chery!" bellowed Dwayne, slopping barbecued pork onto a toasted bun.

Cheryl appeared out of the small office next to the kitchen. Cheryl Ford was one of those women who would draw people's attention when she was seventy. She had a voluptuous figure, close-cropped black hair, and creamy brown skin that didn't have a flaw. Her eyes were her finest feature, drawing you in with their warmth and sincerity.

"What?" she shouted at him, then spotted Zion. Coming over, she gave Zion a hug. "How about dinner, sweetie?"

Cheryl was probably ten years older than Zion, but it didn't matter. They'd hit it off from the beginning.

"I'd love some dinner."

Cheryl grabbed two baskets and held them out to her husband. He made two sandwiches and took the baskets, adding coleslaw on the side. He passed them back to her and kissed her cheek. She nudged him with her hip and nodded for Zion to open the door. As Zion did so, Pedro came back in with his bucket full and went to the sink.

Cheryl paused on the other side of the door. "Daryl, bring us two beers," she commanded.

"Anything you want, Princess," Daryl said, bowing.

Zion smiled at him. The Ford family always made her happy. Their love and dedication to each other made her a little envious. She wouldn't mind having that for herself.

She and Cheryl took a seat in an empty booth. Cheryl passed her a basket and they both dug in. A moment later, Daryl appeared with their beers and Zion took a sip, washing the spicy barbecue down. She loved eating here and she probably ate here more than she should, but it was hard to pass up something that tasted this good.

"What's going on?" asked Cheryl, looking at her over the sandwich she held in her hands.

"Nothing. I had the day off and I was tired of sweeping down cobwebs."

"That's not it. Something's bothering you."

Zion looked around the restaurant. "Does Sequoia do anything for Halloween?"

"What?"

"Like decorate the stores or hold events."

"Not really."

Zion considered that. It might draw more people to their businesses if they did. She could present it to the Chamber of Commerce. ""What if we had a Halloween festival? We could offer kids candy to trick-or-treat in our stores. We could put up fliers and post it on the Sequoia social media sites."

Cheryl frowned. "Does Sequoia have social media sites?"

"It sure does. And I heard the fairgrounds are doing a haunted house this year to attract tourists."

Cheryl considered it. "That Sabrina Clark, the event planner at the fairgrounds, sure has brought some new ideas to the town."

"Well, they're not bad. Look how much money we made off *Redwood Stock*."

"And someone died," said Cheryl.

"True, but that was an isolated incident."

Cheryl nodded and took another bite, chewing contemplatively. Her eyes narrowed on Zion. "Something else is bothering you."

Zion shifted uncomfortably in her seat. Damn Cheryl's motherly instincts. It was hard to resist those penetrating brown eyes. "I'm just wondering if I made a mistake leaving everything in the City to come here."

Cheryl set down her sandwich. "Where's this coming from all of a sudden? I thought you loved it here."

"I do, but you're my only friend."

"That's not true. You have Deimos and Dottie." She braced her chin with her hand. "Is this about Tate?"

"What?" Zion reared away. "No." She shook her head, her red curls bouncing. "No, not at all."

"Mmmhmm," said Cheryl, eyeing her.

Zion pushed the basket away and leaned on the table. "I feel horrible about David. He won't even talk to me."

"Do you want to talk to him?"

"Well, I'd like to be friends."

Cheryl waved that off. "I've never been friends with an ex in my life. It doesn't work." She took a sip of beer. "Do you like Tate?"

"What? No, no!" she said emphatically.

Cheryl's brows rose. "Really?"

Zion held up a hand and let it fall. "I don't know, okay? I felt so guilty about David that I wouldn't return Tate's calls. We've been avoiding each other for months now."

"Why do you feel guilty about David?"

"We were supposed to go away for the weekend and then I kissed another man, in my store, in front of people."

Cheryl gasped, fluttering a hand against her chest. "Heavens to Betsy," she said dramatically.

Zion laughed. "Stop it."

"You hussy!"

Zion laughed harder. "You're impossible." She picked up her own beer and took a sip.

"Just answer a simple question, okay?"

"Okay," Zion said.

"Did you like the kiss with Tate?"

Did she like it? It's all she'd thought about for months now. "It's not that simple."

"It is that simple. Did you like the kiss? Yes or no?"

"The thing is Tate has issues. He left the police force – why? He got divorced – why? He moved here – why?'

"Yes or no?"

"And when I look into his eyes I can see shadows. I see that he's seen or done things he shouldn't have. It scares me. I need a guy that's stable and collected and grounded."

"Yes or no?"

Zion closed her eyes briefly and drew a deep breath. "Yes," she said reluctantly.

"Then why don't you give it a try? What have you got to lose?"

My heart, thought Zion, but she kept it to herself. "Nothing I guess. It's better than painting nudes."

Cheryl thought about that one for a while. "What?"

Zion pulled the basket back to herself and took another bite of her sandwich. "Let's just say my mother has a new hobby and leave it at that."

Cheryl nodded. "Enough said for certain."

* * *

Zion slowed her car as she drove past Tate's house. His windows were lit from within and she wondered if he was still awake. It was only 8:30, so odds were he'd be up, but she panicked and drove on to her own house. What a coward she was becoming!

She got out of the car and walked up to her door, fumbling to find the right key. She should have left the outside light on, especially now that it was getting dark earlier as fall moved toward winter. Pushing the right key into the lock, she turned it and shoved the door open, wondering if she was ready for winter in Sequoia. Would she need snow tires on her Optima?

She would have asked Tate in the past, but they weren't exactly speaking to each other. Maybe that was her way back into his life. She could drop by the hardware store and talk about tires. Oooh, that would be such a sexy conversation!

She slammed the door in frustration and Cleo jumped off the couch, making a trilling noise as she walked over to weave around Zion's legs. Zion hung her purse in the closet and went into the bedroom, throwing off her jeans and long-sleeved t-shirt and tugging on her pajamas. She shoved her feet into her fuzzy pink slippers and went into the bathroom to wash her face.

Pulling her heavy hair up into a ponytail, she looked at her reflection in the mirror over the sink and reach for the moisturizer, squirting some into her hand. She smoothed it over the freckles across her nose and cheekbones, then sighed. What was wrong with her today? She usually didn't mope around like this. Why was she feeling so lonely all of a sudden?

Her phone rang on the sink next to her and she looked down, a flush of happiness washing over her when she saw Rebekah's name on the display. She grabbed it up, hurrying out of the bathroom and shutting off the light. She thumbed the phone on and put it to her ear as she climbed beneath the covers on her bed. Cleo jumped up next to her and began kneading the blanket.

"Hey, Becks," she said into the phone. "I'm so glad to hear from you."

In response, Rebekah burst into tears.

"Whoa, whoa! What's going on?"

"I broke it off with Wendel," Rebekah sobbed.

Wendel had been Rebekah's latest doctor boyfriend for the past two years, the one she'd convinced herself was the right one to marry. She'd agreed to move in with him instead of getting an engagement ring. Zion had tried to convince her it wasn't a good idea, since Rebekah had lived with five men since college. Wendel was just the most recent of these. Rebekah always winded up worse off than the men, homeless and without furniture of any kind.

"Oh, honey, I'm so sorry. What happened?"

Rebekah sniffed dramatically. Zion knew this was an ugly crying session by the amount of sniffing because Rebekah was one of those rare women who could cry prettily if she wanted. Everything Rebekah did was pretty. While Zion was tall, buxom, and freckled, Rebekah had a svelte figure that fashion just draped over, gorgeous straight black hair that came to the center of her back, naturally tanned skin, and almond-shaped, heavily lashed dark eyes. If she was sniffling, the breakup had to be serious.

"He's such an ass!" she wailed.

Zion drew a deep breath and settled back in the pillows. This was going to be a long night, she could tell. "What happened?"

"We went to the mall to see a movie and as we were walking by the jewelry store, I suggested we go inside."

"Okay?"

"And he said…" Sniffle. Sniffle. "He said…"

"What, Becks? What did he say?"

She burst into tears again. "Why?"

Zion winced. "God, I'm sorry, honey. That's awful."

"I asked him if he ever saw himself buying a ring and he said he couldn't imagine one reason why he'd want to."

Ouch. That was harsher than usual. "Wow, what an ass!"

"A total and complete ass. I went and grabbed a suitcase, loading it with a few of my things."

Or as most people would call it, a wardrobe.

"And I went to the Fairmont for the night."

"Oh, honey, I'm so sorry. I wish I was there for you."

She sobbed some more. "I wish you were too. I need someone to eat ice cream with me."

Except when they ate ice cream together, Zion ate the ice cream and Rebekah watched. She had an iron will, that one.

"Well, you know you can come here if you want."

Rebekah went silent and Zion knew it was a silly gesture. Rebekah hated quiet, little Sequoia and would never think of leaving the City. Besides, she had a good job with the insurance company Zion used to work for.

"I thought he was the one," sobbed Rebekah. "I thought we were going to get married."

"I know, honey. I know you did."

"I did it again, Zion. I'm homeless. Can you believe it? I'm homeless again. When will I ever learn? When will I stop letting men treat me like a doormat?"

Zion thought of Tate and David. They both treated her well, but David had been too possessive. She wasn't sure what might have happened if she pursued something with Tate. Maybe he would have become possessive too, but he let her work the murder cases with him, so that spoke well for his ideas of equality.

"Are you listening to me?" Rebekah whined.

"I am, I'm listening, Becks."

"What's wrong with me, Zion? Why can't I keep a man?"

Then the tears became a waterfall and Zion felt drowned out. She snuggled back into the pillows and waited. Yep, it was going to be a long night all right.

CHAPTER 2

Tate's phone buzzed as he got near the door of the *Hammer Tyme*, his hardware store. He pulled it out and looked at the display. A text from Logan flashed at him. *Something came up. I won't be in today. Sorry.* Tate frowned. He didn't ever remember Logan calling in sick or asking for a day off. The kid worked like a machine. Of course, school had started up again and Logan was trying to go to regular classes, rather than the continuation school he'd been going to. Tate had urged him to complete his senior year with his class. Maybe he had something for school he had to take care of, or maybe he just needed time to study.

Tate unlocked the door and went to the back to turn off the alarm and turn on the lights. When he returned, Bill Stanley, his morning help, stepped inside, pulling a *Hammer Tyme* ball cap over his grey hair. Tate had succumbed to Bill and Logan's urging to brand the store. He'd gotten aprons and ball caps for them to wear while they worked. For some reason, Tate couldn't remember to bring his ball cap with him, so he left it in the back of the store with his apron.

"Hey, Bill," he said, smiling at the older man as he went to open the blinds.

"Morning," said Bill, lifting the counter to duck under it. He carried a carton with two coffees on it.

Tate tried not to salivate, but he loved his morning cup of coffee from the *Caffeinator*, even though he couldn't go get it himself anymore. He'd screwed up his friendship with Zion by moving too fast and now he didn't feel right going into the store and making her uncomfortable.

He stared out the window at the street. He could just see the awning over the coffee shop door from here and he knew her white Optima was in the municipal parking lot. He looked for it every morning without fail.

He wished he could take back the impulsiveness that had made him kiss her in her store, in front of everyone, but he didn't regret it. He hadn't wanted her to go away with David. He knew it wasn't his place to ask her not to go, but he couldn't help himself. Except now, they weren't even friends anymore and that hurt.

Although being friends with Zion had been eating him alive, especially because he wanted so much more. When they saw each other at social functions, it was awkward, but the pull he felt toward her hadn't diminished in the months since he'd made his monumental blunder.

"You gonna stand there, looking outside all day?"

Tate squared his shoulders and turned around, walking to the counter. Bill picked up a paper cup and held it out to him.

"Dottie made this special for you. She said it was your favorite. I don't hold with all those fussy drinks, but people seem to love them."

Tate took a sip. Bill usually just brought two black cups of coffee, which was fine with Tate, but Dottie must have figured out the second cup was for him. The coffee that touched his tongue now was sweet with a hint of mint, the very drink Dottie had introduced him to six months before.

"She's the best," he said, smiling.

"She wanted to know how you were. Why don't you go down there?"

Tate drew a deep breath. That was a conversation he wasn't having with Bill Stanley. "I'm trying to save money," he lied as he lifted the counter and grabbed his apron off a peg just inside the storeroom door. Tying it around himself, he watched Bill grab the basket of return items that needed to be restocked. Walking into the storeroom, Tate took his hat off the shelf and pulled it on, then he went to the safe and got money for the cash register.

He'd just finished counting out the money, when the buzzer sounded and the door opened. Deimos, Zion's hippy barista, stepped into the shop, hovering by the door. Tate frowned at the anxious look on Dee's face.

Deimos Hendrix had blue eyes, shaggy blond hair, and lately he begun growing a patchy beard on his jaw. He wore a pair of faded jeans and a t-shirt that said *Caffeinator* on it. A few months ago, he'd been a suspect in a murder case and he'd had a rough go of it, but he was cleaning up his act. Zion's mother, Gabi, had helped him get off pot and start eating healthy. The two of them had done yoga in Zion's front yard for weeks. Tate smiled now in memory of Deimos in hot pink yoga pants, bending in ways the human body just shouldn't.

"Hey, Dee," he said, lifting the counter and approaching him.

Bill Stanley was arranging the screws and nails in the bins, giving Dee a skeptical look from the corner of his eyes. Bill Stanley was a hard worker, but he could be judgmental. Tate would probably let him go if he didn't need the help, especially with Logan back in school.

Dee's worried blue eyes flashed to Tate's face and he gave a breathless laugh. "Tate dude, how's it hanging?" He held out a hand and when Tate accepted it, he pulled him in for a hug, patting his back.

Tate smiled, extricating himself. He'd always liked Dee. "Good, how are you?"

"Dude, I'm all sorts of awesome." He shot another anxious look around. He hadn't left the doorway yet. "So, I thought I'd come see you, see the store." He tucked his hands in his back pockets and rocked on his heels. "See the nails."

Tate gave him an amused frown. "Right, you don't like nails."

"Dude, I so don't like nails. Jesus and all."

"Right, I remember." Tate glanced over and saw Bill Stanley not even trying to hide his disapproving glare. "So, you just came to visit."

"Yeah…no."

Tate's brows rose.

"I mean, sure, I wanted to see you. You haven't been in the *Caffeinator* in months, Tate dude. Look, whatever happened with Zion, man, you and me, we're cool, right?"

"We're cool, Dee."

"Awesome," said Dee, jerking his chin up. "But I also came 'cause stuff needs fixing at the shop."

Tate crossed his arms over his chest. "What's broken?"

"The bar door, you know? The hinge is loose. It's hanging all wonky."

"Okay, you probably just need to tighten the screws."

Dee pointed at him. "That's it. But I don't have one of them screw doodads." He made a twisting motion with his hand.

"A screwdriver."

"That's it," he said again, laughing and pointing at Tate.

"Phillips head or slot head?"

"Yes," Dee said, nodding.

Tate glanced at Bill Stanley, who gaped openly at Dee. "What else?"

"The toilet just keeps running, all the time."

"You probably need a new flush valve gasket."

"Probably," said Dee enthusiastically.

Tate fought his smile. "You don't have any idea what I'm talking about, do you?"

"Not even a little."

Tate laughed. "What if I come down…"

"No way, hombre," said Dee, holding up his hands. "I can't authorize that."

"Look, Dee, Zion and I are adults."

"Dude, you kissed her in front of everyone."

"I know, but…"

"When she was going away with another dude."

"Right, but…"

"And she had to break it off with the other dude."

Bill Stanley made a disapproving noise, drawing both of their attention.

Tate pushed up his ball cap, rubbing his forehead. "Okay, what if Bill comes down?"

Deimos considered that, studying Bill, while Bill studied him in return. Then Dee leaned toward Tate and whispered, "I don't think he likes me."

Tate held out his hands. "Then I don't know what to do about this."

Dee held up his index finger, pointing it at Tate. "Tell you what. I got a key now. I'll sneak you in after the coffee shop closes and Zion goes home. She's working late tonight, doing the books. What do you say? We can be like little fixit elves and get it done before she comes in the next morning. You know, like that fable about the guy who makes shoes and the elves come in to make the shoes for him while he sleeps."

"*The Elves and the Shoemaker*," Tate told him.

"Right." Dee scrunched up his face. "That's a little on the nose, don't you think? The title, I mean. It's a little disappointing."

Tate shrugged. "It was a simpler time."

"True that," said Dee, scratching at his blond head. "So, how about tonight and you can bring the Phillip thingy and the valve whatchamacallit."

"Sounds good."

"I'll text you when Zion leaves."

"Fine." The whole situation made him sad, but he shoved it aside. He had to stop getting his hopes up where she was concerned. She clearly didn't want anything to do with him anymore.

Dee backed to the door. "Later, Tate dude."

"Later, Dee."

Then Dee was gone.

* * *

Bill left at 2:00. Usually that meant that Tate would be by himself for an hour until Logan came in, but there was no Logan today. He fussed with straightening the shelves and helped a few customers that wandered in, then he pulled out his glasses and put them on, dragging a stool behind the counter and opening the paperback he'd stashed on the shelves for just such an occasion.

For some reason, he gravitated toward mysteries, which always frustrated him. He usually figured out *who done it* before the investigators in the story did, but he still kept picking them. Maybe it was his past as a cop, maybe it was his innate need to figure out puzzles, but he didn't really like any other type of books.

He'd actually lost himself in this one when the buzzer over the door sounded. He glanced up, blinking myopically as Jaguar entered the shop. Jaguar, Jerome Jarvis, had been a talented, famous rockstar for many years, but recently he'd discovered he had a daughter and his mother had died. He'd come home and wound up staying. He and Tate had struck up a friendship in the time that Jaguar had been back. In fact, Tate had been helping Jaguar get his music store up and running.

Jaguar was in his early thirties with spiky white blond hair and recently, he sported a clean-shaven face, instead of his usual scruffy beard. His arms were covered in full-sleeve tattoos and he had a number of piercings in his ears, although Tate thought there were a few less than the last time he'd seen him. Jaguar's most remarkable feature, however, were his pale blue eyes, eyes so stunning that they drew your attention away from the artwork on his arms.

Tate removed his glasses and put them in the book, shutting it. Jaguar swaggered up to the counter, shooting a look around. He didn't really like Bill Stanley and the feeling was mutual. Tate smiled, glad for the distraction.

"So, what chore do you have for me today?" he said, crossing his arms on the counter.

Jaguar leaned a hip against the counter and rested on his elbow. He crossed his feet at the ankles. He wore a band t-shirt, jeans torn at the knees, and run-down Converse sneakers. He exuded a cool that Tate would never be able to pull off.

"Can't I just come in to say hi?"

"Sure, but that's never how it goes with you," said Tate, chuckling.

Jaguar gave a nod. "True, true. How are you at hanging shelves?"

Tate shrugged. "I manage."

"Buy you a beer at the *Bourbon Brothers* afterwards?"

"How 'bout you buy me dinner instead?"

Jaguar held up an empty hand. "I could do that."

"I have to do some repairs at the *Caffeinator*, but it needs to be done after Zion goes home. I can come down, help you hang your shelves, then we could grab dinner, and that should make it late enough for me to go over to the *Caffeinator*."

Jaguar gave him a disgruntled look. "How long you gonna keep this up? Why don't you go down there right now and ask her on a date? You shouldn't be dating me all the time."

Tate reared back. "Hell no. And you and I aren't dating."

"Aren't we? You have dinner with me more often than you do…" His voice trailed off.

"Than I do what?"

"That's the point. You have dinner with me, no one else."

"I go out with Daryl too," he protested. "We went to *Corkers* just the other night."

Jaguar drew a deep breath and released it. "Sorry. So you're dating around."

Tate gave him an arch look. "It's complicated with Zion."

"How's it complicated? You like her, she doesn't hate you."

"She might hate me."

"Well, I mean, yeah, that was a monumentally stupid thing to do. What made you think you could just go in there and kiss her in front of everyone when she was going away with another dude?"

Tate blew out air. He'd heard this same thing over and over again. From everyone. It was getting boring.

"You're one to talk," he scolded. "When are you going to ask Kallista out?"

"She's Sophia's teacher. It's not kosher right now, but I'll get around to it."

"When she's no longer Sophia's teacher? What if she decides to date someone else?"

Jaguar turned to face him. "You're deflecting. Classic defensive posturing."

Tate stared down at the cover of his paperback. "Fine. Look, can we talk about something else?"

Jaguar looked around the hardware store. "Where's the kid?"

"He called in sick today."

"That's weird. He never misses a day."

"I know, but he just went back to school, so maybe he's got stuff to take care of."

"Maybe. So, you think you can get me a spot on the Chamber of Commerce?"

Tate burst out laughing. He could just imagine the reaction of the business people on the Chamber to Jaguar with his piercings and tattoos, but Jaguar was a legitimate business man now and his store was certain to be a boon to the economy in Sequoia. He'd never seen anyone draw a crowd the way Jaguar could.

The buzzer sounded and Jaguar's driver stepped inside. Hakim had driven a taxi for years until Jaguar came to town and hired him as his personal assistant/bodyguard. He lifted a hand in greeting to Tate.

"Hey, Hakim," Tate said.

"We got that appointment at the bank," Hakim told Jaguar.

"Shit, that's right." Jaguar pointed an index finger at Tate. "See you around 5:00?"

"It's a date," Tate quipped.

Jaguar rolled his eyes and followed Hakim from the store.

* * *

Tate stood, looking out the window of the *Bourbon Brothers*, waiting for Zion to make her way to the car. Daryl and Jaguar watched with him. Jaguar leaned against a table, his tattooed arms crossed, while Daryl had his hands fisted on his hips, his legs shoulder distance apart, a frown creasing his smooth brow.

"How long you gonna do this?" he asked Tate.

Tate ignored him, feeling a longing in his chest whenever he watched Zion. She wore a pair of jeans and a light jacket, her red hair flowing down her back as she hurried to the municipal parking lot. He leaned forward to keep her in sight. He didn't like her leaving this late by herself. It was starting to get dark.

"It's creepy is what it is," said Jaguar.

"Definitely creepy," said Daryl.

"Shut it, both of you!" Tate said with a swipe of his hand.

A Mercedes pulled up in front of the *Bourbon Brothers* and Jaguar pushed away from the table. "That's my ride," he said, going to the door. "Thanks for the help with the shelves."

"No problem," said Tate, his gaze still fixed on the corner of the parking lot he could see from the barbecue's window. He knew Zion's Optima would be pulling out and heading back down the street any minute now.

Jaguar jogged to the car and pulled open the passenger side door as the Optima came into view. When Zion honked at him, he looked up and waved at her. Tate ducked behind the door, so she couldn't inadvertently see him spying on her.

Daryl made a disgusted sound. "Seriously, this has gone too far. Do I got to get involved?"

Tate gave him a horrified look as the Optima drove out of sight. "God, no. Don't say a word to her about any of this."

Daryl went over and turned off the open light beside the door, pushing Tate out of the way. "You've got it bad, brother. It's pathetic."

Tate slumped against the door, watching him and Pedro, the busboy, begin putting the chairs up on the tables to prepare for the janitor who came in the middle of the night. "Look, it's just awkward right now."

"Yeah, because you're making it awkward. Grow some cojones, man." He gave Pedro a questioning look. "I said that right, didn't I?"

"Yes, you said it right and I agree."

Tate's eyes widened. He'd only exchanged a few words with Pedro since he started working here and he didn't know him that well.

"Life is short, hombre. Stop wasting it."

"Truth," said Daryl.

"That's enough out of both of you. I've got plenty of cojones. I was a cop."

"*Was* being the operative word," said Daryl. "Now you just hide in your hardware store."

"And what about you?" Tate said testily.

"I'm not peeking out of a window at a girl or sneaking over to fix her toilet in the night."

"Shut up!" Tate said, yanking open the door and picking up his toolbox off the floor. He wasn't really angry at Daryl. He was frustrated with himself and frustrated with the situation and frustrated that everyone around him was right and he knew it.

He hurried down the street to the *Caffeinator*, peering in the glass door. Dee waved to him from behind the counter and hurried over, turning the lock and pulling it open. The bell jingled as Tate ducked inside.

"Zion just left," Dee said in a hushed voice.

"I know. I saw her go."

Dee frowned, but he motioned to the bar doors that led to the kitchen and Zion's office. "The doors need to be fixed first," he said.

Tate set about working on the hinges, while Dee continued to clean the espresso machine. When he was done, Dee led him into the bathroom and Tate began replacing the valve in the toilet. Dee leaned against the wall, watching him, his arms crossed.

"Where you learn all this handy stuff, Tate dude?" Dee asked.

Tate looked up, both hands deep in the reservoir. "My dad," he said.

"Huh, good guy, eh?"

"No," said Tate. "He was not a good guy. My dad was a tough old bastard who believed a man's worth was measured in how much booze he could hold and how many women he could bed."

"Dude, is he dead?"

"Naw, he's still alive, but I don't see him."

"What about your mom?"

"She's with him. I talk to her on the phone, but that's about it. I don't really know why she stayed."

"You have any sibs?"

"Nope. Just me."

"How come your mom puts up with that mess?"

Tate glanced up from the toilet. "That's been an issue since I was in high school, Dee. I just couldn't understand why she put up with the abuse."

"He ever hit her?"

"Not that I saw, but I honestly don't know."

"Man, that's rough."

Tate cleared his throat. He didn't really want to talk about this. Not with anyone. "You know, you could learn to do some of the minor repairs around here?"

"Naw, I don't think so. I got that phobia, you know, about the nails?"

Tate finished and flushed the toilet. They both leaned over and watched the tank fill. The running water noise finally shut off. Dee clapped his hands together.

"That's the ticket," he said, beaming.

Tate went to wash his hands. "Look, I know you got a phobia about nails."

"Don't much like screws either." Dee shuddered.

"Right, but they have a good purpose too." He dried his hands and began packing up his tools. "I mean, it's kinda that way with everything. For instance, I don't like guns. They're scary, but they sure do have a purpose when you're a cop."

"I don't like guns either."

"Right." Tate picked up the toolbox and they made their way out of the bathroom. "But my point is you can get over a phobia if you just try. I mean what would we do without nails and screws? Nothing would stay up and we'd still be eating dinner around a boulder…" His voice trailed away as they stepped out of the short hallway and found Zion standing in the middle of the room with her keys in hand.

"Hey, boss," said Dee brightly, shooting an uncomfortable look at Tate. "I thought you went home."

"I left my wallet in my desk and I realized I didn't have it when I stopped to get some ice cream." Her eyes lowered to Tate's toolbox. "What's going on?"

Dee hurried over and pushed the bar door. "Look, it's fixed."

"I see that."

"I had Tate come over to fix a few things," said Dee, pushing the door again.

"He asked me to help," offered Tate.

Zion's gaze shifted to her barista. "We could have taken care of it ourselves."

"Well, I don't know about that. We didn't have no Philips."

"Philips?" she asked skeptically.

"Screwdriver," Tate offered. "Look, he was just trying to help you out. We did it after you left, thinking it wouldn't make you uncomfortable."

Zion's green eyes shifted to Dee again. "You can go, Dee. It's getting late."

"Are you mad at us? I mean, it's not Tate's fault. I asked him."

"I'm not mad, Dee. I appreciate you looking out for the store and me, but I want to talk to Tate alone for a minute."

Tate shot a panicked look at Dee. Dee gave him a regretful look in return. Tate wanted to spend time with Zion, but he suspected she was about to unleash her wrath on him and he wasn't prepared for it. He was so raw and vulnerable where she was concerned.

"Sorry, dude," said Dee, untying his apron and shoving it under the counter. "Thanks for the help."

"No problem," Tate said, his gaze fixated on the red-headed woman who'd dominated his thoughts since she'd moved here.

Dee headed toward the door, his head hanging. Zion touched his arm. "Thank you, Dee. I appreciate it."

He gave her a sad smile. "Don't be too harsh on him, boss. He's a good guy inside."

Zion shook her head in amusement and looked over her shoulder, watching Dee go out the door, then she turned back to Tate.

Tate held up a hand. "I know I shouldn't have come in here without your permission," he said, his eyes widening as she stalked toward him. Was she going to slap him? Well, he probably deserved it, but he didn't have to like it. "Dee just wanted to help you. He's a really good guy and he meant only the best."

Zion stopped in front of him, looking into his eyes. She was tall for a woman and didn't have to look up too far to meet his six-foot gaze. "Shut up!" she hissed.

"Yes, ma'am," he answered.

Then she did the most surprising thing. She rose on her tiptoes and kissed him. Tate wanted to crush her against him, but he curled his hands into fists and let her kiss him, tilting his head to grant her access. The kiss was hot and salacious, especially since neither of them touched the other one.

Then Zion broke it off, making Tate weave. He took a step back.

"Yeah, it's still there," she said, touching her lips.

Tate blinked, the passion of their kiss fogging his brain. "What? What's still there?"

"The something between us."

"Oh," he said, then he frowned. "What?"

"Look, Tate, you shouldn't have kissed me a few months ago."

"I know."

"I was supposed to go away with David and even though I wasn't sure the relationship was going anywhere, I needed to make that decision by myself, but you took that out of my hands. I had to tell David what happened and I had to end the relationship."

"I'm sorry."

"No, you're not."

No, he wasn't, but he was sort of confused.

"I was so angry with you."

He nodded in agreement. She hadn't really talked to him in months, so he'd kind of figured that out himself.

"But that doesn't mean I don't feel the attraction."

"Yeah?" he said, a stupid grin crossing his face.

"That doesn't mean I've totally forgiven you."

His face fell. "Zion, I'm not gonna lie, my head's spinning a little. If you haven't forgiven me, why'd you kiss me?"

"To see if the spark was still there and because my mother's painting nudes now."

Tate blinked a few times, knowing he'd completely lost control of the conversation. "Cool?" he said skeptically.

"No, it's creepy, especially since she's painting my dad." She pressed a hand to her forehead. "I did not need to see that."

Tate squinted, staring up at the ceiling. "Um, okay?"

Zion sighed as if he were the stupidest man in the world. "The point is this, my mother keeps reinventing herself, taking risks, trying new things. Maybe I should do the same thing."

Was he a risk? He didn't think of himself as a risk. He was a pretty vanilla sort of guy. Jaguar would be a risk, but he, he was just your average Joe. He straightened a little, rubbing the panther tattoo on his arm. Maybe she thought he was some sort of bad boy, like a wicked temptation. He took a step closer to her, but she blocked him with a hand on his chest.

"Nope. It would be too easy just to have a crazy affair with you."

He couldn't help the devilish smile that crossed his lips. She laughed, but her hand continued to block him.

"You're going to take me on a real date, do you hear me?"

He nodded rapidly. He could take her on a date. "How about tomorrow?"

She laughed again and he loved the sound. "No, Friday night."

It was Tuesday. He could do Friday. "Friday night. Definitely." He covered the back of her hand with his own.

Her look softened and he thought maybe she'd let him kiss her again. He really wanted to kiss her again.

"Zion, I'm sorry about what happened…well, I'm not sorry. I mean, I didn't want you to go away with David, but I shouldn't have kissed you like that, except I'm not really sorry about that either."

Zion blew out air, removing her hand. "You're making it worse."

He gave her a sheepish look. "What I'm trying to say is I really like you."

She smiled and her smile made his heart pound faster. "I really like you too."

He smiled in return and started toward her, but her hand came back up.

"Nope. None of that. I'm not hopping into bed with you, Tate Mercer. That would be a mistake."

"Right, right," he said, tapping his hands against his thighs. "A mistake." Although, Tate couldn't deny it was a mistake he was probably willing to make. "So, Friday night."

"Friday night, and it's just a date. No hanky panky."

"Right." He crossed his heart. "I'll be a perfect gentleman."

She gave him a skeptical look from her green eyes, then she walked around him, headed for her office. "Get out of here," she said, pushing the bar door open. Then she looked over her shoulder at him. "And thanks for the repairs."

Tate beamed with happiness, his heart soaring. "Anytime," he said loudly. "Anytime."

CHAPTER 3

Zion entered the Chamber of Commerce meeting with a little trepidation. David usually attended for his father's firm and although they tried to remain on good terms, the fact that she'd just accepted a date with Tate might make things tense. Tate was also on the Chamber and she hoped he would keep his distance just so it wouldn't make David uncomfortable.

The meetings were held in the breakfast room at the *Tumble Inn Beer & Breakfast,* a pretty building with blue gingerbread shingles and white trim. A large porch ran across the front of the building and the breakfast room was filled with sunshine and painted a cheerful yellow. A long table against the sidewall groaned under plates of pastries and donuts, and a spot waited for the two coffee urns Zion had brought with her.

She set down her stuff at one of the round tables with a floral tablecloth covering it and went back into the lobby, smiling at Daisy McCoy, the co-owner of the *Tumble Inn.*

"Hey, Daisy, I'll just bring in the coffee."

Daisy bustled around the front counter. "Let me help you," she said.

Daisy was middle aged with grey flecked hair. She was pleasantly plump and had round cheeks that made her whole face light up when she smiled. They hurried down to the parking lot and Zion pressed the button to unlock her car. Pulling open the backseat, she handed an urn of decaf to Daisy and reached in for the leaded coffee.

As she straightened again, a black Lincoln Town Car pulled into the lot. It looked like a moving hearse. Zion shut the back door with her hip and turned to follow Daisy back into the inn. The door opened on the Lincoln and Jim Dawson climbed out. Jim Dawson was president of the

Chamber and he owned the *Cut & Print* in town. He had a paunch and thinning salt and pepper hair with a full moustache and beard. He was a gruff ex-school teacher, but he was also a fair man and Zion liked him despite his tendency to bark at her.

"Hey, Jim," she called as she followed Daisy up the stairs.

"Let me get the door for you," said Jim, hurrying to catch up to them. He jogged up the steps and tugged the door open, holding it so the two of them could pass through.

Jim always ran the meetings with efficiency and order. He didn't tolerate off-task behavior of any kind. While Zion set up the urns, he arranged his leather folder on the podium in front of the windows.

A few moments later the other Chamber members began to arrive. Trixie Taylor, a woman in her early forties, was the proprietor of *Trinkets by Trixie.* She came in wearing a stylish pair of skinny jeans with six inch heels and a button-up shirt in rose colored silk. Trixie had platinum blond hair and a svelte figure. She always wore the latest fashions and had her nails manicured regularly. Next came Barney and Betty Brown, who owned the *Fast & Furriest Pet Store.* Their brown hair was neatly combed into a bowl cut and they wore denim shirts and denim pants that matched. Betty was round and full figured, while Barney was thin as a rail. They waved enthusiastically to Zion and she waved back.

Trixie came over and reached for a pink paper cup that said *Caffeinator* on it. "How you doing, darlin'?" she asked Zion.

"Good, how are you Trixie?"

"Fit as a fiddle," she said, pressing the valve to get coffee.

A massive man, with arms so large they looked disproportionate, entered next. He carried a tray of lunch meat and cheese, setting them on the table next to the pastries. He jerked his chin at Zion and Trixie, and Trixie fanned herself, giving him a wink.

Serge owned *Up to No Gouda*, the deli outside of Sequoia. He didn't speak much, but he was a loyal member of the Chamber, never missing a meeting. Everyone loved his contributions, since the rest of the food tended toward the sweet.

"Ladies," he said, coming to get some coffee himself.

Although Trixie was happily married, she got a kick out of flirting with the huge deli owner every month.

"Hey, Serge," Zion said, taking her cup of coffee over to the table.

Trixie immediately sidled up to him and began asking him about his business. Serge answered with one word responses, but Trixie didn't seem to mind. Zion smiled, thinking the flirtation was harmless, but Jim Dawson glared at the two of them. Jim disapproved of a lot of things.

Beatrice Sanchez and her sister-in-law Carmen arrived next. They ran the *Knitatorium* next to the *Caffeinator*. Beatrice was in her late sixties with her grey hair in a tight perm. She wore polyester and knit tops she made herself, and her glasses were always perched on the end of her nose. She had a tendency to overshare and that just set Jim Dawson on edge. He gave Beatrice a sour look, but Zion liked her.

Zion hugged the older woman, then hugged her sister-in-law. Carmen patted her shoulders, smiling at her. "You look so pretty today, Zion," Carmen said.

"Thank you," she replied, but her smile dried as Dwayne Ford and Tate entered the room side by side. Tate gave her an uncomfortable smile, but Dwayne headed immediately toward the refreshment table. Behind Tate came David.

The lawyer caught sight of Zion and gave her a jerk of his head. Zion straightened, clasping her hands before her. Tate glanced over his shoulder, seeing where her eyes had gone and decided to detour after his friend.

David came up to her. He was dressed immaculately in a black suit with a crisp white shirt and a navy blue tie. His brown hair was neatly combed away from his face and his brown eyes were gentle as they looked on her.

"How are you, Zion?"

Zion gave him an uncomfortable smile, disappointed when Beatrice and Carmen made a hasty retreat.

"That's the ex-boyfriend," stage-whispered Beatrice, so of course everyone heard.

Zion felt her face heat with embarrassment. "I'm good. How are you, David?"

"Excellent," he said a little too brightly. "Well, I better get some coffee. You know how Jim likes to start this meeting right on time?"

"Right," she said.

David went to the refreshment table as Zion turned to take her seat. Her eyes lifted and met Tate's. He gave her a pointed look. He wanted to sit with her, but she gave a shake of the head, surreptitiously pointing at a table across the room. His shoulders slumped and she felt bad, but she didn't need a scene here. David would be so hurt that she'd agreed to see Tate after everything that had happened and she didn't want to hurt David.

He was a good guy, he just wasn't *her* guy.

To her relief, Trixie came over and took the seat next to her. Zion blew out air. Trixie gave her a curious look. "You don't drink coffee?"

Zion laughed unexpectedly. She felt a little manic with both men in the room. "No, isn't that ironic?"

Trixie gave her a puzzled look. "Is something wrong, honey?"

Zion leaned toward her. "It's just awkward with both Tate and David here," she whispered.

Trixie frowned, sipping at her coffee. "Why? You broke it off with David months ago and you never started anything with Tate."

"Well," Zion said, dragging the word out.

"Well?" said Trixie, turning toward her.

Beatrice and Carmen arrived at Zion's table, carrying plates of food and coffee cups. Zion knew she couldn't talk around Beatrice or the whole room would know her business.

"I'll tell you later," she said, glancing up as Jim Dawson banged his gavel on the podium.

For the first half hour, Jim took care of business. He insisted on calling roll, although the regulars always came and the others never did. Then he read the minutes of the previous meeting and went over the budget ad nauseam. Zion wished that for once Jim wouldn't have to be so thorough.

Finally, he opened it up for new business, calling Daisy in to take the minutes. Zion jabbed her hand into the air, but to her surprise, Tate did the same thing. Jim glanced between the two of them, then he pointed the gavel at Zion.

"Ladies first," he said.

When all eyes turned to her, Zion felt her heart kick up and her mouth went dry. She wished she'd gotten some juice or water from the refreshment table. She glanced at Tate.

"Tate can go first," she said.

Tate shook his head, his eyes wide. "No, you go."

"I don't mind," she said. "I can wait."

"I insist," he said, giving her a tilt of his head. A smile touched the corners of his mouth and he looked up at her flirtatiously.

Zion's face heated and she blushed, tilting her chin toward her shoulder.

"Oh for God's sakes, someone go!" shouted Jim.

Zion and Trixie both jumped and Beatrice fumbled her roll, sending it bouncing into the middle of the table.

Jim pointed the gavel at Tate. "Mercer, speak!"

Tate cleared his throat. "Jaguar wants to join the Chamber."

Silence met that pronouncement. Zion looked around the room. If no one else seconded Tate's motion, she'd have to. Jaguar deserved to be part of their community. Still, she and Tate had already drawn enough attention to themselves.

She didn't want to look too eager to support him, especially because she could feel David's curious gaze pinned to her.

Jim stroked his beard. "I'll second it," he said. "I've known Jerome Jarvis for a long time and he's straightened himself out. I think he'll definitely add to our organization." He shot a baleful gaze around the room. "Does anyone object?"

"Not in the least," said Beatrice, fanning herself. "I would love to have him as part of our monthly meetings. He's scrumptious."

She and Carmen giggled, despite the glower Jim Dawson leveled on them. Zion and Tate exchanged a smile at that, but Jim's gavel made them both jump again.

"Then it's settled." He pointed the gavel at Zion. "Now, young woman, have you collected yourself and are you ready to bring forward your motion?"

Zion nodded and rose to her feet, wiping her hands on her jeans. She hated to speak in public, especially when so much tension zipped around the room. Her eyes involuntarily tracked to Tate and he gave her an encouraging smile.

"I think we should have a Halloween festival on Main Street."

No one said anything and the silence weighed heavily in the room.

Jim Dawson made a face. "What do you mean a festival?"

"I think we should decorate all of the shops and we should wear costumes on Halloween. I think we should have apple bobbing and hay rides and a hay maze all set up in the municipal parking lot. We could all pitch in and get cloth bags with Sequoia embroidered on it to give the kids as they arrive and each shop could have candy, so the kids could trick-or-treat down Main Street."

Still no one said anything. Zion felt foolish. They all stared at her as if she'd lost her mind. She felt her shoulders slump and she sank into her chair, staring at the tablecloth, her cheeks heating with embarrassment.

Tate shifted forward in his seat. "Maybe Jaguar could push back the opening of his store a few weeks to coincide with Halloween, then his band could play."

Zion glanced up and smiled at him. He gave her an encouraging wink, then nudged Dwayne's shoulder with his arm.

Dwayne gave him a glare, then raised his hand. "The barbecue could offer a discount on beer for the parents if they bring their kids in and you could print up fliers, Jim," he said.

Trixie's hand shot up next. "What if we could get one of those carnival haunted houses? You know, the ones they bring on a flatbed truck and maybe the high school could get kids to volunteer to run it, in exchange for part of the ticket sales."

Zion smiled at her.

"We could put coupons in the goodie bags for all of our establishments, so those of us not on Main Street could still participate," said Serge.

"We could even put together some baskets with Halloween themed treats from all of our stores and have a raffle. We could donate the winnings to a charity," said Beatrice.

Betty and Barney raised their hands simultaneously. "Halloween is on a Saturday this year," said Betty.

"So we could have something for the adults after the kids' party ends," said Barney.

"We could shut down Main Street."

"And *Anaconda* could play."

"Leaving the street open for dancing."

Zion looked around, stunned by the ideas being floated. It would be fantastic. Nothing like this had ever been done in Sequoia before.

Jim turned to David. "What do you think? Can we legally do it?"

"I'll draw up the permits, but we need to get Sheriff Wilson on board. We'll need patrols and a strong sheriff's department presence."

"I'll talk with Wilson," said Tate.

Jim held up his gavel. "All in favor?" he said loudly.

Every hand in the room shot up.

Jim banged the gavel. "Then it's set. Sequoia will have its first Halloween Celebration."

* * *

After the Chamber meeting ended, Dwayne and Tate carried the urns to the Optima for Zion. She thanked them both, being careful not to show Tate too much attention. She caught sight of David glancing over at her as he headed for his car.

Driving back to Main Street, Zion parked in front of the coffee shop. Dee wasn't scheduled to come in until noon, so she carried the urns in herself, while Dottie manned the espresso machine and the cash register.

After she'd stored the urns in the kitchen, she moved the Optima down to the municipal parking lot. Walking back, she saw Jaguar laying a doormat down outside his shop door. She slowed as she came up to him and he straightened, smiling at her.

"Heya, girl," he said, giving her a wink.

"Heya, boy," she said in return. "Can I take a peek?"

"Nope," he said, shutting the door. "I'll let you see it just before the Grand Opening."

"You're part of the Chamber now," she told him.

"Awesome," he said, rubbing his hands together. "I always knew I was destined for great things."

Zion laughed. "We're having a Halloween Festival."

"Really?"

Zion looked toward her shop. A number of customers were heading inside. "I gotta get to work, but I'll fill you in later, or you can have Tate tell you."

He held up a hand to stop her. "I hear you and Tate are going on a date." He barked out a laugh. "Oh, lord, that rhymes."

"Funny," she said, giving him a disapproving look. "Don't go spreading rumors!" she scolded.

He splayed a hand in the center of his chest. Every finger, including his thumb sported a ring. Most of them were skulls and crossbones. She wondered where Jaguar shopped for his stuff – *Pirates Are Us*. She smirked at her own cleverness.

He made a production out of crossing his heart. "They'll have to cut it out of me," he said dramatically.

She swatted him, but she was smiling as she jogged across the street to the *Caffeinator*. She and Dottie worked in tandem the rest of the morning, baking cookies and pastries to fill the display case. Dottie usually ran the espresso machine since it hated Zion, but Zion handled the cash register. Zion loved her days. The morning sped past and at noon, Dee would arrive. Dee always brought fun with him.

When Dee came in, Dottie gathered her things and prepared to leave. Zion stopped her. They had a few customers sipping coffee on the couches and a young woman sketching on a pad at a table in front of the windows. The shop would remain quiet until the high school let out at 3:30. Then the students would descend on the *Caffeinator*, wanting sweets and coffee, sitting around and chatting or studying until closing. Tallah came in after school and she would help Dee close up for the night.

"What's up, sugar?" asked Dottie, laying her jacket on the counter with her purse on top of it. This month, Dottie sported orange and black hair. The black hair was at the ends of her short bob, the orange on top. Zion envied her a little. She wished she could pull off such bold looks.

"We're having a Halloween Festival," she said, clapping her hands. "We're gonna put hay mazes in the municipal parking lot, have apple bobbing and a haunted house. All of the businesses are going to decorate and we're going to pass out candy to kids that trick-or-treat at the shops."

Dee's eyes grew wide with excitement and he bounced on his feet. "Seriously?"

"It gets better," said Zion. She couldn't believe how happy this plan made her. "After the kids go home, we're going to shut down the street and have *Anaconda* perform. We'll have adult beverages and dancing. And costumes!"

Dee threw his arms around her and they danced around in a circle. Dottie laughed, watching them. Zion came over and clasped Dottie's hands.

"We have to come up with Halloween themed treats."

"Like monster cupcakes and Frankenstein cookies," said Dee.

"Witches brew coffee," added Dottie, rubbing her hands together.

"Exactly! And I'm going to go shopping on my next day off to get decorations in Visalia," Zion said. "This is going to be so much fun."

"What are they going to call it?" asked Dee, his blue eyes dancing.

Zion shrugged. "Right now it's just the Halloween Festival."

Dee scrunched up his face in concentration. "It has to be grander than that. What about Spooktacular?"

"I think that's been done," Zion told him.

Dee tapped his chin. "I'll keep working on it."

Zion patted his shoulder. "You do that."

Dottie smiled at her, picking up her coat and putting it on. "I'll look up some cute Halloween treats."

"Oooh, candy coated apples," said Dee.

"Popcorn balls," said Zion.

"Green rice crispy treats!" shouted Dee. "We can call them Frankensweets."

Dottie waved over her back as she went out the door. "Have fun!" she called.

* * *

After Tallah arrived, Zion gathered her things and headed out. Some days she stayed until closing, but she was trying to give herself more downtime and she trusted Dee and Tallah to run things. They hadn't let her down once so far.

Out of habit, she glanced at Tate's house as she drove down her street, but his truck wasn't parked in the driveway. A red convertible sat in her driveway, however. She squinted at it as she pulled in next to it. The little sporty Fiat Spider in the cherry red color was familiar to her. She'd gone out on the town many nights in it when she lived in San Francisco.

She grabbed her purse, pushing open the Optima's door. She climbed out and hurried around the corner of the cottage. An entire collection of suitcases in pale pink with black fleur-de-lis were lined up along the front porch and Rebekah had curled up in the wicker lounger, her bare feet tucked to the side. She was staring morosely at her phone and didn't notice Zion.

"Becks, what are you doing here?"

Rebekah's head snapped up and she swung her legs down, slipping her feet into sparkly silver Jimmy Choo heels. She wore a pencil skirt in charcoal grey and a silver blouse with rhinestone buttons up the front.

"Oh, Zion, you're finally home. I couldn't remember how to get to that little coffee hut of yours." She glided forward and wrapped her arms around Zion's neck, laying her head on Zion's shoulder.

Zion patted her back, eying the mountain of luggage all around them. "Becks, how did you get all of this into the Spider?"

"I'm a genius at Tetris," she said over Zion's shoulder.

Zion figured she was, but the number of bags spoke to a visit of a certain duration and Zion wasn't sure she was up for that, no matter how much she loved her friend. She held Rebekah off and looked at her.

"What's going on?"

Rebekah fluffed out Zion's hair. "I wish I had the courage to go natural like you have." She peered closer at her, squinting. "You're not even wearing any concealer."

Zion touched her cheek, then forced a smile. "Becks, stop stalling. What's going on?"

Rebekah backed up and picked up two smaller bags. "Help me get this stuff in and get me a glass of wine, then I'll tell you."

Zion pulled out her keys and unlocked the door, then gathered as many bags as she could, following Rebekah into the house. Cleo greeted them at the door, meowing, then she followed them down the short hallway on the right to the guest room directly across from the little bathroom.

Rebekah deposited her bags and turned a circle, giving the decor a jaundiced eye. Zion hadn't really done anything to this room, preserving it the way Vivian, her biological mother, had decorated it. Vivian had been partial to vintage furniture. Zion suspected the bed, nightstands and dresser were antiques. The walls were papered in beige with soft pink roses cascading down them. The curtains were also a soft rose-colored gabardine, and a rag rug in pastel colors covered the hardwood floor.

Zion didn't ask Rebekah what the face was about. She didn't care. The room was clean and she liked it. It felt homey. Rebekah had come unannounced, so she could just manage with what she was given.

She went over and pushed back the curtains, looking out at the trees that lined the side and back of the property. "It's just like camping," she said with a tight smile.

Zion scooped up Cleo as the little cat started to jump on the bed. "Look, I'm gonna change into some sweats, then I'll open a bottle of wine. Why don't you change into something more comfortable and we'll meet in the living room for some girl talk?"

Rebekah gave her a sad look, then said, "Oh!" and hurried to a bag, unzipping it. She pulled out a bottle of wine and held it out to Zion. "I brought you a Napa Zinfandel. The last time I was here, it was obvious you didn't get any decent grapes in the sticks."

Zion looked at the bottle and her smile grew brittle. Rebekah knew she didn't like red as well as she liked white, but she was determined to convert her. Rebekah thought drinking red wine somehow imparted culture on a person.

"Thanks," she said, carrying Cleo and the bottle with her to her room.

She changed into sweats and a pair of socks. There was a definite nip in the air tonight. Going into the kitchen, she opened the wine and poured two glasses. When she came back out, she found Rebekah on the couch, wearing a jogging suit that probably cost more than Zion's entire wardrobe.

Zion handed her the wine and set the bottle on the coffee table. She figured this would probably be a full bottle sort of talk. "What's going on, Becks?"

Rebekah sniffed the wine, then swirled it around her glass, holding it up so she could study it. "I had three weeks of vacation coming, so I took it."

Zion nearly choked on the sip she'd taken. "You took all of your vacation at once?"

"I did," said Rebekah, lowering the glass. "I had to get out of there. I've been so depressed."

"Ooh, sweetie," said Zion, rubbing Rebekah's arm where it lay along the back of the sofa. "I'm so sorry.'

Rebekah sighed. "Do you know I've lived with five different men since college?"

Zion looked away, sipping at her wine. She wasn't touching that, no way.

"What's wrong with me, Zion? Why can't I find a good man?"

"I think you're looking in the wrong place, Becks."

"What's the right place?"

Zion set her glass on the coffee table and tucked her legs under her. "That's not what I mean. I mean you're looking for someone who has money and can take care of you. You're not looking for love and devotion."

Rebekah made a face. "God, that's so turn of the century."

Zion's brows lifted in question. "Turn of the century?"

"The aughts?" When Zion still looked confused, Rebekah said, "2000 and so forth."

"Oh," said Zion, nodding, then she gave her a puzzled look. "Wait. Do you really not believe in love, Becks?"

Rebekah's dark eyes widened. "Do you really believe in it?"

Zion considered that. As she thought about the question, Cleo jumped on her lap. She stroked a hand down the cat's back. "I do. I really do."

Rebekah reached out and played with one of Zion's curls. "Oh, honey, you're going to be so disappointed. There just aren't any men out there worth all that fuss."

"I don't believe that, Becks. There's a lot of good men out there."

"Name one," she said.

Tate immediately came to mind, but she wasn't ready to talk to Rebekah about him. "Sheriff Wilson's a good man."

"Sheriff Wilson? Who's that? Is that a cartoon character?"

Zion laughed. "No, he's the sheriff in Sequoia."

"You have a…" Rebekah held up a hand and closed her eyes. "Don't even say it. Of course you have a sheriff."

"So what is your plan?"

Rebekah reached over and took Cleo from Zion, placing her on her lap. She gave the little cat a gentle scratch with her long, manicured nails and Cleo began to purr. "I'm going to stay with you for a while."

"Me?" Zion's voice came out in a squeak and she reached for the wine again. She took a gulp, her eyes watering. "You want to stay in Sequoia?"

"Yes." She leaned forward, grasping Zion's hand. "I promise I won't be a bother. You won't even know I'm here, but I need this, Zion. I need to get away from the City and get some perspective." She shot a sour look around the cottage. "This should do it."

Zion's brows rose. She loved Rebekah, she really did, but three weeks…lord help her, three weeks was a very long time in Rebekah Miles' Universe. She leaned over and grabbed the bottle of wine, refilling her glass, but she wasn't sure there was enough wine in all of Sequoia to save her now.

CHAPTER 4

Tate and Bill Stanley had just opened the *Hammer Tyme*, when the buzzer sounded and Sheriff Wayne Wilson swaggered in. Wilson always reminded Tate of a 1950's cowboy sheriff with his hat tilted to the back of his head, his thumbs tucked into his gun belt, and his severe widows peak. He was a slight man with a concave chest and a thin moustache perched above his upper lip.

"Bill," Wilson said, nodding at the older man.

"Sheriff, nice to see you. Beautiful morning, isn't it?"

"It is." His watery brown eyes shifted to Tate and narrowed. "Tate, how are you?"

"Good. What can I get for you, Sheriff?" Tate felt a sinking in his gut. He never saw Wilson that the man didn't have something unpleasant for him.

Wilson drew a breath and let it out slowly. "Got a call late last night for the ambulance to head out to the Baxter place."

Tate straightened and Bill put down his coffee cup.

"Logan's place?" asked Tate, the feeling in his gut becoming a knot.

"Yeah, for his mom."

"Is she in the hospital?"

Wilson pressed his thin lips against his teeth and shook his head. Tate knew what that meant.

"Where's the kid?" asked Bill, voicing the question that was circulating in Tate's mind.

For some reason, he couldn't get his head around Logan's loss. For so long he'd worked to support his mother while she battled breast cancer, going to continuation school instead of regular high school so he could work full time. Tate had talked the kid into going back to school for his senior year and Logan's mother had agreed. Tate had hoped that meant she was doing better. Logan wanted her to see him graduate, so he'd been on board with the change.

Tate closed his eyes and fought the wave of despair that swept over him. Logan had wanted her to see him graduate. That had been the only thing they both were looking forward to. Logan hadn't really talked about going to college, even though Tate had brought him brochures, urging him to consider it. He just wanted his mother to see him finish high school.

"He's at the house. A social worker showed up this morning, and his uncle and aunt are there."

Tate looked up at Wilson. "How's he taking it?"

"He's a strong kid. I know he's upset, but when I asked him how he was doing, he said he was fine."

Tate reached in his pocket for his keys, taking the *Hammer Tyme* ball cap off his head and setting it on the counter. "I've got to go see him," he told Bill Stanley.

"No worries," said Bill. "I'll hold down the fort."

Tate nodded. "You might have to stay later than noon."

"I'll let the wife know." Bill took his phone out of his pocket and walked into the storeroom to make the call.

Tate grabbed the wind breaker hanging on the peg just inside the storeroom and put it on. "What the hell is Logan going to do now?"

"He's under eighteen, Tate. He's going into foster care, unless the uncle agrees to take him."

Tate's jaw hardened. "That's not acceptable. This kid's been through enough."

"It'd only be for a year. Then he could do whatever he wanted. They age out of the system as soon as they turn eighteen."

"What does that mean?"

"It means he'll be on his own."

"How's he supposed to support himself at eighteen?"

"He's already been doing that."

Bill came out of the back room. "She's not happy, but I promised to take her to *Corker's* for dinner. I told her the extra hours would buy their best T-bone steak. That helped."

"I don't know when I'll be back, Bill," Tate said.

"Leave me your store keys and I can lock up for you."

Tate stared at the keys in his hand, hesitating. Everything he had was tied up in this store and Bill had only worked for him a few months. He'd trust Logan to lock up more than Bill at this point.

"I'll swing back by tonight and help Bill shut everything down," offered Wilson, "then I'll get the keys and bring them by your house. I want to know how the kid's doing, anyway."

Tate nodded. He didn't have time to debate it, so he took the keys off his ring and passed them to Bill, then he lifted the counter and ducked under it. "I'll call later to make sure everything's all right," he said to Bill, headed for the door.

"Don't worry. I'll handle it."

Tate pushed open the outer door and Wilson followed him. "Don't worry about the store. I'll have someone patrol by the front the rest of the day," said Wilson.

"Thank you, Sheriff," said Tate, turning toward the parking lot. He hesitated when he reached the truck, looking over at the *Caffeinator*. He knew if he asked Zion to go with him, she would. She liked Logan and she'd be better equipped to handle his sorrow, but something told Tate that he needed to do this himself.

He opened the truck and climbed in, the roar of the engine loud on the quiet street. As he pulled onto Main, he wondered why some people just got more than their share of misery. Logan Baxter was a good kid, kind, hard working, smart. Why couldn't the doctors have given his mother just a little more time? Just a few more years?

He banged the heel of his hand on the steering wheel and turned for the interstate. Nothing was guaranteed. He knew that. But a kid shouldn't lose his mother before he was fully grown. That just didn't seem fair no matter how he looked at it.

* * *

Tate arrived at the Baxter residence, pulling up in front of the house. It looked worse than it had the last time he was here. The yard had a foot of weeds in it and there were more dead plants in the planter beds before the front door. A sedan was parked in the driveway and a battered pickup stood beside it, the paint rusting off the doors.

Tate hesitated a moment, staring at the closed curtains on the front windows, wishing he was anywhere else but here at this moment. Forcing himself to push open the car door, he climbed out and headed up the walkway, marking the weeds pushing their way through cracks in the concrete. He climbed the stairs and knocked on the door, glancing back at the street.

A moment later it opened and a woman peered out at him. She had short brown hair and brown eyes, her cheeks round and full. "Yes, what can I do for you?"

"Hi, I'm Tate Mercer. I'm Logan's employer. I just wanted to give him my condolences."

She narrowed her eyes on him, then she opened the door wider. Tate could see furniture being gathered in the living room until there was hardly any room left to move. "Come in," the woman said. "I'm Esther Carson." She motioned to a man in jeans and a t-shirt wearing cowboy boots who was moving a couch into the center of the room. "This is my husband, Ernest, Peggy's brother."

Tate moved forward to shake the man's hand. He had a firm grip and gave Tate a closed-mouth smile.

"Nice to meet you. Logan talks about you a lot," Ernest said. He wore a ball cap, but brown hair peeked out beneath it. His brown eyes were red-rimmed and he tucked his hands into his back pockets, rocking on his heels.

"I'm sorry for your loss."

Esther looked down and Tate noticed her eyes were puffy and her nose red. She dabbed a tissue at her tear ducts.

"Thank you," said Ernest. "No matter how much you prepare yourself, it's still a shock."

"I know," said Tate. He glanced around the room. "Are you moving stuff out?"

"We're selling it. To help pay for the funeral," said Ernest, looking around, "but most of this stuff just needs to be junked. It's not worth much."

Tate didn't know how to respond.

Ernest motioned toward a doorway across the room. "Logan's meeting with the social worker. They're trying to find a placement for him in foster care."

Tate's eyes whipped to Ernest's face. "Foster care?" He'd just assumed, upon seeing that Peggy had a brother that Logan would stay with him.

Ernest started to speak, but Esther looked up, her eyes glistening with tears.

"Don't judge us like that!" she snapped.

Tate's eyes widened in surprise.

"Esther," said Ernest wearily.

"No, I heard his tone." She squared off in front of Tate, dropping her voice to a hiss. "We asked him to come with us, but we live in Redding. He refused. He said he wanted to stay here and finish out school. That his mother wanted that." She choked on a sob, covering her mouth with a hand. "What are we supposed to do?"

"I understand," said Tate, trying to placate her. "I'm not judging anyone. I'm so sorry. I know how hard this must be." He glanced toward the kitchen. Jeez, what was this kid going to do? He didn't even have enough money for a funeral for his mother, and clearly his uncle didn't either or they wouldn't be selling old furniture for a few bucks. "What about Logan's father? Could he help?"

Esther's lips thinned and Ernest quickly shook his head.

"I hope Mitchell Baxter is dead and in his grave. He was a vile man," said Esther. She glanced over her shoulder at the kitchen doorway. "He beat Peggy for years, then he started on Logan."

Tate felt his heart catch. Good God, he hadn't known any of this.

"The first time he struck Logan, Peggy wised up and got a restraining order. Mitchell skipped town and good riddance," said Esther. "We haven't heard from him since. Peggy didn't even try to get child support. She wanted nothing from that man."

"I understand," said Tate, feeling the weight of Logan's predicament land heavily on him.

Esther's eyes filled with tears again. "Peggy went through so much and just when it seemed like she had her life in order, she got cancer. How is that fair? Tell me. How the hell is any of this fair?" Before Tate could answer, she shook her head and held up a hand, then hurried out of the room.

Ernest gave Tate an uncomfortable smile. "Sorry about that. She and Peggy were real close. She's not taking this well and she really thought Logan would come with us."

Tate nodded. God, he felt so inadequate to deal with this.

"Go ahead and talk to Logan. I'd better go see about her," said Ernest, then he headed off after his wife.

Tate screwed up his courage and wended his way through the furniture to the doorway. It opened onto a sunny kitchen painted in yellow with bright white cabinets and vintage teapots on every surface. Logan and an African American woman were sitting at the table. The woman wore a blue suit and skirt with black heels, her badge affixed to the pocket on the jacket. Her black hair was styled away from her face and she had large, dark eyes that assessed him the minute he entered the room.

Logan looked up. The kid seemed thinner than he had just a few days ago, his eyes heavy, his hair mussed. He wore a t-shirt and a pair of khaki shorts, sneakers on his feet. "Hey, Tate," he said.

"Hey, kid," answered Tate, moving to the side of the table and gripping his shoulder. "How you holding up?"

Logan lifted both hands and let them fall again.

Tate held out his hand to the woman. "I'm Tate Mercer, Logan's employer."

She shook his hand. "I'm Mary Singleton. I'm the social worker assigned to Logan's case." She laid her hand on the file sitting on the table before her. "Mr. Mercer, Logan actually told me he wanted to discuss his situation with you. Maybe you can help me convince him that foster care is his best option if he wants to stay in Sequoia."

Logan gave Tate a pleading look. Tate pulled out the chair and took a seat perpendicular to both of them. He didn't really want to get into a discussion of this nature, but Logan needed some guidance since he was all alone now.

"I don't think there's much choice, unless you go with your uncle, Logan," he said.

"I'm not going to Redding. Mom wanted me to finish school here and that's what I'm going to do."

"Then you have to go into foster care," said Mary.

"Not if I get emancipated."

Mary shifted to face Tate. "Tell him what a bad idea that is. If he goes into foster care, he'll have his college tuition paid. It's not something he should take lightly."

Tate grimaced. He really had no place saying anything either way.

"I'm not going into foster care. I'm not living with some family that I don't know like I'm some trash that needs dumping somewhere."

"It's not like that at all, Logan. I would never place you with a family that didn't want you. I have a few good candidates in mind. They have other foster kids…"

"So, I'll just be part of a crowd. That's awesome. All this time I've been living on my own, doing my own thing, and you want me to suddenly start answering to someone else."

Tate had never heard him so angry before.

"You should have been under someone's supervision before this. If we'd have known how sick your mother was…"

"You would have taken me away from her? You would have denied me the last few months of her life?"

"We could have gotten her hospice care and you could have gone to school full time."

Logan stood up, leaning on the table. "I don't need your help. I do fine. I'll go back to the continuation school and I'll work full time for Tate. I supported us before."

Mary's eyes widened and she looked around the kitchen. "How do you figure that? I looked in that refrigerator, Logan, and there's nothing inside. The yard's overgrown, the house needs serious repairs. How are you going to pay rent? You were barely holding it together!"

"I'm not going to a stranger's house!" Logan shouted, banging his fist on the table.

Tate and Mary jumped.

"This display just proves to me that you're a child still!" she said, just as angrily.

Tate lowered his head and closed his eyes. He could understand both sides of this argument, but this wasn't solving anything. The kid had just lost his mother, the only person he had. He needed someone who understood him, who cared about him, who wanted the best for him.

"What if I do it?" he heard himself say.

Silence fell instantly.

He opened his eyes and looked up at Mary. "What if I become Logan's foster parent?"

Mary stared at him, mouth agape. He glanced up at Logan to see the same expression on his face.

"Look, I was a cop in L.A. I can get character witnesses to vouch for me. I'm also a consultant here in Sequoia for Sheriff Wilson. I know he'll vouch for me. Then there's Zion Sawyer. She owns the coffee shop in town, and Cheryl and Dwayne Ford. They can all tell you what sort of a man I am."

"Mr. Mercer…"

"No, hear me out. I've known Logan for two years. We've worked together every day without a problem. I know his situation. I know what sort of a kid he is."

"Mr. Mercer…"

"I have my own home. It has three bedrooms and two baths. Two of the rooms aren't even being used and I own my own business. I'm financially stable and I make a good income."

Logan sat down hard, staring at him.

"Look, Ms. Singleton, Logan's a good kid. He's been through a lot, but he knows me. He knows what I expect out of him and he's never failed me. Not once. I think this could work out."

"You don't know what you're getting into. Being his employer is one thing, but he's a teenager and he's grieving."

"I'll get him into grief counseling." He held up a hand. "You've got to admit this is a better solution than him being emancipated."

She hesitated, considering. "You said you were a cop, Mr. Mercer. Does that mean you have guns in your house?"

"I have a gun, locked in a wall safe, and I keep the key on my person at all times."

"I'd have to inspect your home."

"Understood."

"We'd have to get an emergency hearing with a judge."

"That's fine."

"Sheriff Wilson would have to vouch for you in person."

"I'll call him right now."

"Why don't we wait for a few days, Mr. Mercer? Give yourself time to think this through completely."

Tate chewed on his inner lip. He probably should think about it a bit more, but it just felt right. "Where would Logan go for those few days?"

"Either to a foster home or he'd have to go with his uncle."

"No. If that's the case, let's try to get a hearing today."

Her eyes shifted to Logan. "Is this what you want?"

Logan glanced between Tate and the social worker. Tate held his breath, not sure how the kid was going to react. He couldn't believe how much he wanted Logan to say yes. He cared about this kid and he couldn't stand the thought of him winding up with strangers either.

"Hell yes!" said Logan.

Mary waggled a finger in front of his face. "Hold on a minute, young man. This isn't a ticket to run wild. You will be expected to follow all of Mr. Mercer's rules and I will be checking up on you frequently. One hint that you aren't doing what you're supposed to be doing and I pull the plug on this experiment. Do you understand me?"

"I understand," said Logan. "Seriously, Ms. Singleton, you don't know anything about me. I'm probably more responsible than Tate is."

Tate had to agree that might be true.

Mary Singleton shook her head, reaching for her phone. "Don't make me regret this, Mr. Baxter," she scolded.

* * *

Tate closed the door after Mary Singleton went down the walkway, the click of her heels echoing back at him. He pressed his forehead to the door and breathed out a sigh of relief. She'd been thorough in her inspection, even going through his underwear drawer. The judge had only granted Tate temporary custody. He and Logan had to report back in a month with Logan's school attendance record, Mary's weekly reports, and Logan's grades.

"Is she gone?" asked the kid from the hallway.

Tate turned around, looking at him. Ernest had driven Logan's bed and dresser and clothes over after the judge made his ruling. Logan had chosen the room at the end of the hallway, which suited Tate just fine. It would be harder to sneak out, since Tate's room was the closest to the living room and the front door. Unless he went out the window, but Tate didn't think Logan was that sort of teenager.

"Yeah. What do you want for dinner?"

Logan shrugged. He'd been quiet. He was a quiet kid, but this quiet was even more pronounced. Tate didn't want to push too hard. His mother had just died and Logan didn't know how he was going to pay for her funeral. It was a whole lot for anyone to take.

"A pizza?" Tate suggested.

"Sure," said Logan.

"Do you have homework?"

Logan gave him a skeptical look. "I don't know. I sort of missed a week of school."

Tate motioned to the armchair next to his recliner. "Come sit for a minute, okay?"

Logan walked over and sat on the edge of the chair, clasping his hands. He watched Tate from the corner of his eyes warily.

Tate sat down so he wasn't looming over him. He really didn't want to intimidate. He braced his forearms on his thighs and clasped his hands. "Look, kid, I know how incredibly hard this must be for you."

"Yeah, I'd rather not talk about it."

"Sure, I get that," said Tate. "But you've got to talk to somebody. Ms. Singleton gave me a list of grief counselors and I'm going to call them tomorrow. Would you rather have a woman or a man?"

"Man," said Logan sullenly.

"I also think you need to go back to school tomorrow."

Logan's eyes snapped to his face. "What?"

"I'm sorry, but I think it's best. You need to be with your friends, get your mind off things."

"I've got to arrange my mother's funeral!" he said angrily.

Tate stared at him. He could honestly say he'd never seen Logan angry before, but he figured he probably had a right to be for now. "We'll do that this weekend. I promise you. I'll get Bill Stanley and Daryl to cover at the shop for us and we'll go plan her funeral." He didn't tell him that he was going to see if the merchants on Main Street would pitch in. He'd tell Logan that after he got donations.

Logan looked down. "Fine. I'm not trying to be difficult."

"I know that. This is all strange for you. You have a right to be a little angry right now."

A knock sounded at the door. Tate pushed himself to his feet and headed toward it. Zion waited on the other side and her expression was anxious as she peered past him into the house.

"Is he here?" she said.

"Yeah," answered Tate, stepping back to let her inside.

Logan had climbed to his feet when the knock sounded. Zion went right over to him and wrapped him in her arms, hugging him tight. Logan gave Tate a startled look over her shoulder and Tate shrugged, then the kid hugged her back, pressing his face into her wild red hair. In that instant, he looked like a little boy, needing comfort. Tate couldn't help but admire how perceptive Zion was.

After a moment, she pulled back and clasped his shoulders. "I ordered dinner," she said. "It should be here in a bit. Are you hungry?"

Logan forced a smile. "Sure," he said, although he didn't sound convincing.

"Dwayne put together some sandwiches and coleslaw. Daryl said he'd deliver it on his way out of town."

"Thanks, Zion," said Logan. He stepped back. "I think I'm just going to go back to unpacking." He pointed a thumb over his shoulder into the kitchen. "After I get a soda."

Zion watched him walk into the kitchen, then she faced Tate, giving him a searching look. "You okay?"

He nodded, leaning over to see if Logan could hear them. He took a step closer to Zion and lowered his voice. "He needs help with the funeral expense. Do you think the other merchants will pitch in?"

"I know they will. I'll start a collection tomorrow."

"Good."

She glanced over her shoulder as well. "Are you sure about this, Tate?"

"As sure as anyone can be. I couldn't let him go with strangers and he refused his uncle. It seemed like the best solution." He scratched the back of his neck. He wanted to pull Zion into his arms and hug her. He felt like he deserved a hug too after his day. "We'll work it out. I'm going to find a grief counselor tomorrow."

"Good," she said again. "Do you think we should cancel our date tomorrow night?"

Tate's eyes widened. No, he didn't want to cancel tomorrow night. He'd been looking forward to it for months, but he knew Logan might not want to stay here alone. "I don't know. Maybe we should. Damn it."

"Cancel what?" said Logan, coming out of the kitchen.

Tate didn't know how to respond.

Zion shifted to face him. "We were just going to dinner, that's all."

"You were going on a date," said Logan.

"Well…" answered Zion.

"Go. Look, Tate, if this is going to work, you can't walk around me like you think I'm going to fall apart. Go with Zion. You both deserve it. Besides, I'm so sick of everyone acting like I'm some tragic character in a movie. I'm fine. I'll be fine. I can stay by myself for a few hours."

Tate didn't like that, but maybe he could get Jaguar to help out. He didn't say anything, in case Jaguar had other plans, but Jaguar had recently lost his mother too. He might be a good sounding board for Logan.

Logan drank from his soda can. "The two of you have been moping around each other for months. It's disgusting. Go on your date and get it over with, then the rest of us can get back to living our lives."

Both Zion and Tate burst into laughter. The comment was so like the Logan of old that Tate felt the tension ease inside of him a little. Logan rolled his eyes and walked to the hallway, heading toward his room.

Zion turned to face Tate, dropping her gaze. A blush painted her cheeks and made her freckles more pronounced. God, he found everything about this woman so damn enticing. He reached up and tugged on a curl.

"Well, what do you think?" He smoothed the curl between his fingers, thinking how soft her hair was.

She lifted those green eyes to him. "I don't like him being alone."

"What if I see if Jaguar would come over and stay with him?"

Zion nodded. "That's not a bad idea." He knew she immediately got the connection. She gave him a sideways look that had all sorts of flutters coursing through him. "I have a special dress I want to wear for tomorrow night."

He licked his lips and let the backs of his fingers trail over her cheek. "Yeah. Then I'll have the coach and horses polished by six, milady."

She giggled, but Tate heard a groan from the hallway. He ignored it.

"Are the horses street legal?" she asked, giving him a sultry look.

"Not even a little. We'll be going rogue. Care to walk on the wild side with me."

"Oh kill me now!" came Logan's moan.

Zion burst into giggles and pressed her forehead to the middle of Tate's chest. Tate slid his hand under her chin and lifted her face until their eyes met again.

"I'll be over at 6:00 tomorrow night," he said, starting to lower his head.

She pressed two fingers to his lips to stop him. "Date first," she said, then she brushed by him for the door. He got a whiff of her vanilla shampoo and he wanted to bury his face in the thick locks, but he let her go.

When she opened the door, Daryl was waiting on the other side, his hand lifted to knock. He held up a bag and the smell of barbecue wafted into the house. "Dinner!" he said brightly, sliding past Zion and heading for the kitchen.

Zion smiled over her shoulder at Tate and stepped outside. "See you tomorrow night, Prince Charming," she said and Tate could hardly wait.

CHAPTER 5

Zion filled Cleo's bowl, stroking her hand down the kitten's sleek back, then she grabbed her purse off the kitchen table and turned for the door. Rebekah stood in the entrance, her eyes heavy from sleep, her hair disheveled, wearing pink silk baby doll pajamas and fuzzy pink slippers.

"Where are you going?" she said, rubbing her eye with a fist. "It's 6:30 in the morning."

"I know," said Zion, coming forward and kissing her cheek. "I have to get to work."

"Work? I thought you owned the business."

"I do, which is why I have to get to work." She pushed past her and into the living room, going to the closet near the door and pulling it open. She reached inside for her hoodie, setting her purse on the floor at her feet.

Rebekah followed her. "What am I supposed to do today?"

"For starters, go back to bed and sleep in, then…" Zion looked around the cottage. She didn't have much that would entertain someone like Rebekah. "…read a book."

Rebekah made a face. "I did that yesterday. Are you going to work everyday?"

Zion shut the closet and picked up her purse. "Every single day," she said. She hadn't told Rebekah that she was going on a date tonight. She didn't think that was going to sit very well. She hurried to the front door. "I'll call you later. Why don't you come down and meet me for lunch?"

"Okay. But we're not going to that barbecue place again." She pointed a finger at Zion. "No more barbecue."

"No barbecue. We'll go to *Up to No Gouda.* It has salads."

Rebekah made a face. "The names of these places. Honestly," she said, shuffling back toward the bedroom.

Zion smiled after her, then went out the door, closing it behind her. Fallen leaves skittered across the walkway as she climbed into the Optima. When she drove by Tate's house, she noticed his truck was gone. She wondered if that meant he'd taken Logan to school this morning.

She arrived at the municipal parking lot a few minutes later. No one else was around, so she climbed out and hurried down the street. A brisk wind made her clutch her hoodie tighter around her and she hunched her shoulders. Fall was definitely here now.

The wind blew the door to the *Caffeinator* open. Dottie looked up from kneading dough, watching her struggle to push the door closed again. The little bell above the door jingled merrily. "Morning, Dottie," Zion called, pulling a leaf from her hair.

"Morning, sugar, how are you?"

"Good." She hurried around the counter and into her office, stuffing her purse in her desk. She started to remove her hoodie, but it was still too cold in the coffee shop without it. She needed to get some thermal shirts to go under her *Caffeinator* t-shirt.

Removing the money from the safe, she came back out and grabbed a clean apron from under the counter, tying it around her waist and running the ties behind her hair, then she twisted her hair into a bun and secured it with pins she'd stuffed into her jeans pocket.

"It's really windy out there," she told Dottie, setting the money bag next to the register. "I wonder if we're getting a storm."

"You never know. The weather in the Sierras can be unpredictable."

Zion counted the money into the register as Dottie prepared the second batch of her famous cinnamon breadsticks. The first batch was already in the display case, steaming up the glass. After she finished with the money, Zion washed her hands and counted the pastries in the display.

"We need some chocolate chip cookies. I'll go put on a batch," she told Dottie.

"Sounds good," said the older woman as one of their regulars walked through the doors.

While Dottie waited on him, getting his coffee, Zion pulled the frozen cookie dough out of the freezer and laid a layer of cookies on the cookie sheet, then popped it in the oven. The first thing Dottie did when she came in at 6:00 was turn on the ovens to heat them.

When Zion came out again, Dottie had served a few more customers. One older couple had taken the seats in front of the window, while a teenager had tossed himself down on the couch, reading a book. Zion figured it must be for his English class because he'd occasionally highlight something on the page.

Going out to wipe off the tables, Zion took a detour into the bathroom to make sure the soap dispenser and the toilet paper roll were both full. She checked the towel dispenser as well. When she came out, Dottie handed her her favorite Chai tea.

Zion sipped it as she moved behind the cash register. "Thank you."

"I heard about Logan's mother," Dottie said, beginning her next batch of cinnamon breadsticks.

"Tate agreed to be his foster father," Zion said, leaning her hip against the counter.

"No kidding," said Dottie, her brows lifting behind her cat's eye glasses. "Well, I guess that makes sense. Poor kid. I feel for him."

"So do I. Hey, when the other businesses open, I'm gonna step out for a bit. Tate mentioned that Logan didn't have enough money to pay for the funeral. I'm going to see if some of the other merchants might be able to pitch in."

"That's a good idea," said Dottie, glancing up as the bell over the door tinkled. "Count me in for $200.00."

"Dottie, that's too generous," said Zion, watching as the tall, handsome man strolled in, glancing around. He had dark hair parted on the side and combed back from a striking face. A five o'clock shadow dusted his cheeks and his eyes were so dark, it was hard to distinguish his iris from his pupil. He wore an LAPD t-shirt with a white long sleeved t-shirt under it and a pair of jeans with hiking boots. He smiled crookedly at Zion as he approached the counter.

"Good morning," he said. His shoulders were broad, his biceps straining the lines of the shirt. Zion's attention was snagged by the LAPD logo on his chest. He had an intimidating aura about him and she could feel Dottie's alertness beside her.

"Good morning," Zion said in return, setting her tea on the counter. "What can I get for you?"

"I'll have an espresso. I like my coffee strong and bitter."

Zion smiled at him and glanced at Dottie, but the older woman was already moving to fix his drink. Zion rang up the total and the man handed her a debit card. As she swiped the card, he took a look around the coffee house.

"This is nice. Homey. I've never been to Sequoia before."

"Well, welcome," said Zion, handing him back his card and a receipt. Her eyes drifted back to the LAPD logo on his shirt. "Are you from LA?"

"I am. I'm on vacation. A friend of mine owns a shop in Sequoia. I'm trying to find him, but I can't remember the sort of shop. Maybe you know him? Tate Mercer?"

Zion fought to keep her face neutral. Dottie peered at her over her shoulder, but Zion ignored the question. She didn't know who this guy was and she sure wasn't going to give Tate up before she talked to him. Tate had left LA for a reason, one he hadn't shared with her, and she knew he didn't like to talk about it. Whenever she brought it up, he changed the subject.

"What's your name?"

He held out his hand. "Keith Poole. Me and Tate worked the force together for years. I hated it when he left."

When Zion gave him her own hand, he crushed her fingers. She didn't understand why so many men felt that was necessary.

"Zion Sawyer," she said.

"So, do you know where I can find him?"

Dottie set his cup on the counter in front of him and exchanged a look with Zion.

"How about something sweet to go with your espresso? Dottie makes the best cinnamon breadsticks. We're famous for them."

He chuckled, lifting the coffee to his lips. "Sure. Sounds good."

Zion got a couple of breadsticks out for him and a small cup of the frosting that Dottie prepared with it, while Dottie rang up the second sale. Handing the warm pastries over to him, Zion dropped her eyes, hoping he'd leave and not question her about Tate anymore.

He lifted the bag to his nose and sniffed. "Man, this smells heavenly." Then he reached into his pocket and pulled out a business card, sliding it across the counter to Zion. "Look, if you see Tate, will you give him my card? Tell him Poole says hi and I'd like to take him out for a beer."

Zion picked up the card, turning it in her fingers.

He rapped the knuckles of his right hand on the counter, gave her a wink, and strode to the door, pushing it open with his back. Then he headed to the left away from the rest of Main Street. Zion blew out a sigh and put the card in her back pocket.

"How come you didn't want to tell him where to find Tate?" Dottie asked, wiping her hands on her apron.

"I don't know," said Zion, staring at the door. "I just want to talk to Tate first before I give him away." She turned to face Dottie. "Tate left a promising career as a cop to become a hardware store owner. Something happened in LA, but he never talks about it. I just figure he might not be too excited to see someone from his past and I thought I might give him a warning."

Dottie nodded, going back to her dough. "You're sweet on that guy," she said. "Why don't the two of you just get it over with and go out on a date or something?"

Zion made a scoffing sound. "Dottie, look at you, playing matchmaker."

Dottie chuckled as she picked up her rolling pin. "When you go protecting a man the way you just did, you have feelings for him. No sense in pretending otherwise. You forget. I was here to see *the kiss*."

Zion felt a blush paint her cheeks and she swatted the air near Dottie. Dottie pealed off into laughter and dusted the cutting board with flour.

* * *

"What am I supposed to do now?" whined Rebekah as they walked into the *Caffeinator* from lunch. "I don't want to go back to your place."

The coffee shop wouldn't get busy again until after the high school let out. Then, teenagers would take all the bistro tables and lounge on the couches and armchairs. Another spat of customers would enter when people got off work.

Dee manned the espresso machine, making a coffee for an older customer with a cane. Zion smiled at him as she made her way to her office, Rebekah trailing behind her. She stashed her purse and watched as Rebekah threw herself into the chair on the other side of the desk.

"Why can't we go see a movie?" Rebekah asked.

"I have to work. You're going to have to find something to do to keep yourself occupied."

"Okay, let me work. I can make coffee."

Zion arched an eyebrow. "You think so? I can't even get that darned machine to work."

"Well, you aren't the handiest person I know. Show me how."

Zion grabbed her apron from the peg behind her door and tied it on. "Okay. I need to bake some pumpkin bars, so you can help Dee while I'm in the kitchen."

She led Rebekah out to the counter and got her an apron. Rebekah gave it a skeptical look. "Do you have something in cyan or maybe magenta? Pink just doesn't go with my complexion."

Zion gave her an arch look.

"Fine," Rebekah said, shaking it out. "I'll wear pink."

Zion gave Rebekah's heels a skeptical look. "Are you sure about this? It's a lot of standing around."

"I'll be fine. I've walked miles in these puppies," she said, turning out her foot so Zion could admire her heels.

Zion had to admit, she preferred her pink tennis shoes over the heels she'd had to wear when she worked for the insurance company. There were definitely some benefits to having her own business.

"Dee?"

Dee turned, all bright smiles, his shaggy hair falling over his eyes. "I thought up another name for our Halloween festival."

"Okay," said Zion, shifting topics. "What is it?"

"Fangs for the Memories." He nodded a few times.

Zion and Rebekah frowned at him.

"*Fangs* for the Memories," he repeated, emphasizing the first word.

"No, I got it," said Zion, patting his shoulder, "but what do you say we keep working on it?"

"No problemo, boss lady."

"Sooo…" said Zion, knowing Dee probably wasn't going to like what she was about to say. "I'm gonna go bake and Rebekah's going to assist you."

Dee's smile dried.

Zion exchanged a look with Rebekah. Dee still didn't move.

"Dee?"

Dee blinked dramatically. "I'm sorry," he said with a laugh, "she's gonna do what?"

"Assist you. She wants to learn how to work the espresso machine."

"She wants to learn how to work the espresso machine," Dee repeated.

"Right. Can you teach her?"

"Can I teach her?"

Rebekah gave Zion a bewildered look. "Did he have a stroke or something?"

Zion started to answer, but she wasn't sure.

Dee narrowed his eyes in concentration. "Tallah comes in at 3:30."

"I know, but until then…"

"We don't have many customers. I can handle it."

"Dee…"

"Fine. If he doesn't want my help, I'll just help you bake," said Rebekah.

Zion felt panic move through her. She enjoyed baking and she didn't want anyone doing it with her, especially not Rebekah. Rebekah wouldn't find baking enjoyable. "Just show her how to use the espresso machine, Dee, please." She gave him a look, hoping he'd understand she wanted him to cooperate.

"Fine," he said. "Come on."

"Well, don't act like you're being asked to clean toilets," groused Rebekah.

Zion felt a little guilty as she beat a hasty retreat into the kitchen. She snatched her headphones off her desk and put them in her ears, turning on her music. It didn't take long for her to get lost in what she was doing. Baking was one of Zion's favorite things and she'd discovered that she was almost as good at it as Dottie.

When she'd made enough for the next day, she turned off her music and pulled out her earphones. Tallah was just heading to Zion's office to drop off her backpack and she pointed emphatically over her shoulder into the coffee house.

"You might want to get out there," she said as she disappeared from sight.

Zion frowned, but a moment later, she heard voices raised in argument.

"That does not look like a heart. Honestly, how hard is it to make a proper heart?" said Rebekah.

"I don't know. Maybe it's about the hardest thing anyone can do, dude!"

"Dude! Are you calling me dude? Let me have the spoon. I'll show you how to do it."

"You literally learned how to work the machine just an hour ago, but you suddenly know how to make coffee art?" Dee made a scoffing noise. "You couldn't even make the whip cream dispenser work."

"It was clogged. When was the last time you cleaned the damn thing?"

Zion scrambled around the stainless steel prep table and hurried out into the coffee shop. Dee and Rebekah were faced off against each other, a cappuccino held hostage between them and a wide-eyed teenager on the other side of the counter looking like she was about to bolt.

Zion grabbed the spoon out of Rebekah's hand and turned her toward the office. "We'll just take off now that Tallah's here, Dee."

Dee put his hand on his hip. She'd never seen mild-mannered Deimos Hendrix so worked up.

"Hold on, I'm not done," said Rebekah, digging in her heels.

"You're done," Zion said, sidestepping Tallah. She pushed Rebekah into her office and Rebekah whirled to face her.

"I could have done it better."

Zion clasped her hands and held them before her. "Please, Becks, please. I need Dee. He works harder than anyone I know. You can't get him all worked up like that."

"Well, what am I supposed to do for the next two weeks? I'm not moping about your house. It makes me too sad and I start missing Wendell."

Zion held up her hands. "Okay, look, you can come with me in the morning. Maybe that will work out better for you."

"You promise."

"Yes," said Zion. "Come on. Let's go home. I think you earned a glass of wine." She felt like a coward for not telling her about her date, but she figured Rebekah would be in a better mood once she got the heels off.

* * *

Zion stepped out of her bedroom and found Rebekah sitting on the couch in her high priced jogging suit, holding Cleo and sipping a glass of wine. Rebekah's eyes widened when she saw her. Zion had chosen a black sheath dress that came to mid-thigh. Rhinestones lined the bodice and the end of the sleeves around her wrist. Black Ferragamo pumps with rhinestones trailing from the instep to the toe covered her feet. She'd pulled her red curls into a loose chignon and pinned it with a rhinestone comb.

"Oh my God," said Rebekah, setting her glass on the table and climbing to her feet. "You are gorgeous." She stopped and put her hands on her hips. "You're going on a date."

Zion nodded, feeling horrible. "I'm sorry I didn't tell you."

"Are you kidding me? I'm happy for you," she said with a brilliant smile. "Who's the guy?" Then her eyes snagged on the shoes. "Oh my God, are those the Ferragamos?"

Zion nodded again. The Ferragamo pumps had been an impulse purchase and she'd never worn them. They cost her $500 on sale and she'd never bought anything that extravagant before, but Rebekah had talked her into it, saying every woman needed one pair of ridiculously expensive shoes.

Rebekah stopped in front of her. She had her black hair pulled up in a ponytail and she'd washed all the makeup off her face. She looked younger. Zion liked seeing her this way. She seemed more herself.

"You brought out the Ferragamos? Who's the guy?"

"Tate," Zion said, pulling at the hem of her dress.

Rebekah caught her hands in her own. "Hardware man?"

"Tate," said Zion again, emphasizing his name.

"I thought you weren't going to see him."

"Well…"

Rebekah put a hand on her hip. "Hold on. Does he know he's getting the Ferragamos?"

"He wouldn't even know what that was."

Rebekah's mouth hung open. "Lucas didn't even get the Ferragamos. This is serious."

"This isn't serious. It's just a date."

Rebekah shook her head. "You like him."

"Of course I like him. I wouldn't be going on a date if I didn't like him." She fussed with the dress some more.

Rebekah tapped her finger on her bottom lip. "I don't like the lipstick and you need a clutch."

"I don't have a clutch."

"I do," she said and grabbed Zion's hand, dragging her to her room. She rummaged around in her bags and brought out a silver clutch, then went into the bathroom.

Zion trailed after her, her eyes widening when she saw the makeup counter at Nordstrom's laid out across the bathroom vanity.

"You brought all this makeup with you?"

"Of course I did," said Rebekah, looking through the tray of lipstick. She selected one and grabbed Zion's chin, applying it. "Do this," she said and smacked her lips together.

Zion did as instructed when the doorbell rang. Rebekah shoved the lipstick tube in her hand and pushed past her. "Stick that in your clutch."

"Rebekah," Zion called after her. She wanted to be the one to open the door. She was a little afraid Rebekah might scare Tate off.

Taking one last look in the mirror, she tried to walk as calmly as she could into the living room, but butterflies had taken up residence in her belly and she felt jittery. She didn't know why she was so nervous, but she was.

Tate had stepped into the room and was talking with Rebekah. His eyes immediately tracked over to her and stuck. He wore a pair of black slacks, a silk collared shirt in navy blue, and a sports coat. His brown hair was combed back from his face and he was cleanly shaven. A pair of loafers covered his feet.

"Wow," he breathed, moving toward her.

Zion ducked her head and smiled up at him.

"You are stunning." He sounded a little breathless.

"Thank you, sir."

He gave her a crooked smile and motioned to the door. "Your carriage awaits, milady," he said.

Zion heard herself giggle as she walked toward the door. Rebekah kissed her cheek, holding the door open for them. "Have a good time," she said.

"Thank you," said Zion, stepping outside.

Tate lightly put his hand in the center of her back to guide her down the walkway and to his truck parked on the street. He opened the door for her and gave her an apologetic look. "It's not much of a chariot. I should probably get a better car for things like this."

She eyed the climb into the cab, then eyed the short skirt of her dress. Tate placed a hand under her elbow and lifted her easily onto the running board. Zion settled herself and smiled at him as he hurried around the front of the truck and climbed in beside her. He smelled like soap and aftershave.

She glanced up when she felt his eyes on her. "What?" she asked him.

He shook his head, smiling. "I'm just feeling like the luckiest man in the world right now."

Zion blushed and dropped her eyes as he started the truck. They pulled out and drove back down the street.

Zion noticed Jaguar's Mercedes in Tate's driveway. "Jaguar agreed to stay with Logan tonight?"

"He did. He brought over two guitars and he was giving him a lesson when I left."

"He's a nice guy."

"He is."

"How's Logan doing?"

Tate tapped his hands against the steering wheel. "He went to school today, although he didn't want to. I think it's gonna take some time, though. I found a counselor and he's going to see Logan next week."

"That's good." She watched the road go by. "Oh, I forgot to tell you. Someone came into the coffee shop today looking for you."

Tate glanced over, giving her a skeptical look. "Looking for me?"

"Yeah, he had an LAPD t-shirt on and he said he worked with you on the force."

Tate went still. "Did he give you a name?"

"Keith Poole. Did you work with him?"

Tate's jaw clenched, but he nodded. "We were on a gang task force together. Did he say what he wanted?"

"He said he was here on vacation and he wanted to touch bases with you. I didn't tell him where you were. I wanted to talk with you first."

Tate glanced over at her again. "Thanks. I appreciate that." He reached out and took her hand. "I don't have too many people watching my back. Thank you, Zion."

She folded her other hand over his and the tension eased between them. She'd always felt so at ease with Tate, but this date had made her more nervous than she'd expected. It was nice to get back on an even footing with him.

They pulled into the crowded parking lot of *Corkers*. Tate parked and then hurried around the truck to open her door. He held out his hand to help her down and she accepted it, then he placed his hand in the middle of her back again to guide her to the door. The intimate gesture sent the butterflies to fluttering in her stomach again.

The hostess seated them immediately and Zion felt a little apprehensive as she realized they were sitting at the exact same table she'd sat at with David not that long ago. Tate gave her a curious look.

"You okay?"

"Yeah," she said, not wanting to spoil the evening by talking about another man. She focused her attention on the candle in the center of the table and shook out her napkin to place on her lap.

A waiter appeared. He looked like he was a college student, wearing a white button up shirt, a red bowtie, and a black apron tied around his waist. He handed them both menus and gave Tate the wine list.

"The prime rib is our special tonight. Prepared with a horseradish sauce on the side and our red skinned mashed potatoes."

"Thank you," said Tate.

Zion smiled up at him.

"We'll have a bottle of the Riesling," Tate said, giving the wine list back to the waiter.

"Excellent choice. I'll just give you a moment with the menu." And he went off.

"Why did you pick Riesling?" Zion asked.

Tate's eyes widened. "I'm sorry. Did you want something else?"

"No," she said with a laugh, "it's perfect."

"I remembered you told me you like white wine and I like Riesling, so I hoped you did as well."

Zion felt a flush of pleasure and relaxed again. He'd remembered she liked white.

He studied her in the candlelight and she watched him in return. Tate wasn't as handsome or as polished as David. He certainly didn't have as much money, but there was so much about him that she liked. He gave her goose bumps when he looked at her like this, something that had never happened with David, and the few times they'd kissed had been electric.

"Do you miss LA?" she asked, still thinking about the visit from Keith Poole.

Tate shook his head, playing with his silverware. "No, LA holds a lot of bad memories for me."

"Your divorce?"

He glanced up. "That and leaving the force."

"Do you miss being a cop?"

"Not as much as I thought I would," he said. He leaned forward and held out his hand for hers. "Do you miss San Francisco?"

"I miss my crazy parents." They both laughed.

"How long is Rebekah staying? I saw the Spider in your driveway, but I haven't had a chance to ask you about it."

So he watched her house the way she watched his. She liked thinking he was looking out for her. She traced her thumb over the back of his hand. "She showed up earlier this week. She broke up with Wendell the doctor. Of course, she moved in with him and when they broke up, she had nowhere to go."

"How long is she here for?"

"Another two weeks. She took all of her vacation to get away and figure things out."

"That's hard. It was hard starting over again after my divorce."

"Well, this is the fifth time Rebekah's had to start over."

Tate's eyes grew wide and they both burst out laughing. The waiter returned with the wine and they went through all the wine tasting ritual before Tate pronounced it acceptable.

"What can I get for you?"

Tate ordered the prime rib special, but Zion didn't feel like eating that much red meat. She got the chicken in a wine reduction with medallion potatoes and string beans.

She took a sip of her wine. "You know, I went to UCLA."

He nodded. "Why didn't you stay down there? People usually stay where they went to college."

"I didn't feel at home in LA. It was so crowded and everyone seemed to be scrapping for everything they got."

"Try being on the force."

"Still, I keep thinking about your friend coming all the way up here for a vacation. Why did *you* pick Sequoia? I mean, how did you even hear about it?"

"I came up here with some buddies to go on a camping, fishing trip." Tate gave a careless shrug. "One thing I'm not is a fisherman."

Zion laughed.

"Poole's on leave because of an officer related shooting. He knew I was here, and he doesn't have family, so I guess he thought he'd check it out."

"That makes sense. So, we won't be going on a fishing date, huh?"

Tate shook his head darkly. "I got so frustrated with the whole thing, I wanted to take out my gun and shoot the damn things."

Zion laughed.

The rest of the dinner passed pleasantly. Zion told him about growing up with her parents and her mom's crazy retirement hobbies and Tate talked about things that happened at the hardware store. After the dishes were cleared away, Zion felt sure she couldn't eat another bite, but Tate ordered a lemon bar and they split it. The refreshment of the lemon was just what she needed to complete a perfect meal.

Unlike with David, her conversation with Tate never lagged. She was a little frustrated that he wouldn't discuss the force any more than he did or his marriage, but everything else was so easy. He guided her out to the car and when he helped her in, his hand lingered a little longer this time. She looked down at him, her lips parting. His eyes zeroed in on her mouth and he drew a deep breath. Stepping back, he walked around the truck and climbed inside, starting the engine. The parking lot of *Corkers* had only gotten more crowded as the night went on.

They didn't talk much on the ride back, but Zion was okay with the silence, looking out at the shadows of trees as they drove back toward their neighborhood. However, once they got to her house, she was suddenly more aware of Tate.

He helped her out of the truck and walked her to the door. She marked that the placement of his hand had gravitated down, until she could feel it in the small of her back. Her pulse picked up and her butterflies returned. He smelled so good and the warmth of his hand sent tingles up her spine.

At the door, she turned to face him. He smiled at her, moving closer, licking his bottom lip. Zion shivered and it wasn't from the cold. There was definite chemistry between them, had been from the moment they met.

"I had a really nice time, Zion," he said. "Will you go out with me again?"

"Yes," she said, gripping the clutch tighter.

"Can I kiss you?" he asked, a mischievous glint in his eyes.

Zion laughed because the question was so unexpected. Neither one of them had asked for permission before. "Yes," she barely got out before he cupped her face in his hands and pressed his warm mouth to hers.

Zion gasped and dropped the clutch, then she was winding her arms around his neck and kissing him back. A moment later, his hands dropped from her face and he pulled her hips in against him, tilting his head and deepening the kiss. Zion threaded her fingers into his hair and felt her back come up hard against the door, but she didn't care. She suddenly couldn't get close enough to this man and they were wearing entirely too many clothes.

That's when the door was wrenched open and they stumbled apart. Tate caught Zion, pulling her against him to prevent her from falling into the house on her ass. They were both breathing hard and Zion was sure her lips were swollen as they stared at Rebekah.

"That's enough of that. Say goodnight, Hardware Man," she told him.

"Becks!" Zion gasped in horror.

Rebekah gave her a stern look. "Two minutes more," she said and closed the door again.

Zion sputtered in outrage, but Tate chuckled. He kissed her on the nose. "She's probably right. I mean, where would we go? I have a rockstar and a teenager at my house and you…you have a drill sergeant."

"I'm so sorry."

He put his hand under her chin. "Don't apologize. I just had the best first date of my life."

Zion blushed.

He kissed her sweetly again and released her, then he reluctantly backed up. "Maybe this is for the best. Prolong the agony."

She laughed and watched him hurry down the walkway to his truck. He waved before he got inside, then he wheeled around and parked in his own driveway.

Zion pushed open her door and stepped inside. Rebekah and Cleo were both waiting for her.

She opened her mouth to reprimand Rebekah when the other woman held up her hand.

"Before you get all angry at me, I did it for you."

Zion crossed her arms. "You did it for me?"

"Look where I always end up, Zion. I jump into bed with them right away and then it never works. You like this one. Take your time and let it develop."

Zion sighed and realized Rebekah was right. If this didn't work with Tate, she would have two men in this small town she had to avoid. "Fine," she said, taking off her pumps.

Rebekah frowned at her. "Where's your purse?"

Zion whipped back around to look at the door and her cheeks heated with embarrassment when she realized she'd completely forgotten it. Wow, Rebekah was right. She hadn't gone this far with David and they'd dated for months.

Biting her inner lip, she walked barefoot back to the door and retrieved the bag, shutting it again and then hurrying to her room.

Rebekah's laugh followed her.

CHAPTER 6

Tate walked into his house to find Jaguar sitting in his recliner, his guitar braced on his thigh, showing Logan different chords. Logan sat on the sofa, listening to the tattooed rockstar as if he were imparting to him the secrets of the universe. This was the same place Tate had left them when he went to pick Zion up, except an empty pizza box sat on the coffee table, filled with soda cans.

"Hey," said Jaguar, glancing up at him.

"Hey," said Tate, putting his keys on the hook beside the door. "You're still at it?"

"Yep. He's a natural," said Jaguar, nodding at Logan.

The kid beamed. He was clearly smitten with his famous music teacher.

"It's good practice for me. I've never formally taught anyone before, so this helps a lot."

Tate shrugged out of his sports coat. "Aren't his fingers going to be sore?"

Jaguar considered that, then turned to Logan. "He's right. We better stop for tonight." He hooked the guitar case with his foot and laid the guitar gently in it. Logan did the same with the guitar case that lay on the couch next to him.

The kid buckled it shut and picked it up, rising to his feet. Holding it out, he offered it to Jaguar. "Thanks a lot. I had fun."

Jaguar leaned back and looked up at the kid. "I brought that for you. It's yours."

Logan shook his head. "I can't take this. It's too much."

"Look, kid. You've agreed to let me practice my teaching on you. It's the least I can do. Think of it as payment for helping me out."

Logan glanced over his shoulder at Tate.

"Seems fair to me," Tate said.

Logan clutched the guitar case against his chest. "Thank you. Man, that means a lot."

Jaguar waved him off. "You're doing me an even bigger favor."

"If you ever need help in the shop…I mean, after I'm done working for Tate…well, I can come by."

"Sounds good," said Jaguar, flashing a smile.

Logan scratched the back of his neck. "Talk to you later."

"Later," said Jaguar.

"Night, Tate," the kid said, carrying the guitar toward his room.

"Night, Logan," Tate answered, watching him go.

"How was the date?" asked Jaguar, pushing the guitar case to the side and leaning back in the chair.

Tate walked over to the couch, tossing his sports coat onto the seat next to him. "It was pretty damn awesome, but her friend Rebekah ruined it."

"Ruined it? How?"

"She yanked open the door when we were…" Tate's voice trailed away.

"Oh, yeah, that sucks."

Tate gave him a nod, reaching forward to shut the empty pizza box. "Thanks for what you did with the guitar. I'll buy it from you."

"No, you won't. That transaction was between the kid and me. It didn't involve you."

"Well, I appreciate it."

Jaguar reached into the pocket on his shirt and pulled something out, passing it to Tate. "Here, I meant to give you this earlier. This is for the funeral expenses."

Tate took the check and unfolded it, studying the amount written on it. He folded it again and held it out to Jaguar. "I'm not accepting this. It's too much, Jaguar."

"Don't be an ass. It's not for you."

"I know it's not, but it's still too much."

Jaguar shifted in the chair to face him. "Look, Tate, I'm in a position where I can help. Let me do that. I'm a little offended that Zion asked everyone else and avoided me. My money's not tainted, you know?"

"I know, but you can't keep bailing out the entire town like this."

"Why not? This is where I grew up."

"Because you'll go broke," said Tate sternly.

Jaguar tilted his head. "Give me a little more credit than that. I'm not stupid."

"I didn't say you were."

"Well, then don't insult me. I'm a good financial planner and I've got the money. Why are we arguing this? I know what that kid's going through right now. If I can ease the burden just a little, let me do it."

Tate looked at the check again. "You're insane, you know that?"

"Whatever. At least I don't make out with my girl on the porch like some randy teenager."

Tate glared at him. "You didn't see her in that little black dress," he said.

"Hot, huh?"

"Hot, yeah, but don't ever let me hear you saying that about her again."

Jaguar laughed, then he reached into his pocket for his phone and looked at the display, pushing himself to his feet. "That's my cue to head out." He picked up his guitar. "Tell Logan I'll see him next Saturday morning at my shop for his lesson."

Tate rose also and walked him to the door. "I'll tell him. Thanks again."

Jaguar held up a hand as he went out the door and down to the street where Hakim waited with the Mercedes.

"You owe Hakim a raise!" Tate called to him.

"You just told me I was being irresponsible with my money," said Jaguar as he pulled open the rear door and tossed his guitar case inside.

"I never said irresponsible."

Jaguar paused, his hand resting on top of the passenger side door. "That's what I heard," he said.

Tate shook his head in amusement, watching as Jaguar climbed inside and closed the door. Hakim leaned forward and waved, then he sped off, heading out of town.

* * *

Tate walked down the rows of shelves in the storage room, counting inventory and marking it on the pad of paper he had. He knew it would be easier if he just logged it directly into the laptop, but some habits were hard to break.

He heard the buzzer over the door, but Bill Stanley was in his spot behind the register, reading the *Sequette*, the local paper. Tate usually avoided the paper. For the most part, it was a gossip column and advertisers weekly, but the Chamber had taken out a full page ad for the Halloween Festival, asking for volunteers to help organize it, and he was curious about whether they'd get any responses. A meeting was scheduled for Tuesday night at the *Caffeinator.*

Bill stuck his head inside the storage room. "Tate?"

Tate leaned out, lowering his glasses on his nose so he could see Bill.

"Guy's here to see you."

Tate frowned, taking the glasses off and tucking them into his shirt pocket. He dropped the pad of paper on the table and walked out to the counter.

Keith Poole stood on the other side, looking large and relaxed in a flannel shirt and jeans.

"Tater Tot!" he boomed, holding out his arms. "Man, you are one hard mother to track down."

Bill gave him a searching look, but he ignored it. "Keith, what the hell are you doing here?"

"Came up from LA to get in touch with nature. Darcy said you brag about this place all the time, so I thought I'd come see it for myself, spend some time with my old friend."

Tate offered his hand and Poole took it, squeezing so hard Tate fought a grimace. "You staying at a motel?"

"Naw, I got a cabin out by a little creek."

"Which creek?"

"Bearpaw. The lodge is called the *Back-of-Beyond.* They got about six cabins arranged in a horseshoe."

"Yeah, I know where that is," said Bill. "Take a left off the highway at Canyon Ravine Road. You know where *Perfect Ten Body Shop* is?"

Tate nodded, uncertain why Bill had suddenly become a tour guide.

"You go about five miles up Canyon Ravine and you'll find it."

"That's the one," said Poole. "Rented it for a month."

"A month?" said Tate in surprise. Darcy had told him Poole was on leave for shooting a fourteen-year-old kid, but Tate couldn't believe he was staying away from LA so long. He wasn't going to fight his suspension?

Poole's expression darkened. "Captain thought it would do me good."

Tate wasn't willing to discuss the situation with Bill Stanley standing right here, absorbing everything. He'd taken a seat on the stool again and was pretending to read the paper.

"How the hell are you, Tater Tot?" Poole said, giving him a huge smile. Jason had given Tate the nickname and it had stuck. Damn Jason, always thinking he was so clever. He didn't mind when Darcy used it, but he and Poole hadn't been that close. It was grating.

"Good."

Poole looked around the store. "Man, I never pictured you for this. You really like it out here in the middle of nowhere?"

"I do," said Tate.

Poole shook his head, bracing his hands on his hips. "What about nightlife? Women?"

Tate caught Bill Stanley's disapproving glance over the top of the newspaper. "I left LA to get away from nightlife. It gets old after awhile."

"Women?" said Poole, tilting his head.

Tate drew a breath for calm.

"Although, I did see a cute, little redhead at the coffee shop down the street. I asked her where I could find you and she wouldn't tell me. I might have to go back down there to get some coffee, if you know what I mean."

Tate felt his jaw clench. "She's seeing someone!" he blurted out, drawing a speculative look from Bill. Tate avoided looking at the older man.

"Ah, that's too bad. She's really cute."

"So, what are your plans?" said Tate, trying to change the subject.

"I thought I'd pick up some fishing equipment and see what I can catch in the creek, but we should grab a beer or something tonight."

"Tonight?"

"Yeah, you got plans."

Tate wished he thought quicker on his feet, but he didn't. "No, um, I don't."

"Then let's do it. Where's a good place to grab some burgers and a pitcher?"

Tate drew a deep breath and released it. He wasn't getting out of this. Poole had come all this way for some reason and he wasn't going to take no for an answer. "There's a barbecue down the street. *The Bourbon Brothers*. Let's meet there about 6:30."

"Sounds like a plan," said Poole, tapping his fist against the counter. "I'll see you then."

He turned and walked out of the store. Tate watched him head toward the coffee shop and he wanted to go after him, but he forced himself to stay where he was. Poole wasn't a threat, he told himself. Zion wouldn't go for a guy like that – a guy who was self-confident, handsome, and over six feet tall.

"Zion's seeing someone?" asked Bill conversationally.

Tate pushed away from the counter, headed for the storeroom and his inventory. "Yeah, she is," he said, wishing it hadn't come out like a growl.

* * *

"So," said Tate, tapping his fingers on the steering wheel, "how come you don't have a driver's license?"

He could see Logan pursing his lips out of the corner of his eyes. They'd just come back from the funeral parlor after making arrangements with Esther and Ernest, Logan's aunt and uncle. The kid was really quiet. When Tate had presented the money from the town, he'd dropped his head and covered his eyes. He hadn't said much beyond that.

"Didn't really think about it," Logan said, shrugging.

"What if we go get your permit and start practicing?"

"I guess," Logan answered.

Tate chewed on his inner lip. This is where he didn't feel equipped to deal with a teenager. He wasn't sure how much to push. "So, I'm meeting an old friend tonight for dinner at the *Bourbon Brothers.* You wanna come?" He couldn't leave the kid alone after making arrangements to bury his mother and Jaguar had his daughter this weekend.

"Naw, Uncle Ernie wants me to come over to the old house and help them pick out some pictures for Mom's memorial slide show. Can you drop me off there?"

"Sure. Look, Logan."

"Tate," he said, holding up a hand to stop him. "I'm fine. Just give me some space and time, man. I'm not going to go hitching a ride on a freight train or anything."

"Good," said Tate, concentrating on the road. "Good." But he wasn't sure if not hopping a freight train was the greatest way to evaluate someone's mental state. "I just need you to know that you can talk to me if you want."

Logan turned and looked out the side window.

Tate forced himself to concentrate on the road. Logan was a strong kid. He'd proven that when he'd gone to continuation school to help his mother by working full time, but he was still a kid and a kid needed his mother. Tate's own relationship with his mother was fraught because of his father, but that didn't mean he wouldn't be devastated if he lost her.

"Did Mr. Stanley's wife get mad that he was working another full day, so you could go with me?" Logan finally asked.

"I actually think she likes the break."

"Who's the old friend you're meeting?"

Tate didn't really want to talk about Keith Poole with anyone, but he figured if he wanted Logan to open up to him, he might have to do some opening up himself. "Guy I worked with on the force. He came up here for vacation."

He felt Logan's eyes on him. "You don't sound too excited to see him."

Tate twisted his hands on the steering wheel. "Poole's on administrative leave. He shot a fourteen-year-old kid and killed him."

"Shit!"

Tate shot Logan a stern look.

"Shoooot," he corrected, drawing the word out.

Tate smiled.

"Was the kid armed or something?"

"I don't know much about it. Poole and I worked together on a gang task force. The kid apparently hung around gang bangers, but he wasn't one himself."

"That would mess you up something good."

Tate shot another look at him.

"Killing a kid?"

"Yeah, which is probably why Poole came here. He needed to get away. That's ended the careers of a lot of cops."

He pulled up outside of Logan's old house. His uncle's beat up truck sat in the driveway. The kid didn't move for a moment, just staring at the overgrown front yard. A *For Rent* sign stared back at them.

"You okay?" Tate asked. If possible, the place looked even more forlorn than the last time Tate had been here.

"I don't know. I haven't been back since Mom…" His voice choked off.

Tate placed a hand on the kid's shoulder. "You're the strongest person I know, Logan. You can do this."

Logan looked over at him in surprise. "Seriously? You think that?" he asked.

Tate nodded. "I think that, yeah."

Logan gave a half-smile. "Thanks, Tate." He picked at a stray thread on his jeans. "You know that money you gave Mr. Bonds?"

Barry Bonds was the mortician in Sequoia, who ran the oddly combined *Barry Bonds Mortuary & Notary.*

"Yeah."

"Do you have a list of everyone that contributed and how much they gave?"

"Zion might. Why?"

Logan pulled the thread free. "I want to pay them back."

"No, Logan…"

He looked up, his expression stern. "I appreciate what you all did. You'll never know how much, but I want to pay for my mother's funeral. I don't know how long it'll take me, but I want to pay everyone back."

Tate felt a swelling of pride for this kid. He nodded, his throat too tight to speak.

Logan gave him another wane smile and pushed open the door of the truck. "I'll have Uncle Ernie drop me off when we're done."

"Wait." Tate remembered he had a key for Logan. He opened the glove compartment and pulled the key out. He'd attached it to a Sequoia keychain that he'd found in *Trinkets by Trixie* the other day. "This is yours."

Logan stared at the key, then palmed it. He swallowed hard. "Thanks, Tate. I mean, for everything, you know?"

"I know," Tate said.

Logan shut the truck door and started up the walk. Tate watched him until he got to the front door and opened it. Esther was waiting on the other side and pulled him into her arms for a bear hug. Tate put the truck in drive and pulled away, amazed at how much his life had changed in two years. He'd never seen himself as father material. Not that he felt like a father now, but he was glad he'd stepped up for Logan. That kid deserved so much more in his life than he'd been given, and yet, he'd turned out to be an exceptional young man.

* * *

The *Bourbon Brothers* was slammed on weekends. When Tate arrived at the barbecue, he found a line nearly out the door of people waiting to place their orders. He had to dodge Pedro, the busboy, as he sped past with a bucket filled with dirty dishes.

"Estar atento, amigo," he said.

"Lo siento," Tate answered, weaving his way to the counter.

Daryl shot him a quick look. "Hey, Tate man, can you pull a few pitchers of beer? I need a light and a regular, the microbrew stuff. We're slammed right now."

Tate slipped around the counter and quickly washed his hands, grabbing two pitchers at a time and placing them under the taps. He glanced up to the order window and caught sight of Dwayne and Al Wong, the short order cook, whipping up pulled pork sandwiches. His stomach grumbled as the delicious smells wafted out of the kitchen.

The swinging door opened and Cheryl, Dwayne's wife, appeared, carrying a tray with baskets on it. "Come to pitch in, Tate," she called to him.

"Just pulling some beers," Tate called back.

Cheryl was one of those women who just got more beautiful with age. She had a curvy figure, flawless brown skin, and large dark eyes. She kept her hair close cropped, but with her high cheekbones, it suited her. Her daughter, Tallah, would be just as beautiful when she grew up. She was already a stunning teenager.

Tate stopped the taps and carried the pitchers over to the counter, adding some plastic cups. A young man grabbed them and shoved the cups under his arm, walking to a table in the middle of the room.

"You need to hire some weekend help," Tate told Daryl.

Daryl rang up another order and pointed to the beer taps. "Another two, both domestic," he said. "You know anyone looking for weekend work?"

"I'll ask around," said Tate, grabbing two more pitchers.

"Hey, Tate, tell Daryl dinner's on us tonight," called Dwayne through the window.

Tate shook his head, turning off the taps. "I'm meeting an old work buddy, Dwayne. I'm buying." He carried the pitchers back to the counter and glanced up to see Poole enter the restaurant.

Tallah stepped out of the swinging doors, tying an apron around her waist as Cheryl came back with the tray. "I'll get the tables, Mom," she said, taking the tray. "You help Uncle Daryl."

Cheryl hugged her daughter. "You're a lifesaver, darlin," she said, then she went behind the counter, kissing Tate on the cheek. "Thank you for the help, cutie pie."

He beamed, but when he caught Dwayne glaring at him, he hurried around the counter to meet Poole. Poole's dark eyes lit up when he saw Tate walking toward him. "What? Do you have to moonlight here too just to make ends meet?"

Tate shook his head, motioning to a booth in the back corner that was just opening up. "We just help each other out when necessary." He pointed to the bench seat. "I'll get us a couple of beers."

Poole pulled out his wallet and threw a $20 on the table. "Get us a pitcher. I feel like getting drunk."

"Guess you'll be taking Uber back to Bearpaw Creek, huh?"

"Guess so."

Tate wove his way back to the counter.

"What can I get you, darlin?" called Cheryl.

"A pitcher of the domestic."

As she pulled the pitcher, Daryl gave him a piercing look. "He's from LA?"

"Yep."

"Cop?"

"Sort of," said Tate, but he didn't elaborate. He didn't think Poole would appreciate him telling everyone his business.

Cheryl put the pitcher on the counter and added two glasses. "You want the usual?" she asked.

"You know it."

She smiled and walked toward the kitchen as Tate carried the pitcher and glasses back to Poole. Poole grabbed the handle the moment Tate set it down and filled both glasses. He shoved one over to Tate and lifted the other.

"To old friends," he said over the cacophony of the other patrons.

Tate touched his glass to Poole's and took a sip. "Catch any fish today?"

"Naw." He downed half the glass. "You know what?"

"What?"

"Fishing is hella boring."

Tate laughed. He'd thought much the same thing when he tried it. He ran his finger through the condensation on the glass as Poole looked around the restaurant. "So is this the only place in town to eat?"

Tate laughed. "You'd think so, but we have a few other choices." He wasn't sure how to make small talk with

Poole. They'd never really been friends. He knew Poole had never married, but he dated around. He didn't have kids, but beyond that, Tate didn't know much more about him.

Poole finished off his beer and poured himself another one. "So, Tater Tot, you really happy here?"

"I am," said Tate, trying not to bristle at the nickname.

"You don't feel suffocated by all the trees."

Tate shrugged. "They're a little better than being suffocated by buildings."

"True. True." Poole sighed. "Man, I already miss LA though."

Tate leaned back in the seat. "How long do you think the investigation's going to take?"

"Who knows? You know how slow Internal Affairs moves. It's such bullshit."

"Well, I can kinda see the need for it. Do you have to see a shrink?"

"If they determine I'm not fit for duty, yeah. Anyway, I have to have a psych evaluation when I return." He pointed the glass at Tate. "That's also bullshit."

Tate bit his inner lip. "You killed a fourteen-year-old kid, Keith."

"Who was a gang banger."

"So they've proven that?"

Poole looked out at the restaurant. "Look, can we not talk about that? Can we talk about something else?"

Tallah appeared at the table, carrying two baskets. Poole's eyes lit up when he saw the food. "Holy hell, that smells good."

Tallah smiled as she set a basket in front of him. "Enjoy," she said and left.

The two men ate in silence. Poole brought up a lot of memories for Tate about Jason. He and Jason had had a competition going on to see who could bulk up the largest. Tate had never been part of that. Much as he loved Jason, he'd never had the inclination to spend hours lifting weights. Jason had definitely been closer to Poole than he was.

As if he guessed the train of Tate's thoughts, Poole reached for a napkin from the dispenser and wiped his mouth, swallowing the last of his sandwich. "You talk to Rachel much?"

Tate reached for his own napkin. He knew he should have been better about keeping in touch with Jason's wife, but it was just so hard. The only thing they'd had between them, Jason, had been taken away, and Tate felt guilty whenever he saw her.

"No." He swiped his tongue over his teeth, then reached for his beer. "Darcy says she's doing okay, but I haven't called her."

Poole nodded, blowing out air. "Yeah, I haven't seen her either, not after the funeral. I heard she sold the house, though, and got a condo."

"That's probably good."

"Yeah, they planned kids in that house."

Tate tossed the napkin in the basket and glanced up as the door opened and a familiar redhead came in. "Zion?" he called, desperate to change the subject.

Rebekah followed Zion through the door, wrinkling her nose at all the patrons. She heard Tate and pointed to the booth, touching Zion's shoulder. Zion had her hair pulled up in a loose ponytail, wearing jeans, a pink *Caffeinator* t-shirt, and keds on her feet. A hot pink hoodie completed her ensemble. Rebekah, on the other hand, had on a pair of slacks, a white sweater that was off the shoulder, her black hair a silky curtain down her back, and she wore six inch heels.

"Hey," said Zion, smiling at him. "God, it's crowded in here." Her eyes swept the restaurant, then returned to the table, narrowing on Poole. She held out her hand. "I'm Zion Sawyer. We met the other day."

Poole took her hand and shook it, but his eyes were on Rebekah. "And you are?"

Rebekah gave him a cool look down her nose. "Rebekah Miles." She didn't offer her hand.

Poole slid over and climbed out of the booth. "Please, have a seat. I'm just going for another pitcher of beer." He gave Rebekah a searching look. "I'm sure you don't drink beer though, do you?"

"Wine. Zinfandel if they have it."

Poole gave her a nod and strode toward the counter.

"Sit down," said Tate, patting the bench next to him.

"We don't want to interrupt," said Zion, shaking her head.

"Please, save me," he begged.

Zion laughed, glancing over at Poole, then she slid in next to him. Rebekah took the opposite side, pulling a napkin from the dispenser and wiping the table. Tate draped his arm across the back of the booth, toying with a lock of Zion's hair.

"How are you?" he asked.

She leaned into him. "I'm fine. We were just going to pick up dinner and head home. It's been a long day."

He nodded. "How about a hike tomorrow? Logan's coming in around noon and he can manage the store by himself for a few hours. What do you say? Think you can get away?"

"I'd like that," she said, resting her hand on his leg.

"I'll pick you up at 1:00 at your house? That'll give you time to change into hiking clothes."

"Sounds perfect," said Zion.

Tate breathed in the smell of her perfume and wanted to bury his nose in her hair, but Poole returned to the table with Rebekah's wine and another pitcher of beer.

"Thank you," said Rebekah as he slid in next to her.

He braced his left arm on the table and turned to face her. "So, tell me everything there is to know about you, Rebekah Miles."

She gave him a sultry look and picked up her wine. "You don't have that much time."

Tallah appeared beside the table. "Hey, Zion."

"Hey, Tallah. You're working here tonight?"

Tallah nodded. "It gets so busy on the weekends. What can I get you?"

"The usual." Zion looked at Rebekah. "A sandwich okay with you?"

Rebekah ran her finger over the top of her wineglass. "Fine, but go light on the barbecue sauce."

Tallah's eyes widened as if she'd never heard such nonsense before.

Zion gave her an apologetic look and Tallah shrugged, hurrying away.

"So, Rebekah Miles, are you from around here?" asked Poole.

Rebekah placed a hand against her chest. "Heavens no. I'm from San Francisco."

"What brings you out here?" said Poole, bracing his other hand on the back of the booth.

"Vacation."

"Ah," said Poole, smiling. "Then we have a lot in common."

Rebekah's eyes tracked down his body and she licked her lips. "You don't say," she purred.

"Oh dear God," whispered Zion, laying her head on Tate's shoulder. "Here we go again."

CHAPTER 7

Zion looked up from her computer, finding Dottie looming in the doorway, her hands on her hips, her orange and black hair in disarray. Zion had been trying to get caught up on the bookkeeping, while Rebekah helped Dottie work the counter, but the look on Dottie's face suggested Zion's day was about to get a lot harder.

"Either she goes or I do," said Dottie between clenched teeth. "If you keep her out there, I'm gonna brain her with my rolling pin."

Zion scrambled out from behind the desk. "Okay, okay," she said, placing her hands on Dottie's shoulders. "I'll get her out of there. Why don't you go take a break?"

Dottie nodded, staring straight ahead, her body rigid. Zion eased past her and into the coffee shop. The place was crowded with people at every table and some were even sitting on the floor around the couches and armchairs.

Rebekah stood behind the cash register, a curious look on her face, her index finger tapping against her upper lip. Zion slid up beside her.

"Hey, honey, how's it going?"

Rebekah tilted her head. "You know, this place isn't arranged right at all. You could get more tables in here and make it more cozy, so people will stay longer."

Zion glanced over her coffee shop. She liked the way it was arranged. She hadn't changed anything from the way her biological mother, Vivian, had decorated it. And people seemed to like the homey decor. Before Vivian had bought it, the previous owner had opted for a more industrial vibe, hence the name the *Caffeinator.*

She shook away the distraction and turned to face Rebekah. "So, here's the thing…"

Rebekah's eyes tracked to Zion's face and narrowed. "The harpy with the orange hair doesn't like me."

"No, no…" Zion paused. "Actually, she hates you."

"So the hippy hates me and the witch hates me too?"

"Maybe you could stop calling them names?"

Rebekah stamped her foot. A customer approached the counter with an empty cup and Rebekah glared at him. "What?" she growled.

He backed up a step.

"Rebekah!" scolded Zion, turning to the customer. "I'm sorry, sir. What can I get you? It's on the house."

He approached cautiously again. "Just another black coffee."

Zion quickly refilled his cup and added a cookie to his saucer, then she took Rebekah by the shoulders and urged her through the swinging bar doors and into her office. As soon as they passed the kitchen, Dottie moved back into the coffee shop to cover the counter.

Zion shut the door and turned, watching Rebekah throw herself down in Zion's chair.

"What am I supposed to do with myself? You're going to work until noon, then you're going on your hiking date with Hardware Man." She shuddered at the word *hike*.

"Tate," Zion corrected mildly. "Look, Becks, I love you something fierce, but you're killing me here. I have to work. I can't entertain you for the next two weeks. You're going to have to find something to occupy yourself."

Rebekah burst into tears, leaning forward and covering her face. Zion hurried around the desk and knelt before her, placing her hands on Rebekah's knees.

"Oh, honey, what in the world is going on?" She grabbed some tissues out of the dispenser on her desk and held them out to Rebekah.

Rebekah took them and wiped her eyes. Her mascara had smeared, so Zion knew this wasn't just a manipulation tactic. "I don't have a home."

"You'll get one."

"How? I don't have a job."

Zion reared back. "What?"

"I don't have a job, Zion. I quit."

"What happened?"

"I got into it with Franklin. They denied a cancer drug for this kid. She was seven and it would have cured her, but they said it was considered experimental for children. We just got FDA approval two weeks ago for adult treatment. The studies all point to it being effective in children as well, but *Judicious* denied it." She dabbed at her eyes. "It's just weeks away from being approved for children. They could have gotten a special waiver, but Franklin refused. That little girl might not have weeks, Zion, so I told the mother to contact her senator. Franklin heard me on the recording and ordered me to attend retraining like they did to you, but I told him to retrain his ass and I quit."

Zion burst into laughter.

Rebekah gave her a watery smile. "It was just after Wendell told me he didn't want to marry me." Rebekah sniffed and shook back her long hair. "I remember standing there in Franklin's office as he was yelling at me and thinking about Wendell saying why in the world would he ever marry me and that little girl with cancer and I just thought…" She stopped and scraped her teeth over her lower lip. "I just thought, what's the point of any of this."

Zion reached up and hugged her. "I get it. I'm so proud of you."

Rebekah hugged her back, giving a mirthless laugh. "Well, you're the only one. My mother hit the roof. She told me I wasn't coming home. That I was a disgrace."

Zion leaned back. "Seriously?"

"Yeah, so I came here, but now…" She motioned out to the coffee shop. "I can't even make coffee apparently."

Zion took her free hand. "Look, we'll figure it out. Let me get done working today and go on this date with Tate, but tonight is yours. We'll sit down with a bottle of wine and figure this thing out."

Rebekah gave her a sad smile. "Okay."

Zion kissed the back of her hand. "Go wash your face and then come back in here and shop online for shoes you can't afford anymore."

Rebekah laughed. "Sounds good."

They both stood up and Zion hugged her tight.

"It's gonna be okay, Becks. I promise you," she said.

Rebekah hugged her in return. "I know, but I may just have to move in with you permanently."

Zion went still and Rebekah laughed again.

"Relax, sister, I'm just kidding," she said, then she moved around her toward the door.

Zion blew out a sigh, hoping she was kidding, but with Rebekah one never knew.

* * *

Dee stepped through the door at noon, looking around warily. Zion had just let Dottie go home and she was wiping down the glass counter, scrubbing off the fingerprints. She watched Dee sidle into the room, standing on tiptoes to see beyond the bar doors.

"She's in my office," Zion told him, amused by the way he was sneaking around.

Dee eased up to the counter, taking off his jacket. He lowered his voice. "Is she working with me this afternoon again? Dottie said she threatened to bash Rebekah's brains in with a rolling pin, so I figured I'd get stuck with her."

Zion planted her hand on her hip. "Seriously, Dee. You're a grown man."

Dee leaned closer to Zion. "She makes me want to smoke the ganja again."

"Everything makes you want to smoke the ganja."

"Yeah, but that one…" He shuddered. "She makes me want to smoke the ganja and pierce my eardrums with a hot poker."

Zion burst out laughing. "Relax, Braveheart. Tallah's coming in at 1:00 and Rebekah's going home with me."

Dee visibly relaxed, striding around the counter. He started to go into the back to store his coat in Zion's office, but he stopped and looked over at Zion, clearly not wanting to beard the lion in her den. Zion rolled her eyes, then took the coat from him.

"There's a clean apron under the counter. Since you're here, we'll be on our way."

Dee nodded vigorously and reached for the apron, tying it around his waist. Zion went through the bar doors and opened her office. As she hung up Dee's coat, she realized Rebekah was still messing on her computer, her attention completely absorbed by it. Those must be some shoes she was buying.

"Let's head out, Becks. How about I pick us up some salads from *Up to No Gouda* for dinner after my hike with Tate?"

"Sure," said Rebekah, barely glancing up. "Come here a minute."

Zion went around the desk. "What? Can't decide between the kitten slippers or the stilettos?"

Rebekah gave her an arch look. "No." She pointed at the screen. "I did your payroll and messed with the taxes. You had the wrong percentage on the deductions. Then I took a look at your vendors' list and your supply orders."

"You did what?" said Zion, feeling alarmed. She leaned over Rebekah's shoulder to look at the screen.

"You spend way too much money on paper cups."

"Well, we are a coffee shop…" she began, panic edging to the surface. "What did you do?" She pulled the rolling chair back. "Let me see."

Rebekah sighed in annoyance, but she climbed out of the chair and went around the desk, throwing herself into the guest chair. Zion pulled up her payroll program and began reviewing everything that Rebekah had done.

"Here's the thing. You get those cute little pink printed cups, but they cost a fortune," continued Rebekah.

"They have the store logo on them," said Zion, clicking on the various windows.

"Well, you could get the same pink cups without the logo for about half the price. Then you could order a stamp with the logo on it. Your baristas could stamp the cups during their down times, saving you a lot of money. Maybe even making it possible for them to get a raise."

Zion looked up. "You did the payroll?"

"I know."

"And it's right."

"Of course."

"You also fixed the taxes?"

"Yep."

"How do you know how to do this?"

"Despite popular opinion, I'm not stupid."

"I never said that," said Zion.

Rebekah shrugged. "I'm good with numbers."

"Better than I am."

"Obviously," said Rebekah, looking at her fingernails. "Now, about the cups?"

"Tell me again."

So Rebekah did. She even showed her the product on the computer.

"I don't know if they're going to want to stamp cups in their downtime," said Zion, skeptically.

"They will if they ever want a raise. You need to work on the bottom line, sister. You're spending too much on supplies. There's some other areas where I think we can cut or get new suppliers." Rebekah straightened. "I also have some ideas for increasing your customer base, if you want to hear them."

Zion did. She was impressed with what Rebekah had already done, but looking at the clock above the door, she didn't have much time to get ready before Tate would arrive. She pulled her purse out of her desk. "Tell you what," she said. "After the morning rush tomorrow, you and I will sit down and discuss all of these things."

"Sounds good."

"But right now, I need to get home and get changed."

Rebekah grabbed her own purse and walked to the door. "That's right. You better not keep Hardware Man waiting."

"Tate," said Zion, following her out into the coffee shop. "His name's Tate."

"Whatever," said Rebekah, crossing the dining room as if she were the queen of England.

"Bye, Dee," Zion called to her barista. "I'll be on cell if you need anything."

"I got it covered, boss lady," said Dee. "Oh, hey, I thought up another name for the festival. I think you're really going to like it this time."

Zion caught the outer door as Rebekah went out. "Sounds good," she called over her shoulder.

"What do you think about *Sequoia's Fangtastic Howl-o-ween Monster Bash*?"

Zion stopped and looked back at him. "Actually, that's really good, Dee. I think you've found it."

Dee clapped, his face breaking into a brilliant smile.

"I'll text Jim Dawson and tell him."

"Awesome," said Dee, doing a jig behind the counter. A few patrons laughed and Zion smiled.

"Tomorrow I'm going into Visalia to get our decorations. We can put them up on Tuesday."

"Sounds good, boss lady. Looking forward to it. Enjoy your hot date."

Zion stopped, wondering how he knew about her date with Tate, but she shrugged it off. Nothing was a secret in a town like Sequoia.

* * *

"Oh, my God, this is crazy beautiful," said Zion, turning a circle in the middle of the trail, her arms extended to the sides. She'd changed into a pair of jean shorts, a flannel shirt, and popped a beanie on her head. She also wore her new hiking boots, the ones the guy at the sports shop had said were guaranteed not to rub.

She felt Tate's eyes on her and stopped spinning. He was smiling. He looked rugged and delicious in jeans and a forest green Henley that strained across his shoulders. He had the sleeves pushed up to his forearms, showing off his panther tattoo, and he had broken-down hiking boots on his feet. A five o'clock shadow darkened his jaw.

"Don't you think it's amazing out here. It smells so fresh."

He nodded, moving toward her. Zion felt a flutter in her belly as he stopped so close to her their bodies almost brushed. "It's amazing, yes." He reached down and took her hand. "I'm glad you could join me. I'll bet Rebekah wasn't happy."

Zion shrugged, linking her fingers with his. "I promised to bring home dinner and spend the night talking with her. Did you know she quit her job?"

"No, I didn't know," he said in amusement.

Zion laughed and leaned forward, brushing her nose along his jaw. "You smell like pine."

He made a low growl in his chest and she backed up. Another couple hiking by on the trail gave them smiles. Zion waved with her free hand, then she tugged Tate forward to get him walking again.

"We need a dog."

Tate choked out a laugh. "*We* need a dog. We?"

"Just for walking. Relax. I'm not asking you for a diamond ring."

He tugged her back beside him. "I'm not against having a dog with you," he said significantly.

Zion looked away, feeling her face heat. God, she wished she didn't blush so easily. "How did it go yesterday with Logan at the funeral home?"

"As good as it can. It's the most miserable thing to have to do."

"I know. Even though I didn't know Vivian, I hated planning her burial. And she made all of the decisions for me."

"Logan wants to pay everyone back. He asked if you kept a list of who donated to her funeral."

"I did, but people donated that money to him. They don't want it back," she said, frowning.

"I know. I told him that, but he insisted he wanted to pay for his mother's funeral himself."

Zion sighed. She understood that. She couldn't fault him for wanting to do one last thing for his mother. "When's the service?"

"Next Saturday."

"I'll let everyone know."

"I thought I'd have a reception back at the house afterward."

"I can help with the coffee and stuff."

"Sounds good."

Zion swung their hands between them. "How was it talking with your old friend?"

"Poole and I weren't really friends. He hung around with my partner more than me."

"I see. Did your partner stay on the force after you left?"

She felt the sudden tension in Tate's hand and turned to face him. They were at a curve in the trail where a massive sequoia shadowed the path. "Tate?"

"He's dead, Zion," he said, his jaw clenching. "He died in the line of duty."

Zion felt a drop in her belly. He never talked about his time on the force. She knew so little about his past, but she'd sensed there was a darkness inside him. This must have been it. "I'm so sorry, Tate. Is that why you left?"

"Yeah." He said, then he looked away, out over the land.

The trees rose on all sides of them and they could hear insects and birdsong floating in from a distance. The trail was covered with pine needles and the ground beneath the trees was dense with fern and lichen.

Zion waited for him to speak again. Finally he turned to face her, then he stepped forward, cupping her cheek with his hand. He brought his mouth to hers and Zion responded immediately, kissing him back.

A moment later, she found her back pressed up against the trunk of the tree, Tate's body melded to her own, her hands gripping his shirt to hold him against her. He deepened the kiss, pressing tighter against her, and Zion ignored the jab of bark and sticks into her back, needing to be closer still.

A cough sounded behind them and someone made an ahem sound. "We came out here to see nature, not see *nature*!" said a snide voice.

Tate tore his mouth from hers and looked over his shoulder. An older couple and a dog were standing in the trail. The dog wagged his tail, but his people did not seem amused.

"Sorry," said Tate in a husky voice, then they both burst into laugher.

* * *

Tate walked her to the door, carrying her bag from the deli. Zion was surprised to find the Spider gone, but she figured Rebekah had run out to buy some more wine. If she remembered right, Rebekah had finished off the last of it the previous night.

She turned to face Tate and took the bag from his hand. She wished she could invite him in. She didn't want the date to end and she felt like she probably should question him a little more about his partner's death, but he hadn't brought it up again.

"I had a really nice time," he told her. "I don't remember the last time I went hiking."

"I enjoyed it too. I don't get enough time to explore around here."

He drew a deep breath. He seemed reluctant to leave. Zion wondered if she should just invite him in, but they had such undeniable chemistry between them, she was a little afraid things might get out of hand if they were alone for very long.

It had never been this way with David, but with Tate, she found herself not wanting to put on the brakes. Even so, she knew that would be a mistake. There was a lot of pain lurking behind those brown eyes and she needed to figure out what it was exactly.

"When can I see you again?" he said.

"I have tomorrow off, but I'm working the rest of the week and I don't think Rebekah is going anywhere anytime soon."

"No, I guess not. What about tomorrow? We could go see a movie. Bill Stanley usually runs the store on Mondays until Logan comes in after school, so I can have a day off."

"I have to go into Visalia for Halloween decorations." Her eyes brightened. "What if we go together? We can buy some decorations for the *Hammer Tyme* and have lunch."

"Sounds good."

"Rebekah will probably come. Is that okay?"

"Fine by me," he said, but she could tell he was disappointed.

She moved closer to him. "How about a rain-check on the movie? We could go Friday night?"

He pulled her close. "I like it and I could take you to dinner also."

"Sounds like a date."

He kissed her gently and backed up. "I'd better go before Rebekah gets back and scolds me."

Zion hugged her arms around her middle. She couldn't believe how badly she didn't want him to go. This relationship felt so different from the one with David. Actually, it felt different than any relationship she'd ever been in, but she was reluctant to bank too much on it this soon. Once the newness of it wore off, maybe they'd find they didn't have that much in common.

"Good night, Zion," he said.

"Good night, Tate," she answered and watched him as he turned and jogged to his truck, climbing inside. He waved to her as he turned the vehicle and headed back down the street, bypassing his house. She figured he was probably going to lock up his store and pick up Logan.

Going inside the cottage, she found Cleo waiting for her. The kitten meowed as Zion walked into the kitchen and put the bag in the refrigerator. Bending over, she picked the cat up and Cleo started to purr, nestling against Zion's neck. Zion carried her to her room and changed into her sweats, then came out and curled up on the sofa with her, waiting for Rebekah to come home.

She woke when she heard a car horn honk outside the house. At first she was disoriented. The room was dark and she'd curled up in the corner of the couch, her head resting on the arm. Cleo had snuggled against her belly, but she stretched now, yawning. Zion reached over and turned on the table lamp, grabbing her phone off the coffee table and thumbing it on to check the time.

She blinked and rubbed her eyes, staring at the display. It was 1:00AM. What the hell! She climbed off the couch and walked to the front windows, pulling back the curtains. A silver Chevy Camaro had pulled up in front of the house and Zion could just make out two people entwined in the front seat.

A moment later, Rebekah got out of the car, shut the door and leaned in the open window to say something, then she weaved her way up Zion's walkway toward the door. Zion hurried over and unlocked it, pulling it open as the Camaro honked and made a wide turn to head back down the road.

Rebekah stopped on the walkway and waved after the car, laughing.

Zion hurried across the porch and down the stairs, grabbing Rebekah as she weaved. Rebekah laughed, throwing her arm around Zion's shoulders. She was wearing a silver mini-dress with stiletto heels and no jacket, her silver clutch grasped in her other hand. She smelled of booze and cigarette smoke.

"Hey, sister," she said, slurring her words. "Did you wait up for me?"

Zion struggled to keep her on her feet, getting her to the stairs. "Where's your car?"

"Itz at the club," she said, stumbling and catching herself on the banister.

"You left it there."

"Well, I couldna drive."

Zion staggered under Rebekah's weight, but she got her into the house and to the couch where they both tumbled onto the cushions. Cleo jumped off and stalked away, furious. Rebekah laughed, dropping her clutch on the floor.

"Who brought you home?"

Rebekah thought about that for a moment, squinting at Zion. Zion shook her head and went back to shut and lock the door, then she detoured into the kitchen and poured Rebekah a large glass of water. She carried it back to her and curled Rebekah's hands around it, taking a seat beside her.

"Drink," she ordered.

Rebekah tried to drink, but she slopped some down the front of her dress, making her body shiver. When she leaned over to put it on the coffee table, Zion steadied it so it didn't tip over. Then Rebekah collapsed onto the couch, resting her head against the back.

"Where the hell did you go? I brought us dinner. I thought we were going to talk."

"I know, but I just couldna stan sitting here anymore. I wenz to the club."

"What club?"

"The Rockin…the robins…the rockin in the robin?"

"*The Rollicking Robin*?"

Rebekah pointed at her. "Thaz the one."

"How much did you drink?"

"Not thatz muchz."

Zion gave her a stern look, but Rebekah's eyes drifted closed. "Rebekah!" she said sternly.

Rebekah's eyes popped open. "What?"

"Who drove you home?"

"Thatz nize cop from laz night."

"What cop from last night?"

"Hardware Manz friend?"

"Keith Poole. You went to the club with Keith Poole?"

"Don'tz be ridicu…ridic…" She waved it off. "I ran into himz there."

"You ran into him at the *Rollicking Robin*?"

"Yep."

Zion closed her eyes, bracing her head in her hands. "This is a mess, Rebekah. You promised me you weren't going to jump into these things anymore, and yet here you are just a few nights later, meeting a virtual stranger in a club and making out with him in his car." Zion shifted on the couch and glared at her. "You promised me you weren't going to do this anymore."

She stopped herself. Rebekah was asleep.

Zion shook her head in disgust, then pulled off Rebekah's ridiculous stilettos. Standing up, she pulled Rebekah's legs straight and rolled her to her side in case she got sick, then she grabbed the throw off the armchair and draped it over Rebekah, moving the water so she wouldn't have to reach to get it. Brushing back the tangle of hair from her face, Zion gave Rebekah a shake of her head, then eased out from behind the coffee table, headed for her room.

No use trying to get her to listen right now, but come morning, she and Rebekah Miles were having a long overdue talk, and this time Zion didn't care if she had a hangover or not.

CHAPTER 8

Visalia had a population of around 130,000 and unlike Sequoia, it had all of the most popular department stores. Tate didn't get down here too often, but when he needed something a little more commercial, Visalia usually had it.

Zion and Rebekah had picked him up at 10:00, later than they'd planned, but it had given Tate time to open the hardware store and make sure Bill didn't need anything. Logan would be in after school, and Tate knew the kid could run things on his own.

Now, he watched the buildings going by outside the window of Zion's Optima, drumming his fingers on the armrest. They had talked hardly at all and the tension was starting to make him edgy. Rebekah had climbed in the backseat, wearing a hoodie and dark sunglasses, then curled against the door and went to sleep.

Zion had muttered something that Tate didn't catch, but he wasn't sure she felt like repeating herself today. He probably should have begged off when he noticed something wasn't right between the friends, but he'd wanted to spend time with Zion.

She pulled into the parking lot of a warehouse that had a *Halloween Store* sign hanging from the marquee. It had obviously been another sort of establishment that went out of business and someone had opened a temporary Halloween store in its place.

Zion set the brake, then reached between the seats and swatted Rebekah's designer-jeans clad leg. "Wake up! We're here!" she shouted, much louder than necessary.

Rebekah groaned and kicked the back of Tate's chair. Tate's eyes widened. What the hell had happened last night between these two?

"Rebekah, I am not kidding you! Get out of the car!" said Zion, sounding like a fed-up mother. Tate gave her a curious look and she flashed a tense smile at him.

"I'm up!" snapped Rebekah, throwing open the door and smashing it into a shopping cart.

Zion made a hissing sound and got out herself, stomping around the car to see the damage. "I can't believe you! I took you in and this is how you repay me!"

Rebekah climbed out, but Tate was frankly a little afraid to move. Zion shoved the cart into the shopping cart receptacle and stomped back, squaring off in front of her friend. Rebekah bent over to examine the door.

"I didn't do anything to it," she said adjusting her sunglasses and pulling her hoodie around her. Tate figured it was probably Zion's hoodie, because he didn't remember ever seeing Rebekah in anything that wasn't designer brands. Even now she wore pumps with ridiculous heels. "Why couldn't you let me stay home?"

"Because you wanted to go with me, remember? You didn't want me working while you sat at home, and the one time I leave you for a minute, what do you do?"

Rebekah made a growl of frustration and pushed past Zion, headed for the store.

"You act like a damn fool!" Zion shouted after her.

A few people getting out of their cars glanced over, but Rebekah just shot her hand in the air, her middle finger extended.

Zion huffed, then glared at Tate, who was still sitting in the car. He gave her a false smile and she tilted her head, frowning. "Are you coming or not?"

Tate looked at the dashboard. "I'm not sure," he told her through the closed window.

"Fine. Stay there." And she turned on her heel, headed for the store.

Tate scrambled out of the car and hurried up beside her. "Look, I'm not trying to pry, but is something wrong?"

She stopped walking and gave him a wild-eyed look.

He held up a placating hand. "Okay, let's try this again. How can I help?"

Zion burst into laughter and moved closer to him, giving him a light kiss on the mouth. "I'm sorry. I didn't mean to take it out on you. I'm just frustrated with Rebekah." She hooked her arm in Tate's and started walking him toward the building. "So, they sell Halloween costumes here too."

Tate gave her a skeptical look. He didn't remember the last time he'd dressed up for Halloween.

"Come on. It'll be fun. We have to dress up for the kids."

"Do we though?" he asked, but he let her drag him into the store.

The interior of the store was hung with dark drapes and black lights flickering from gothic candle sconces affixed to the walls. Spooky music filtered through the speakers and occasional moans and screams sounded in various parts of the building. Artificial cobwebs covered all the surfaces and red blinking eyes peered out from beneath shelves. Animatronic figures dripped blood and gore, making herky jerky movements.

As they passed a grave scene, something popped up and Zion gave a squeak, clutching his arm tighter. Tate laughed and patted her hand, picking up a severed leg and waving it at her. She shook her head and detoured to get a cart.

For the next few moments, they wandered the store, picking out decorations. Tate wasn't opposed to some of the gorier creations, but Zion had a tendency toward the less scary side of the holiday – black cats with big lantern green eyes, pumpkins with smiling faces, and puppies in mummy wrap.

"They're just kids," she said. "I don't want to permanently damage them."

He nodded, wondering where Rebekah had gone to in all of this. They found her sacked out in a bone chair, holding a French maid's costume, her head braced on a fist. He couldn't tell if her eyes were closed behind the dark spectacles.

"Of course, a French maid, what else?" grumbled Zion, pushing her cart to the side and looking through the costumes herself.

Tate turned her to face him. "What's going on with you two?"

Zion let out a frustrated breath. "Last night I brought dinner home. I promised Rebekah I'd stay home and talk with her about her situation. When I got there, she was gone. She apparently got bored and went to the *Rollicking Robin*."

"Okay?" he said, trying not to sound like he didn't get the significance of that.

"We had plans and she broke them."

"I see."

"No, you don't," said Zion, shoving angrily at the hanger. "She ran into your buddy at the bar."

Tate felt confused. "My buddy?"

"Keith Poole. She came home last night at 1:00AM, drunk as a skunk, and making out with Keith in front of the house."

Tate looked beyond Zion, considering that. Poole wasn't the most monogamous man he'd ever met, but then he suspected Rebekah wasn't either. Maybe they both just needed to blow off some steam together. Each of them were facing life altering events and it seemed reasonable they'd be drawn to each other.

"I'm sure it's not a permanent relationship, Zion," he said.

She slammed the hanger again. "She promised me she wouldn't do this again. She's lived with five different men and every time they've cleaned her out." She looked over her shoulder at Rebekah's sleeping form. "And then who has to bail her out?" I do." She tapped her index finger in the middle of her chest.

"No, you don't," said Rebekah.

"Yes, I do."

Tate waited until they stopped arguing. He tugged Zion's arm, drawing her out of earshot of Rebekah. "Look, I understand you're trying to look out for her."

"But?" Zion said, an edge to her voice. Tate knew he was treading on thin ice, but if he and Zion had a hope of anything real, he couldn't just keep his mouth shut all the time.

"But she's a grown woman, Zion. She can handle herself."

Zion didn't look like she agreed; however, she finally nodded. "Okay." She kissed him. "I'm sorry. I'm ruining our fun date together."

He arched an eyebrow and looked into the cart filled with Halloween decorations. They apparently had different ideas of fun.

"This *is* fun," she said, coaxing him. She pulled out a Wolverine costume and he vehemently shook his head. "Come on, you'd be adorable in it."

"Just what every man wants to hear," he said.

Zion giggled. "Fine, then let's go look at scars," and she pulled him away to pick out scary makeup.

* * *

Tate jerked awake, his heart pounding, his body covered in sweat. He tented his knees and dragged his hands through his hair, trying to calm the rapid pounding of his heart. The dream was the same. The street, the gunfire, the lights being blown out, the police cruiser…the blood.

Jason's face was still so clear. After all this time, he could still see Jason's staring eyes, the bullet hole in the middle of his forehead. Why didn't it ever dim? Other things about Jason had dimmed. He couldn't remember his voice. He barely remembered his cologne. Only once in a while would a man come into the *Hammer Tyme*, wearing Jason's cologne, and he'd be transported back.

He used to give Jason a bad time that the perp would know they were coming by the cloud of cologne Jason wore. To get back at him, Jason would grab him in a headlock and tell him he was transferring his scent. Tate smiled, remembering that. He missed Jason. Jason had been like a brother to him. They'd been partnered out of the gate and Tate had never had another. He'd never wanted another, to be honest.

He threw back the covers and climbed out of bed. The wood floors were cold against his bare feet, but he ignored it, going to the bedroom door and yanking it open. He padded in the dark through the living room to the kitchen and grabbed the teapot, carrying it to the sink.

He filled it with water and put it on the stove, turning on a burner, then he grabbed the tea and a teacup out of the cabinet, placing it on the counter next to the stove. He tore open a tea bag and settled it into the bottom of the cup, then he turned to throw the wrapper in the garbage.

Logan stood in the doorway, his hair sleep tousled, his eyes heavy. "You okay?" he asked.

"Yeah, want some tea?"

Logan shrugged. "Sure."

Tate got another cup out of the cabinet and set it next to his, then he put a tea bag in it. Finally he got out the honey and carried it to the table, setting it in the middle. Logan took a seat at the table, bracing his chin on his hands.

The water began to boil and the pot shrieked. Tate turned off the burner and filled the two cups, carrying them back to the table. He slid one across to Logan and dunked his own tea bag a few times.

"Can't sleep?" he asked the kid.

"It's off and on, you know?"

"Yeah, I'll bet. Sorry if I woke you by banging around."

Logan sniffed at the tea, giving it a skeptical look. "That wasn't what woke me. You were talking in your sleep, or yelling actually."

Tate glanced up at him, then he rose and grabbed a saucer out of the cabinet, placing his used tea bag on it. Logan did the same, then he took a tentative sip of the tea and grimaced.

Tate pushed the honey at him.

"Try this. You might like it better."

Logan poured honey into his cup, but his eyes were on Tate. "You know, that counselor you found for me sees adults too."

"How do you know that?"

"I looked him up online. I'm not just gonna spill my guts to some shrink if he doesn't have the credentials."

Tate smiled, sipping at his own tea.

"It wouldn't hurt to talk to him," Logan suggested.

"I don't need a grief counselor."

"You sure about that?"

Tate set the mug down, studying Logan. "This stuff happened more than two years ago."

"Your partner dying?"

Tate nodded, reaching for the honey. "This guy Jason and I worked with, Keith Poole, showed up in town and it's messing with my head. It'll go away as soon as Poole leaves."

Logan didn't look like he believed him. He sipped at his tea again. "That's better," he said and Tate smiled. He curled his hands around the cup and gave Tate a level stare. "Look, Tate, here's the thing. With you and Zion seeing each other now, you're gonna want to knock boots with her at some point."

Tate frowned. "Knock boots?"

"My mother's expression," said Logan.

Tate found it completely insane that he was getting a sex talk from a seventeen-year-old kid. "And your point?"

"What are you going to do when you start shouting and thrashing around in your sleep and she's in the bed next to you?"

Tate sat back. He hadn't thought about that.

Logan stared into the tea. "Just saying. I mean, if you're still shouting at shadows two years later, maybe you need to talk to someone."

Tate started to answer, but he could hear his phone ringing on the table in the living room. He got up and walked into the other room, snatching the phone up. Sheriff Wilson's name flashed on the screen. Feeling a drop in the pit of his stomach, he thumbed it on and held it to his ear.

"Sheriff?"

"You know a man named Keith Poole?"

Tate swallowed, running a hand through his hair. "Yeah."

"He told me to call you," said Wilson. "You think you can come down to the *Back-of-Beyond Lodge*."

"Now?"

"I'd appreciate it."

"Okay. What's going on?"

"Your buddy…"

"He's not my buddy."

"Your acquaintance then…shot someone and killed him."

Tate scrubbed a hand over his jaw. Shit, shit, shit! "Who did he shoot?"

"Well, that's why I want you to come out here."

"On my way," said Tate, disconnecting the call. He turned and found Logan in the doorway watching him. "I've gotta go."

"I heard."

"I'll be back in time to take you to school. If not, I'll see if Zion can drop you off."

"No sweat." Logan started to go back into the kitchen, then he turned back around. "Hey, Tate?"

"Yeah, kid."

"Be careful, okay?"

"You got it," said Tate.

* * *

Every police cruiser in Sequoia seemed to be parked in the semi-circular parking lot of the *Back-of-Beyond Lodge*, their lights flashing. A number of guests were standing around in clusters, wearing bathrobes and slippers, huddled against the early morning chill.

Tate pulled in and parked, climbing out of the truck. He showed his badge to Jones, one of the patrol officers, then glanced up as Emilio Vasquez came toward him. Vasquez was a senior deputy in his early forties with a lean build and dark hair and eyes. Vasquez lifted a hand to Tate, holding up the crime tape so Tate could duck under it.

They passed a late model Chevy Impala in a midnight blue color, its suspension modified so it was nearly touching the ground. A flame ran up the hood of the car and Tate stopped, feeling a wash of recognition sweep over him.

"Sweet, huh?" said Vasquez.

Tate glanced at him, realizing he hadn't heard what he said. "What?"

"Sweet car, huh?"

"Yeah…" he said.

"This way," said Vasquez, pointing to the brightly lit open door of a small log cabin.

Tate hesitated, trying to pull the memory to the front of his mind. He'd seen this car before, or a car very similar to it, but he couldn't remember where.

"Tate?"

Tate tore his gaze from it and followed Vasquez into the cabin. Before him was Poole, wearing a pair of basketball shorts and a tanktop, his feet bare. He was pacing back and forth in the small living room. As Tate started to speak, someone launched out of the chair on his right, throwing her arms around his neck.

Tate staggered, then curled his arm around Rebekah's back. She was trembling as she buried her face against his shoulder.

Wilson walked through the doorway behind Poole and gave Tate a relieved look.

"What are you doing here, Rebekah?" Tate said, but she wouldn't answer him, just tightened her hold. Although she was wearing a thick bathrobe, she was shaking violently in his arms. Poole's gaze settled on him and he stopped pacing.

"Thank God you're here, Tater Tot."

Tate shifted his attention to Sheriff Wilson. "What's she doing here?" he asked.

"You know her?"

"Yes, this is Rebekah Miles, Zion's friend from San Francisco."

Sam Murphy, Wilson's other senior deputy, stepped out of the kitchen, carrying a notebook in her hand. Wilson nodded at the pad. "You got that?"

"I got it," said Murphy. Murphy was in her late forties, early fifties with short grey hair and lines around her eyes and mouth.

"We couldn't get anything out of her," said Wilson, stepping around Poole.

Tate extricated himself, holding Rebekah by the arms. There were no tears in her eyes, but her teeth chattered. He figured she was in shock. "What are you doing here, Rebekah?"

"He tried to break in the window. He tried to break in. We were in bed…" she gasped, her hands clawing at his arms.

Tate eased her back into the armchair. "Can you call Zion to come down here?" he asked Wilson. "And tell her to bring some street clothes?"

Wilson jerked his chin at Vasquez and the deputy nodded, leaving the cabin. Tate focused on Poole. "What the hell happened, Keith?"

Poole rubbed his hand over his mouth and chin. "We were in bed, Tate, and he came through the window. I had the gun in my nightstand and I got it out. He had a hard time getting through the window. He got stuck in the screen. I fired off a few rounds and he fell back out again. When I went outside, he was already dead." Poole held out his hand. "Look, I'm giving you this information freely. I'm not even asking for a lawyer. It was self-defense."

Tate knelt before Rebekah. "Zion will be here shortly."

She nodded jerkily, her hands clasped in her lap.

"I need you to wait here, Rebekah, okay?"

"Okay." She was making a strange hitching sound. He squeezed her hands and rose to his feet.

Wilson jerked his chin toward the other room. Tate followed him into a rustic kitchen with an old fashioned gas stove and a modern icebox made to look like it was from the 1950's. Tate could see a number of cops moving around in the harsh glare of spotlights through the open back door.

"Tell me about this Poole fellow," said Wilson, turning to face him, his thumbs hooked in his belt.

Tate looked over his shoulder, but Poole had gone back to pacing, muttering to himself, and raking his hands through his hair.

"We worked together on a gang task force in LA. Recently, I heard he was placed on leave."

"For what?"

"Shooting and killing a fourteen-year-old kid. There were some racial undertones. Internal Affairs is involved."

"Of course," said Wilson.

"Of course," answered Tate. "His captain told him to get out of town for a while, so he remembered I'd moved to Sequoia and decided to come here to get away."

"But you're not friends?"

Tate shrugged. "Not really. He was closer with my partner than me."

"And yet this is where he decided to come?"

"Look, Sheriff, I don't know. He doesn't have family and he wanted to get away." Tate's attention was captured by the gun in an evidence bag on the table. "Is that his gun?"

"Yeah, doesn't look like his service revolver."

"It's not. They would have confiscated that during the investigation. That's his own private gun."

"He says he has a conceal carry permit, but I haven't had a chance to check it."

Tate shifted weight. "He probably does. I have one."

Wilson nodded. "He ever get suspended for anything before this?"

"Not that I know."

Wilson scratched the back of his neck. "The registration on the low rider in front lists an LA address."

Tate felt a wash of apprehension snake over him. "I guess I better see the body."

Wilson nodded, holding out his hand toward the door. Tate stepped out into the back of the cabin. It butted right up to the forest and Tate could hear the gurgle of Bearpaw Creek in the distance.

A group of cops were hovering around a window at the back of the cabin and Tate recognized the county logo for the coroner. Wilson led him over to the group, pushing his way to the center. A body under a drape lay sprawled beneath the window, the screen caught around a boot clad ankle. A switchblade lay by the vic's outstretched right hand.

Wilson nudged Lewis, one of his other patrol officers, and Lewis bent, pulling back the drape. Tate grimaced as he took in the man's blunt featured face, his staring black eyes, and the hole in the side of his throat. He'd bled out pretty fast by the look of the wound. He wore a flannel shirt over a white t-shirt and jeans rolled up around his ankles.

A frisson of anxiety peppered down Tate's back. He looked over at the coroner, Angela Davenport. He'd never met her, but he'd talked to her on the phone during the last case when Merilee Whitmire had died. She had long coppery colored hair, pulled up in a ponytail, and piercing brown eyes. She had to be Wilson's age or just a few years younger.

"Can you see if he has a tattoo on his left pectoral muscle?" Tate asked her.

She pulled the penlight out of her tool belt and placed it between her teeth, then she hunkered down at the head of the body and tugged on a clean pair of gloves. Pulling back the flannel shirt, she reached for the bottom of the white t-shirt and drew that back until she reached his neck.

Tate looked away, but Wilson stepped closer, squinting in the light from the coroner's beam. "What does that mean?"

Tate looked at the tattoo, a devil with a forked tongue poking out of his mouth and smoldering horns on the top of his head. "He's part of a mixed race gang in LA. They call themselves the Devil's Tongue. They deal in drugs mostly, but once in a while one of them gets popped for racketeering."

"What's he doing here?"

Tate looked back at the cabin. He felt sick to his stomach. He'd left this stuff behind in LA. Scratching his head, he forced his voice to stay steady. "The gang task force I told you about?"

"Yeah?"

"Well, we were investigating the Devil's Tongue."

"You and Poole worked a gang task force to stop the Devil's Tongue?"

Tate nodded, staring at the tattoo. Nothing good was going to come of this. They weren't equipped to deal with the fire power a gang like the Devil's Tongue could bring. Damn Poole anyway. What the hell was going on? Why would a member of the Devil's Tongue come all the way up here to Northern California and how had he found out where Poole was anyway?

"But they're still operating?"

Tate drew a calming breath, his palms sweating. "Yeah."

Wilson turned and faced him, crossing his arms over his chest. "I think you better tell me everything."

Tate's eyes drifted up to him. "Okay."

Rather than going back into the cabin, Wilson led him around the side to the front parking lot. His cruiser was parked at an angle, blocking Poole's Camaro from leaving. He motioned for Tate to get inside.

Tate pulled the door open, surprised when his hand shook. Wilson climbed in behind the steering wheel, shifting to keep Tate in his line of sight. Red and blue lights from the patrol cars cut across Wilson's face, creating an eerie flicker in his eyes.

"I'm waiting, son."

Tate scrubbed his hands on his pants and sank into the passenger seat. "Our captain and the commissioner thought we had a good chance of bringing down the Devil's Tongue. They weren't that organized and their numbers had diminished – a lot of infighting since they were mixed race. The LAPD set up the task force to finish them off. They hand selected me, my partner Jason Black, and Keith Poole. There were a few other junior officers, but they were mostly support."

"Okay."

"We did surveillance on the Devil's Tongue for months. We knew who went in and out of the tenement where they stayed. We were getting close to cracking their banking records, we thought we knew what firepower they had, and we were even pretty sure we knew how they were smuggling the drugs into the country."

"Something went wrong?"

Tate nodded, staring at the display on the sheriff's dashboard. "All of a sudden there was more activity at the complex. More people we didn't recognize going in and out, and cargo vans, no license plates, start pulling up." Tate scratched his forehead. "It's just the sort of thing you don't want happening. Either they're bringing in reinforcement or they're bringing in guns."

"Or both?"

"Or both. We get the order to take them down. It just comes out of nowhere. We weren't prepared, we didn't have enough backup, but they tell us we've got to take them out this night." Tate wrung his hands. "They've got cop killers. They're firing thirty rounds per minute. Bullets are just flying everywhere."

Wilson rubbed his forehead wearily.

"There were women and children in that complex. You could hear them screaming. Jason and I get pinned down on the street in front of the complex. They shoot out the tires on the left side of the car, then the street lights, the mirror." Tate drew a deep breath and let it out in a shivery pant. "I know I've got to get away from the cruiser. They're peppering the side of it. The windshield shatters and I duck below the door. I start crab walking back to get around the end of the car. I'm not sure where Jason's gone and I keep waiting to hear backup coming our way, but there's nothing."

"Jesus," breathed Wilson.

"When I get to the back of the car, I step in blood. At first I thought it was gasoline, but it's pretty clear what it was. When I look around the back of the car, Jason's lying there, a bullet hole in the middle of his forehead."

Wilson shifted in his seat.

"We were outgunned, outmanned, and out finessed. It was like shooting fish in a barrel. I kept waiting to hear the sounds of sirens, waiting for backup to get there, but it never came."

"How did you get out?"

Tate looked over at Wilson, his jaw clenched. "The tenement where the gang was crashing…"

"Yeah."

"It blew up. They were cooking meth in there."

"Holy hell!"

"Thirteen people died in the explosion."

"I never heard about it."

Tate shrugged. "The majority of them were illegal immigrants," he said, unable to hide the bitterness in his voice. "I guess to the media it didn't matter that five kids lost their lives."

Wilson was silent for a moment, letting the weight of what Tate told him sink in, then he cleared his throat. "That's when you left the force?"

Tate nodded. "I couldn't take it anymore. We were supposed to protect and serve, but we destroyed a whole apartment complex. Homes for people who didn't have much to start with."

"Why'd they order you in prematurely?"

"No idea. They just did."

"How many of the Devil's Tongue were left?"

"Hard to say. They scattered."

Wilson looked over at the cabin. "Well, at least one survived."

"Appears that way."

"Why'd he come here, though?"

Tate looked over at Wilson. "Now, that, Sheriff, is going to give me nightmares for another two years, I'm guessing."

CHAPTER 9

Zion stepped into the cabin, looking around warily. She didn't really want to see a dead body. Rebekah sat in a chair in the small, rustic living room, her hands clasped in her lap. She wore a white robe, her feet bare, the blue nail polish on her toenails showing beneath the hem. Her black hair was tangled around her face and she looked pale.

She looked up as Zion hurried over to her, dropping the duffle bag and her purse on the ground, then she gathered Rebekah in her arms. Rebekah melted against her and a hitch in her breath told Zion she was crying.

"Are you okay?" Zion asked her.

Rebekah's hold tightened. "I'm so sorry. I'm so sorry. I did it again, but this time I really messed everything up."

Zion hunkered down in front of her, brushing the tangle of hair away from Rebekah's face. "It's okay, Becks. I'm sorry I got so judgmental."

Rebekah sniffed. "Well, look where I ended up." She gave a mirthless laugh.

Zion sighed.

After the disastrous trip to the Halloween store that Zion had forced on Rebekah, they'd gotten into a fight at the cottage. They'd both said some pretty horrible things to each other and Rebekah had driven off in a fit of rage. Zion had tried to call her for hours, but Rebekah wasn't answering.

When she'd gotten the call from Deputy Vasquez, Zion had felt so guilty for some of the things she'd said to Rebekah. It wasn't her business what Rebekah did with her life. She had no right to try to curb her personality.

"What happened? Can you tell me?"

Rebekah looked up. Zion followed her look, seeing Poole come out of the bedroom wearing jeans and a sweater, a uniformed officer escorting him. He glanced at Rebekah, but she looked away. The officer escorted Poole out of the cabin and Zion shifted to watch their departure.

"I can't believe this happened to me. What is wrong with me, Zion? Why do I keep jumping into bed with these men?"

Zion clasped Rebekah's hands in her own. "It's a defensive mechanism."

Sheriff Wilson and Tate stepped through the cabin door. Zion couldn't believe how relieved she was to see Tate, but he had shadows in his eyes as he gave her a nod. Wilson stopped beside Rebekah's chair.

"Ms. Miles, I'd like you to come down to the station and make a statement. Do you feel up for that?"

Rebekah looked at him, her eyes wide and vulnerable. Zion felt so guilty for this. It was her fault Rebekah had left the house and gone with Poole. She knew how weak Rebekah was when there was a man involved and she should have tried to make peace.

"I can do that," Rebekah finally said.

"Did you bring her some clothes? The clothes she had before are evidence now."

Zion picked up the duffel bag.

"Go change, Ms. Miles. You'll ride with me."

Rebekah gave Zion a panicked look. "Can Zion ride with me?"

"Of course," he said.

She took the bag in a hand that trembled and rose to her feet, hurrying toward the bathroom to change. Zion rose and gave Wilson a grateful look. "Thank you."

"No problem. I'll be out front when she's ready." He tipped his hat to her and turned for the door.

Zion walked over to Tate. He reached out and took her hand, pulling her closer. "What's going on?" she asked him, leaning into the warmth of his body.

"It's a long story. I'll have to tell you later."

Zion touched the stubble on his cheek. "You look upset."

"Yeah, I should have known that Poole was going to make things difficult."

She leaned away from him. "Tate, I know there are things you don't want to talk about, but…"

He tugged her closer again. "Look, I'll tell you everything, just not now, okay?"

"Okay," she said, realizing she was going to have to be okay with that.

He kissed her forehead. "I promise, but right now, we need to get Rebekah cleared and away from Poole."

Zion nodded.

"He's not good for her, Zion."

"I know. I'll talk to her."

Rebekah appeared out of the bathroom, wearing her sweats and a hoodie. She had the hood pulled over her head and she'd washed off the makeup. She looked so vulnerable, Zion left Tate's side and wrapped an arm around her waist.

"It's gonna be okay, sweetie," she told her.

* * *

Zion sat with Rebekah in the interrogation room at the sheriff's office. She'd seen this room before, but never from this side of it. Rebekah sat in the chair, staring at her chipped nail polish, and her silence was unnerving. Zion had never seen her like this and when she tried to question her, all Rebekah would say was she was tired.

The door opened and Tate entered. He carried a recorder which he set in the middle of the table. Rebekah looked up at him, her expression anguished. "Are you going to arrest me?"

Tate gave her a gentle smile and squeezed her shoulder as he took a seat across from her. "No, you're not in any trouble, Rebekah. How about a cup of coffee?"

She nodded stiffly and Tate lifted his chin to the two-way glass, then he focused on Rebekah again. "Sheriff Wilson thought you might be more comfortable talking to me. Do you mind if I ask you a few questions?"

"No, that's fine," she said, clasping her hands on the table.

Tate reached for the recorder. "I'm gonna record our conversation if that's acceptable to you."

"Fine," she said. "Can Zion stay with me?"

"Yeah," said Tate, giving Zion a grim smile. "How did you meet Keith Poole, Rebekah?"

She glanced at Zion and Zion nodded for her to tell Tate. "I met him at the *Rollicking Robin.* I went there for a drink the other night because I was tired of sitting alone in the house."

"Okay. What happened at the club?"

"We talked, he bought me a few drinks, and we danced some. We really hit it off, so when I wanted to go home, he agreed to take me. I knew I shouldn't drive. We exchanged phone numbers and he dropped me off at Zion's house."

"Then last night you met up with him again?"

Rebekah wrung her hands. "Zion and I got into a fight. I called Poole and asked him if he wanted to take me out. We went to dinner at that place off the highway, the nice place."

"*Corkers*?" Tate asked.

"That's the one."

The door opened and Vasquez stepped inside with a cup of coffee and two packets, one of creamer and the other sugar, which he placed in front of Rebekah.

"Thank you," said Rebekah, glancing up at him and Zion noticed it was probably the first time she didn't flirt with an attractive man.

"No problem," Vasquez said and left the room.

"So after *Corkers,* where did you go?"

Rebekah curled her hands around the coffee cup and closed her eyes.

"Rebekah please, I need you to be completely honest with me."

"I didn't want to go home. I was still mad at Zion." She reached over and took Zion's hand. "He asked me to come back to his cabin, so I did. We had some more to drink and the next thing I know…"

Tate gave her a significant look.

"We were…um." She waved her hand in the air and stopped, closing her eyes. "Why do I always do this, Zion? Why?"

Tate's gaze shifted to Zion in alarm.

"I meet a man and next thing you know I'm moving in with him. It's a sickness. There has to be something wrong with me. Why do I need the validation like that?"

Zion shifted uncomfortably, opening her mouth to respond, but Tate leaned into Rebekah's line of sight.

"Rebekah?"

She seemed to remember he was there. "We slept together," she said bluntly.

Tate narrowed his eyes, then looked down. "Okay. So, um…"

"I fell asleep and the next thing I know I hear this crash."

"What time was that?"

"I don't know. A little after 1:00." She rubbed her forehead, then she picked up the coffee and took a sip. "Keith launches out of bed. I tried to get up, but he pushed me back down. I'm completely disoriented, and then…"

"Then?"

Rebekah swallowed hard and stared at the recorder. "The gun starts going off. It was so loud, I screamed, but I couldn't even hear myself."

"How many times?"

She glanced up. "What?"

"How many times did it go off?"

"I don't know, once or twice. I heard some weird sound, this gurgling sound, and Keith tells me not to leave the room. I got up and put on the robe. I was so scared and my ears were ringing. I didn't know what was going on, but I could see the window was shattered. There was…" She shuddered and hugged herself. "There was blood on the wall."

Tate nodded. "Besides telling you to stay in the room, did Poole say anything to you?"

"No, I called to him through the window, but he didn't answer. All I could do was pace back and forth. I wasn't sure what was going on. Eventually, I heard sirens."

"Poole never came back into the room?"

"No."

"He never spoke to you again?"

"No." She leaned forward. "Who was that man? Why did he try to break into our cabin?"

Tate studied her, but he didn't immediately answer.

Zion rubbed Rebekah's back.

"Is there anything else you can remember?" Tate asked her.

"No, that's it."

"Did you notice any strange cars in the parking lot of the lodge or any strange people hanging around?"

Rebekah frowned. "How would I know? I've never been there before."

"Did Poole call out a warning to the intruder? Did he tell him he had a gun?"

"Is that required?" Rebekah asked.

"I just need to know. Did he give the guy any sort of warning before he shot?"

"I don't remember anything," she said. "I just remember the gun. It was so loud."

Tate thought for a moment, then he nodded. "Why don't you go home and get some rest?"

Rebekah nodded and rose to her feet. Zion rose with her, but Tate touched her arm. "Can I talk to you in the hallway for a moment?"

"Sure," said Zion, taking her car keys out of her purse. She handed them to Rebekah. "Go ahead and wait in the car for me. I'll be right out."

Rebekah took them and went through the door. Zion followed Tate into the hallway as he turned to face her.

"I know you have to get to the shop and you're probably tired, but I still have to talk to Poole. Can you take Logan to school?"

"Of course," she said, feeling a wash of happiness. He was asking her to do something for him.

"And let Jim Dawson know I'll be missing the meeting about the Halloween Festival. I'm sorry."

"I'll take care of it."

He kissed her lightly. "I'll come by and see you both later, okay?"

She touched his cheek. "No worries. Come by when you can."

He walked her out to the working part of the police station. As they headed for the inner door, she noticed Keith Poole sitting in a chair next to Sam Murphy's desk, his forearms braced on his thighs, his hands clasped. He looked up and watched them as they crossed the room and his eyes were filled with worry.

* * *

Zion glanced over at the quiet teenager in the car next to her. "How do you like being a senior?" she said. She wasn't sure how to get him talking and she sure didn't want to bring up his mother, but she didn't want to drive all this way and pretend he wasn't there.

"It's fine."

"Do you like your classes?"

"Sure."

Zion adjusted her *Caffeinator* ball cap. This was like pulling teeth. Between a catatonic Rebekah on the ride back to her house and now this, Zion was wanting a little human interaction. She wondered what would get a teenager talking. She didn't really know what music Logan liked or any of the latest video games.

"When you saw Tate at the sheriff's office, he was okay?" he asked, a worried tone in his voice.

Zion shot him a look. "Yeah, he was fine. I mean, he seemed a little tired."

"Okay," said Logan, nodding and staring out the window.

Zion sensed something in the kid's question. "Why do you ask that? Is everything all right with Tate?"

He turned and regarded her. Sometimes Logan seemed a lot older than seventeen. "No reason," he said.

"You must have asked for a reason," said Zion, turning off the highway.

Logan shrugged. "He's not too happy this Poole guy's here. I don't know. There's history between them, you know?"

Zion sensed there was, but Tate hadn't really told her much about him. When she thought about it, Tate hadn't told her much at all about his previous life and it was starting to become a thing between them. It was one thing when they were just friends, but since they were dating now, it was starting to loom large.

"I think it has something to do with his partner's death."

Zion's grip tightened on the steering wheel. "You know about that?"

"Yeah, he told me awhile ago. That's why he left LA."

Zion felt a rush of anger, then tamped it down. She didn't really have a right to get angry that Tate hadn't told her before, but now, he was going to have to come clean if they were going to go any farther with this relationship.

She pulled up in front of the high school.

"Thanks for the ride, Zion. Tate says he's going to teach me how to drive soon."

"That's good. Have a good day, Logan. One of us will be here to get you after school's over."

"Don't worry. I can get a friend to give me a ride to the *Hammer Tyme*. I'll text Tate and let him know."

"Okay." She watched the kid get out and hurry toward the buildings, a backpack slung over his shoulders. Logan was a great kid. She was glad Tate had decided to take him in. Maybe they'd be good for each other.

* * *

She was feeling a little groggy when she arrived at the coffee shop, but she didn't have time to get her usual Chai tea before she and Dottie were swamped with customers. She dropped the Halloween decorations in the office and hurried out, tying an apron around her waist.

Nearly an hour later, the traffic died down and she made her tea, grabbed two of Dottie's cinnamon breadsticks, and sat down on the sofa to rest. As she sipped the tea, she sighed, enjoying the warmth spreading through her body. There had been frost on the windows today when she arrived.

"You okay, sugar?" called Dottie from her breadboard.

"I'm fine, Dottie, just tired."

She waved over her shoulder and went back to sipping. She was surprised when the bell jangled and Rebekah walked through, freshly showered and wearing slacks, an angora scoop neck sweater in rose-pink, and black heels. Her makeup was perfectly applied and her hair hung in loose curls to the middle of her back.

Dottie made a groan behind them, but Zion sat forward, surprised. "What are you doing here? I thought you'd be sleeping."

A shadow passed over Rebekah's eyes, but she took a seat in the armchair perpendicular to Zion and settled her purse on her lap. "I didn't want to stay home. My mind just won't shut off."

Zion rested a hand on her knee. "I know, honey, I'm sorry."

"So, I decided to work."

Zion quirked a brow and Dottie started coughing. "Work?" Zion said.

Rebekah rolled her eyes and it was so Rebekah-like that something eased in Zion's chest. She hadn't realized she'd been so worried about her friend until that moment. "Not as a barista." She made an airy motion toward the espresso machine. "I think I can help you increase business and make a larger profit."

"Honey…"

"Just hear me out. Did you think any more about the cups?"

"Not really."

"Well, not only that, but some of the distributors you're using for your supplies are charging too much. I found a number of suppliers that are cheaper and closer to Sequoia. You'll be helping the local markets."

Zion sat back, listening. "Go on."

Rebekah opened her purse and pulled out a computer tablet, swiping her fingers across the display. "I made a business plan." She handed it to Zion. "We can print it out if you're interested." She looked around the coffee house and twisted her lips to the side. "I also think we should redesign the layout of this room and get you more space for tables." She pointed to the area before the windows behind them. "Plus, you could make a reader's nook over there, which would get people to stay longer."

Zion glanced over the information on the tablet. "You sure I'd save that much?"

"Yes, and with the changes, you'd be able to offer your workers a raise…"

"Listen to her, sugar," said Dottie from behind the counter.

"And open a satellite location near the highway."

Zion looked up, intrigued. "What do you mean open a satellite location?"

Rebekah crossed her legs. "Can I get a sugar free cafe latte with a splash of cinnamon in it, Dottie?"

"Coming right up," Dottie said, dusting her hands on her apron.

"You miss a lot of morning traffic because it's too hard for commuters to come into town to get their coffee. If you opened a place out by the highway, you could have a drive-up window and entice a whole new clientele to you."

"Where would I find a place by the highway?"

Rebekah reached back into her purse and pulled out a flier.

Zion smiled. "Is that Mary Poppins' magical bag?"

"Don't be silly." She passed the flier to Zion. "I noticed this place when we went to *Up to No Gouda.* It's at the corner of the strip mall, an A-frame building, very small, but perfect for a coffee kiosk. It was a real estate office, so it'll need a little renovation, but it hasn't been rented in three years, so I think we could negotiate a good deal."

Zion stared at the flier. "I'd have to get a loan to do the remodeling."

"Sure, but with my new market plan, your bottom line will be stronger."

"It's not a bad idea," said Dottie, bringing Rebekah's coffee to her. "Dee and I have talked about that before. We miss a lot of traffic in the morning."

Rebekah held up a hand to indicate Dottie was right.

Zion took a deep breath. "Okay. What do we do first?"

"Give me two days to rearrange this entire room. I'll draw up the plans tomorrow and then the next day, can you get the hunky rockstar and hardware man to move furniture? The cute barbecue guy would also be good."

Jaguar, Tate and Daryl, Zion translated in her mind.
"Okay," said Zion.

"Today, I'm gonna look at your books again and see where else we can trim the budget. Are you okay with me going through everything?"

Zion held out her hands. "If you're sure about this, yeah. Can I pay you for this?"

Rebekah waved her off. "Don't be silly. You're letting me stay at your house for free."

Zion gave her a smile, feeling a sinking in her belly. She hadn't heard an end time to Rebekah's visit in there.

* * *

Zion handed Jim Dawson a bag filled with some of the cookies they'd set out on the table for the meeting about the Halloween Festival. Jim gave her a rare smile. "Good meeting. We got a lot done," he said.

"We did, Jim. I think the festival's going to be a lot of fun."

He looked at Dee, where the barista was cleaning off the counter. "Great job on the name, Deimos," he said. "I knew you had a brain in that shaggy head of yours."

Dee held up a hand in acknowledgement of the dubious compliment. Zion smiled wryly.

The Chamber had voted to use Dee's name – *Sequoia's Fangtastic Howl-o-ween Monster Bash*. Jim was going to print up the fliers the next day and give them to every business on Main. Jaguar had agreed to get *Anaconda* to play a concert for the adults that night, and Trixie was going to have trick-or-treat bags made up with the festival's name on it to give to the kids.

"Do you think the high school will agree to send volunteers to man the games?" asked Zion.

Jim shrugged. "I don't see why not. I still have some contacts on the front lines. I'll give them a call tomorrow."

He made it seem like teaching was a military offensive. Maybe it was, she agreed, seeing as Dawson had taught less than stellar students like Deimos Hendrix and

Jerome Jaguar Jarvis. She patted his arm. "That's great. We should probably try to get our stores decorated by the end of the week. If you need help, my friend Rebekah and I could come over."

Jim frowned. "Help? I can decorate my own store. I've been known for my holiday whimsy."

Zion fought a laugh. Whimsy and Jim Dawson didn't seem to share the same zip code, but she left it at that.

"Well, I better be going."

"Later, Mr. Dawson dude," shouted Dee, waving his rag.

"Good evening, Deimos, Zion," said Jim and he turned for the door, pushing it open just as Tate was trying to get inside.

"Sorry, Jim," Tate said, sidestepping him.

"No worries," said Jim, walking out into the night.

"Hey, Dee," said Tate, holding up a hand.

"Tate, my man, how's it hanging, dude?"

Tate gave Zion a wry look, kissing her on the cheek. "Better now," he said.

Zion touched his stubbly chin. "You look exhausted."

"So do you," he said. "Look, can we talk?"

She motioned to the couch area. It was a bit more private and comfortable. She figured this might be a long talk. As they took seats, Tate laid his arm across the back of the couch and curled the other into a fist on his thigh.

"Logan told me you guys talked about stuff this morning," he said.

"Stuff?" she questioned.

"Me," he answered. "Look, I'm sorry I didn't tell you before, but it's difficult to talk about."

She tucked a leg under her and turned toward him. "I know, Tate, but if we're serious about this dating thing…"

"I'm serious," he said urgently.

"Then you need to talk to me."

He sighed and scratched the side of his head. "I know."

She reached out and took his hand. "Why is it so hard for you to tell me?"

"It's not that. It's just hard to talk about period."

"Start with your partner. Tell me about him."

"Jason?" He looked toward the windows. "Jason was an ass." He laughed and looked back at Zion. "He was my best friend. We got partnered on the force almost from the first day. We were both so green, rookies. Jason was already married to Rachel and I was dating Cherise."

Zion almost held her breath as he started talking about his time with Jason, some of the cases they worked together. Dee quietly finished up and left, leaving the two of them alone in the coffee shop, while the night pressed in outside.

When Tate got to the night Jason died, Zion moved closer to him, stroking the back of his hair as he talked. He curled his hand around her hip and pulled her closer still, his fingers flexing against her side.

Tate paused. "It was surreal, that night. After it was over, I just kept reliving it again and again, the sounds, the smells, the sights. I thought I was going to die that night. I was sure of it." He looked away. "And then I didn't."

"Survivor's remorse," she said softly.

His gaze swung up to hers. "Yeah, yeah. For days, I just sat at home. I ate and I did things. I remember gardening for hours and I hate to garden. You've seen my yard. I only mow when I can't see the house anymore from the street."

They both laughed.

"I lost track of time. I went back to work and they put me on desk duty, and honestly, I don't remember any of it. It's like I was in a fog. Like I wasn't really participating in my own life."

"What brought you out?"

Tate toyed with a lock of her hair. "Cherise told me she was leaving." He scraped his bottom lip with his teeth. "She said she'd met someone. A gardener." He laughed and Zion frowned. "Irony, yeah. Johnny Delcaro. He was younger than Cherise, but…" Tate shook his head. "I was actually surprised. I didn't know we'd gotten to such a bad place."

Zion swallowed hard, wanting to comfort him, but not knowing what was the best way to do it. "Did you still love her?"

Tate's gaze flicked up to hers. "I honestly don't know. I think I loved her, once, but…" He shook his head. "I don't know." He drew a breath and released it. "When we got married, it was sort of because we should. We both had steady jobs, we'd been seeing each other for a long time, living together, but I'd watch Jason and Rachel together and I'd think we didn't have what they had. Jason was always touching her, some small thing, and the way she looked at him." He rolled his shoulders to ease the tension. "Rachel was destroyed by his death, and I remember thinking that Cherise wouldn't have been that upset if I died."

"Tate…"

"No, I'm serious. That's not self-pity. She wouldn't have been. It didn't seem fair, you know?"

"What? What didn't seem fair?"

He thought about it for a moment. "That Jason died and left a woman who really loved him, a woman he wanted to build a family with, and me…I lived and no one really gave a damn." Tears filled his eyes and he blinked them away, turning his head to the side. "Not my parents, not my wife. Jason had so much more to live for."

Zion did the only thing she could think of and eased up as close to him as she could get. She wrapped her arms around him and brought his head down to her shoulder, holding him. He sank against her, letting her support him.

"Cherise asked for a divorce and I didn't argue. I signed the papers the same day I gave the LAPD my resignation. Then I looked for some place the exact opposite of LA to go. I found the hardware store for sale and I had the money from the sale of our house, my retirement from the force, and some stocks I'd bought before our marriage."

Zion stroked her hands down his back. "That must have been scary, picking up everything and starting over in a new place."

He shrugged. "It was either that or…"

"Or?" she said, feeling a tightening in her chest.

"Or, I honestly don't know, Zion. I just honestly don't know."

CHAPTER 10

Tate stepped into the sheriff's office and pressed the button on the counter. He rocked on his heels and stuffed his hands in the back pockets of his jeans, looking out the door. He needed to get to the *Hammer Tyme*. He'd been leaving the business to Bill Stanley too much lately, but he wanted to make sure he shared his ideas with Wilson first.

He thought of the previous night in Zion's coffee shop. The way she'd comforted him when he'd told her about Jason's death and his divorce. He didn't sense any judgment in her. He'd been hesitant to share that much intimacy with anyone since Cherise, but Zion was different. He'd known that from the first moment he'd met her. Of course he was attracted to her physically. That had never been in doubt, but he sensed so much more depth in her and he gravitated toward it. Last night she'd proved that right.

If they both hadn't had people in their houses, he suspected their relationship might have taken an even more intimate turn, but as it was, he'd walked her to her car, kissed her good night and followed her back to their street, waving to her as he went in his house to his teenage roommate.

The frosted window before him opened and Sam Murphy gave him a speculative look. "What's up, Tate?"

"Can I talk to Sheriff Wilson?"

She hit the buzzer. "He said to bring you back if you showed up today."

Tate walked to the door and pushed it open. He knew his way to Wilson's office well, but Sam accompanied him. "You want some coffee?" she asked.

He shook his head. "No, I'm gonna stop by the *Caffeinator* on my way in to town this morning."

"Right. So, you and the Ginger are dating I hear."

Tate gave her a tense smile. "Zion. Her name's Zion," he said firmly.

"Right." She pushed Wilson's door open. "Tate Mercer here to see you, Sheriff."

"Come in, Tate," said Wilson, sitting behind his desk. He motioned to the chair across from him and Tate sank into it, bracing his forearms on his thighs. "How you doing, son?"

"I'm fine."

Wilson raked his fingers through his hair, making his widows peak more prominent. "Let me guess, you're here to talk about the case."

"I am. Look, Sheriff, I get why you didn't want me to interview Poole, but I need to be on this case. I have insight into the Devil's Tongue that you don't and I still have my contacts in LA. I'm guessing you didn't identify the body yet."

"Nope, not yet. I'm hoping the coroner will get a fingerprint match on AFIS, but I haven't heard from her yet."

"Where's Poole?"

"He's back at the cabin as far as I know. I couldn't hold him. He had a valid concealed carry permit and the gun was registered. I need to identify the victim and see if we've got a motive, so I ordered him not to leave town."

"I want to work this case, Sheriff."

"Tate, I think you're too closely involved."

"Yeah," said Tate, holding out his hands. "I am too involved. The Devil's Tongue killed my partner. You don't know the firepower they have, Sheriff. You aren't equipped to fight them. You need my help."

Wilson studied him a moment, rubbing his fingers along the pencil-thin moustache on his upper lip. "Okay, but if I tell you to back off, you back off, is that clear?"

Tate nodded enthusiastically.

"I need to hear the words, son."

"I'll back off if you tell me to back off."

"Okay. Murphy's heading this investigation. Give her any information you can from your contacts in LA as soon as you get them."

"I will, sir." Tate rose to his feet. "Can you tell me what you found out about the Impala?"

"You're not going to let this go, are you?"

"I can't, sir."

"The Impala was reported stolen from Los Angeles two nights before."

"I thought so," he said.

"Tate?"

Tate hesitated and looked back at Wilson.

"Sometimes our need for revenge can make us forget why we got into law enforcement."

"I understand, sir."

Wilson quirked a brow. "Do you, son? Are you sure?"

Tate gave him a nod. He had no intention of crossing a line with this case, but the Devil's Tongue had to be ended, that was all.

* * *

Instead of driving over to the *Hammer Tyme*, Tate drove to the coroner's office. He was surprised to find Angela Davenport just getting out of a Toyota Forerunner a few cars away from him. He threw open the truck's door and hurried after her.

"Dr. Davenport?"

She turned and gave him a cool appraisal. He took out his badge and showed it to her.

"Dr. Davenport, I'm Tate Mercer. I'm a consultant for the sheriff's department and I was on scene yesterday morning when you were called out for the shooting at Bearpaw Creek."

"I remember you, Mr. Mercer," she said, pulling her briefcase in front of her. "How can I help you?"

"I was just wondering if I could get a copy of your report on the autopsy for the John Doe when you finish it."

"You could have put in a call to my office, Mr. Mercer. You didn't have come out here on your own."

Tate shifted weight, studying the single story, grey building behind him. A sign stood under two redwood trees, proclaiming it the *Tulare County Coroner*'s office. "Actually, I wanted to talk to you in person. The John Doe, did you run his fingerprints through AFIS?"

"I did."

"And did it ping on anything?"

She crossed her arms over her chest. She wore a suit in pale brown with a dark brown blouse beneath it. "I'm guessing you know it didn't, am I right?"

"I suspected as much. The sheriff said the car was stolen."

"Well, the body didn't have any identification on it either. I'm at a dead end."

Tate considered that. "I might be able to help."

"And how is that?"

"I was a cop in LA."

"I heard you mention that to Sheriff Wilson the other night." She shifted weight, her gaze steady. This wasn't a woman to mess with, Tate decided. He needed to just tell her what he knew. "You knew about the tattoo on the man's chest," she added.

"I did. I still have contacts in LA. There was one specific tattoo parlor that did those tattoos. If I can have a picture of the vic, I might be able to get an ID on him."

She thought about that one for a moment, chewing on her inner lip. "If Wilson gives the okay, I'll send you the report and the pictures I took."

Tate nodded. "Thank you."

"Mr. Mercer," she said levelly, "it's never good to get personally involved in an investigation."

"I'm aware of that, Dr. Davenport."

"Aware and believe it are two different things though."

Tate didn't answer. He wasn't sure she expected one. He watched her walk away, headed for her office, then he turned for his truck, climbing inside. He understood that he shouldn't get personally involved in this investigation, but they didn't understand what the Devil's Tongue could do to a town like Sequoia.

* * *

He made it back to Main before he was scheduled to open the hardware store. He detoured down the street and opened the door to the *Caffeinator*. The coffee shop's morning rush had ended and Zion stood on a step ladder, stringing black tinsel around the bar door frame that led to the kitchen. Dottie gave him a smile as she pounded on dough.

"Hey, sugar, can I get you a mint mocha chip Frappuccino?"

"Can you make it hot rather than cold?" he asked, frowning as Zion teetered on the ladder. He hurried around the counter and steadied her. "You're gonna break your neck."

She finished affixing the last pin and hopped down, wrapping her arms around his neck and kissing him. "Oooh, you're cold."

He felt Dottie's smiling eyes on them as he encircled Zion's waist and drew her closer, nuzzling her throat. "You could warm me up," he whispered against her ear.

She shoved him back. "Not in front of the customers."

When he looked at the customers, they were all smiling and didn't seem to mind.

"Wait here," she told him. She hurried through the bar doors and into the back.

Tate moved around the counter and leaned on it as Dottie finished his drink. She set it in front of him and he took out some money, but she waved it off. "Keep our girl off the ladder and I'll buy."

"That may be easier said than done," he said, looking around at the decorations. Fake cobwebs draped off the glass counter top and a fuzzy black spider hung directly over the cash register. Decals of smiling black kittens sitting inside pumpkins were affixed to the windows and cutouts of puppies wrapped in mummy bandages were stuffed into the corners of the picture frames. Orange and black tablecloths covered the bistro tables and a small pumpkin candle sat in the middle of each one.

Zion appeared out of the back, carrying a bag overflowing with more Halloween decorations. "Take these down to your shop. When I get off, I'll come down and help you decorate."

He gave the bag a weary look, then took it. "No ladders," he said.

"How are we going to hang the pumpkin lights then?" she said, placing her hands on her hips.

"Pumpkin lights?"

"Pumpkin lights."

Dottie chuckled and went back to beating her dough.

"If I let you do this to my shop, I want something in return," he said, giving her a stern look.

"What?" she replied, scandalized.

"I want you to go bowling with me at *Spare Me the Lanes.*"

"The bowling alley?" she asked in horror.

"That's the one."

"With rental shoes in two different tones?" She shuddered. "And chili cheese fries?"

Dottie and Tate both laughed. "I even have my own bowling glove," he said. "And a custom made ball."

She gave him a disgusted look. "If I'd have known that, I would have said no to our first date."

He leaned on the counter, bringing himself close to her. "Pumpkin lights for bowling shoes, Zion," he said in a growl. "You decide."

She licked her bottom lip. "Fine," she said a little breathlessly.

He gave her a smile, then leaned in for a slow kiss. Drawing away, he reached for his coffee cup and lifted it for a sip. "Thanks for the drink, Dottie," he said and sauntered out, carrying the bag of fluffy Halloween decorations.

* * *

He was just selling a chainsaw to a customer when the buzzer sounded and Keith Poole walked through the door. As Tate took the customer's credit card, he kept his eyes on Poole as he wandered around the store. Sharing a look with Bill Stanley, the older man took over the customer, while Tate went to the counter and lifted it, moving toward Poole.

Poole put a can of oil back on the shelf and turned to meet him, smiling broadly. "Hey, Tater Tot."

"What are you doing in here, Poole?"

"I needed to talk to you."

"I don't think we should be talking. I'm consulting on the shooting."

"I know. I figured you would be. It was self-defense, Tate."

Tate tucked his hands in his jeans pockets. "That's what you said."

"You don't believe me? You heard Rebekah. The guy broke through our bedroom window in the middle of the night. He had a switchblade. What was I supposed to do?" Poole rubbed the back of his neck, his sweater straining against his chest. "Seriously, Tate, what did you expect me to do?"

Tate looked away, watching as another customer entered his store. "I guess I don't know."

Poole nodded. "You're the only one I know in this town, the only one I trust. The sheriff said I couldn't leave town until he figures out who the John Doe is. He took my gun and I had to pay all the damages on the cabin so they'd let me stay. It's a hot mess."

Somehow hot messes always seemed to find Poole. "He had a Devil's Tongue tattoo on his chest, Keith."

Keith flinched and his mouth drew into a tight line. "You sure?"

"I saw it myself."

"Wow."

"Yeah." Tate glanced around to be sure no one else was listening to them. "What's the Devil's Tongue doing in Sequoia, Keith? How did they find you?"

"I don't know, Tate," he said, holding out his hands. "You think I'd know something like that?"

Tate leaned closer to him, punctuating his words with his index finger. "These people can't handle the Devil's Tongue. We couldn't handle them in LA. Why did you come here? Why did you bring them here?"

"I didn't know they'd find me, Tate." He shrugged. "They might be following you too. Did you ever think of that? Maybe they just figured out where you moved."

Tate gave him a frown. He'd been here for two years and the first person from his past to find him was standing in front of him right now. "They came for you. Why, Poole?"

"I don't know!" shouted Poole, then he also looked around. Bill Stanley and the two customers were watching them. "I haven't had anything to do with them since the night Jason died. You know that." He dropped his voice. "Our task force was disbanded that night, Tate. After the tenement went up, the Devil's Tongue scattered. The LAPD took them off their watch list."

Tate absorbed that. He knew the task force was disbanded, but he didn't know about the watch list.

"You gotta help me, Tate. This isn't going to look good with internal affairs." When Tate gave him a skeptical look, he amended, "Me being in another officer involved shooting."

"You weren't on duty."

"It doesn't matter. I shot another person. You know how they're going to view that. I mean, both were justifiable, but it's gonna make it harder to get my badge back now. You've got to prove that it was in self-defense. You've got to help me, Tate."

Tate didn't have to do a damn thing. He owed Poole nothing. They'd never been partners, they'd never been friends. They'd barely been colleagues. "I don't owe you anything."

"Then I guess saving your life means nothing?"

"What?" Tate gave him a disbelieving look. "What the hell are you talking about?"

"The night Jason died, you were pinned behind the cruiser. You remember?"

Remember? He never forgot it.

"They would have picked you off. You were a sitting duck."

Tate felt sweat pepper down his spine. "Yeah?"

"I saved you, Tate. I drew them off."

"How?"

Poole's phone rang. He pulled it out of his pocket and looked at the display. "I've got to take this," he said, holding it up. "It's the captain." He thumbed it on and held it to his ear, stepping around Tate.

Tate turned to watch him walk to the door.

"Yeah, I'll hold," said Poole, placing his free hand on the door. He gave Tate a tense smile. "Hey, you think Rebekah would…"

"No!" said Tate firmly.

Poole shrugged and shoved the door open. "Yeah, I figured as much. Later, Tater Tot," he said and walked outside, the phone pressed to his ear.

Tate stared after him, mulling over what he said. A lot of that night was a blur, but he didn't remember anyone drawing the gunfire away from him. The explosion of the meth lab had ended it, followed by the sirens. What the hell did Poole mean he saved Tate's life? As far as Tate could remember, he didn't even know where Poole was during much of the gunfight. He just remembered him showing up after the area had been secured. Something wasn't right about this whole thing.

* * *

Tate took a break when Logan arrived and went into the storage room, sitting down at the table with a can of soda. He opened his laptop and googled the Devil's Tongue, but what he found was incidental mentions of the night Jason died. He didn't want to read those articles, so he reached for his phone instead. He dialed Darcy Reyes, his friend on the force. Darcy had never failed him in the past when he'd asked her for help.

"Hey, Tater Tot, let me guess, you're calling me about Poole."

Tate smiled. "I really hate that nickname right now," he told her. "How are you, Darce?"

"I'm good, but you don't really give a damn about that."

"Did you get the case of wine I sent you?"

"Yep, and the building blocks for Mikey. He loved them." Mikey was her five-year-old son. "Me, not so much. Do you know how damn painful it is to step on those things in the dark?"

Tate chuckled. "Yeah, I can imagine. How's Mikey doing?"

"Trying to butter me up by pretending you care about my kid?"

"No, I genuinely care about your kid, Darcy. You know that?"

"He's awesome as always, Tater Tot. So, what do you want this time?"

Tate sighed, brushing away some lint on the laptop keyboard. "I need everything you can find me on Poole. Any prior suspensions he's had, the results of the investigation into the shooting death of the kid, anything else that you can think of."

"I could lose my job for this, Tate."

"A hit man from the Devil's Tongue was here in Sequoia, Darce."

"The Devil's Tongue hasn't been in operation for years, Tate."

"I know what I saw. He had the tattoo and he found Poole here. How did he locate him?"

"I have no idea. Are you sure it was the same tattoo?"

"It was the same. What I can't figure out is why a member of the Devil's Tongue would follow Poole to Sequoia just after he's put on leave for killing an African American teenager. What's the connection between the two?"

"Maybe they're not related, Tater Tot. Have you thought of that?"

"Then why did both events happen within weeks of each other?"

She fell silent. He waited, knowing Darcy's conscience was the quickest way to get her to cooperate. "I could lose my job," she said again.

"Innocent people could die. The sheriff's department here isn't equipped to deal with the Devil's Tongue, and you know it."

She sighed and Tate knew he had her. "Okay, fine. I'll send you everything I can dig up on Poole, but if I get caught, you're putting Mikey and me up in your house."

"Deal."

"Give me a few days."

"You've got it."

"And Tater Tot?"

"Yes, Darcy.

"Do not tell Poole what I'm doing, no matter what. You got me?"

"I got you," he answered and disconnected the call.

* * *

"Okay, we have webs and I thought we could put these cute spiders in the webs. Then we've got the little skeletons. I thought we could hang these off the shelves. And the pumpkin lights can go along the counter here. We can tape them down."

Tate glanced up from the pile on his counter and caught Logan smirking at him. He glared at him and nodded at the broom. Logan gave a low laugh and got the broom, pushing it across the floor behind the counter.

Pulling out a sheet of decals, Zion held them up. "Look at this. Isn't it adorable?"

The black kittens on the decal spelled out happy Halloween with their bodies. Tate didn't know what to say. He had to do something before his manly hardware store became Halloween cute, not that he'd ever believed there was such a thing before Zion blazed into his life.

"What about scary stuff like ghouls and ghosts and ax-murderers?"

"You have spiders," she told him, holding up a packet of plastic spiders.

He arched a brow, realizing he wasn't getting out of this. She grabbed the cobwebs and began pulling them apart.

"Come on, it's going to be fun."

It was fun, but the fun he had was flirting with Zion while they decorated the store. Every chance he got, he somehow had to wrap his arms around her and give her a kiss on the cheek or neck before he could complete the task she gave him. She scolded him mildly, pushing him away, but one time he caught her in the corner and bracing his hands on either side of her head, leaned in for a deeper kiss. She responded, until Logan made a retching noise behind them, driving them apart.

Once they had hung and strung and pinned everything where Zion wanted it, she made Logan plug in the lights and illuminate the space. Clapping her hands together, she turned a circle in the store and exclaimed how beautiful it all was.

Tate wasn't sure beautiful was the right theme for Halloween, but he loved seeing the way her eyes danced with pleasure. He couldn't take his eyes off her. Throwing her arms around his neck, she hugged him. He smiled, her mood infectious, and felt the tension ease inside of him. He didn't think he'd taken a deep breath since the night he got the call to go out to Bearpaw Creek.

"Okay, now it's time for bowling," he said.

She made a face and drew away a little. "Seriously? I thought you were joking."

"Not even a little."

A mischievous glint entered her eyes. "I can't leave Rebekah home alone and you can't leave Logan."

"He can leave Logan," Logan said. "He really can."

"No, if we're going bowling, we're all going bowling."

Tate gave her a severe look, but she kissed him quickly and danced off, going to the storage room to collect her purse and jacket.

Tate felt Logan's eyes on him.

"What?"

"You've got it bad, dude," said Logan.

"I know," said Tate with a sigh.

"All I can say is thanks a lot, man. Thanks a freakin' lot. I hate bowling and she's not my girl."

Tate didn't answer as Logan stormed into the back for his own coat. He figured Logan would understand his predicament someday himself. It was inevitable.

* * *

Tate watched in amusement as Rebekah dropped the bowling shoes on the floor and grabbed a napkin off the score panel, wiping her hands. "You can't be serious? I'm not wearing someone else's shoes and I'm not wearing shoes that look like two different discount shoes have been cut in half and shoved together."

Tate and Zion exchanged a smile and Zion stretched out her feet. "I don't know. I think they're kinda cute."

"Do you think the smell of pine disinfectant is cute too?" said Rebekah, opening another napkin and laying it down on the seat before sitting down. "I'm going to get a fungus. I can just feel the fungus trying to attach itself to me."

Tate laughed and stood, going to the ball return and grabbing his bowling ball. He positioned himself before the lane and held the ball in front of his face, then he took his three steps and released. The ball sailed down the lane and smashed into the pins, sending them all flying. Zion clapped her hands for him.

Logan jogged down the stairs onto the lane, carrying a tray filled with nachos, chili cheese fries, and sodas. He set the tray on the table next to Rebekah and she slid away, giving it a jaundiced look. Logan handed Tate back his credit card.

"You think you got enough?" asked Tate wryly.

"I don't know, Tate. You think there's enough polyester in here," he grumbled. "And back sweat."

Rebekah shuddered. "Oh dear God," she whispered.

Zion shook her head in amusement and grabbed a pink ball she'd found on the rack. She stepped up in front of the lane and then shuffled forward quickly and threw the ball right into the gutter. She turned and gave Tate a pout. He smiled at her.

"You need to aim. Have you ever bowled before?"

"When I was a little girl."

Rebekah looked around the bowling alley. "What if someone sees me in here?"

"You don't know anyone here," said Zion, waiting for her ball to return.

When it bounced onto the rails, Zion picked it up, but Tate said, "Let me help you." He curled his arms around her from behind and she leaned into him, kissing his cheek. He smiled at her. "See the triangle on the floor."

"Mmmhmm," she said, but she wasn't looking.

Logan shoved a bunch of chips in his mouth. "Jesuf, yew moaking me soick," he said with his mouth full.

Rebekah crinkled her nose at him, then she nodded. "I agree. Play grab ass some other place, hardware man."

"Rebekah!" Zion said, glaring at her over Tate's shoulder.

"Ignore them," he said, turning her back to the lane. "Look at the triangle on the floor and aim for it," he urged her.

She nodded, then she took a few mincing steps forward and heaved the ball. It landed with a thud in the lane and began creeping toward the pins. Both Rebekah and Logan leaned over, watching it make its way down the lane in slow motion. Tate glanced around to be sure none of the workers had seen her throw the ball.

Eventually the ball reached the pins and tapped them. Two in back fell over. Zion leaped into the air, whooping with delight, then she ran back to Tate and threw herself at him, kissing him on the mouth. He staggered back, but he caught her, sinking his hands in her hair and kissing her in return.

"So gload I coame hoere," said Logan with his mouth still full. "I noeed to boe oembarrassed. Toeenagers loove to be oembarrassed by adoults, you know? I thoink I'll roun awoay now!"

Rebekah crossed her legs and jogged her foot up and down. "Tell me about it, kid," she said, glancing at him, then away in disgust. "For God's sake, chew with your mouth closed," she groused.

CHAPTER 11

"Where...exactly...is Tate?" grunted Daryl, shoving one of the couches up against the windows in the *Caffeinator.*

"He's busy doing something at the sheriff's office," said Zion.

"Move it more to the right," said Rebekah, tapping the end of a pencil against her lower lip.

Daryl nodded for Jaguar to grab the other end and they shoved it over into the corner of the store, the back against the windows. Zion wasn't sure about that. She didn't think her customers were going to like having their backs to the windows.

"Pull it out a little. You've got to hang the curtains behind it."

"Hang curtains?" said Jaguar. "I don't hang curtains. That involves power tools."

"Well, how do you think you're going to build the bookcase, Rockstar?" she said, giving him a look that said he was daft.

Jaguar's pale blue eyes shifted to Zion and widened. "Bookcase?"

Zion looked away. She didn't know about the bookcase until Rebekah had shown up with it this morning in the back of the Spider and made poor Jim Dawson haul it in with his hand truck.

"Dee can put the bookcase together," said Daryl.

"Dee's afraid of nails," said Zion quietly.

Daryl glared at her.

"Don't just stand there. I want the other couch along this wall, perpendicular to the first," ordered Rebekah.

As the men lifted the second couch and positioned it, Rebekah motioned to the open area. "The coffee table will go in front of the couch by the windows and we'll position the two armchairs side by side in front of the table. The bookcase will go along here." She motioned to the area to the right of the door. "It'll guide the customers directly to the counter and provide privacy for those in the reading nook."

"Do you really think people want their backs to the windows?"

"You want them looking at the display case, Zion. Seeing all that sugary goodness will make them want to buy."

Zion had to agree she had a point.

"I got a reading lamp to go in the corner between the two couches to soften the light and make it conducive to reading and I picked up a whole bunch of hardbound books at a used bookstore in Visalia on the cheap. The longer you keep people in here, the more money they might spend."

Once the men had the couch positioned, Rebekah had them lay out a dusky pink rug with a scallop pattern and place the coffee table on it. Then she positioned the armchairs herself.

Motioning to the open area where the couches had been just this morning, she said, "We need to go to some garage sales this weekend and see if we can pick up a few more bistro sets. I don't want them to match. We'll mix them with the other tables and create ambiance."

"Okay," Zion said, skeptically. "I gotta go wait on customers right now though."

"Don't you worry. I'll get this all whipped into shape in no time." Rebekah clapped her hands together. "That bookcase isn't going to build itself, gentlemen," she ordered.

Zion could feel Jaguar and Daryl pelting her back with visual daggers, but she hurried behind the counter and whispered to Dottie, "We'd better make them something special to drink."

"I'm on it," Dottie said, going to the espresso machine.

* * *

Zion was baking cookies in the kitchen when Tate stepped through the bar doors.

"Hey," she said, feeling a flush of pleasure at his arrival.

"Hey, yourself." He leaned over the baking table and kissed her. "I thought I might entice you to lunch."

"We can't go to the barbecue," said Zion, going to the sink and washing her hands. "I don't think Daryl's talking to me."

"Yeah, he's not talking to me either," said Tate, leaning on the counter next to her. "So I've been told I have to hang curtains after the hardware store closes."

"I'm sorry."

"Are you kidding? I don't mind. It means I get to spend time with you."

"And Rebekah."

"Right, and Rebekah."

She dried off her hands. "So, should we go to *Up to No Gouda* for a sandwich."

"Actually, I picked up Chinese food when I was at the sheriff's office. I thought maybe I could get you to come to my storage room for a bite." He growled and nipped at her neck.

She giggled and wrapped her arms around him.

"Oh, dear God, no more of this," complained Rebekah, coming out of Zion's office.

Zion grabbed Tate's hand. "Let's go out the back. That way we don't have to hear any more complaints."

"Sounds good," he said.

"I'm going to lunch, Dee," she shouted into the coffee shop.

"Okey dokey, boss lady," shouted Dee in return.

Zion dragged Tate into the alley behind the shops. It was cold and she'd forgotten her jacket, so she curled into his side. He kissed her temple and wrapped his arms around her as they hurried down to the *Hammer Tyme.*

Bill Stanley had on his coat when they slipped inside. "You need to me stay?" he asked Tate when he saw Zion.

"Nope, I've got it."

"Hi, Bill," Zion said, sidestepping the other man as she followed Tate toward the back.

"Miss Sawyer," said Bill, nodding his head.

"You can call me Zion, Bill. I'm okay with that."

"Have a nice rest of your day, Miss Sawyer," Bill answered.

Tate gave her a shrug as he lifted the counter and pulled her toward the storeroom with him.

"Should we leave the store unattended?" she asked him.

"I can hear the buzzer when people come in."

He had the Chinese food arranged on the table in back with two paper plates and napkins. He handed her a pair of chopsticks and motioned to the chair. "Sit. What can I get you to drink? I have cola or water or cola?"

She laughed, taking a seat. "Cola sounds good."

He went over to the little refrigerator and bent over, opening it. Zion couldn't help but admire his backside in his jeans. He got out the sodas and brought them back to the table, handing her one.

"You were pretty sure I'd join you," she said, looking at all the food.

"Actually, I wasn't, but I figured if you couldn't join me, I had a teenager arriving in a few hours who would devour the rest of it."

She laughed and popped the tab. "The funeral's in two days. How's he holding up?"

Tate shrugged and took a seat. "He gets quiet sometimes and I know he's thinking about his mom. I think it'll be good when the funeral's over. He goes to the grief counselor tomorrow." He grabbed a takeout box and opened it. "So, you have your chow mein and your fried rice. In this box is your broccoli beef and your moo shu pork."

Zion smiled and accepted the chow mein. "Do you have everything you need for the wake?"

"Yeah, everyone I've talked to has said they're bringing food. You're still bringing coffee, right?"

"Right."

"We should be good. Logan's aunt Esther is bringing food too. I think they ordered a platter of sandwiches from the deli."

"Okay, good."

Tate dished up the rice. "How's Rebekah? I haven't asked you how she's holding up after the other night."

"She seems okay, but I catch her up in the middle of the night, making tea."

Tate handed her another box and she tilted it to dish a little onto her plate. "I know something about that," he said grimly.

"Getting up in the middle of the night?" she asked, setting the box down.

He nodded.

"How often does that happen?"

He considered, his eyes drifting upward. "A lot more lately. I keep reliving the gunfight."

Zion covered his hand with her own. "Have you ever thought of talking to someone? I mean a professional."

He nodded. "Logan suggested that too. Maybe." He handed her the last box.

She took it, placing a spoonful on her plate. "What were you doing at the sheriff's office this morning?"

He reached over to a manila folder sitting on the table next to him. "Trying to figure out where this tattoo came from." He pulled open the folder and picked up a photograph of a devil tattoo and passed it to Zion.

She studied it. "Was this on the guy Poole shot?"

"Yeah, it's a tattoo members of the the Devil's Tongue gang get. Only one tattoo parlor in LA does this very tattoo, but we've never been able to locate it."

"Then how do you know only one does it?"

"We confirmed that with a few informants when I was on the case."

"Is this the gang that killed Jason?"

"Yeah."

"So one of the gang members followed Poole here to Sequoia."

Tate met her gaze, chewing his food and swallowing before he responded. "Yeah, Zion, that means one of the gang members followed Poole here."

"Why?"

Tate motioned with his chopsticks. "That's what's keeping me up at night. The gang was scattered when the tenement blew up, the same night Jason died. Most of the members were illegal immigrants and they realized they had the LAPD on their trail. When the task force was disbanded, it was believed the Devil's Tongue wasn't really a threat anymore."

Zion set the picture down. "Did the coroner ID the body?"

"Not yet. She's supposed to get me the autopsy today or tomorrow. I spent the morning trying to track down all the tattoo parlors in LA."

"You think they'll tell you if they do a gang affiliation tattoo?"

"It's the only thing I've got to go on right now." He leaned forward. "I'm worried about this, Zion. That's why I'm telling you. Sequoia's not prepared to have a gang war start here." He tapped his finger on the photo. "This guy was part of the Devil's Tongue at some point in his life. He came here specifically to find Poole. Poole knows more than he's telling me."

"Okay, give me half the list."

"What?"

"I'll make half the calls." She took out her phone and snapped a picture of the tattoo.

"How do you think you're going to get them to tell you anything if I can't?"

She made her face appear grief-stricken. "I'm going to tell them that my fiancé had this tattoo on his chest and he was killed in a car accident. Then I'm going to start crying and tell them I want to get a copy of the tattoo to honor his memory."

Tate smiled, pointing his chopsticks at her. "You lady, may have just figured out the best way to bust this case wide open."

* * *

Zion covered the mouthpiece on the cell phone as the knock came on her office door. She got up and opened it, surprised to find Dottie standing on the other side, her purse slung over her shoulder. Dottie had left at her usual time, so why was she here now?

Zion waved her in. "Yes, yes, I would appreciate any help you can give me. It means so much to me," said Zion. "You don't know how hard it's been since he was killed." She motioned Dottie to a seat before her desk and took a seat herself, picking up the pencil off the blotter and staring at the list of tattoo parlors Tate had given her.

"I need to talk to my supervisor," said the man on the line.

"I understand, but you have my number, right? You'll get back to me?" she asked

"I'll get back to you, miss," he answered.

"Thank you so much," Zion gushed, giving Dottie a wry look.

"Okay, talk to you later."

"Bye." Zion disconnected the call and set the phone on the blotter. Dottie frowned at the unfamiliar device. "I'm helping Tate on a case," she said, lifting the phone. "He insisted I use a burner cell."

"Okay. What's the case?"

"We're trying to figure out the identity of the guy that his ex-cop friend shot at the lodge when Rebekah was there.

He's trying to identify him by his tattoo." Zion held up the picture she'd printed off her phone. Dottie took it, studying it closely. "Apparently, only one tattoo parlor in LA does this sort of tattoo."

"It's ugly."

"It's a gang affiliation, so…"

"Ah. So Tate thinks if he can locate the tattoo parlor, they might have a record of who got the tattoos."

"Exactly."

"That's a long shot."

"I know, but it's the only lead he has. Hopefully, the coroner will come back with an identification, but until then, I'm helping him out. I told him a grieving fiancée might get further than a cop."

Dottie nodded.

Zion folded her hands before her. "Why are you back here? Did you forget something?"

"No," said Dottie, shifting in her chair. Her legs barely touched the floor. "I wanted to talk to you about something."

Zion felt a catch in her heart. Was Dottie going to tell her she wanted to quit? Zion didn't know how she'd run the business without her. She'd learned a lot in the last six months, but there was still so much that she didn't know.

"Dottie, please don't quit on me."

Dottie blinked at her. "What?"

"Isn't that why you're here? You're going to quit?"

"No, sugar, that isn't why I'm here."

Zion let the breath whoosh out of her and she slumped back in the seat. "Okay." She placed a hand over her heart. "You don't know how relieved I am."

"I know you're being about as dramatic as your friend Rebekah," said Dottie.

Zion laughed.

"I've been thinking a lot about the coffee kiosk plan that Rebekah brought up."

"Okay?"

"It's a good plan, Zion. I think we need to move on it before that location's snapped up. We can get a good deal on it now since it's been sitting empty for so long."

"I understand that, Dottie, but I just don't have the capital right now. I mean, Vivian left me a little cash, but I'm scared to use it all. I'm sort of holding on to it for a rainy day."

"That makes sense." Dottie twisted the handle on her bag. "Here's the thing, sugar. I'm all alone. My husband died at fifty and he left me with a little bit of money. I mean, I do fine with social security and what I make from here, plus he had a pension, but let's be honest, I don't necessarily have ten more years in me for pounding dough. My arthritis is getting worse."

"I see," said Zion, but she wasn't sure she did.

"I love working here, I love being with you and Dee and Tallah, and I love the customers. It keeps my brain young." She looked down. "I don't want to sit at home all alone when the time comes that I can't make my baked goods anymore."

Zion didn't know what to say. She knew Dottie's hands ached at the end of a shift, but she seemed so vibrant and energetic other than that.

"Like I said, Gary left me with a little money that I've hoarded all these years. It makes diddly squat in interest, but I was thinking that if I invested with you in the kiosk, we could have it up and running by spring at the latest."

Zion blinked. "You want to invest in the kiosk?"

"Yep. We'd set it up with David as a contract. I'd put up the money for the first six months of rent on the place and the renovation. Then you'd take over the rent after that. We'd split the profits equally if there were any and when I die, I'd put it in my will that the kiosk goes to both you and Deimos in equal share."

Zion thought about it. She liked the idea of reaching the traffic they missed headed out of town and the little A-frame in the *Up to No Gouda* parking lot was a great location.

She felt pretty sure they could turn a profit out of it and it was small enough that the overhead wouldn't be too much more than the *Caffeinator*.

"I think we need to look at the place before we make a commitment to it," she told Dottie.

"I agree."

"I mean, if it needs too much work, we might have to find another location."

"I understand."

Zion felt a flutter of excitement in her belly. "Are you sure about this, Dottie?"

"I haven't been able to stop thinking about it since Rebekah brought it up. Do you think we'd be good partners?"

Zion had no doubt about that. She smiled at her. "I know we'd be good partners."

"Okay, then what do you say? Should we start working on it."

Zion held her hand over the desk. "I say, let's go for it, partner."

Dottie laughed, then her eyes fell on the list sitting on Zion's blotter. "You know what generates more sympathy than a grieving fiancée?"

Zion frowned. "No, what?"

"A grieving grandmother. Why don't you let me give your list a shot? I've got nothing else to do all afternoon and you've got a hunky guy in the coffee shop, trying to hang curtains."

Zion smiled at that and pushed back her chair. "You got it, partner. Go guilt some information out of these guys."

Dottie beamed at her in return.

* * *

A thin, rectangular box sat on the doorstep of Zion's cottage when she and Rebekah got home that night. Zion eyed it suspiciously, knowing she hadn't ordered anything online. Rebekah gave it the same skeptical look.

"What's that?"

"I don't know," said Zion, picking it up. It was addressed to her and the return address label said…Gabrielle Sawyer. "Oh no," moaned Zion, shifting the package in her hands. It was the perfect size for a canvas.

"What's oh no? It's from your mother." Rebekah tilted her head. "Although it's a strange shape."

Zion fished her keys out of her purse and passed them to Rebekah who opened the door. Cleo trilled at them from the darkness, but Rebekah threw on the lights. Zion walked past her to the kitchen and set the box on the table, backing away from it.

Rebekah followed her inside. "Why are you acting so weird? Open it."

"It's from my mother."

"I know that."

Zion curved her arms around herself. "Do you remember the piano?"

"Yeah, she made the neighbors sell their house."

"And the yoga?"

"You said she did it in the front yard in yoga pants."

"And the kale?"

"She made your father's stomach bleed."

Cleo jumped up on the kitchen chair, purring.

Zion stroked the kitten distractedly. "Her new thing is painting."

"Well, that's not bad."

Zion looked over at Rebekah. "Nudes."

"Nudes?"

"Nudes."

Rebekah pointed at the box. "You don't think?"

"I don't know. She painted a nude of my father." They both shivered. "I accidentally saw it."

"Dear God," whispered Rebekah, then she shoved Zion in the shoulder. "Call her."

"Call her?"

"Call her. She's gonna wanna know what you think. Get her to tell you what's inside, so we can prepare ourselves. I'll get us some wine."

Zion pulled her phone out of her pocket and thumbed it on, pressing the icon for her mother. Gabi picked up on the second ring. "How's my sweet girl?" she said.

"Fine, Mom. Um, I…" Zion hesitated. This was going to be awkward no matter what. She held the phone away and pressed the speaker button, setting it on the table. "You're on speaker now, Mom. Rebekah's here too." Zion knew she was stalling.

"Oh, good, how are you, Rebekah dear?" Gabi said.

"I'm fine, Mrs. S. How are you?"

"Just excellent."

"I hear you're painting now," said Rebekah, smirking.

Zion shoved her, nearly making Rebekah slosh her wine.

"Oh, I am. I'm taking a nude figure drawing class and we built an atrium so I can have my own studio and you should see all the canvases I've been working on."

"Back up, Mrs. S," said Rebekah. "Did you say you're taking a nude figure drawing class?"

"I am. At the junior college."

"Real people?"

"As real as it gets, Rebekah."

Rebekah covered her mouth to hold in a laugh. Zion figured she'd better take control.

"Mom, I got a package today."

"Oh, good, I was waiting for you to say something. What do you think? I made it for your kitchen."

Rebekah snorted. "Don't you mean bedroom?"

"Well, I guess it could go in the bedroom, but I think the colors will complement the kitchen more. You need to put it somewhere where it'll get good light, otherwise it won't bring out all the subtle shades of color."

Rebekah snorted again.

"I haven't opened it yet, Mom."

"Well, open it. What are you waiting for? I really want to know what you think. DeManuel said I really got the strokes down perfectly this time."

Rebekah nearly choked with laughter. Zion glared at her. "Oh, just open it," Rebekah said.

Zion grabbed the box and tore the top open, then she and Rebekah both leaned forward, peering in the opening, but the painting was wrapped in butcher paper.

"Zion, I wanted to tell you, I met the most interesting young man in my class. His name's Luther."

"What?" asked Zion in alarm.

"Yes, he's quite the looker if you know what I mean."

Zion and Rebekah exchanged looks. "He's a student in your class, Mom?"

"Goodness no, he's one of the models. Like I said, he's quite handsome."

Rebekah clapped both hands over her mouth, holding in the giggles.

"Anyway, I was telling him about you. Do you have the painting out of the box yet?"

Zion blinked, unable to follow the rapid change in topic. "No, I don't have it out. Mom, is this…"

"What's taking so long?"

"I don't know," said Zion with a sigh. She reached for the box again.

"Anyway, Luther is really interested in you. I think the two of you would hit it off famously. I told him I'd try to get you down to San Francisco in the next few weeks."

"You told him what?" said Zion, grimacing as she slid the canvas out onto the table.

Rebekah leaned over her shoulder, looking at it too. "Just rip the paper off. Like a bandage."

Zion drew a deep breath and gripped the paper at the top.

"I thought maybe we could double date – me and your father, you and Luther."

Zion's hand jerked and she tore the paper, flinching as it peeled away. She and Rebekah both looked at the painting from the corner of their eyes and then sighed. They were looking at the back.

"You want me to double date with you and Dad? A guy you've seen in the nude in your class, Mom?"

"Don't be a prude, Zion. I didn't raise you that way."

Rebekah brayed in Zion's ear. Zion shrugged her off.

Rebekah picked up the wine and took a drink. "You're going to have to turn it over. You might as well see Luther in his all-together before the date."

Zion grabbed her own wine and downed half the glass, then she reached for the canvas. Counting to five, she flipped it over and set it back down on the table. Both she and Rebekah leaned forward.

"What is it?" Rebekah asked.

"I'm not sure."

"Well, did you get it out of the box?" asked Gabi.

Rebekah and Zion tilted their heads to the side, then Zion turned the canvas around 180 degrees.

"Oh," they both said at the same time. "It's a bowl of fruit."

"Of course it's a bowl of fruit. What did you think it was?"

Zion and Rebekah shared a look, but neither of them said anything.

"Oh, dear God, Zion, you didn't think I sent you the nude of Luther did you?" Which pretty much confirmed there was a nude of Luther. Gabi started laughing, drawing Zion and Rebekah along with her. "Oh, my goodness," gasped Zion's mother. "Oh, heavens, that's hysterical. And you thought I wanted you to put it in the kitchen?"

Tears blinded Zion and she collapsed onto the kitchen chair, blinking at the painting of an abstract fruit bowl her mother had done. Rebekah went to refill their wine.

"So," said Gabi when she'd regained control. "What do you think about the double date?"

Zion braced her chin on her hand, missing her mother so much. "Mom, I'm dating Tate right now."

Gabi didn't say anything, then she let out a breath. "Oh, sweetie, I'm so glad. I mean, I figured that would happen sooner or later, but I'm so glad you've finally decided to take the chance."

Zion smiled, accepting the wine glass from Rebekah again. "Thanks, Mom."

"Oh, boy," said Gabi, "this is awesome. I know exactly what my next painting's going to be."

Zion sat up straighter, her eyes widening, while Rebekah coughed. "What does that mean, Mom?"

"I gotta go, sweet girl, I'll talk to you soon."

"Mom! What does that mean?"

"Bye, Rebekah," she called.

"Bye, Mrs. S," answered Rebekah.

Zion swiveled and looked up at her friend where she leaned against the counter. "She didn't mean what I think she meant, did she?"

"You mean that she's going to paint a nude of Hardware Man, no." said Rebekah, waving her off. "Your mother? That's ridiculous."

"Whew!" Zion said, slumping in the chair, then she replayed Rebekah's words over in her mind again.

They brought her upright once more, her eyes going wide.

CHAPTER 12

Tate had to leave Bill Stanley in charge of the *Hammer Tyme* for another morning, while he took Logan to his first appointment with the grief counselor. The psychologist's office was in the hospital, where he also functioned as a pastor to give solace to dying patients and their families.

As they pulled in the parking lot of Sequoia General, Logan stared out the window, not speaking, his seatbelt still in place. Tate glanced over at him, wondering what was on the kid's mind. Tomorrow was his mother's funeral and that would be enough to make even the most stoic person pensive.

"You ready?"

"I guess," said Logan.

"We agreed this was a good idea, right?"

"We agreed I had to do this in order to stay with you. Mrs. Singleton's coming to the funeral tomorrow and she wants to see how I'm doing."

"Right. I know that, but I still think this'll be good for you, Logan."

"Then why don't you agree to come see him too? I heard you up again last night."

Tate scratched the side of his throat. "I just wanted some water. I'm fine."

Logan gave him a disbelieving look.

"Listen, I talked to Zion like you suggested, so she knows about it now. I'm working on things, okay?"

Logan unbuckled his seatbelt and shoved the truck door open. "Keep telling yourself that. That's how people go postal."

Tate climbed out after him. "That's not how people go postal."

"Keep telling yourself that."

"Would you stop saying that?" said Tate, rounding the back of the truck.

"Fine," said Logan with as much teenage angst as Tate had ever heard.

They entered the hospital and Tate pointed to the left where the medical offices were located. They found Dr. Jeffrey Martin's office and pushed the door open. A woman behind the counter opened a frosted glass window. She had dark skin and a brilliant smile. She wore a pink sweater that strained across her ample bosom, and she had short black hair and pink glasses that hung off a chain around her neck.

"How can I help you?" she said in a sweet voice.

"Logan Baxter to see Dr. Martin," said Tate, giving her a smile.

She typed on the computer as Logan shot Tate a glare.

"I know my own name," he grumbled.

Tate frowned at that. The kid was sure cantankerous today and Tate was rapidly getting tired of it. "I'm trying to help."

"Well, stop. I'm seventeen."

Tate sighed. The receptionist looked up and gave them both a smile, then she picked up a clipboard and placed it on the counter. "I'll need you to fill this out," she said. "Do you have your insurance card?"

Logan dug it out of his pocket, continuing to glare at Tate as he handed it over. Tate met his gaze and refused to look away, not until Logan dropped his eyes first. Score one for the older dog, Tate thought.

After the receptionist handed him back his insurance card, Logan picked up the clipboard and went to take a seat. Tate sat down next to him, curious about the questions he saw on the form. Logan unhooked the pen from under the clip and began checking things off.

Tate pretended not to watch him, but he couldn't help stealing glimpses whenever he could. He wasn't trying to be snoopy, he just really wanted to know Logan's mental state after his loss. Finally Logan slapped the pen on the clipboard.

"Do you want me to just hand it to you so you can read it?"

Tate's eyes snapped up from the clipboard. "No…no! I wasn't trying to look. I just wanted to get some insight into how you are."

"So you *were* trying to look?"

"NO…NO!" Tate blew out air. "Yes."

Logan chuckled. "You suck at this, you know?"

"What?"

"This whole foster parent thing."

Tate felt a little hurt. He was trying his hardest. "This sort of got sprung on me rather quickly. I mean, it's like instant parent, just add water."

Logan chuckled again. "I know. I'm sorry. I don't mean to be an assh—."

Tate cleared his throat.

"Assassin."

"Assassin?" said Tate, giving him an *are you serious* look. "That's the word you flip to? And I'm not supposed to be alarmed."

"It sort of fits," Logan said, then he turned the clipboard sideways and folded his hands on the edge. "You know what word I was really going to say. Anyway, I know you're trying. I appreciate that, but I'm not suicidal. I've never been suicidal, and what's more…"

Tate glanced up at him.

"If I were suicidal, I sure as hell wouldn't put it on this stupid questionnaire."

Point to Logan, thought Tate. He stared at the lines in the carpet. "I just think this has got to be the hardest couple of weeks in anyone's life and I get why you're pissed off right now."

Logan drummed his fingers on the edge of the clipboard. "I'm pissed off because…" His voice trailed away.

"Because?" Tate shifted in the chair. "You're right, I suck at this foster parent thing, but I want to do better. You gotta talk to me, kid."

"I don't want you to think I'm ungrateful or anything."

"I won't. I promise you."

Logan cast him a sideways look. "I had a life before this. I mean, maybe it wasn't a traditional life. Maybe it wasn't even the best life, but it was mine. I went to work, I did my lessons, and I took care of my mom. I did it myself. For a long time. Now, all of a sudden someone comes along and says, hey you can't do that anymore, even though I *was* doing it."

"Yeah, I get that."

"Logan Baxter?" came a man's voice.

They both looked up to see a large man with a rectangular shaped head, massive hands, and a crew-cut staring down at them. He had to be six two or six three wearing a cardigan knit sweater, slacks, and a checked button-up shirt. He held a pair of glasses in his hand. With the other, he extended it to Logan.

"I'm Dr. Martin," he said, shaking Logan's hand, then he shifted to Tate.

Tate rose to his feet and accepted the hand. "Tate Mercer, Dr. Martin. I'm Logan's…um…foster…uh, guardian."

Martin gave him an understanding smile, then he turned back to Logan and held his hand out for the clipboard. "Why don't we talk alone for a bit, Logan?" he said, motioning with the clipboard to the open doorway. He glanced back at Tate. "Stick around. If you don't mind, I'd like to talk to you when our session is over."

"Sure," said Tate, watching Logan disappear through the door with the doctor.

* * *

Tate wandered around the waiting room, picking up magazines and setting them down. Nothing interested him. Especially not *Mental Health Today*. He wasn't opening that can of worms, so to speak. He thought a lot about what Logan said, about him needing therapy himself.

He wasn't sure he believed in therapy. Well, not for him. Other people did find some benefit in it and he was hoping it would help Logan. His own father definitely needed therapy, but he'd never agree to get it.

Tate sat down and braced his forearms on his thighs, staring at the carpet again. Did he need therapy? Would he become like his father if he didn't do something to get over Jason's death? He didn't think he was depressed. He had a great girl now and a job he loved. So he woke up in the middle of the night in a cold sweat. He was still functioning, he was still meeting all his obligations.

His phone buzzed and he pulled it out, looking at the display. A text message from Angela Davenport, the coroner, flashed on his screen.

Autopsy finished. Report sent to your email.

Putting on his glasses, Tate pulled up his email and clicked on the icon for the report, waiting for it to load. The first thing he saw was the name. John Doe. Damn it, she hadn't been able to get a positive identification, which meant the victim didn't have any fingerprints in the system, no driver's license, no social security card. He was likely an illegal immigrant.

The cause of death had been listed as *exsanguination caused by a gunshot wound to the carotid artery.*

His phone rang and he pressed the call button, lifting it to his ear. "Murphy?" he said into the receiver.

"You got the autopsy report?" said Murphy without introduction.

"I got it."

"No identification."

"I know, which probably means he's an illegal immigrant." Tate thought for a moment. "Can you tell me who reported the Impala missing?"

"It was stolen. The perp picked it up on the street."

"Yeah," said Tate, rubbing his forehead. "But I feel like I've seen it before. I know I've seen it before. Can you give me the name of the person who reported it stolen?"

"Karina Mason," said Murphy.

"That's strange," said Tate.

"Why?"

"Does that seem like the sort of car a woman would drive?"

"Are you saying women can't drive hopped-up cars, Mercer?"

"I'm saying it doesn't feel like a car a woman would drive. Was there any personal effects in it?"

"You mean like lipstick or tampons," said Murphy with an edge to her voice.

Tate stretched, feeling tired after his difficult night. "Actually, yeah, was there anything like that in there?"

"No," she said shortly.

"Let me get back to you. I want to snoop around a little on my own."

"Fine. Make sure you update me on whatever you figure out."

"Got it," he said, disconnecting the call.

Just as he did so, the door opened and Logan walked out with Dr. Martin. Tate rose to his feet.

Dr. Martin put a hand on Logan's shoulder and offered them both a smile.

"We had a good session. Logan's pretty open about how he's feeling, so that's good. I don't want to wait until next Friday to see him again though. Can you bring him Monday around 4:00?"

Tate opened his mouth to respond.

"I can find a ride. I know you need to man the store."

"No, um," said Tate. "Monday at 4:00 it is. I'll make sure he's here."

"You're gonna make Zion drive me, aren't you?"

"You get Zion or her friend Rebekah."

"I'll take Zion. Just tell her to stop looking at me as if I'm a wounded puppy."

Tate shared a smile with Dr. Martin. "Did you need to talk to me?"

"Not unless you have some concerns."

Tate did, but he remembered what Logan had said about everyone thinking he couldn't take care of himself anymore and he decided to trust Logan to be open with Martin about his state of mind. "I think I'm good," he said. "Come on, kid, let's get you to school."

"Ugh," said Logan, walking toward the door with his shoulders slumped.

* * *

Tate called Darcy as soon as Bill Stanley left for the day. He sat in the storeroom, his feet propped on a chair, the laptop open on the table. Darcy picked up on the second ring.

"You are going to get me fired, Tate. The captain just asked me if I'd heard from you. Apparently your sheriff called him about Poole."

"Really? Shit. What did he say to you?"

"He wanted to know if I'd heard from you. I said we talked regularly. He said Poole had shown up in Sequoia and was in another shooting. He wanted to know if I knew anything about it."

"And what did you say?"

"I said we hadn't talked about it."

"Okay. So that's good. Did you get me the files on Poole?"

"I'm working on it. I'm having to pull a bunch of favors to get that information, Tate. I don't want internal affairs knowing I pulled it."

"I understand. I also need anything you can get me on the raid."

"The Devil's Tongue raid?"

"Yeah, I need to know who ordered it."

"The commissioner, Tate. You know that."

Tate pushed the bridge of his nose. He was getting a headache. "They told us an informant gave them information that made them pull the trigger on the raid, but they protected their source. Who was the informant, Darcy?"

"Okay, Tate, I'll try to track that down."

Tate picked up his glasses and put them on. "I need you to do something else for me."

"Damn it, Tate."

"Darcy, this is too important. I don't want to put you at risk, but I need your help. I need you to do this for Jason."

"That's really low, Tater Tot."

"I can't help it. I've got to know what happened that night, Darce. I can't pretend it isn't eating me alive anymore."

"I don't want Poole to know I'm helping you. Do you understand me?"

"I understand." He pulled the laptop closer, staring at the autopsy report. "Can you tell me why you're worried about that, though?"

She hesitated. "I don't know. Something about Poole has always set me on edge. I just want to be kept out of this as much as you can."

"Got it."

She sighed. "What do you need me to do?"

"I need you to look up DMV records on a Chevy Impala."

Tate could hear her clicking on her keyboard. "Give me the license plate number."

Tate read it off to her and heard her clicking some more.

"What do you want to know? The car was reported stolen three days ago."

"Who's the registered owner?"

"Karina Mason."

"How long had she owned the car?"

Darcy clicked some more and Tate rose to his feet, going to the mini-fridge and taking out a soda. He popped the top on it and carried it back to the table, sitting down again.

"It was transferred into her name a little over a year ago."

"Can you trace the original owner?"

"Um, hold on."

Tate took a sip of the soda.

"It belonged to Lon Edmonds. It's listed as a family member transfer."

"Lon Edmonds?" Tate stared at the screen on the computer. That name was vaguely familiar. He tried to pull it to the foreground. "Can you search for Edmond's driver's license and send me the picture?"

"Give me a second."

Lon Edmonds? Why did that seem so familiar?

"Huh, his license is suspended."

"Why?"

"I'm sending you the picture."

Tate held the phone away from his face and waited for the text to come through. He hit the button to put Darcy on speaker and pressed the picture icon. The screen opened to a man with sharp features and a hooked nose. Tate felt his mouth go dry. He remembered where he'd seen the Impala before.

He and Jason had followed the Impala to a tattoo parlor. They suspected the tattoo parlor was fronting meth sales, but when they'd gotten a warrant to search the place, it had been clean. He needed to remember where the tattoo parlor was. If he had access to his reports with LAPD, he'd be able to figure it out, but his log-on had been taken away when he quit.

"Why was Edmonds' license suspended, Darcy?" He put his feet up on the chair again and leaned back

"He's serving a life sentence for murder in Atascadero. He was convicted shortly after the car was transferred to Karina." Darcy made a strange noise. "Let me get into the prison records."

Tate felt a little concerned that she was digging so deep. Someone might get suspicious the more she poked around in this stuff, but he wanted to know. He needed to know.

"Edmonds was shanked shortly after he arrived and wound up in the infirmary."

Tate sat up straight, dropping his feet to the floor. "And?"

"The prison doctor noted a tattoo on his upper chest."

Shit, thought Tate, holding his breath. "Of what?"

"A devil." Darcy drew in a breath and released it. "Tate, Lon Edmonds was the Devil's Tongue."

The buzzer on the door sounded and Tate rose to his feet, closing the lid on his laptop. He walked to the doorway and looked out. Poole had stepped inside, gazing around the store, but as soon as he saw Tate, he headed for the counter.

"I gotta go," Tate said.

"I'll get the report on the raid, but I gotta do this carefully."

"Sounds good. Talk to you soon," he said.

"Bye, Tater Tot," she answered and disconnected the call.

Poole placed both hands on the counter, leaning on them. "So, my captain called me today. Appears your sheriff told him about the shooting. I thought we were going to keep this on the DL until we got an ID on the guy."

"I don't control the sheriff, Keith."

Poole hung his head. "He's getting the report from the sheriff and sending it to Internal Affairs as well."

"This might be to your benefit. If you're right and the Devil's Tongue's coming after you, you had no choice but to fire your gun."

"Do we have an identification on the break-in?"

"No, his fingerprints aren't in the system." Tate sighed. "Is the name Lon Edmonds familiar to you?"

"Lon Edmonds?" Poole gave it some thought. "That sounds familiar. Why?"

"He owned the Impala before he wound up in Atascadero."

Poole shook his head. "Okay, so this guy got the Impala and used it to come up here. Why? Why would he come after me? The raid was more than two years ago."

"Is there something you're not telling me about the kid you shot?"

"I'm telling you everything I know."

Tate gave him a speculative look.

Poole briefly met his eyes, then looked away, raking his hands through his hair. "What would be the point of keeping stuff from you, Tate? I'm already in enough trouble. And now my damn life is on the line." He punched the center of his chest with his fist. "I'm getting scared. They tracked me all the way up here from LA. How?"

"I don't know how."

"Exactly."

"What did you mean when you said you saved my life during the raid?"

Poole gave him an annoyed look. "You were pinned down behind the cruiser. I gave them something new to fret over."

"What was that?"

"What?"

"What do you mean you gave them something new to fret over?"

"I took the focus off you."

"How?"

Poole shook his head and held up a hand. "I made myself a target. What the hell do you think? Can we get back to my problem now?"

Tate didn't want to get back to Poole's problem, but he didn't know what more to ask him. It still felt too glib an answer. When he'd said it before, he'd meant more than just giving them another target to aim at, he meant he'd done something to actively draw the gunfire away from Tate. Of course, Poole wasn't beyond manipulation when he wanted something and he wanted Tate to prove he'd killed the unidentified man in the cabin through self-defense. He could have said he'd saved Tate just to guilt him into helping him now.

Tate rubbed the tattoo on his forearm. "Lon Edmonds was also Devil's Tongue, Poole."

"I figured as much. I knew the name sounded familiar."

Tate leveled a hard look on the other man. "This is why I think you're keeping something from me. The raid was more than two years ago. Why are they coming after you now?"

"How should I know? Maybe because my name has been all over the damn news lately. My damn picture for the force with it? Maybe they remember I was part of the task force and they suddenly have a renewed interest in getting back at me?" He scraped both hands through his hair again. "I'm freaking out here, man. I can't even leave and get back to LA because of the damn sheriff. Now he's called my captain, so I'm trapped here or my career is over, but I feel like a damn sitting duck."

"Did he return your gun to you?"

Poole nodded, his features tortured. "I got it yesterday."

Tate wasn't sure how he felt about that, but Poole did have a point. If the Devil's Tongue had seen him on the news, decided they wanted revenge, they'd found him already.

He didn't like the thought that they might send someone else after him. Still, it seemed too convenient, all of it. Tate felt like he was still missing a piece of the puzzle.

"I'll keep trying to figure out what's going on," said Tate.

Poole's shoulders slumped. "Thank you, man."

Tate pointed a finger at him. "But you'd better have told me everything, damn it, Poole. You'd better not have left anything out."

Poole held up his hands. "I haven't. I swear to God," he said. "Come on, Tate. We're brothers. You know the sort of man I am."

Tate didn't answer because the truth was he didn't know. He didn't know Poole that well at all.

* * *

Tate passed Logan a soda and leaned against the counter in the kitchen. "What do you want for dinner? I could barbecue up some burgers?"

Logan popped the soda open and took a swig. "That sounds good."

Tate watched the kid messing on his phone, texting someone. He and Zion had talked about going for dinner and a movie tonight, but when it came down to it, he couldn't leave Logan the day before his mother's funeral. Zion had promised she understood, but breaking dates this early in their relationship might not be the best idea either.

"You got homework?"

Logan's eyes briefly lifted from the phone, then returned to it. "Seriously? Homework?"

Tate shrugged. He wasn't sure where his duty lay. Logan was a senior. Clearly he'd been taking care of his homework for a number of years now, but Tate figured urging kids to do homework was something a parent was obligated to do. He was saved by a knock at the front door.

Pushing away from the counter, he walked into the living room and pulled the door open. Zion stood on the other side, holding a baking dish in her hands with something wrapped in tinfoil on top of it. "Hey," she said, smiling brightly.

A flush of pleasure swept through him and he leaned over to kiss her. "What are you doing here?" he said, then stepped back. "Come in." A cold breeze blew through the door, making her hair dance.

"I brought you and Logan dinner. It's not much. It's just tuna casserole, but I also have garlic bread." She made her way to the kitchen, setting it on the counter. The wonderful aroma of garlic and butter followed her.

"That smells amazing," he said. "Beautiful and smart, and you cook. You're the girl of my dreams."

Logan looked up from the phone and caught Tate's eye, giving his head a slight shake. *Too desperate*, he mouthed.

Tate glared at him.

Zion turned. "Hi, Logan."

"Hey, Zion." He pushed himself out of the chair and approached the counter, sniffing. "You wanna stay and eat with us."

"No, I brought it for the two of you."

Tate wrapped his arms around her from behind, resting his chin on her shoulder. "You've got to eat something."

She curled her arms around Tate's where they banded her waist. "I promised Rebekah we'd have dinner together. I made a second casserole for us. I need to get back before she drinks an entire bottle of wine by herself." Her cell phone buzzed and she dug it out of her pocket, looking at the display. "Yep, that's her." She showed the phone to Tate.

Shake a leg, sister. This tuna's getting cold.

"Sister?" asked Tate.

"That's what she always calls me. If she likes you, she never calls you by your real name. You're Hardware Man, Jaguar's Rock Star, and Daryl's Cutie Pie."

Tate gave Zion a frown. "Jaguar and Daryl get cool names and I get Hardware Man?"

She kissed his cheek. "Sorry. She calls Dottie the Orange-Haired Witch, so it could be worse."

Logan and Tate laughed. "And that means she likes her?"

"The jury's still out on Dottie, I'm afraid." She turned and hugged Tate. "I'll see you tomorrow morning."

Tate's expression sobered and they both glanced at Logan, but the kid was busy dishing up his dinner and didn't seem to notice. Tate walked Zion to the door and drew her in for a kiss, lingering on her mouth.

"Rain check on the dinner and a movie?" he asked.

"Of course," she answered, then her phone buzzed again. "Argh! She's killing me!" she groused, staring at the display.

Tate pulled Zion back to him. "Any chance she'll find her own place soon."

Zion gave him a regretful look and touched his cheek. "I wish I knew, Tate," she said wistfully. "I wish I knew."

CHAPTER 13

Zion pulled the ends of her coat closer about herself. The temperature had dropped again overnight and frost lay in a crystalline blanket on the grass as she opened the front door to meet Tate for the funeral. Logan had gone to the church earlier with his aunt and uncle to make sure the pastor had everything he needed for the slideshow.

Tate wore a black suit and tie and a black wool coat with the collar turned up. He gave her a grim smile and leaned forward, kissing her cheek. Zion had opted for black tights and a black sheath dress. Rebekah had lent her a black raincoat with a fuzzy lining.

"I'll see you over at Hardware Man's house later," Rebekah called from inside. "And don't worry about the coffee. I promise it'll be there."

"Thank you," Zion said, shutting the door. She'd given Rebekah the keys to her Optima, so she could pick up the coffee from Dottie for the wake after the funeral. The big silver urns just wouldn't fit in the Spider.

"How are you this morning?" Tate asked, taking her elbow and guiding her down to the truck.

"I'll be glad when this is over."

He nodded and helped her inside, shooting a look at the clouds overhead. "We might get rain."

She leaned forward and looked out the front windshield. They just might and that would make a miserable occasion all the more miserable. They didn't talk much as they drove to the church.

A man with thinning brown hair in a navy blue suit and cowboy boots stood on the stairs, greeting people as they arrived.

Zion and Tate got in line behind Jim Dawson and his wife. Dawson gave Tate and Zion a head bob. "Mercer, Zion?"

"Hi, Jim," said Zion. She held her hand out to the woman. "You must be Mrs. Dawson."

The woman had strawberry blond hair that was strictly trained with hairspray and cat's eye glasses. She wore a black suit with a colorful scarf around her neck. "Minnie, dear," she said, taking Zion's hand.

"I love your scarf."

"Thank you. I thought a splash of color might help to lessen the gloom, but I suppose nothing will."

Zion nodded and hooked her arm through Tate's. He patted her hand and leaned close to her. "The man at the top of the stairs is Logan's uncle, Ernest."

A few minutes later, they arrived and shook hands with him, Zion offering her condolences. Then they were entering the warm interior of the church. Walking into the sanctuary, they found Logan standing with a woman who had short brown hair and round, rosy cheeks. She must have been his aunt. They were talking to Bill Stanley and his wife, but when Bill guided his wife away, Logan's eyes lifted and fixed on them.

He motioned them to approach him.

Tate and Zion hurried up the aisle to him. He stepped away from his aunt and said something to Tate. Tate touched Zion's arm and whispered in her ear. "I'll be right back."

She nodded, then held out her hand for the woman. "You must be Logan's aunt?"

"I am. Call me Esther." She shook Zion's hand, but her eyes drifted past her to where Logan and Tate were making their way to the back of the church.

"I'm Zion."

"Why don't you sit with me, Zion?" she said, pointing to the pew in the front row.

Zion wasn't sure that was acceptable. The first pew should be reserved for family, but her eyes landed on the white coffin draped with yellow roses and she moved to the seat Esther indicated. This wasn't the time to argue funeral protocol. Esther sat down, but she twisted so she could look back down the aisle. Zion wasn't sure what to do.

More people entered and the church filled up. A few moments later, Ernest came in and took a seat next to his wife. Still no Logan. Esther and Ernest began a whispered conversation, but Zion tried not to eavesdrop.

A few minutes later, the pastor approached the altar and laid his Bible on its surface. Zion shifted to see if she could spot Tate and Logan, but they weren't visible. There were very few seats left, Zion noticed. Most of Sequoia seemed to have turned out.

Esther nudged her husband. "Go find him," she urged.

Ernest looked torn. He glanced behind him and then to the pastor, shrugging his shoulders.

Zion leaned forward. "I'll go find them," she said.

"Thank you," said Ernest.

Zion rose to her feet and walked down the aisle, hurrying to the back door. A few people nodded at her, but most were busy reading the memorial about Peggy Baxter. She found Logan and Tate sitting on the stairs outside, staring at the street.

Tate looked up as she left the church, but Logan didn't acknowledge her at all.

"They're ready to start," she said.

Tate gave a shrug and looked at Logan, but Logan didn't budge. Zion took a seat on Logan's other side, clasping her hands before her. She glanced up at the kid, catching the bleak expression on his face. What did you say when someone had lost the most important person in his life?

"This is probably the most awful moment in anyone's life, Logan. I'm not going to pretend I understand what you're feeling right now because I can't, but I know I would feel gutted if I lost my mother. I can't even get my head around the pain I'd be in."

Logan cuffed his polished dress shoe on the stairs. "My dad beat her," he said suddenly.

Tate and Zion exchanged a look over the kid's bent head, but they didn't say anything.

"He used to fly into a rage and then he'd backhand her. I was just a little kid. Maybe five or six. I don't know, but I have these images in my mind of his voice." He shuddered. "He'd clench his teeth before he was going to strike, clench his teeth and talk through them. Have you ever seen anyone do that?"

"I have," said Zion. She wanted to touch him, but she wasn't sure he'd appreciate it and she didn't want him to stop talking.

"Sometimes he'd hit her with his fist. Aunt Esther said he made her have a miscarriage. I was supposed to have a brother or sister, but he punched her in the stomach and killed his own baby."

Zion put her hand over her mouth, her eyes welling with tears.

"I don't remember her crying. I never remember hearing her cry no matter how bad he beat her. I know it doesn't seem like it, but she was so strong, so brave."

He scraped his bottom lip with his teeth. "I remember hearing conversations between my mother and Esther. She would insist Mom leave him, but Mom said she couldn't. She had to provide for me and she didn't think she could do it on her own."

Zion finally did put her arm around him, resting her head against the side of his. He leaned into her. "Then he hit me."

Zion tightened her hold.

"I was coloring at the table while she made dinner and I had these pens. They were washable. I mean, it's not like they would stain anything permanently, but I missed and I drew a line across the table. He was sitting there, I remember it. He was sitting there with the newspaper, drinking a beer, and he looked up."

Logan drew a shivery breath and released it.

"I froze. I froze solid. I will never forget that feeling in my chest, the way my heart pounded."

"Jesus," whispered Tate.

"It was so sudden. One minute he was looking at the paper and the next…" Logan shivered. "The next I was on the floor, his handprint on my face."

Zion closed her eyes, fighting back the tears.

Logan sniffed and tossed his head. "You know how some memories are so clear in your mind, you can almost see them still."

"Yes," said Zion, opening her eyes again.

"That's how that memory is. My mother put down the spatula, turned off the burner, and picked me up in her arms. Then she walked out." He gave a little laugh. "I don't mean walked out of the room. She walked out of the house and the next thing I remember is a deputy giving me a cherry cola. She took me to the sheriff's office and he never bothered us again."

Zion leaned away from him. "She *was* brave, Logan."

Logan nodded. "She was. God, she was everything to me. Even after she got sick, taking care of her gave me a reason, you know? She needed me. I don't want to say goodbye. I just don't want this to be happening."

"I know, Logan. And I wish it wasn't, but she'd want you to be as brave as she was. She'd want you to face even this."

"She was in a lot of pain at the end. Sometimes she didn't make a lot of sense." He glanced at Zion. "The drugs or something."

Zion nodded.

"But just before she died…" He gave a wounded smile. "Just before she died, she told me it was all worth it. Everything she went through with my father, with the cancer, she said it was worth it just to be my mother." His face crumpled and he shook violently, then he bowed his head into his hands and wept.

Zion wrapped her arms around him and held him, knowing nothing else would be enough at this point.

* * *

Zion grabbed a spatula and began cutting the lasagna into squares for the guests. Tate eased up behind her, wrapping his arms around her waist and kissing her cheek. "I'm so glad you're here today," he said.

She smiled and nuzzled her cheek against his. "I wouldn't be anywhere else. Where's Logan?"

"Messing on the guitar with Jaguar in the living room. They have a crowd around them."

Zion finished cutting and reached for a clean plate. "Have you eaten anything yet?"

He released her and accepted the plate. "Not yet. Have you?"

"No, but I'm going to get something now." Moving around the kitchen table, she dished up some of the food. The entire Sequoia community had come out in force and provided a feast for this wake. There were casseroles and salads and sandwiches. She didn't know what Tate was going to do with it all.

She waited for him to finish, then they went into the living room. Finding a spot on the floor where she could put her plate on the coffee table, she sat down. Someone got up and offered Tate a seat on the couch behind her. He motioned for Zion to take it, but she shook her head. She'd rather have the coffee table to eat on, so Tate took a seat, balancing his plate on his thigh.

As Zion ate, she watched Logan and Jaguar messing with their guitars. Jaguar was patient as he instructed the younger man and Logan seemed to eat up the attention. He hadn't said much after the funeral, but he'd stood for a long time over the grave after the casket had been lowered inside. Tate and Zion had stood with him as everyone else got into their cars and drove away.

Zion finished eating, then she leaned back against Tate's legs, listening as Jaguar began to play a soft ballad. The song transfixed everyone and conversation hushed as they stopped to take in the music.

She felt Tate's hand as he stroked it down the back of her hair and she realized how content she was in that moment. It felt right to be here with him, sharing this moment in their community.

It didn't last long because the door opened and David stepped inside. Zion felt the tension in Tate's body as David looked around the room, then spotted Logan and headed in his direction.

He handed Logan an envelope. Logan looked up at him curiously, then he reached out and took it, leaning the guitar against the chair.

"What's this?" he asked and Jaguar stopped playing.

"This is a trust account that has been set up in your name for college. I can explain all of the details to you later, but suffice it to say, when you decide what college you want to attend, you have funds to help you get books and tuition."

Zion's gaze shifted to Jaguar, but the rockstar was looking at the floor, his expression unreadable. Zion looked back at Tate and he shrugged.

"Where did the money come from?" asked Logan, rising to his feet.

"The donors asked to remain anonymous, but you should know you mean a lot to the people of Sequoia."

"I don't know what to say," said Logan, staring at the envelope.

"You don't have to say anything," answered David, resting a hand on his shoulder.

When Jaguar finally looked up, he gave Zion a wink, then he went back to strumming on his guitar. Zion sighed, then pushed herself to her feet and took Tate's plate, adding it to her own. She eased out from the couch and went into the kitchen where Rebekah was cutting a carrot cake. Zion paused, surprised. She'd never seen Rebekah make herself useful like this before.

"Hey," she said, setting the plates in the sink.

"Hey, yourself."

Zion moved to her side. "What are you doing?"

"Trying to help out. I feel for the kid." Rebekah pulled the knife out, holding it up. "As much as I fight with my mother, I don't know what I'd do if I lost her."

Zion nodded. "I feel the same way."

Rebekah wiped the icing off the knife and put it in her mouth. Zion didn't think she'd ever seen Rebekah eat sweets before. Just as she was about to say something, David walked into the kitchen. Rebekah went still, her gaze sweeping over his tall form.

David paused also. "Sorry. Tate told me to get something to eat, but I don't mean to intrude."

Zion backed up. "No, you're not intruding. Thank you for coming." She picked up a plate and handed it to David. "David, you remember my friend, Rebekah Miles."

David accepted the plate, then held his hand out to Rebekah. "Yes, how are you, Rebekah?"

Rebekah set down the knife and shook his hand. "I'm great," she said. "How are you, David?"

"Great," he answered smiling, his eyes fixed on her face.

Zion frowned, then backed up, feeling like she'd been forgotten.

"I hear you're staying here for a while," said David.

Rebekah touched a hand to her throat. "I am. I'm between jobs and…homes."

"Ah, I see."

Zion backed from the room, running into Tate as she left the kitchen. He caught her elbows. "Whoa," he said, laughing.

She turned and placed her hands on his chest. "Rebekah and David are talking and they completely forgot I was there."

Tate leaned over a little and peered into the kitchen. "Well, that's…" He shook his head. "I'm not sure what that is."

Zion thought about it. David was Rebekah's type, that was certain and Rebekah was most men's type, but she wasn't sure how she felt about her ex-boyfriend and her best friend hooking up. Still, if it made them both happy…

Dottie stepped through the door behind them. She held a paper in her hand and she waved it at Zion. Zion patted Tate's chest. "Dottie's here," she said, easing out of his hold and walking across the room to her employee.

Dottie's face was urgent. "Come outside," she said, stepping back through the door. "Bring Tate."

Zion and Tate followed her onto the front porch. Dottie waved the paper again. "I got a hit."

"What?" asked Tate.

"On the tattoo parlor for the devil tattoo. I got a potential hit."

Zion and Tate exchanged a look. "How?" asked Zion.

"I finally got the manager of *Tattoos by Emilio* to admit he used to do skull tattoos. I sent him the picture of the one on the perp…"

Zion smiled at her use of slang.

"…and he admitted it looked like one of theirs. So I printed out the Yelp review with the address. I thought Sheriff Wilson might want the information. By the way, they've got some really great Yelp reviews. This is definitely the place to go if you want a devil tattoo."

Zion smiled at her. "Good work."

Dottie beamed and held out the paper to Tate.

He took it. "She's right. Good wor…" He stopped in mid-sentence, his expression sobering.

Zion looked at him in alarm.

"Tate?"

His eyes flicked up to hers.

"You okay?" She touched his arm.

"Yeah," he said, forcing a smile. "I'm fine." He folded the paper in half. "Hey, Dottie, there's a ton of food in there. Why don't you help yourself?"

Dottie gave him a speculative once-over, then she eased around them and opened the front door again. Zion turned to face Tate.

"You recognized something?" she said.

He held up the picture. "See the picture here?"

"Yeah." She looked at the squat brown building in a strip mall. "You've seen this place before?"

"Jason and I followed the Impala to this location, Zion, when we were on the task force. This is the tattoo parlor that inked the Devil's Tongue." He sighed. "I need to call Wilson. I'm getting more and more worried about what this means. This isn't just coincidence."

Zion frowned. "Okay. Hold on a minute, Tate. You and Jason followed the Impala that was outside Poole's cabin just a few days ago?"

"Yeah, I knew I'd recognized the car when I saw it. When Jason and I followed it, we thought the tattoo parlor was a front for drug distribution. A guy named Lon Edmonds got out of the Impala and went inside. We got a warrant for the place and searched it, but it was clean. Yesterday, I called Darcy and had her look up the license on the Impala. It had been registered to Lon Edmonds before he sold it to a family member, Karina Mason."

"Okay, I'm with you. You think the guy Poole killed is Lon Edmonds."

"No, Lon Edmonds is serving time in Atascadero."

"So who did Poole kill then?"

"I don't know, but we're getting closer to figuring that out, but what I do know is Lon Edmonds got shanked in Atascadero and the medic on call reported a devil tattoo on his upper chest." He stared at the picture of the tattoo parlor. "Lon Edmonds was Devil's Tongue and the Devil's Tongue was the target of our task force. Whatever's going on, Zion, has to do with the raid that killed Jason, but that was two years ago. Why is it just now boiling over?"

Zion curled her arms around herself. "I don't know, but I don't like it."

Tate nodded. "Neither do I," he said.

* * *

Zion crossed her legs and stroked a hand down Cleo's sleek coat. She had her sweats on and her pillows fluffed behind her. The night pressing in outside was cold and rain clouds had moved across the sky. The wind whipped a tree branch against the side of the cottage. She needed to get a gardener out to trim everything away from the house.

"So, what are you going to do with all that food?" she asked Tate on the phone.

Even though they'd spent the whole day together, he'd called her to say goodnight, causing a flush of pleasure to heat her cheeks. She didn't remember David ever calling to tell her goodnight before.

"I gave as much of it away as I could, then Minnie Dawson got every storage container out of my cabinets and filled them, then filled my freezer. Logan and I have dinners for the next six months inside that poor, damn thing."

Zion laughed, leaning back against the pillows. "Did you contact Sheriff Wilson about *Tattoos by Emilio*?"

"I did. He made contact with the LAPD and they're going to take the vic's picture to the store and see if they recognize him. I also suggested they make contact with Karina Mason."

"She might know who he is too, right?"

"Right."

A knock sounded at the door. Zion frowned, glancing at the clock on her nightstand. It was after 11:00. "Someone's at the door," she told Tate.

"Don't answer it," he said.

"I'll get it," called Rebekah from the hallway.

"NO!" shouted Zion, scrambling off the bed and upsetting Cleo. "Rebekah!" But she was already gone. "I gotta go, Tate."

"Zion…" he began, but she'd already hung up.

Zion tugged open her door and hurried out into the hallway. Rebekah already had the door open and she was talking to someone on the other side. Zion glanced around for a weapon, but didn't see anything. She really needed to see about getting pepper spray or something.

"I jest wanna talk to you," said a slurring male voice.

"I told you I don't want to talk to you. I told you that a hundred times when you called me on the phone."

Zion grabbed the door and pulled it back, glaring at Poole where he leaned against the door jamb. "What are you doing here, Poole?" she said furious.

"I jest wanna talk to Becksah." He had his arm braced on the door frame and he rubbed his forehead against it. "Jest five min-utes."

Zion drew Rebekah out of the doorway and put herself between her and Poole. "You're drunk, Keith. You need to call a cab or Uber and go back to the lodge." She could see his Camaro parked half-assed near the curb in front of her house. The idiot had driven over here drunk like this.

"Jest let me come in. You can give me coffee." His eyes drooped.

Zion didn't know what to do. She couldn't let him leave here like this, but she wasn't letting him in her house. "I'll call a cab for you. Just stay there." She gave Rebekah a pointed look and Rebekah hurried off to get a phone.

"Becksah!" Poole shouted, rolling his forehead along his arm. "Becksah, talk to me!"

Zion glanced out at the street, worried her neighbors might hear him. "Poole!" she hissed.

He opened bloodshot eyes and stared at her. "You know, I thoughtz you're cute too. Remember when we met." He tried to ease into the house, but Zion put a hand in the center of his chest and shoved him back out.

"Stay!" she told him.

Rebekah returned with the phone. "Who do you want me to call?"

"Look up a cab company or something," Zion said, still holding Keith off.

"There you are," Keith said, leaning forward. "I thought you wenz away. I'm so glad to see you. Remember when we slept together."

"Oh, Jesus," said Rebekah. "I've really got to do something with my life." She clicked on the phone.

"It was sooo good." He motioned between the two of them. "We really connected, we did, dinna wez, Becksah? We connected." Then he gave a drunken laugh.

Rebekah curled her upper lip in disgust and pressed an icon, holding the phone to her ear. "Yes, I can hold."

"Who you calling, Becksah? Who you calling?"

Rebekah glared at him, not answering. Zion shoved Poole back as he leaned further into the house.

"Yes, I need a cab at…"

"No, no, don't do it, Becksah, I jest need coffee. You give me the coffee and I be fine."

Rebekah ignored him, placing her finger in her other ear to hear better. Zion wasn't sure what they were going to do to keep Poole from driving away while they waited for the cab to arrive, but maybe if she could get his keys, that would be enough.

"Can I have your keys?" she asked.

He shook a finger in her face. "No, no, no. I waz not born yesterday."

Zion fought her rising disgust. Suddenly she saw movement behind Poole and Tate appeared in the light from the door. He wore only a t-shirt and pajama bottoms, a pair of sneakers hastily thrown on his feet. Zion couldn't believe how grateful she was to see him.

"Hey, Keith," he said, loudly to warn the idiot he was approaching. "What's going on, man?"

"Tater Totz," said Keith, turning and dropping an arm across Tate's shoulder. "I'm so glad to see you. I jest wanna talk to Becksah, but your girl is blocking me."

"You're drunk, Keith. That's why. What if we go back to my place and we can talk?"

"Hold on a minute," said Rebekah, talking into the phone. "Am I getting a cab or not?"

"You'll talk to me?" asked Poole, leaning heavily on Tate, his free hand pressed against Tate's chest. "You keep saying you don't wanna talk."

"We can talk now." Tate gave Rebekah a glance. "You don't have to call a cab."

"Fine," said Rebekah in an aggravated voice. "Apparently, we don't need your assistance tonight," she told the guy on the phone.

Tate struggled to turn Poole around. "Come on, Poole. Let's go get some coffee."

"You sure you want to do this?" Zion asked Tate.

"We'll be fine," he said, getting Poole to the stairs. They staggered down them and Poole laughed as he nearly took them both over.

Zion felt a wash of gratitude for Tate coming to their rescue. She still wasn't sure what she would have done with Poole while they waited for the cab. The thought of bringing him into her house made her skin crawl. As Tate and Poole stumbled down the walkway, Zion caught sight of something resting against the small of Tate's back.

He'd brought his gun.

CHAPTER 14

"Here," said Tate, nudging the couch with his foot.

Poole opened his eyes and squinted up at him, then he rubbed his hands over his face and rolled to a sitting position, the blanket dropping to the floor. Finally he reached up and accepted the mug of coffee, taking a sip.

"I'm sorry about last night, Tater Tot."

Tate sat down on the coffee table in front of him. "You're spiraling, Keith. What the hell's going on?"

Poole shook his head. "I don't know. I wish I did." He cradled the mug in both hands. "You don't know what it's like looking over your shoulder all the time. After I shot the kid, the media was all over it, showing up at my apartment, banging on my door. They even followed me into the grocery store one time. I didn't ask for this. I didn't ask for any of this."

Tate wasn't sure what to feel about it. Poole had killed a fourteen-year-old boy, but he was also a cop. He had a job to do and sometimes that job wasn't pleasant. "Look, no one knows you're here. The kid and I are going to work, but you can stay here. Just rest and think about your next move. You need to think hard, Poole, 'cause this isn't working for anyone."

Poole nodded and took another sip of his coffee. "I appreciate it. Can I take a shower?"

"Yeah, I put a towel in the bathroom. I also left a pair of sweats in there that should fit you. There's food in the refrigerator from the funeral." He scratched his eyebrow. "When I get home tonight, we'll talk about what you're gonna do, okay?"

"Okay. Again, I really appreciate this."

Tate glanced over as Logan walked out of the hallway. He tossed the kid his keys. "You get to drive to the end of the block."

Logan stared at him with big eyes. "Seriously?"

"Yep, I'll take over after that."

They made it to the *Hammer Tyme* around 9:30. Rain had started to fall and the windshield wipers made a swishing sound as they whisked the water away. Logan grumbled about getting wet, but Tate just threw open the truck's door and bolted for the store, slamming the door behind him. Logan shouted at him, then he gave chase.

They were both laughing as they reached the door. Logan easily beat him, slapping a hand against the glass panel with a triumphant smile. Tate shook his head and stuck the key in the lock, turning it. Running both hands through his wet hair, he went in back to deactivate the alarm and turn on the lights, while Logan began opening the blinds.

Shucking off his jacket, Tate reached for the apron and tied it on, then stuck the ball cap on his head and got the money for the cash register. A moment later, Logan appeared, grabbing his own apron and ball cap. Bill Stanley usually got the weekends off, so they weren't expecting him.

"You know, now that it's raining, you should put a bucket or something by the door so people can drop their umbrellas inside. And we need a doormat so they can wipe their feet," said Logan.

Tate agreed it wasn't a bad idea. He went to the cash register and began counting out the money, brushing aside one of Zion's cobwebs. Logan turned on the pumpkin lights and grabbed the broom, starting his sweeping in the far back corner where the power tools were.

Once the cash register was ready, Tate went into the storeroom looking for an umbrella bucket. He found an old tin bin that had once been used for flowers. He'd gotten it to hold American flags for the 4th of July. It was perfect for holding umbrellas. He came out and placed the tin by the door, then grabbed his credit card out of his wallet.

"Hey, kid."

Logan appeared from the end of an aisle. "What's up?"

"Take this and go by Trixie's place. See if she has a welcome mat. I don't want anything fancy. Then go by the *Caffeinator* and get us two coffees and some of Dottie's cinnamon breadsticks."

Logan's eyes danced with happiness and he took the card Tate held out to him, passing him the broom. "So no flowers or butterflies on the mat? Or unicorns and rainbows?"

Tate didn't answer, just gave him a narrow-eyed look.

Logan laughed and Tate felt pretty damn glad to hear it after the day Logan had had yesterday. "What sort of coffee do you want?"

Tate walked toward the counter. "Dottie will know. Just tell her my regular.

"Huh," said Logan, scraping the card against his chin. "I probably need to get a regular too."

"You do that," said Tate, lifting the counter and setting the broom inside the storeroom. He grabbed Logan's jacket. "Hey kid!"

Logan turned and Tate threw the jacket at him.

"Don't catch a cold."

Logan slipped the damp jacket on. "Man, you should have taken biology when you were in school. That's not how you get a cold."

"Whatever, just go already."

Logan pulled his ball cap down lower and headed for the door. Tate looked around for some last chores to do and saw a basket with return items in it. He picked it up and began replacing things on the shelves where they belonged.

Once he finished, he pulled the stool up to the counter and reached under it for his mystery novel, taking the glasses out of his shirt pocket and putting them on. He'd barely opened the book when the buzzer sounded.

He looked up to see a man he didn't know walk into the store. The man looked around, his profile backlit from the weak light seeping in through the front windows. Tate took off his glasses and put them in the book, estimating the man was just under six feet, broad shoulders, thick forearms. Tate couldn't really make out much else, until the man turned to look at him, striding across the room toward the counter.

He had sharp features and a hooked nose. If Tate didn't know any better, he reminded him a lot of Lon Edmonds. He gave Tate a slow perusal, then tilted his head to the side, his vertebrae popping. Tate tried not to make a face at the sound.

"How can I help you?" he asked.

The man's heavy brows lifted. "I'm looking for someone."

"Okay." Tate kept his voice neutral. He didn't want to jump to conclusions. This man might just be out doing his Sunday errands and he needed a power drill or something. "Not sure I can help you, since this is just a hardware store."

The man leveled a severe look on him. "Where's Poole?"

Nope, he definitely didn't want a power drill. Tate slowly rose to his feet and slipped his hand into his pocket, his fingers curling around the fob that unlocked his gun safe. He eased down the counter until he was right over the spot where his gun lay.

"I don't know what you're talking about. I'm sorry."

The man leaned on the counter. "Let's not get cute, okay?"

"Okay," said Tate, reaching his free hand under the counter and holding it over the latch to open the safe.

"I know you were a cop. I know you know Poole. And I know Poole is here." He placed the other hand on the counter. "I also know you went after the Devil's Tongue two years ago. Blew up a tenement where my mother lived and that..." He shook his head. "...that is not good."

Tate stared him down. "I'm not a cop anymore. I don't know anything about the Devil's Tongue and I don't know where Poole is."

The man gave a crooked smile. "Oh, see that's not an acceptable answer." He looked around the store, then back at Tate. "My mother, she lived in that tenement for thirty years. The fire took everything."

"I'm sorry about that."

"It would be very bad if that happened here, no?" His upper lip twitched. "If this place went up in flames? All the oil and gasoline in here? It might catch the whole neighborhood on fire. And that would be very bad."

Tate didn't break eye contact. "Are you threatening me?" He pressed the fob and heard the gun safe click open.

The man heard it too. He lowered his chin. "Are you going to pull a gun on me?"

"Do I need to pull a gun on you?"

The dark eyes narrowed. "You and me, we understand one another. We know how things work, no?"

Tate didn't bother to answer, his fingers closing around the grip.

"Poole's not worth this." He motioned to the shop. "I will forgive you for my mother. I will let you go, but you've got to tell me where Poole is."

Tate swallowed hard and tightened his grip on the gun, sliding it back toward him. He didn't want to draw it because he sensed if he did they'd be at a point of no return, but he wasn't going to be intimidated in his own store.

Suddenly the door flew open and the buzzer sounded. Logan walked through, oblivious to what was going on. "Dottie said to tell you she added something special to your drink today."

Tate pulled the gun out of the safe and brought it down to his side. Logan glanced up, shaking rain off his cap and spotted the man. His eyes flicked over to Tate and he stiffened, gripping his packages with two hands.

"Logan, go down to Jaguar's right now," said Tate, never taking his eyes off the gangbanger.

Logan backed out immediately, shoving open the door and disappearing from sight. Tate let out a breath when he was gone.

"Now, I'm going to tell you one time and one time only," Tate said, his voice edged. "Walk out of here and leave Sequoia. I don't want trouble and as far as I know, we have no quarrel with each other. If you go, that'll be the end of it, but if you mess with anyone in this town, I can promise you I will come after you and it won't end well."

The man stared at him a moment longer, his lip twitching. Tate never broke eye contact, not even for a moment and his fingers flexed on the grip of the gun. Finally, the man blinked and looked away, turning on his heel and striding for the door without looking back.

Tate lowered his head and breathed out, closing his eyes. Then he set the gun on the counter, stripped off his apron and cap, and grabbed his jacket out of the storeroom. Picking up the gun again, he tucked it into the back of his pants and walked to the door, yanking it open. He took out his phone and pressed the icon for Murphy's number as he locked the door. The rain had slowed to a drizzle.

Holding the phone to his ear, he started down the street for Jaguar's shop, glancing in the municipal parking lot for a strange car, but he could hear a large engine roaring as it turned off Main. He stopped at Jaguar's door and banged on it.

"Murphy," came the voice in his ear.

Tate banged on the door again. Jaguar peered out around a tear in the butcher paper, then he unlocked it and pulled it open. Tate stepped inside.

"Murphy, I just had a guy from the Devil's Tongue threaten me in my store," he said, searching the dim interior for Logan. The kid stood at the back of Jaguar's shop, his eyes wide with fright.

"Just now?" said Murphy.

"Yep. He was looking for Poole, but Poole's at my house. He came there last night drunk out of his head."

"What exactly did the guy say to you?"

Tate gave Jaguar a questioning look. Jaguar held a trombone in his hand. "I thought you played the guitar?"

Jaguar frowned. "What?"

Tate shook his head and concentrated on Murphy. "He said he knew I was a cop and that I worked with Poole. He knew I was part of the Devil's Tongue task force and that we were responsible for the tenement burning down. He said his mother lived in that tenement and she lost everything. He threatened to burn down my store."

"You said Poole's at your house?"

"Yeah, I think we should bring him in."

"We're on it," she said. "I'll keep you posted."

"Thanks." Tate hung up and shoved the phone into his pocket, giving Jaguar another bewildered look. "What's with the trombone?"

Jaguar looked at the instrument, then back at Tate. "When the kid came down here saying someone was robbing you, I grabbed the first thing I could find."

Tate laughed. "You were going to beat the guy off with a trombone?"

"Don't laugh, ass. I was coming to your rescue."

Tate couldn't stop laughing. "Gives new meaning to the song *When the Saints Go Marching In*."

Jaguar shook his head, but he was smiling.

Tate's gaze shifted to Logan. "Hey, kid, it's okay now. Come here."

Logan walked across the store, still holding his bags. "I got the coffee," he said in a tremulous voice.

Tate grabbed him behind the neck and pulled him close. "It's okay now. You hear me?"

Logan put his forehead on Tate's shoulder. "I thought he was going to kill you," he whispered. "I couldn't stand another funeral."

"I'm fine." Tate held him off. "Where's my coffee?"

Logan dug it out of the bag, passing it to Tate. Tate took a sip, drew a deep breath, and released it, then he focused his attention on Jaguar.

"I'm going to the *Caffeinator* to make sure they're okay, then I'm heading to the sheriff's department. I'm going to close the *Hammer Tyme* today. Can Logan stay with you?"

"Of course he can." Jaguar glanced around the store. "I've still got a lot to do before I'm ready to open."

Tate looked around as well. Jaguar wasn't kidding. There were unopened boxes and half painted walls.

"Tate," he said, setting the trombone down on the counter. "Do you think we should hire security to keep watch over our stores during the day, or maybe at least at night?"

Tate considered that. He didn't like the idea of changing the atmosphere in Sequoia. If a security guard was patrolling around, would it lessen the wholesome, homey vibe Main Street had? "I don't know. Let's bring it up at the Chamber meeting next time. Right now, I've got other things I'm worried about."

Jaguar nodded, but Tate could see he was feeling anxious. When he'd been a famous rockstar, he'd had two permanent body guards that followed him around. Tate shifted his focus to Logan.

"You did good, kid. When I told you to leave, you did good, exactly what you should have done."

Logan nodded, but he still looked terrified.

"Help Jaguar out today, okay? I'll be back as soon as I can."

Logan nodded again.

Carrying his coffee, Tate headed for the door.

"Tate," called Logan, starting after him.

Tate turned. "What's up?"

Logan swallowed hard and looked away. "Nothing. Just…"

Jaguar put a hand on Logan's shoulder. "Come on, kid. I got a freakin' mess in here and I'm supposed to open in less than a week."

Tate gave Logan a smile and went to the door, pulling it open. "Come lock this, Trombone Man," he called to Jaguar.

"You're a regular comedian, Mercer. Anyone ever tell you that. See if I ever come to your rescue again."

Tate laughed and let the door close behind him, but he hated the fear he saw in both their eyes. Damn it, he wasn't going to let the life he'd left behind in LA ruin the life he'd built here. He just wasn't going to have it.

He walked across the street and opened the *Caffeinator*, breathing a sigh of relief when he saw Zion working the cash register and Dottie pulling an espresso. A number of customers were sitting at the bistro tables, and the couches in the new reading nook were full. Tate couldn't deny Rebekah had done a good job rearranging everything to make it more appealing.

Zion looked up as he entered and immediately she knew something was wrong. The fact that she was already attuned to his moods made him feel a surge of emotion towards her. Cherise, in all the years they'd been married, had never picked up on his state of mind.

Dottie turned and frowned at him. "You don't like the secret ingredient?" she said.

Tate realized he hadn't even noticed. He'd been a bit preoccupied. He took another sip and thought about it. Vanilla? "You added a splash of vanilla?"

Dottie smiled. "That's it. What do you think?"

"It's amazing, but it always is." Vanilla reminded him of the scent of Zion's hair. He wondered if Dottie had realized that or if it was just coincidence. Tate paused at the counter, watching as Zion handed the customer his credit card and a receipt. She smiled for the customer, but when she looked back at Tate, her expression sobered.

"What's wrong?"

"Can I talk to you in back?"

She nodded and gave Dottie a significant look, then she walked to the bar doors and pushed them open. Tate followed her into the kitchen, setting the coffee on the stainless steel baking table. Moving close to her, he pulled her into his arms and held her. He just needed to hold her for a moment.

"Tate, you're scaring me."

"Where's Rebekah?" he said, easing back from her.

"I'm right here. What's going on?" She came out of Zion's office.

Tate felt his shoulders lower. He hadn't realized how tense he'd been.

"Why do you have your gun?" asked Zion, her hand against the small of his back.

"A man came into the *Hammer Tyme*, looking for Poole."

"What?" they both said.

Tate told them about the incident and explained how Logan had walked in, breaking the stalemate between them. He reassured them that he'd called the sheriff's department and they were going to pick Poole up from his house.

Zion hugged her arms around her middle. "This just keeps getting worse," she said, miserably. "Should we cancel the Halloween Festival?"

"No, not yet. I've got my friend Darcy working on a few things. Once we figure out who the John Doe is, we can decide whether Poole was in the right to shoot him or not. Then, as soon as Wilson releases him, Poole's out of here."

Zion didn't look convinced.

Rebekah came over and wrapped her arms around her friend. "I'm so sorry about this, sister," she said.

Tate started to tell Rebekah it wasn't her fault when his phone rang. He pulled it out of his pocket and saw Wilson's name flash on the screen. Thumbing it on, he put the phone to his ear. "Sheriff?"

"Tate, there's been an officer involved shooting on Conifer Circle."

"What? That's my street."

"I'm aware. The shooting happened in front of Zion's house. One of the neighbors said a prowler was lurking around, peering in the windows and trying to get in the backyard. Jones was already in route to pick up Poole. When he got on scene, the man was still there. Jones warned him to surrender, but he pulled a gun."

"Where's Poole?"

"Murphy's in route to get him."

"Is the suspect dead?"

"Not yet. Jones called an ambulance and he's being transported to Sequoia Memorial."

"What's going on?" demanded Zion.

Tate's head was buzzing. How the hell had the suspect known Poole was at his house? And why had he gone to Zion's house instead?

"Someone was prowling around your house. Jones confronted him and they exchanged gunfire."

"My house? What are you talking about?"

"We're bringing Poole into the station. Can you come here?" said Wilson. "I think it's time for someone to get him talking and you might be the only one who can."

"Yeah, I'll be there. Sheriff, are you sure he was prowling around Zion's house, not mine?"

"Jones shot him in the street right in front of her driveway, Tate."

Tate thought about that. "Why would he be at Zion's house? I'll bet he's the same guy who confronted me in the shop, but how would he know Poole was anywhere on Conifer Circle and if he knew that, why would he go to the wrong house?"

Zion's green eyes went wide. "Poole's car. It's still in front of my house."

Tate went still. Shit. Poole's car. "Sheriff, we need to tow Poole's car. Can you get your CSI to go over it?"

"What are you thinking, Tate?" asked Wilson.

"There's only one way the Devil's Tongue's finding Poole. We need to search the car, and we need to do it now."

"On it. Are you coming in?"

"I'm on my way."

Wilson disconnected the call.

Zion shivered. "Did he get in the house? Cleo's there."

"No, Jones stopped him outside." He glanced at Rebekah, who still held Zion in her arms. "I have to go to the sheriff's office. They're bringing Poole in and they're going to tow the car to impounds."

"Can I go with you?" She stepped out of Rebekah's hold, looking him directly in the eyes. "This is getting too close to us, Tate. What's going on?"

He cupped her face in his hands. "I don't know, but I need you to stay here. Please."

She shivered again. "Someone threatened you already. What if there are more of them out there?"

"I'll be all right. Please stay here. I'll come by this afternoon and escort you and Rebekah home, but I need to know you're safe here."

She nodded, resting her hands on his chest. "Okay. I'll stay here."

He kissed her. "It's going to be okay. I promise you. I'm not going to let anything happen."

She eased forward, wrapping her arms around his waist again and resting her head on his chest. Tate tightened his hold on her and met Rebekah's gaze over her shoulder. "Please wait here until I get back."

"You got it, Hardware Man, but in exchange, I want you to teach me how to shoot a gun."

Tate didn't answer. He wasn't sure what was scarier – the Devil's Tongue or an armed Rebekah Miles.

* * *

Poole sat at the table in the interrogation room at the sheriff's office, his head on his crossed arms. He wore Tate's LAPD sweats and a cup of cold coffee stood by his elbow.

Tate pulled open the door and walked in, tossing a device onto the table in front of Poole.

Poole lifted his head and looked at it, then he looked up at Tate. "What's that?"

"That was on your car, under the back bumper. It's a tracking device. You can buy them online." Tate took a seat, glaring at the other man. "Surprisingly effective."

Poole lifted it and turned it over in his hands. "This is how the Devil's Tongue found me?"

"Yep. They've apparently been tracking you for a while. Now, why would the Devil's Tongue be tracking you, Keith?"

Poole set the device on the table and pushed it away. "I get you're pissed, Tate."

"A man came into my store and threatened to burn down the entire street. I'm a little past pissed, Poole."

Poole leaned back in the chair. He picked up the coffee and took a sip, then grimaced. "Could I get this warmed up?" He held the paper cup up to the two-way glass.

Tate fought against the anger that moved through him. "Why is the Devil's Tongue following you, Poole? Don't lie to me anymore."

Poole set the cup down and clasped his hands together. "It's because of the kid."

"The kid?"

"The one I shot."

Tate shook his head. "You said he had nothing to do with this."

"I figured you wouldn't help me if you knew he did."

Tate bit his inner lip for composure. "Tell me!" he growled.

Poole scrubbed his hands over his face. "The kid ran messages for the Devil's Tongue."

Tate frowned. That didn't seem likely. "The kid was African American, right?"

"Right, but the Devi's Tongue is mixed race. He grew up in the tenement. He started running messages for them to make some extra money. He had a mother and two younger brothers to support."

"I thought he wasn't gang affiliated?"

"Yeah, well, he wasn't technically in the gang, but he was affiliated."

"How did you wind up tangling with him?"

"He was on my radar two years ago when we went after the Devil's Tongue."

"What? He had to be twelve or so."

Poole held out his empty hands. "He was running messages for them already, Tate. I don't know what else to tell you." Poole reached for the coffee and swirled it in the cup. "I thought maybe we could redirect him, he was so young, get him some help from a social worker or something."

"Okay. What happened?"

"He disappeared after the tenement went up, but I ran into him recently. He tried to hold up a liquor store. They brought him in to the precinct and told me to talk to him, so I did. I even got him hooked up with a community group. He said his mother was struggling. She got laid off and the unemployment was about to run out."

"Tell me his name again."

"Fine," said Poole, giving Tate a frustrated look. "Davonte Walsh. You act like I have something to hide."

"You have been hiding things, Poole!" Tate said too loudly. He needed to get his anger under control. "So you met with the kid and got him set up with a community group."

"Yeah, but I kept thinking about him. I mean, he was just a kid and he had so much riding on his shoulders. So I went out to the new place where he was living. He wasn't there, but his mother told me he'd just stepped out and was going to the grocery store on the corner." Poole rubbed the stubble on his jaw. "I was going to get in my car and drive away, but suddenly alarms start going off down the street. I ran down there and realized someone was robbing the store. I pulled my gun and entered the store, yelling for everyone to drop to the ground."

Tate wasn't sure he wanted to hear the rest. He was pretty sure he knew how this ended.

"The kid came around the back of an aisle and he pointed his gun at me. I just reacted on instinct, Tate. That's all it was. I just aimed my gun and fired. The kid was dead before he even hit the floor."

Tate narrowed his eyes on Poole. Something didn't sit right with him. Poole's confession was too glib, too rehearsed. And the idea of the kid running messages for the Devil's Tongue seemed farfetched. Then there was the fact that the precinct had asked Poole to talk to the kid in the first place. That didn't make sense.

"Here's what I don't get, Poole," said Tate, leaning forward on the table. "Why the hell would they ask you to intervene with the kid? Why wouldn't they just contact a community organizer themselves?"

Poole sighed. "God, it hurts that you don't trust me, Tate. We were brothers. We were on the force together."

"Just tell me the truth."

"After you left the force…after Jason died, I needed something more. I needed to feel like I was making a difference. I started taking classes in conflict management and I joined a task force that tried to redirect troubled youth by offering them resources, education, jobs. I did that for eighteen months, Tate. Check with the captain if you don't believe me."

Tate stared into Poole's eyes, but he didn't back down. "Okay, then how did they put the tracker on your car?"

"I drive a silver Camaro, Tate. Everyone knows it's my car. I was in those neighborhoods all the time."

"But why? Why would they track you?"

Poole shrugged. "You think I know that? Why do they do anything they do? But they did and they're coming after me. Do you doubt that now?"

"No, I don't doubt that."

Poole held up his hands again. "I'm trapped. I can't go back to LA, and yet they know I'm here. My life is completely screwed. What am I going to do?" He raked his hands through his hair. "Everything I've ever known is in LA. That's my whole life and I don't know if I can go back to it."

Tate looked down. He couldn't deny he felt a wash of pity for Poole.

"I'm on everyone's radar. If I move, someone will find me. I can't leave here or the sheriff will put out a statewide BOLO on me. Did he tell you that? Well, that's what he told me. If I go back to LA, the Devil's Tongue's there. I'm a hunted man." He raked his hands through his hair. "Davonte Walsh's mother is suing me for wrongful death. The lawyers tell me not to touch a damn penny of my own money." He dropped his hands into his lap. "I'm so tired and I can't think straight. I don't know which way to jump and I'm afraid I'm going to make a huge mistake if I do. Clearly coming here was another mistake."

Tate exhaled, leaning back in his chair. He didn't know what to tell Poole. Any one of them might have ended up in this situation. Things happened when guns and desperate people combined. Tate didn't know how many times he himself had almost pulled the trigger, almost made a decision that could have ruined so many lives. He could feel for Poole, and yet, something twisted in his gut. It just still wasn't adding up for him.

"I need to talk to the sheriff," he said, pushing himself to his feet.

Poole reached over and caught his wrist. "If you don't help me, Tate, no one will. I just need time. I need time to figure it all out. I need a place to lay low until the heat is off me. You've got to make them see I didn't murder anyone. I killed that guy in self-defense."

Tate stared down at him. "I'll do the best I can, Keith. That's all I can say, but you're right. Making a rash decision will only make this ten times worse. Whatever you do, don't do another stupid thing." He tugged his wrist free and headed for the door.

When he stepped into the hallway, Wilson and Murphy were waiting for him.

"Do you have news about the guy Jones shot?" he asked them.

"He's in surgery, but it doesn't look good. The hospital will let us know as soon as he's out," said Wilson.

Tate nodded. "We need to call Poole's captain again. We need to know if he was really on a task force for troubled youth. I just don't buy it. Poole isn't the sort of guy to put his neck out there…" He trailed off when he saw Murphy and Wilson exchange a look. "What?" he snapped.

Wilson arched a brow and Tate closed his eyes, fighting for composure.

"I'm sorry. This whole thing's got me spooked."

"I know, son," said Wilson, "but we're not your enemy."

"I know." He brushed the side of his hand over his upper lip. "Okay, so you obviously called his captain about that."

Wilson nodded.

"He did receive training in crisis management and youth services," said Murphy. "And he was appointed to the task force just like he said."

Tate shook his head, clenching his fist. Damn it, why did he still feel like Poole was lying to him?

CHAPTER 15

The bell jingled above the door as Jaguar stepped into the *Caffeinator.* Zion smiled at him and handed the coffee to the young woman who was waiting at the counter. Jaguar's usual spiky blond hair was finger-combed away from his face and damp from the rain outside. His jeans had tears in them and his t-shirt had a rip across his six-pack belly. With his pale blue eyes and his cocky grin, Jaguar oozed sex appeal.

"How's my favorite rockstar?" she said.

"Wet." He shivered. "I forgot how rapidly winter comes on up here."

"Well, most sane people wear a jacket and carry an umbrella, Mr. Jarvis. You want a Cafe Au Lait?"

"Yeah, but I'll make it."

Zion laughed as he came around the counter. Jaguar had worked the coffee shop as a teenager and he'd never forgotten how to charm the old espresso machine.

"Hey, Dottie," he called into the kitchen as he passed the bar doors. "I got this."

"Hey, sugar, I know you do," she called back. "You wait a moment and I'll have some gluten-free coffee cake to add to your drink."

"Sounds perfect," he said, then he stroked his hand down the machine. "Hello, old girl, how is Zion treating you?"

"Old witch you mean," Zion said, playfully.

Jaguar gave her a jaundiced eye and started working his magic. A few minutes later, he had a perfect Cafe Au Lait. He reached into his pocket and dropped a twenty on the counter. Zion picked it up and held it out to him.

"Seriously? You make your own drink and you overpay by three times the amount. You're gonna be broke before you're forty the way you're going. I know you set up that trust for Logan."

He put his finger to his lips. "Shh, besides that's for Dottie's coffee cake too and that's worth millions."

Dottie came out of the kitchen then, carrying a platter of cut slices, one on a china plate that she handed to Jaguar. He kissed her cheek as he took it, then gave Zion a delighted smile. Zion shook her head.

"You're gonna be broke."

"Would you stop worrying about that? I'm a savvy businessman, which is actually why I'm here. Is Rebekah around?"

"Rebekah? Yeah, she's in my office. Why?"

"I want to hire her."

Dottie and Zion exchanged a look. "You sure about that, sugar? She'll chew you up and spit you out," said Dottie.

He looked out over the coffee shop. "Look what she's done here. I think she could really help me."

"Okay, come on. Let's see what she has to say." Zion led him to the back and knocked on the office door.

"What?" came Rebekah's voice.

Zion gave Jaguar an *are you sure about this* look.

He shrugged. "All artists are temperamental."

Zion wasn't sure Rebekah was an artist, and Jaguar was an artist who definitely wasn't temperamental. She'd rarely seen a more laid-back millionaire in her life, not that she had much experience with millionaires generally.

She pushed open the door. "Jaguar wants to talk to you."

Rebekah waved them in to *Zion's* office. "Sit," she said, pointing to the chairs on the other side of the desk.

Jaguar obediently sat, placing his coffee on the desk and taking a bite of his cake. Rebekah motioned for Zion to come around the desk and held up a nicely bound folder. "Here is the business plan I've worked up for you."

Zion opened the folder.

"It outlines exactly what you need to do to increase profits here and to be able to get the kiosk we've been talking about. I think if we bring this to the ex-boyfriend lawyer, he'll be able to draw up the contracts for us."

Ex-boyfriend lawyer? "David," Zion corrected mildly, turning the page.

"Whatever," said Rebekah, airily waving her hand. "What do you think?"

"I think this is amazing." Zion couldn't deny she was impressed with Rebekah's business acumen.

"I didn't get that business degree for nothing," she said, then she focused on Jaguar. "What do you want?"

"Rebekah!" Zion scolded.

Jaguar looked up, his mouth full of cake. He chewed rapidly and swallowed. "Sorry," he said, taking a sip of his coffee. "It's just Dottie's baking is amazing."

Rebekah gave him a bored look. "I don't have all day, Rockstar," she said.

"Right." He put the plate on the desk and used his tongue to dislodge something from his teeth. Rubbing his hands together, he pointed his index fingers at Rebekah. "So here's the deal. I'm supposed to open in less than a week and my store's not ready. I'm not sure where to put things, I'm not sure if the layout's right. I'm not even sure if I've got enough merchandise."

Rebekah picked up a pen and grabbed a pad of paper. Zion watched her over the folder. "Go on," she said, waving the pen at him.

"I don't have bookkeeping software, I don't have payroll set up. I actually don't have employees."

Zion frowned at him. Why the hell did he think he could open in a week?

"Logan came and helped me unload boxes, but everything's just sitting on the floor. I don't have display cases and I'm not really sure how to install the shelves I bought." He leaned forward, bracing his arms on his thighs and giving Rebekah the full force of those remarkable eyes. "I really need your help, and I'll pay you."

Rebekah's mouth dropped open, staring at him. Zion felt a flush creep up her neck. Damn, the man knew how to work those eyes. Rebekah shook herself.

"Enough of that!" she said sharply. "I'll help you, but you've got to agree to make all the changes I demand."

"Done."

"No complaining, no balking, no arguing."

"Done."

"I can't come until Wednesday. I'm finishing up with Zion's books, and they are a mess. Then we're going to see the ex-boyfriend lawyer about the kiosk."

"David," whispered Zion.

"Wednesday?" Jaguar's face fell. "Do you think we can get everything ready for the opening the following Monday?"

"We'll open on Monday. We may not be completely ready, but I'll have things in motion." She tore part of the paper off her pad. "I'm going to write a number on here for my services. If it's agreeable to you, I'll draw up a contract. Are you going to need me to maintain your books for you on a regular basis?"

Jaguar glanced at Zion and back to Rebekah. "Can you? I mean, are you planning to stay here?"

Rebekah considered that, placing the end of the pen against her lips. "I'm thinking about it. At least I can get everything set up and running while I'm here."

"Great."

"You haven't seen my price yet, Rockstar." She wrote something on the paper, folded it in half, and slid it across the desk to him with two fingers. Jaguar reached for it, glancing up at Zion. Zion found herself leaning forward, trying to see what she'd wrote.

Jaguar opened the paper and stared at it, then he gave Rebekah a cool look without speaking. Rebekah arched a perfectly manicured brow.

"Well?" she said.

Jaguar nodded, stuffing the paper in his pocket. "Done."

"Zion and I will be over around noon on Wednesday. Have your checkbook ready 'cause we'll need to do some shopping?"

"Wait. Why am I going?" asked Zion.

"Because, sister, you're taking notes. I need an assistant and until I can afford one, you're it."

Zion huffed.

Jaguar rose to his feet and held his hand out to Rebekah. "I appreciate it."

She took his hand and they shook, then he picked up his coffee and cake, and walked toward the door. "Talk to you Wednesday, then," he said and headed out.

Zion sat down in the chair he'd vacated and placed the business plan on the desk. "You know, this might be the answer to all your problems."

"What?" said Rebekah, leaning back in her chair.

"You could be a business consultant. Help the businesses freshen up their stores, do their books, help them with marketing, and future planning. You're really good at this."

Rebekah's eyes danced. "You think?"

"Yeah. If you did the books for the merchants, that would give you a steady income, and then you could start consulting on improving their bottom lines. Think about it. There's quite a few businesses just here in Sequoia, but if you also advertised in Visalia…"

Rebekah clapped her hands. "Oh, my goodness, you're right. This really could be something."

Zion worried a little that Rebekah's abrasive personality might not make for a good consultant. "You might have to tone things down a little. You know, actually call people by their names."

She waved that off. "They'll have to learn to take me as I am. If they want to turn a profit, then they can't expect me to sugarcoat everything. The clients who are serious won't have a problem with a little cold, hard truth."

Zion raised her brows at that. She hoped Rebekah was right.

* * *

Dee came in at noon, wearing a Superman cap and tights. Zion's mouth dropped open. The tights revealed a lot more of Deimos Hendrix than she really needed to see and she had flashbacks to when he'd done yoga in yoga pants in her front yard.

She grabbed a clean apron from beneath the counter and tossed it to him. "Is there a reason you're dressed as Superman?"

"I'm trying out costumes for the Fangtastic Howl-o-ween Monster Bash. I've got to have the perfect one. It can't be too restrictive, but it's got to match my personality."

"Superman is a good choice then," she said, smiling at him.

He smoothed his hands down over the S on his chest. "I agree." He put one arm straight in front of him and zoomed behind the counter. "Now, go to lunch, boss lady, I got this."

Zion removed her own apron. She promised Tate she'd take Logan to his counseling appointment at 4:00, but she wanted to take Tate lunch before that and see if he'd talk to her about what had happened the previous day.

"What are you going to be for the Fangtastic Howl-o-ween Monster Bash?" said Dee, tying the apron around his waist.

"You don't have to say the whole name every time you say it, you know?" she remarked.

"Is that the name of it?"

"Yes."

"Then I have to say it. Besides, I came up with it, so if I don't use it, who will?"

"Who will?" she repeated, going to retrieve her coat and purse, and the lunch she'd packed for Tate.

Rebekah had left earlier, wanting to spend some time coming up with her own business model for her potential consulting business.

When Zion came back into the coffee shop, Dee pounced on her. "You didn't answer me. What are you going to be for the Fangtastic..."

"I don't know," she interrupted before he could say the whole name again.

"You have to have a costume."

She knew she did, but she hadn't had much time to think about it. Maybe she and Logan could detour to the Halloween store after they went to his appointment. He and Tate also needed costumes.

"I'll get something. Don't worry." She patted Dee's shoulder. Then she went out the door and walked down the street to the Hammer Tyme. The rain had stopped, but clouds still rolled by overhead. She was a little worried it might continue raining during the Festival. If it did, it would put a damper on their plans for a street dance.

She pushed open the door of the hardware shop and the buzzer sounded. Tate looked up from behind the counter where he was reading and a smile lit his face. "Hey," he said, taking off his glasses and tucking them in the pocket of his shirt.

She held up the cooler. "What about some lunch?"

He nodded vigorously and climbed off the stool, then he lifted the counter, so Zion could walk under it. She went into the storeroom and began removing the food. She'd made a large chicken salad for her and Rebekah the previous night, so it made a perfect lunch today.

Tate grabbed two sodas from the mini-fridge and carried them back to the table, stopping to give her a kiss. When he deepened it, Zion curled her hand in his shirt and pulled him closer. Finally, she drew back and motioned to the food.

"Let's eat."

He wrapped his arms around her. "What if we skip lunch?"

"Nope. I'm hungry and all I've had all day is Chai tea."

With a groan, Tate released her and took a seat, dishing up salad onto the plates she'd brought. She pulled the salad dressing out of the cooler with a loaf of French bread. They ate in silence for a few moments, then Zion leveled a serious look on him.

"What happened with Poole at the precinct?" she asked.

His expression sobered and he took a sip of his drink to clear his mouth. "A whole lot of nothing. He won't admit to anything, but he told me he thinks there's a link between the Devil's Tongue showing up here and the death of the kid he shot."

"I thought the kid wasn't involved with a gang."

"He was a messenger for them. He lived in the same tenement we raided, the one that caught fire. He was trying to help his mother and brothers out with money after she lost her job, and I guess that was the only thing he thought he could do."

"That's too bad. I'm sorry to hear that. Did you get any closer to identifying the two men who were shot?"

Tate shook his head, taking a bite of salad. "Not yet."

"What about the one shot outside the house? Is he still alive?"

"He made it through surgery, but he's in a medically induced coma." Tate braced his chin on his hand, giving her a speculative look. "You seem pretty calm about everything that's happened."

She set down her fork. "If you think that, then I'm doing a good job at hiding it." She hadn't been able to sleep all night, thinking about what had happened just a few yards away from her home.

He reached over and took her hand. "I know this is scary."

"Someone was shot on our street, in front of my house, Tate. This isn't supposed to be happening here."

"I know. I'm working on figuring it all out."

Zion leveled a look on him. "Do you believe Poole?"

He thought about that for a moment. "I think there's more he's not telling me. We found a tracking device on his car."

"A tracking device?"

Tate nodded.

"Why would they track him?"

"He said he thought they wanted to know where he was because he was working in their territory. He was apparently working on a task force to redirect youth from a life of gangs and crime."

"Maybe he's right. That car is pretty recognizable."

"That's what he told me."

"But you don't believe it?"

Tate looked down, pushing the lettuce around on his plate. "I wish I did, but that doesn't seem likely."

They both fell silent, lost in their own thoughts as they finished their lunch. Customers came into the hardware store, so Zion packed up her things and hurried back to the *Caffeinator*. She had time to place a few orders for supplies, then she had to head out to pick up Logan.

* * *

"So I thought maybe we could stop by the Halloween store on the way home and get some costumes for the festival. What do you think? I'm sure Tate hasn't even given it a moment's consideration," she said to Logan as they walked toward the hospital together.

"Seriously? Yeah, that would be cool. I got paid, so I can buy my own."

Zion smiled at him. "Sounds good to me. You know what you want to be?"

"I have some ideas. Yeah, I'm pretty sure I know, and I definitely know what Tate should be."

She liked seeing the mischievous sparkle in his eyes. "You wanna share?"

"Nope. It'll be a surprise."

Zion laughed and followed him to the psychologist's office. The receptionist greeted them warmly and told them to have a seat. Zion and Logan sat down where the woman indicated and Logan gave a low chuckle.

"What?" asked Zion.

"The last time I was here, they gave me this questionnaire to fill out. You should have seen Tate trying to read what I wrote on it."

Zion shared a smile with him. "He cares about you and he worries. You've had a lot of responsibilities for someone so young."

"I know. And I know this whole parenting thing was sprung on him too quick. It's a big adjustment."

"I'm proud of you, Logan. You know that? You're pretty amazing."

He blushed and looked down. "I'm sorry you have to drive me around. I'll be getting my permit soon."

"Good." She patted his forearm. "Then maybe Tate will get a car instead of that darn truck. It's too hard getting into it in a dress."

Logan gave her an amused look. "Wouldn't know about that," he said.

Zion laughed and nudged his shoulder. A moment later the door opened and a tall man stepped out.

"Logan, are you ready?"

"Sure." Logan rose to his feet. "I'll meet you back here in an hour, Zion."

"Actually I think I'm going to try to find a coffee shop. You have my cell number, right?"

"Right." He gave a lift of his hand and followed the man through the door.

Zion waited a moment to make sure he was situated, then she walked over to the counter. The receptionist smiled up at her.

"How can I help you?"

"Is there some place I can get coffee? I'm feeling a little sleepy and thought I might get a caffeine jolt to wake me up."

"Of course. Head back into the hospital and there's a coffee cart on the opposite side, near the gift shop."

"Thank you," Zion said, slinging her purse over her shoulder and heading out.

A yellow line on the floor pointed the way back to the main lobby, so Zion followed it. Once there, she glanced around and found a white line that indicated the way to the gift shop. She followed that, discovering the little coffee kiosk in the corner outside the shop.

A teenage girl manned the kiosk by herself and she gave Zion a brilliant smile, complete with braces. Acne marred her chin, but she had a full head of silvery grey hair.

"Wow, your hair is amazing," said Zion, shocked and intrigued by the color.

"I just got it done," the girl said, leaning toward her and lowering her voice as if it was confidential. "What can I get you?"

Zion stared at the menu affixed to the wall above the girl's head. "Do you have a full espresso machine back there?"

"I do. It's the latest model. Smaller than the old one, but more efficient."

Zion rose on her tiptoes to see it. Hm, that might be the sort of machine they needed for their own kiosk near the highway. "I'll just have a cappuccino."

"Coming right up." The girl punched the drink into the cash register, then took Zion's card and swiped it.

Handing Zion the receipt and the card back, she bounced to the espresso machine and began preparing Zion's drink. Zion was impressed with her efficiency. "Do you live around here?"

"I live in Sequoia," the girl shouted over the hiss of the steamed milk.

"Really? Are you in high school?"

"Senior." She pointed at her teeth. "I did not want these on when I took my senior portrait, but it couldn't be helped."

Zion nodded. "What are you doing after you graduate?"

"Going to community college for two years, then transferring to Chico State."

Zion took her business card out of her purse. "I run the *Caffeinator* in town, on Main Street."

"I know it," said the girl, handing Zion her drink.

"If you ever want a job…" She held the card out to her.

"Thank you. Boy, it would be easier being close to home."

"I'll bet." Zion took a sip of the drink. It was perfect. "Very good."

The girl beamed, all silver braces and silver hair. "Thank you."

"Thank you," said Zion in return and turned toward the gift shop.

She couldn't take the drink inside, so she studied the stuffed animals and trinkets displayed in the windows. As she looked at a bear, holding a heart that said *Get well!*, she noticed a familiar figure moving across the lobby of the hospital.

Poole.

He stopped in front of the elevators and seemed to be studying the listing for the floors. Zion edged around the gift shop window and watched him, but she couldn't tell what he was looking at. He scanned down the list with his finger, then tapped the tip on the glass a few times before he walked to the elevator and pressed the button.

Zion waited until he got inside the elevator and the doors closed, then she hurried across the lobby and stopped before the list. She wasn't sure what floor he'd been looking at as she scanned the list. She started to reach for her phone to call Tate and tell him, but she was afraid he'd tell her to stay out of it. He'd gotten a lot more protective since they started dating.

Pacing away from the elevator, Zion felt a wash of frustration. There was no reason for Poole to be here, except the man who'd been shot in front of her house was also here. She had to figure out where Poole was going.

Staring out at the rain steaming up the window outside the hospital, she had an idea. Turning back to the list, she opened the top on her coffee and held it against the list, letting the steam caress the glass. Her eyes stopped on the smudge just visible over the floor that said *Surgical ICU*.

"Gotcha," she said, recapping the coffee and taking another sip. Her heart was hammering beneath her ribs, but she walked over and punched the up button, then she dumped the coffee in the trashcan with a feeling of regret. It had been good coffee.

When the elevator arrived, she walked inside, then she realized she would be way too conspicuous with her red hair. Gathering it in her hands, she wound it into a bun, then reached into her purse, trying to find a hat. She sometimes left the *Caffeinator* with her ball cap in place on her head, forgetting it was there, but she was out of luck today. She found her sunglasses, but she figured it would look suspicious to be wearing sunglasses indoors.

As the doors opened on the Surgical ICU, she peered out, looking both ways to see if she could spot Poole. A reception desk in front of her was empty and she saw no one down either corridor. Stepping out, she saw a box of facemasks affixed to the wall by the elevator and she snatched one, putting it on. Maybe if she hid part of her face, he wouldn't recognize her.

Moving toward the reception desk, she looked at the white board affixed to the wall behind it. She didn't know the suspect's name, but next to the names were the patients' dates of arrival. The most recent one was just yesterday. That had to be him. B. Edmonds in room 314. She leaned back and looked at the wall, seeing a white placard that said rooms 290-315 were to her right.

Moving close to the outer wall, she eased down the corridor toward room 314. When she came to a dead end, she marked another placard that said 300-315 were down a hallway on her right. Zion eased to the corner and peered down the hallway. Poole was striding in the middle of the corridor, peering around to see if anyone was in sight. He was almost to room 314.

Zion clenched her jaw and told herself to be brave. A man's life might depend on it. But just as she was about to turn the corner, the door to 314 opened and a police officer stepped out, taking a seat in a chair outside the door.

Poole spotted him and made an abrupt turn into a room on his left. Zion flattened herself against the wall, breathing hard.

Sheriff Wilson had obviously put a guard on the suspect. There was no way Poole was going to be able to get at him. But what did he want with the guy? Was he going to confront him or do something worse?

A nurse in pale blue scrubs appeared before Zion. "Can I help you with something?"

Zion shook her head. "No, I think I'm on the wrong floor." She touched the mask. "I've got a cold and I didn't want to get anyone sick."

"We appreciate that. What floor did you want?"

"What?" Zion blinked at her.

"What floor did you want?"

Zion's brain couldn't think fast enough. Poole would be coming back down the hallway at any second. "Um, what floor?"

"Yes, what floor were you looking for?"

"Uh, maternity," she blurted out, then they both looked down at Zion's flat stomach.

"That would be the second floor," said the nurse.

"Right. Right. It's not for me. My sister. She's having a baby. Um, today."

"Okay," said the nurse, giving her an odd look.

"I better go. Never can tell how fast these things happen."

"Right."

Zion eased back down the hallway, hurrying to the elevator and pushing the button. "We're all really excited," she said over her shoulder to the woman. "We're hoping for a boy."

Thank God the elevator dinged and the doors opened at that moment. Zion hurried inside and pressed the button to close the door, ripping the mask off her face. She slumped against the wall, breathing fast, her heart hammering.

When she reached the lobby again, she dropped the mask into the trashcan and hurried back toward the coffee kiosk. The teenager gave her a bewildered look.

"Did you want another cappuccino?"

Zion shook her head no, taking up her position by the windows of the gift shop where she could see into the lobby.

"I can make you another one on the house. I was worried that one didn't turn out quite right."

"It was fine," Zion said, waving her off, her gaze fixed on the front doors.

"Are you sure? I feel bad."

Zion ignored her, concentrating. A moment later, Poole appeared, striding toward the doors. Zion ducked back, holding her breath, but Poole never looked her way, stepping outside into the rain and disappearing from sight.

"Do you know that guy?" asked the girl.

Zion released her held breath and closed her eyes. "Ex-boyfriend," she said, then decided she was better off sitting quietly in the waiting room for Logan to return.

* * *

"You got what for our costumes?" asked Tate, staring at the blue overalls and the red shirt with the red ball cap. In the center of the ball cap was a red M on a white backdrop. Tate held up the huge black moustache. "You don't really expect me to go to the festival in this?"

Logan burst into laughter, then gathered up the bags and walked toward the back of the house. "I'll just keep these in my room, so you don't get any ideas about a bonfire."

Tate shook his head, but he seemed amused. He started toward Zion, but she held him off, leaning forward to make sure Logan was out of earshot. Taking Tate's hand, she dragged him into the kitchen.

"I need to tell you something."

"You couldn't have talked him out of those costumes?"

"Tate, please listen to me."

His expression grew serious. "What's wrong?"

"I saw Poole at the hospital."

"What?"

"Poole was at the hospital today."

Tate shook his head. "I'm sorry. I'm really confused."

"When I took Logan to see the psychologist, I wanted a cup of coffee. I'm so tired from being up all night. The coffee kiosk was across the lobby by the gift shop. When I was looking in the windows of the gift shop, I saw Poole."

Tate's lips tightened against his teeth. "Go on."

"I followed him."

"You what?" The expression on his face was savage. "You followed him?"

Zion put her hands on his chest. "Just listen to me, okay?"

He took a deep breath and released it. "Go on," he repeated.

"He got off on the Surgical ICU floor. There was a patient there by the name of B. Edmonds."

Tate's eyes drifted away. "The man shot outside your house was Bruno Edmonds. He's Lon Edmonds' brother."

"The guy in Atascadero that owned the Impala?"

"Yeah. We're pretty sure the guy Poole shot was Luther Edmonds their cousin. The tattoo shop confirmed they did Devil's Tongue tattoos for the whole male side of the Edmonds family. The LAPD tried to get Lon to identify the body through a photograph, but he refused. However, the cops who talked with him said he had a definite reaction to Edmonds' face."

"Why weren't Luther's fingerprints in the system?"

"They're pretty sure he's in the country illegally." Tate put his hands on her shoulders. "Go back to Poole."

"I saw that Bruno was in room 314 according to the nurse's board, so I went after Poole. He was in the corridor, heading for Bruno's room."

Tate's eyes narrowed. "You're sure?"

"Yes, but he didn't make it. A deputy came out of the room and took a seat in a chair in the hallway. Poole ducked into another room, then I saw him leave a few minutes later."

"What if he recognized you?"

Zion shifted weight. She felt ridiculous saying this. "I wore a disguise."

"You did what now?" said Tate.

"I wore a disguise."

"What sort of disguise?"

Zion put her hand over her mouth. "Amske."

Tate leaned closer to her, turning his head. "What was that again?"

"I wore a mask."

"Like Zorro."

Zion frowned at him. "No, not like Zorro. A hospital mask."

Tate smiled, then reached out and pulled her into his arms. "I don't want you tangling with Poole again."

"He never even saw me," she said, resting her head against his chest and hearing his heart beating beneath her ear.

"I don't care. He's a dangerous man."

"Are you going to tell Sheriff Wilson about this?"

"Yes, he needs to know it's important to keep the guard there."

"What about Poole? Are you going to have him arrested?"

Tate sighed. "This is where it gets tricky. If we move before we have evidence, he'll just bolt, but he's getting desperate and that makes him particularly dangerous. I need something more on him. I feel like I'm missing something huge. I still can't figure out why Devil's Tongue was tracking him."

Zion leaned away from Tate. "He was planning to intimidate Bruno or…" She shuddered. "Or kill him. He needs to be stopped, Tate."

Tate placed his forehead against hers. "He will be. I promise you. I just need to figure out what the hell is going on."

CHAPTER 16

Tate stared out the window of his house, watching the rain fall. The mailbox stood in his direct line of sight and he knew he needed to go open it, but he couldn't make himself do it. Logan came out of the hallway, his backpack slung over his shoulder, wearing a hoodie and a light jacket. Tate regarded the boy.

"Do you have a winter coat?"

Logan shrugged. "I make due. Layers, man."

Tate shook his head. "We need to get you a proper coat."

"I don't have the money for that, Tate. I'm trying to pay everyone back for the money they gave me for the funeral."

"It's my job as your guardian to get you appropriate clothes, Logan. Stop thinking you have to pay for everything."

Logan shuffled his feet, looking down.

"How'd it go with Dr. Martin yesterday?"

"Fine."

Tate knew he probably wasn't going to get any more out of him. He took the car keys out of his pocket and tossed them to Logan. "Same thing as yesterday."

Logan jangled the keys in his hand. "You think Zion can take me to the DMV sometime this week to take my permit test?"

"I'll ask her."

Logan smiled and headed for the door. Tate grabbed his own coat out of the closet, putting it on and pulling the hood over his head. As they both ran to the truck, Tate hesitated and looked at the mailbox. Then he jogged down to the street and forced himself to open it, staring at the manila envelope inside. He drew it out and ran his thumb over the return address: *Darcy Reyes*. Shit. He'd known it would be here.

These were the files on Poole and the raid that killed Jason.

Logan honked the horn, startling Tate. He tucked the envelope under his arm and shut the box, then he jogged back to the truck and slid inside.

After dropping Logan off at school, Tate drove to the *Hammer Tyme* and climbed out. He stared at the envelope lying on the passenger seat, then he looked down Main Street at the shops glistening in the rain. Reaching in, he grabbed the envelope and slammed the door, hurrying toward his shop.

Bill Stanley was shifting from foot to foot in front of the store, blowing on his hands.

"Sorry, Bill," said Tate, shoving the key in the lock.

"No problem, but once we get everything open, I'm going for some coffee."

"Understood," said Tate, smiling at the older man.

Tate set the envelope on the table in the storeroom as he and Bill performed their morning routine. When Bill left to get coffee, Tate messed with the shelves and surveyed the store, wondering if he should hire Rebekah to take a look at things. He couldn't deny she'd done a great job with Zion's coffee house.

When he couldn't find anything else to fuss with, he forced himself into the storeroom and sat down at the table, his hands resting on either side of the envelope. He needed to know who ordered the raid. He needed to know why the task force had been sent in before they were ready – underprepared, understaffed, and outgunned. And yet, just thinking about reliving that night had his guts roiling.

He scrubbed his hands over his face and tried to slow his breathing. When the buzzer on the door sounded, he jumped and his eyes whipped to the opening. A moment later, Bill Stanley walked into the storeroom, carrying two steaming cups of coffee.

"Dottie says she wants you to try her pumpkin spiced latte in honor of the season." He handed Tate one of the cups.

Tate stared at it, then he shoved the envelope away and rose to his feet. "Can you put it in the refrigerator for me? I'll heat it up later. I've got something I've got to do."

Bill frowned at him. "Everything all right?" He glanced at the envelope, then back to Tate.

Tate forced himself to pick it up and walk to his wall safe. He opened the safe and shoved the envelope inside. "Yeah, I've just got to talk to someone. Will you be okay here?"

"Sure," said Bill. "I'm thinking it'll be slow today with all the rain."

Tate nodded, then he grabbed his damp coat and put it on. His mind was in turmoil as he walked back down to the municipal lot and got in the truck. His thoughts bounced from Poole showing up at the hospital to the night Jason died.

Why would the Devil's Tongue track Poole all this way for a kid they'd used to send messages? They hadn't done anything to improve the kid's life or help him support his family, but they'd sent two men after Poole just to get revenge? It just wasn't sitting right.

When he pulled into the parking lot of the *Back-of-Beyond Lodge*, he searched for Poole's Camaro. He wasn't sure if it had been released from impounds after they'd found the tracking device. Taking out his cell phone, he called Murphy.

"What?" she snapped.

"Good morning to you."

"Look, do you know where that idjet Poole is?"

"I'm out at Bearpaw Creek and his Camaro isn't here. Do you know if it was released from impounds?"

"Yeah, yesterday."

"Why are you looking for him?"

"Sheriff told me to keep an eye on the fool. Now I can't find him. He's not answering his cell."

"You think he left the area?"

Murphy made a disgruntled noise. "Hell if I know. He's got half an hour to return my calls or I'm putting a BOLO out on the Camaro."

Tate scratched the back of his neck. He hadn't wanted to tell the sheriff what Zion had seen yesterday because he really didn't want her involved in this case. It was too volatile and two people had already been shot, but he figured he didn't have a choice anymore.

"Zion saw Poole at the hospital yesterday. On the same floor as Bruno Edmonds."

"What? Why am I just hearing this now?"

"Because he didn't get anywhere near Bruno, Murphy."

"Tate, the sheriff got called out to the hospital this morning."

Tate leaned forward, looking at the cabin Poole had rented. The lights were off. "What? Why?"

"I don't know. He hasn't called back, but if Poole was there…"

"I'm on my way," said Tate. And he just knew things had only gotten worse.

* * *

Tate arrived at the hospital half an hour later. He drove around the parking lot, looking for the silver Camaro, but he didn't find it. Finally, he got out of the truck and ran to the hospital entrance, his jacket already soaked with rain.

Once inside he pulled the hood off and shook as much of the water away that he could, walking to the elevator and searching for the Surgical ICU. He pressed the button for the elevator and looked around as he waited for it to arrive. He could see the coffee kiosk off to his right and the windows for the gift shop. It worried him to think how visible Zion had been, snooping on Poole in this very location. And with her red hair and freckles, she was easy to identify.

The elevator arrived and Tate waited for an older woman to get off. "Good morning," she told him.

"Good morning," he said.

"Wet outside, isn't it?"

"Yes, it is," he answered, wishing she'd hurry along. He felt a little guilty for his impatience, but he didn't have a good feeling about how everything was shaking down. He watched the old woman cross the lobby as the doors on the elevator closed, then he punched the button for the third floor.

Coming out into a corridor, he saw the nurse's station ahead of him and he walked over to it. A young man manned the desk at the front. "How can I help you?"

"I'm looking for…"

"Tate?" came the sheriff's voice to his right.

Tate turned to face him. "Sheriff Wilson, what's going on? Why are you here?"

"Why didn't you tell me Zion saw Poole here yesterday?"

Damn Murphy. She must have called him the minute she hung up with Tate.

"Look…" Tate began, but Wilson grabbed his arm and propelled him down the opposite corridor to a waiting room with couches, end tables, and a television mounted on the wall.

Wilson pushed his hat to the back of his head, hooked his hands in his belt, and glared at Tate. "You'd better come clean, son, 'cause I'm royally pissed."

"I didn't tell you because she said you had a deputy stationed outside Edmonds' room and when Poole saw him, he took a detour into another room. Zion watched him leave the hospital. I figured everything was okay and I honestly didn't want Zion getting roped into this case. Two men have been shot."

"Two men have died!" said Wilson, narrowing his eyes.

"What?"

"Bruno Edmonds is dead."

"How?"

"The doctors think he died of complications from surgery, but until I see Davenport's autopsy, I'm not ruling anything out." Wilson crossed his arms over his chest. "I really don't want to ask you this, Tate, but I've got no choice."

Tate felt a sinking in his gut. "What?"

"You and Poole worked together in LA. You were brothers in blue. Are you involved in this case, Tate?"

"I'm trying to find out what's going on. I'm trying to find out why the Devil's Tongue is after Poole."

"And why are they after Poole?"

"He says it's because the kid he shot in LA was running messages for their gang and they want revenge."

"But you don't think that's it?"

Tate drew a deep breath. "I'm fairly sure that's not it, but I don't know what else it might be. I'm investigating the same as you, Sheriff."

"And what happens if you find out Poole is deeper involved in this than you think?"

"Then I'll be with you when you take him down."

Wilson gave Tate a severe look. "Are you sure about that, son?"

Tate held Wilson's gaze. "I'm sure. Poole and I served on a task force together, but beyond that, there's nothing else there."

Wilson nodded. Before he could say anything else, his phone rang. He pulled it out and thumbed it on. "Wilson," he said, then he listened intently. "We're on it." He put his phone back in his pocket and motioned to the door. "Let's go. We've got another problem."

Tate frowned, but he followed him out.

* * *

Tate pulled up behind Wilson on the shoulder of the highway. The mountain rose to their right and the steep decline on their left led to the forest not far from where Vivian Bradley had lost her life. Deputy Lewis had flares laid out in the lane and he was directing traffic. Tate opened the truck's door and got out. The rain had stopped, but the sky looked angry.

Up ahead, the flicker of fire danced against the damp asphalt. Tate followed Wilson up the road and stood next to him as they watched the Camaro burn. A fire truck was positioned up the road and the firefighters poured water on it from a distance in case the gas tank blew.

Tate wasn't sure how to process what he was seeing, but the Camaro was a complete loss.

Murphy walked over to them, glancing at her phone. "Impounds confirmed the license belonged to Poole's silver Camaro."

"Anyone inside it?" asked Wilson.

"Doesn't appear to be, but we haven't popped the trunk on it yet. Can't get close enough."

Tate's eyes whipped to Murphy's face and he felt a little nauseous. Sure, Poole wasn't one of his favorite people, but the thought of him being burned alive in the car by the Devil's Tongue sickened him.

"Any sign of Poole?" continued Wilson.

"Nope," said Murphy. "I've been trying to reach him all day."

"Witnesses?"

"A number of people reported the burning car, but no one mentioned anything about seeing anyone near it."

Wilson hooked his thumbs in his belt. "You know anything about this, Tate?" he demanded.

Murphy glanced between them, but Tate knew this only added fuel to Wilson's concern about the relationship he had with Poole.

"I haven't seen Poole since you brought him into the precinct after he came to my house two days ago."

"We know Zion saw him at the hospital yesterday and Bruno Edmonds died today," said Wilson. "Put a BOLO out on Poole."

"On it," said Murphy, moving toward her squad car.

"Would he set his own car on fire?" asked Wilson.

Tate wasn't sure. If the Devil's Tongue wanted to eliminate a problem, and Poole was clearly a problem for them, they might figure this was a fitting way to dispose of him. "We need to get the trunk open."

Wilson nodded.

They stood on the gloomy, damp highway and watched the firefighters extinguish the car. Tate hated the fact that Wilson was questioning him, but he had to admit, he'd be suspicious himself if the shoe was on the other foot.

Once the firefighters were sure the car was completely extinguished, Wilson ordered them to pop the trunk. He told Tate to wait where he was, but Tate couldn't deny he had a morbid fear about what they'd find.

The metal shrieked as the firefighters pried it up with a crowbar. Then Murphy and Wilson peered inside. Tate craned his neck to see also, but his view was blocked by the angle of the road and the bodies of the investigators. Watching them pull on gloves, he held his breath as they searched the trunk, then the interior of the car.

A tow truck lumbered up the road and Lewis waved it through the flares. Once it positioned itself before the burnt-out Camaro, Wilson moved away from the group, pulling off his soiled gloves. He marched down to Tate, his expression fierce.

"Do you know where Poole is?"

Tate blinked. That must mean the trunk had been empty. He glanced at the Camaro again, not sure if what he was feeling was relief or not.

Wilson took his hesitation for hedging.

"Is there something you're not telling me?"

Tate's eyes shifted back to the sheriff. Wilson might not be a physically imposing man, but there was something intimidating about him. "No," Tate finally said, but he knew there was. He had a file in his safe that might hold the answers Wilson wanted, but Tate wasn't ready to tell him about it yet.

He realized that if he told Wilson and there was something in the file, Darcy could get in trouble for pulling it and sending it to him since he wasn't part of the LAPD anymore. He had to find a way to make the connection between Poole and the Devil's Tongue without using Darcy.

"Mercer!" growled Wilson. "I'm going to ask you this just one more time. Do you know where Poole is?"

"I don't," said Tate without hesitation.

Wilson must have sensed this was the truth because he turned and looked back at the Camaro. Finally he faced Tate again. "If you hear from him, you tell me."

"Of course."

"If Zion sees him playing hopscotch in the nursery school, you tell me."

"Um," said Tate, arching a brow.

"Mercer!"

"Yes, yes, she will. I'll make sure of it."

Wilson stared him down a moment more. "Okay," he said skeptically. "Okay."

Tate hated disappointing Wilson or making him doubt for a moment that he was loyal to him, but he had no choice. He didn't know anything more than he'd known yesterday, and most importantly, he had no idea where Poole could have gone, especially now that he didn't have a car.

Murphy walked down to them. "I sent Vasquez by the cabin. Poole has it paid for through the end of the month, but he isn't there. Some of the tenants of the other cabins said he hasn't been back for a few days."

Wilson considered that. "Get a warrant for us to search it."

"On it."

Wilson looked back at Tate. "Keep your phone on."

Tate nodded.

"I mean it, Mercer. If I call, you'd better pick up."

Tate nodded again, his eyes drifting back to the burnt-out Camaro.

CHAPTER 17

"Wow, you weren't kidding. You need my help in so many ways," said Rebekah, walking around the store and taking it all in.

Zion had to admit Jaguar was definitely not ready to open. Boxes were strewn around the shop and merchandise lay on the floor. He had one counter along the left hand wall, but he hadn't even started putting stuff inside of it.

Jaguar made a face, his arms crossed over the top of his head. "Can you help me?"

"Alert your credit card company that we're going to be buying," Rebekah said, making notes on her clipboard. She walked over to a black curtain that had been affixed across an archway at the back of the store and pulled it aside.

Zion leaned to her left so she could see inside too. The curtain revealed a little room with sound proof tiles on the walls and a music stand in the center of it. Rebekah let the curtain fall and wiped her hands on her pants.

"What in the world is that?" she demanded.

"The lesson room," said Jaguar.

"You expect parents to let you take their children behind a black curtain?" she asked horrified.

Jaguar looked over at Zion. Zion shook her head. It wasn't a great idea.

"I didn't want my students to feel intimidated by people watching them play and I figured it was still out here in the open."

Rebekah waved her pen at it. "That needs to come down. We'll get some pretty beads to hang over the archway, which will give the illusion of privacy. Then, in this area right outside the room, we should set up chairs and tables with music magazines on them for a parents' waiting room. Oh, and you should serve coffee and water." She pointed the pen at Zion. "Zion can provide it. It'll be good cross promotion for both of you."

"Okay. That sounds good."

Rebekah made some more notes. "You said you have shelves. I'm gonna need to see them."

"They're in back."

"Why? Why are they in back? Why aren't they up?"

Jaguar shifted uncomfortably. "Tate was going to put them up for me, but he's been distracted lately."

They both looked at Zion. Zion held up her hands. "Don't blame me. It's the case. And Logan."

"Well, what are we going to do? I don't think Hardware Man's going to be available anytime soon and those shelves should have gone up yesterday."

"I can hang them," came a voice from the doorway.

They all whipped around to see a young man poking his head inside the store. He pulled the door open all the way and stepped through. He was around twenty-five or so with brown hair cut into one inch spikes all the way around his head. He had brown eyes, a five o'clock shadow, and very prominent cheekbones. Wearing tattered jeans and an *Anaconda* band t-shirt, he wiped his hand on his pants leg and held it out to Jaguar.

"It's so awesome to meet you."

Jaguar gave him a lazy smile and took his hand. "Thanks. Sorry, who are you?"

"I'm Noah Hart. I just moved back to the area." His eyes darted around the store and he placed his hand in the center of his chest. "I'm a huge fan. You're like a genius."

Jaguar's smile grew bigger. "Well, genius is a bit of an exaggeration."

"Oh, for heaven's sakes," said Rebekah. "Look here, Porcupine, we're busy."

"Rebekah!" scolded Zion, and Jaguar looked horrified.

"If we're going to open on Monday, he needs to focus. Well, what's it going to be, Rockstar?"

Jaguar looked torn.

Noah held up a hand. "I was hoping maybe you were hiring. I'm really handy and I love music. I know how to play bass and I've got experience running a cash register."

"Where's your resume? Where's your references?" said Rebekah, holding out her hand. "We're not ready to hire yet."

"Well…" said Jaguar.

The young man shifted weight. "I can hang the shelves and move stuff around." He leaned over to make eye contact with Jaguar. "I really need a job. I was a roadie for *Oblivion* for a few years, toured with them."

"Why'd you leave?"

Noah rubbed a hand over his head. "Got caught up in it. You know?"

"Yeah. Coke?"

"Coke, crank, lot of weed."

Jaguar nodded. "I've been there."

"But I'm clean now. I swear. I can show you my certificate from my program."

"I believe you," said Jaguar with a smile. "Look, I'm only paying minimum to start."

"What?" said Rebekah. "Hold on just a minute."

Jaguar glanced at her and away. "Is that okay?"

"Jaguar," said Zion. "Can I talk to you?"

He nodded. "Just wait here, okay?" he told Noah.

"Whatever you say."

Zion walked toward the back of the store, pushing open the door that lead to the tiny storeroom choked with boxes and furniture. Jaguar and Rebekah stepped inside too.

"What the hell are you doing, Rockstar?" demanded Rebekah. "That guy walks in here, tells you he's a drug addict, has no resume, no references, and you hire him."

"He said he could put up the shelves," Jaguar argued. "Besides, I know what it's like to be part of that lifestyle. I was getting stoned everyday myself until my daughter came along."

"Well, you have no proof he isn't stoned right now!" Rebekah hissed, motioning out into the store. "How do you know he isn't going to rob you?"

"How do I know that with anyone?"

Zion touched his arm. "You don't have body guards anymore, Jaguar, and he's clearly smitten with you."

"Smitten with me?"

"Yeah, like wear your skin smitten with you," said Rebekah.

Jaguar and Zion shivered. "Calm down," Zion told her. "I just think you need to take it slowly. You've never run a store before."

"Okay, what if we try him out on helping me get this place put together? We won't leave him alone in the store and I'll just pay him for the physical labor. I won't hire him permanently until we see how he works. Does that sound like a compromise?" He looked between the two women.

Rebekah considered it. Zion wasn't sure she liked it, but Jim Dawson and Tate were on either side of him, and Daryl and Dwayne Ford were across the street. Besides, Rebekah would be here for the next few days and no one messed with Rebekah.

"Can Hakim come in?"

Jaguar gave Zion a disgruntled look. "You know I'm not totally helpless."

"I'll be here," said Rebekah. "I can watch the Rockstar's *assets*."

Jaguar smiled at her. "You know, if you want to make this business idea work, you're gonna need your own office."

"What do you mean?"

"I mean some place where you can meet potential clients and show them a portfolio of what you can offer. Besides, if you do their books, you might want to do it from your own office so there's less *assets* to distract you." He winked at her.

Rebekah blushed and looked down. "I don't know how I'd get up the money to rent a place."

Jaguar thought for a moment. "You know," he said, turning to Zion. "Nancy's building, where she had *Cater 2 U*, has been sitting empty for months. They might make Rebekah a good deal and it has an apartment in back."

Rebekah's eyes snapped up to Jaguar's face. "An apartment?"

Zion also found herself intrigued by the apartment idea. She loved Rebekah, but she and Tate had no privacy whatsoever.

"Yeah, I'll bet you could get it for the same amount as you'd rent a place to live around here."

Rebekah's gaze shifted to Zion.

"Is David representing Nancy's estate?" Zion asked Jaguar.

"Yeah, Nancy's sister, Pam, inherited everything, including the business. He's handling the rental for her."

Rebekah clasped her hands together. "It has an apartment?"

Zion shrugged. "I don't know. We should take a look at it this afternoon. I'll call David and see if we can get inside."

"Thank you," said Rebekah, throwing her arms around Zion.

"Hey, I came up with it," protested Jaguar.

Zion patted Rebekah's back. "Look, I gotta get back to work." She peered through a crack in the door at Noah's earnest expression. "Please be careful. I really wish you'd call Hakim to come down."

"Fine," said Jaguar, pushing open the door. "You'd think I was a damn Pomeranian that needed to be carried on a pillow."

"Nope," said Rebekah. "Pomeranians know how to put up shelves."

* * *

Zion hadn't been out to the little pink cottage since Nancy Osborn had been arrested for Merilee Whitmire's death. The place looked a little neglected. The decorative pots on the porch had dead plants inside. A *For Rent* sign half hung off the cross beam, and the front door was padlocked.

Zion pushed open the Spider's door and climbed out. Rebekah looked up at the gingerbread shingles and white trim, giving it a skeptical glare. "It'll have to be repainted."

A silver Range Rover pulled in next to them and David climbed out in a suit, white shirt, and navy tie, carrying a briefcase. He gave Zion a cool smile, then held his hand out to Rebekah. "Miss Miles, so nice to see you again."

"You can call me, Rebekah," she said, taking his hand and shaking it.

Zion prayed she wouldn't call him Ex-boyfriend Lawyer like she had so many times with Zion.

"Of course, Rebekah." His eyes drifted to Zion. "Zion."

"David, how are you?"

"I'm doing well." He looked away and motioned to the cottage. "So I understand you're interested in renting this place."

"I don't know. It needs a lot of work."

Zion frowned at her. She hadn't even been inside yet.

"How so?" asked David.

"The paint outside will have to be changed. I can't open a business in a pink house."

"I see. What sort of business are you thinking? Nancy Osborn ran a catering business out of it."

"Which explains why it looks like a cupcake."

David laughed.

Zion frowned at that. She'd always found it difficult to get him to laugh when they were together. She'd make a silly quip and he'd stare at her, then give her a closed-mouth smile.

"How come it hasn't been rented all this time?" Zion asked.

"I think it has to do with the fact that Nancy Osborn killed someone." He gave Rebekah a quick look. "I don't mean inside the place."

"I know. I know what happened." Rebekah tapped her finger against her upper lip. "You asked what sort of business I'm starting?"

"Yes."

"A consulting business. I'm going to help other businesses be more efficient. Show them how to rearrange their stores for optimum traffic. Do their payroll and taxes for them."

"Ah, we could use something like that here. Do you have experience?"

"I have a business degree and I worked at an insurance company for…" She caught herself and looked down. "…a while. I've already got two clients – Zion and Jaguar."

"Well, good. Would you like to see inside?" He motioned to the stairs.

"Definitely," said Rebekah, sashaying to the stairs and climbing onto the porch.

David fell into step beside Zion. "So, you and Tate are dating?"

Zion gave him a surprised look. She didn't really want to talk about this right now. "How did you hear?"

"I was at *Corkers* the other night, meeting a client."

"I'm sorry. I should have told you."

David shook his head. "You don't owe me anything, Zion. I'm not surprised." He stopped on the stairs and met her gaze. "And I'm not angry at you either. I want you to be happy."

Zion felt a wash of guilt. David was a good guy. "David…" she started, but Rebekah clapped her hands.

"Let's put a shake on, Lawyer. I've got a rockstar's money to spend."

To Zion's surprise, David chuckled and went to unlock the padlock. He pushed open the door. "After you," he said and Rebekah flounced into the little cottage.

Zion followed more slowly, memories swamping her. She'd talked with Nancy in this place, met Sophia, Jaguar's daughter, and she'd like both of them instantly. It was hard to reconcile the woman who'd murdered an innocent girl with the woman that might have been her friend at any other time.

The living room/waiting room was the same. Antique couches arranged around an antique tray table. A beaded curtain led into the dining room that Nancy had used as a conference room to meet her customers. Beyond that was another beaded curtain that led to the small kitchen.

Rebekah waved her to follow as she headed to the right down a long hallway. Zion hadn't been in that part of the cottage, but she'd known Nancy and Sophia lived back there. Rebekah pushed open all the doors and Zion peered in after her.

There were two small bedrooms, both had been emptied, and a dated bathroom with penny tiles and a claw footed tub. Rebekah squealed when she saw it and she clasped Zion's hands with her own. Then in the back was the master bedroom. It too was small, but Rebekah didn't need much room.

The personal effects had all been removed.

The hardwood floors were scratched and needed to be buffed. The walls had furniture marks on them and needed a new paint job. And the curtains looked dusty. Besides, they were too country for someone like Rebekah.

Rebekah walked over to a French door that led out to a small fenced yard off the master bedroom and pulled the curtain back, looking outside, then she dusted her hands together.

"Well, what do you think?" asked David.

Rebekah gave him a cool look. Zion knew her well enough. You never revealed you wanted a bargain too enthusiastically or you lost the advantage. "Would the owner be willing to repaint the outside?"

"I can ask her."

"What's she asking for rent?"

David lifted his briefcase and opened the top, pulling out a piece of paper that he handed to Rebekah. She studied it, tapping her finger against her upper lip. "Well, for this, I'm going to need the outside painted. Is she all right with me painting the interior and…" She scuffed a foot on the floor. "…refinishing the floors? I'll pay for that myself if she agrees to repaint the outside."

"I'll ask her." He gave Zion a nod. "Why don't the two of you discuss it and I'll go call Pam?" He hesitated and turned back around. "Have you thought up a name for your business yet?"

Rebekah glanced around the room, then she looked back at him and smiled.

"*Go the Extra Miles*," she said proudly, and Zion felt pretty sure Pam Rosen had a new tenant.

* * *

After David left, leaving them the keys so they could think about the offer, Zion stepped onto the porch of the pink cottage and called for a pizza, then she called Tate. He didn't answer and the call went to voicemail. She pulled the phone away from her ear and disconnected. She hadn't heard from him all day and that was unusual. Since they'd started dating, he called her multiple times a day and they often talked until she fell asleep at night.

She thought to call Logan, but she didn't want to seem desperate. She'd give him until tomorrow. He might be caught up in the case and didn't have the time to talk to her.

She walked back into the cottage and found Rebekah sitting at the table in the conference room, typing on her laptop. Zion sat down across from her. She hadn't seen Rebekah so focused on anything in years. Since coming to

Sequoia, she was a different person. She hadn't talked about fashion or shopping…well, except to exclaim over how much money she'd spent on Jaguar's store today. And since her night with Poole, she'd been as good as her word and hadn't mentioned finding her next man.

"What're you doing?" Zion asked her.

"I'm trying to see how much money I'll have if I cash out my retirement with *Judicious* and sell some stocks I bought a few years ago."

"I hate for you to do either of those things, Becks."

"This place needs updating and I need at least a few months rent in the bank, just until I can get things going, and I'm going to need an advertising budget."

"Let me pay you for what you did for me."

"No, you gave me a place to stay. I'm going to have to stay with you for a little longer, until I can get some furniture and whip this place into shape. At least I don't have to worry about painting the outside." Rebekah braced her chin on her hand. "I want to do this. I want to start a new life and this is perfect for me."

"Okay. Have you thought of calling your mother?"

Rebekah shook her head violently. "No, no, I want to do this myself. She doesn't believe in me. She thinks I'm a loser. Well, then she doesn't get a say in anything to do with me anymore."

"I understand," said Zion, flattening her hands on the table. "How about me? Let me lend you the money."

"Are you kidding me? You're opening another location and you think you can lend me the money. No, sister. I'm doing this myself."

Zion couldn't deny she felt a wash of relief. She was already scared that she was extending herself too much even thinking of the coffee kiosk, not to mention that Dottie was taking the risk with her, but she really wanted Rebekah to have this opportunity.

She looked around the room. "You know, I think this is going to be brilliant when you get it all put together."

"I know. I'm so excited. I haven't been this excited about anything in such a long time." She sighed. "I think I can make something of this. I think I can really build a future here." She laughed. "Who would have thought that? I mean, me in a place like this, but I think this is a second chance for me and I really need that."

Zion reached across and covered her hand with her own. "I felt the same way when I came here. It is a second chance, Becks, and you're going to kill it."

The doorbell rang.

Rebekah gave Zion a questioning look.

"That's dinner."

"What'd you get?" asked Rebekah.

"Pizza," said Zion, pushing herself to her feet.

"Pizza, pulled pork sandwiches, beer. Why do you hate me!" Rebekah called after her and Zion laughed.

CHAPTER 18

Tate stared at the envelope in front of him, balling his hands into fists on either side of it. He realized this was how he dealt with everything. Avoidance had become his modus operandi. When his father's criticism had become too much, he'd joined the force to get away. When his marriage had been falling apart, he ignored it until Cherise told him she was seeing someone else. When Jason died, he quit the force and moved to Sequoia. When Zion had rejected him after he kissed her in her store, he'd avoided her for months.

He scrubbed his hands across his face. Why was he such a monumental coward? Why did he always try to avoid things that upset him? He couldn't think of one thing in his life that he'd forced himself to face, to confront, to overcome. He just ran away.

He heard the buzzer on the door, but he didn't move. Bill Stanley could help the customer. No matter how long he had to sit here, he wasn't budging until he opened this envelope and read the file.

He lifted his head when he heard Bill greet someone, then a female voice filtered back to him. Zion? He'd been avoiding her for the last day or so, not sure what to say to her. Damn it, he was going to push her away too, lose her the way he had Cherise.

She appeared in the doorway of the storeroom, wearing a knit cap on her red hair and a windbreaker that was slick with rain. He gave her a guilty look and folded his arms on the table. She came over and sat down, shrugging out of the jacket and draping it over the back of the chair.

"Are you avoiding me?" she demanded.

He wanted to hug her. He wanted to kiss her. He wanted to tell her he thought she was just about the best thing in his life. "I honestly don't know. I guess I'm avoiding everything." He stared at his tattoo and rubbed his thumb along it. "I just realized that's what I do with everything in my life. I just avoid it."

"Okay," she said, her expression anxious. "Do you want me to leave?"

He quickly shook his head. That was the last thing he wanted. "No, please don't leave." He scraped his fist along his chin. "Poole's been missing for two days now. We found his Camaro in a turn-out on the highway. Someone had set fire to it."

"Wow."

"Bruno Edmonds, the guy at the hospital, died."

Her eyes widened at that. "Poole?"

Tate shrugged. "Not sure. Wilson's waiting for the autopsy. I think he's worried I might be involved with Poole."

"Wilson?"

"Yeah. He questioned me about it."

"Oh boy, that's a lot to deal with." Her eyes dropped to the envelope. "What's that?"

"A file on Poole and the report on the raid that killed Jason."

Zion's gaze rose to him again. "And you haven't opened it yet?"

Tate shook his head. "This is what I do, Zion. I'm a coward."

"How do you figure that? I've seen you face murderers myself. You're not a coward."

"I run when things get too hard. I didn't fight for my marriage, I just gave up. When Jason died, I left the force." He held up a hand and let it fall. "When you told me you needed time to think after I kissed you, I just let it go. I didn't try to change your mind."

"But that's what I wanted, Tate. If you kept pursuing me, it would have been stalking. And regarding your marriage to Cherise, you said yourself it wasn't a love match." She took off the cap and shook out her red hair. "I don't know if I would have done anything different if I had seen my partner get killed, Tate."

He smiled at her. "You're amazing. You know that?"

She shrugged. "Because I'm telling you what you already know?"

"No, because you're not mad at me for not returning your calls."

"I figured you had your reasons."

He reached over and took her hand. "I hate that I keeping running away from things. Maybe Logan's right. Maybe I am a hot mess."

"Well, there are things you can do about that, but right now, you've got to decide what you're going to do about Poole. Does Wilson have any idea where he might have gone?"

"He's got a BOLO out on him. Poole doesn't have a car, he hasn't been back to the cabin, and his stuff is still inside."

"Could he be…" Her voice trailed off, but she lifted her brows speculatively.

"Dead? I'm wondering that myself. At first I thought he might be in the trunk of the Camaro and that's why they set it on fire, but when he didn't turn up there, I can't help but wonder if he's dead over the side of the mountain."

"Hm, that's upsetting. Do you think he killed Edmonds?"

"Why did he go to the hospital when you were there? It wasn't to bring Edmonds flowers."

"No, I guess not," said Zion. Her eyes dropped to the envelope. "You know you have to open it, right?"

"I know."

"You want me to do it?"

"No, I'll do it."

Their eyes met. He knew the time had come. He had to face his demons. He flipped the envelope over and stared at the flap, then he reached for it and tore it away. Closing his eyes, he took a deep breath and shook the contents onto the table.

Two packets of papers slipped out of the opening and lay on the table before him. He swallowed hard. Internal Affairs had debriefed him after the raid went so horribly wrong and he'd answered their questions, feeling detached, wooden, as if this had happened to another person. He hadn't asked them a single question.

But he had questions. He had a lot of questions. Still, he hadn't asked them. He hadn't wanted to know the truth. Someone had called for the raid, someone had sent them in before they were ready, someone had authorized it, but Tate had never asked them who.

He flipped the first packet over and stared at Poole's name on the top line. He drew a deep breath and pulled it to him, reading through his file. There was nothing remarkable about it. Except…Tate frowned. He'd asked to be on the task force that went after the Devil's Tongue. Jason and Tate had been assigned to it, but Poole had requested it. Why in the world would he request a thing like that? He didn't have any particular training in gangs, he hadn't been on any other gang task forces before this.

Tate flipped through Poole's file a second time and still found nothing, except the request for the task force. Staring at the other pile, he reached for that, but a cold sweat peppered his back and his throat felt tight.

There were pictures of the scene, pictures of Jason. He closed his eyes as he flipped past them and came to the narrative of what had happened. Tate read through it, feeling like he'd been transported back through time to that one night, the night his life had changed forever. He could remember it exactly as it was written. The sounds, the smells, the sights. He was back there, huddling behind the cruiser, listening to the hiss of the air as it left the tire, glancing up to see sparks flickering against the night sky from the bulb that had been shot out.

He shook himself from the memories and flipped forward to the background, the justification for why the raid had happened, and he stopped, his hand hovering over the page. He smoothed his fingers down the bold black line. It had been redacted. The name of the person who had asked for the raid, who had provided sufficient information to make the commissioner order it, that name had been marked out.

"What the hell?" said Tate, turning the page and looking at the back, but the ink had obliterated the name completely.

"What?" asked Zion.

"It's been redacted. They blacked out the name."

"Why would they do that?"

"To protect the person who asked for it because it went horribly wrong." Tate scrubbed his hands over his face. "I'm sorry. This whole thing was a wild goose chase. This isn't going to give us any information."

Zion's gaze was steady on him. "What did you believe you'd find?"

Tate shrugged. "That Poole was involved somehow. That he convinced the commissioner to move on the Devil's Tongue."

"But why? Why did you think it was him?"

"Because I can't understand why the Devil's Tongue is coming after him this way. Two men have now lost their lives pursuing him, and I just don't believe it's to get revenge for a kid they used and discarded."

"Why do you think they're here?"

He rubbed the heel of his palm over his forehead and back through his hair. "I think he's got something they want."

"Like what?"

"The Devil's Tongue operated just like all gangs. They sold drugs, they were into racketeering, they sold guns." Tate stopped. "They had so many guns that night, Zion. I mean, they had these guns with magazines that were firing thirty rounds before they had to reload."

"Are you saying he stole something from them?"

Tate's eyes went distant as he thought. He stared at the report in front of him. "They were bringing in trucks just before the raid. That's why I always thought we were authorized to go in, why they sent us in too early. The commissioner thought they were bringing in more guns and they wanted us to stop it."

"What if Poole got a shipment of those guns? How much money could that be?"

"He'd have to sell them on the black market."

"What about at gun shows?"

Tate focused on her. "He could sell them at gun shows and they just had a gun show at the fairgrounds." He shook his head. "But where would he store them? I saw the Camaro. There was nothing in the trunk."

"Maybe he sold them already?"

"He's been under watch pretty much the whole time he's been here."

"What about the cabin?"

"Murphy got a warrant and searched it. She didn't say they found anything."

"What if they missed it? I mean, they don't have your knowledge of Poole. Couldn't you search it under their warrant? You work for the sheriff."

He considered that. He could search it and she was right. Wilson and Murphy knew nothing of Poole. Plus their experience with an investigation was limited. He'd searched a lot more locations on a warrant than they had.

Tate took out his phone and pulled up his text messages.

"What are you doing?"

"I'm gonna tell Murphy I'm going out to Bearpaw Creek and have a look in Poole's cabin."

"By text?"

Tate looked up at her and smiled. "That way she can't talk me out of it."

"She can tell you no on text."

Tate finished and rose to his feet, putting the phone in his pocket. "Oops, I seemed to have missed my cell," he said.

Zion rose also and grabbed her coat. "Should we take your truck or my car?"

He hesitated. "What? No, you're not going with me."

She crossed her arms over her middle. "You wanna think about that a little more. Two sets of eyes are better than one."

"I don't care." He came around the table and put his hands on her shoulders. "Someone torched Poole's car and two men have been killed on this case already."

She placed her hand against his cheek. "Tate, is this how this relationship is going to go now? You never sidelined me before."

"I didn't like you being involved in the last two cases either."

"But I was and if I hadn't been there when Nancy Osborn pointed her gun at Jaguar, he'd be dead."

"Zion…" he began, but she put a finger over his lips. "Do you believe we're equals?"

"That's not fair."

"Just answer me. Do you believe that?"

"You know I do."

"Then let me go with you. It's just to search a cabin. I'm not asking to hitch a ride to the OK Corral."

"The OK Corral?"

"It was the only gunfight I could think of on the spur of the moment."

He laughed, feeling the tension ease inside of him. She was good for him. She made him feel more at ease. "Okay, just to search the cabin, but if I get a feeling there's any danger, you're getting out of there. Are we clear on that?"

"Clear as a bell," she said.

He kissed her. "We'll take the truck. Poole knows it and if he's around, maybe he'll come out of hiding."

"Good thinking," she said.

They walked out into the store. Bill Stanley looked up from reading the *Sequette*. "I've gotta run an errand, Bill," he said, going over to the counter and removing his key fob. Bill and Zion watched him take out his gun and check it, then he placed it at the small of his back.

"Everything okay?" asked Bill skeptically.

Tate took Zion's arm and lifted the counter, so they both could pass through. "Let's just say I'm taking precautions and leave it at that."

As they walked to the door, Tate felt his phone buzz with an incoming message, but he ignored it.

* * *

Tate spotted Lewis' cruiser parked at the far corner of the *Back-of-Beyond Lodge's* parking lot, tucked behind the office, just the nose poking out. He couldn't see the deputy, but he didn't want to tangle with him just yet if Murphy had called him. He drove past the parking lot and turned on a side street.

Zion glanced over her shoulder as they drove away, but she didn't say anything. The rain beat down steadily and the windshield wiper blades whisked back and forth, sweeping the water away.

He pulled to the side of a residential street and parked the truck. "You ready to do a little hiking." Glancing down, he marked that she had on sneakers, not the best for going overland, but better than Rebekah was probably wearing.

She tucked her red hair under the cap until it was out of sight, then pulled the hood of the windbreaker over her head. "Let's go," she said, her eyes dancing with excitement.

He hoped he wasn't going to regret allowing her to come. He noticed that she didn't have a purse and that worried him a little. She had no identification, no wallet, no money if things went the wrong way, but then again, Lewis was sitting in the parking lot, keeping an eye on things.

"Stay close," he told her, then they both got out.

They walked into an open lot next to where Tate had parked and made their way into the forest, headed toward Poole's cabin. Zion kept up until they got bogged down in the brush along the creek.

Bearpaw Creek wasn't very big, but Tate didn't want to go wading in it. Just walking through the forest in the rain made his own cotton hoodie cling to his body in uncomfortable ways. They walked along the creek for a few yards until he found some flat stones that they could jump across.

"Ready?" he called to her over the rain.

"Yep," she said, looking up at him with a grin.

He went first, slipping on the last stone and landing with one foot in the creek. Water soaked into his boot, drenching his jeans up to the knee. Zion giggled behind him. He finally got out on the other side and turned to see her jump nimbly from rock to rock until she hopped up on the bank, a smile teasing the corners of her mouth.

"This isn't supposed to be fun."

She wrapped her arms around his neck and swung him around into a hug. "It's raining, the forest is beautiful, we're on an adventure, and I'm with my guy. How much more fun could it be?"

Tate went still, holding her close. Her guy? He felt his heart beat faster and he kissed her impulsively. She drew reluctantly away.

"We need to get going," she said softly.

He nodded. "In a moment." Pulling her tighter to him, he kissed her again, right there by the creek, in the rain, under the trees. He kissed her and he realized he didn't want to run anymore.

Finally he drew back and they just looked at each other. He smoothed his thumb across her wet cheek. "I like hearing you say that."

"Say what?" she said, smiling.

"That I'm your guy."

Her smile grew softer. "Well, you are, aren't you?"

"Yeah, I am."

She slipped out of his hold and tugged on his hand. "Come on. I'm soaked."

"You're soaked," he said in disbelief, shaking his waterlogged foot.

She giggled and pulled him along.

They reached the cabin, coming up behind it. Tate surveyed the back from the edge of the trees, but he didn't see anyone moving around the perimeter and he didn't see any sign that anyone had been inside in a while. They hurried across the open ground to the backdoor and Tate tried it, but it was locked. A board had been nailed over the broken window.

Walking over to it, he pulled on it and it came away, showing the bedroom where Poole had shot the John Doe. He glanced at Zion. "Think you can get inside if I boost you up?"

She nodded.

"If you hear anything, you get out of there. You hear me?"

"I hear you."

He made a basket with his two hands and held it down for her. She put her foot in it and placed her hand on his shoulder, the other she placed on the window sill above her head. He lifted her and she hoisted her body onto the sill, then slid one leg inside. A moment later, she disappeared from sight.

He held his breath. God, he hoped he wasn't wrong. If Poole was hiding inside and she surprised him, he might lash out, but he didn't think Poole was anywhere in the area. Either he was dead or he was on his way to LA. This was all a wild goose chase.

Zion appeared a moment later, pulling open the back door.

Tate jogged up the steps and into the cabin's kitchen, grateful for a reprieve from the rain. The interior of the cabin was dark and he walked over, turning on the kitchen light. He didn't think anyone would notice it this early in the afternoon and especially coming from the back of the building. He found a flashlight affixed to a charger just under the counter and gave it to Zion.

"I'll take the bedroom. You search the living room," he told her.

"What am I looking for?"

"Anything that looks suspicious. Anything that looks like it was tampered with. Anything that the sheriff's department might have missed."

She nodded and headed off.

Tate went into the bedroom, noticing the rain was slanting through the broken window and getting the floor wet. He started in the closet, feeling the floor for any irregularities or bumps. He knocked his knuckles on all four walls and dragged a chair over so he could inspect the shelf. He found nothing.

Next he pulled out all of the drawers on the nightstands and the dresser, turning them upside down, then he pulled them all away from the wall, and searched the wall and floor behind it. He still found nothing.

Next he turned to the bed, throwing off the bedclothes and tilting the mattress up. He searched it for holes, looked beneath the bed, pulled it away from the wall and completing the same search all over again. Still nothing.

Then he tackled the bathroom, but there wasn't much in there. He lifted the top on the toilet tank and looked inside, then scoured the tiles to see if any were loose. His search was in vain.

Heading for the living room, he helped Zion look. They checked the seat cushions on all the furniture, even stuck a hand up the flue of the fireplace. Tate searched the walls and floors for irregularities, but once again they came up empty handed.

The only place left to search was the kitchen. They went through all of the cabinets and looked under the sink. Tate even went down into the yard and searched the garbage can, but it was empty. Finally, he pulled open the electrical box and when he found nothing, he went back into the cabin, standing in the doorway, feeling such frustration.

Zion watched him carefully, a look of worry on her face.

His phone vibrated again in his pocket and he took it out. A text from Murphy flashed on his screen. *Tell me where you are.* He exhaled and shook his waterlogged boot.

"What's say we go get something hot to drink and grab some late lunch?"

She gave him a commiserate smile, coming over to rub her hand down his arm. "I'm sorry, Tate. I thought we might be onto something."

He shook his head. "It was silly to think that the sheriff would have missed something if there was something to find." He put his arm around her shoulders and turned her toward the back door. "Come on. I'm buying."

"Well, in that case," she said, leaning her head on his shoulder. She hesitated as they neared the back door, laughing. "Did I tell you about the painting my mother sent me?" She pointed to a cheesy print in a thick wooden frame hanging on the wall just to the left of the back door.

Tate glanced at the bowl of fruit on a brown background. Of all the kitschy stuff in this cabin, this was the worst.

Zion slipped out of his hold and stopped beside it, staring up at the garage sale find. "Rebekah and I thought the package held a nude and we were afraid to open it."

"We're going to have to talk about this nude business. That's twice now you've mentioned it."

She giggled. "Anyway, I finally had to just rip the butcher paper off and see what it was. I didn't even recognize it at first. It was a bowl of fruit, but I'm still not sure if I have it right side up or not."

Tate laughed with her, thinking how much he liked her mother.

Zion's laughter died and she looked at the floor beneath the painting.

"What is it?" he asked, moving closer to her.

"Sawdust," she said, pointing at the floorboard.

Tate peered down as well, then his eyes rose to the painting. In a swift motion, he lifted it off its hook and settled it on the kitchen table. A hole had been cut into the pine paneling between the kitchen and the bedroom. Stuffed inside the hole between the two-by-fours was a black gym bag.

Tate exchanged a look with Zion, then he grabbed a dishtowel off the stove and covered his hands with it, reaching in to get the bag. He drew it out, feeling the weight of it, and set it on the table. Zion followed him over, watching as he found the zipper and pulled it back.

Tugging the two halves of the bag open, Tate and Zion stared down at stacks of hundred dollar bills. Glancing up at her, he felt his heart hammering in his ears. "Well, I think we just figured out what the Devil's Tongue is after."

Zion nodded and took a step back. "You'd better answer Murphy, Tate," she said.

* * *

Tate watched as Wilson counted the money out onto the table in the cabin. Zion leaned against the counter, hugging her arms around herself. They were both still soaked and she was shivering in the cool cabin.

"Well, there's a cool $25,000 here," said Wilson, setting down the last stack and putting his hands on his hips.

"Just $25,000?" asked Tate. He couldn't deny he was disappointed. He was really hoping they'd discovered a hell of a lot more than that. It would explain why the Devil's Tongue was after Poole, but he didn't think they'd come this far and risk so much for a paltry $25,000.

Wilson tipped the hat to the back of his head and looked up at Murphy. "Any stolen vehicles reported in the last 48 hours?"

"None," said Murphy. "I've had Jones monitoring it since he's on desk duty."

"Good." Wilson looked over at Tate. "Where the hell do you think Poole got to without wheels?"

"He's either dead or in LA. He could have hitchhiked into Fresno and got on an airplane."

"Check flight records," Wilson told Murphy. "And bus station ticket offices."

Tate scratched the back of his neck. "It doesn't make sense, Sheriff. Why would the Devil's Tongue send two men after Poole for $25,000?"

"You tell me. That can't even be a drop in the bucket for them."

"What if they did it to save face?" asked Zion. "I mean, they're a street gang. They just can't let people steal from them without retribution."

"Yeah, but for $25,000?" said Tate again. He just didn't buy it. He was still missing something.

"You think Poole's a dirty cop?" asked Wilson.

Tate sighed. "I don't want to believe that, but it's getting harder and harder to ignore. First the raid goes bad, then he shoots the kid, then he kills a guy here in this cabin."

"And possibly one in the hospital."

"When is Davenport finishing the autopsy?"

"I hope soon."

Tate felt guilty about that. If he'd told Wilson what Zion had seen the day she saw it, would Bruno Edmonds still be alive?

"What's our next step?"

Wilson scratched at his widow's peak. "I wish I knew, but for now, why don't you head back to town? Lewis can drive you to your car." He jerked his chin at Zion. "Your partner in crime looks like she's half-frozen."

Tate pulled Zion against his side, feeling her shiver. He kissed her forehead. "Come on, Sherlock," he said. "Let's go get you a shot of whiskey to warm you up."

She nodded and let him lead her from the cabin.

CHAPTER 19

Zion changed into dry clothes and came out into the living room. Rebekah had gone to view the pink cottage again. Zion knew it was a big decision and Rebekah just wasn't sure she could swing it, but she refused to take any help. She desperately wanted to do it on her own and Zion admired that determination.

Tate was sitting on the couch, holding Cleo. The kitten had stretched herself across his lap on her back, sound asleep. He looked up and gave Zion a smile. She sank onto the couch next to him and stroked her hand down Cleo's belly.

"Don't you want to go home and change into something dry?"

"I'm okay," he said. "Cleo had other ideas."

She rested her hand on his shoulder. "What are you thinking? Where do you think Poole is?"

"He's probably gone back to LA."

"He'd leave $25,000 here?"

"I'm sure he figured he wouldn't be able to get it with a sheriff's cruiser sitting in the parking lot."

"You didn't think $25,000 was enough money for the gang to come after him. Do you have any other theories?"

Tate shook his head. "That amount of money is a drop in the bucket for a gang that's moving drugs and guns, but it's about the right amount for them to pay him off."

"You think he was working with the Devil's Tongue?"

"I do. Why would the LAPD redact the name of who authorized the raid? They got that information from someone and it had to be someone on the task force. Jason didn't do it because we just didn't know what sort of firepower they had and he'd never move in early like that. I didn't do it, so Poole was the only other detective that was working with us."

His phone rang and Cleo blinked, rolling over. As Tate shifted to pull the phone out of his pocket, Cleo got up and jumped down, flouncing away. Tate glanced at the display, then pressed the icon with his thumb and held it to his ear.

"Sheriff?"

Zion watched the rain falling as Tate listened on the line.

"Okay, thank you. Yeah, I appreciate that." He disconnected the call and sighed. "Bruno Edmonds died of an embolism, a blood clot the medical examiner thinks was from the trauma of his gunshot wounds or the surgery."

Zion felt a wash of relief. The thought that she might have inadvertently contributed to a man's death by not alerting the sheriff of Poole's whereabouts had been bothering her. She eased closer to Tate.

"You know, we're alone for the first time in a long time. Logan's at school and Rebekah's at the *Cater 2 U* building." She stroked the back of his hair. "Maybe I can take your mind off the case."

His dark eyes lowered to her mouth and he licked his bottom lip, then he placed his hands on her waist and dragged her across his lap. She laughed and wrapped her arms around his neck, leaning close to him.

"It might be hours before she comes home," she whispered against his mouth.

He made a growling noise and the next thing she knew, they were kissing, frantically, trying to get closer to one another. When she was just about to suggest they move to the bedroom, her phone rang.

She pulled away and looked at it, sitting on the table. Tate's mouth moved down to her neck, but Zion could see Rebekah's name flashing on the screen. "Hold on," she said. "That's Rebekah."

"She can wait," he said, rising and lifting her with him, setting her on the floor. His hands snaked under her shirt at the small of her back, roving upward.

Zion looked over her shoulder at the phone, but she couldn't read the text message. If Rebekah was writing to tell her she was coming home, it was going to put a damper on Zion's afternoon plans. She was a little surprised she was ready to move to this next step with Tate so quickly, but it just felt right.

"Let me just see what she wants," she said, turning and grabbing the phone.

He wrapped his arms around her waist and hauled her back into him, nuzzling his face in her hair. "She'll be okay for a little while on her own."

Zion picked up the phone and thumbed it on, fighting not to be distracted by Tate's hands. The text message made her frown and she eased out of Tate's hold. "Hold on, please," she said, frowning.

He exhaled in frustration and scrubbed his hands over his face as Zion stared at the message.

I need you to come here. I want to talk about everything. It's important, Zion. Please come.

Zion felt a sinking in her gut. Something didn't feel right. Rebekah never called anyone by their real names and if it was this important, she would have just called so that she could guilt Zion into dropping everything for her.

"What?" asked Tate.

Zion glanced up at him. "Rebekah wants me to come to *Cater 2 U*. She's thinking of renting it for her business."

"Why does she want you to come out there?"

Zion shook her head, then she typed back *Is everything okay?* She waited for a response, but when none came, she looked up at Tate. "This isn't like her, Tate. She never calls me by my first name. She never calls anyone by their first name."

Tate's expression grew grim. "Does she say why she wants you to come out there?"

"Just to talk," said Zion. She went over to the closet and took out a dry raincoat, slipping it on, then she grabbed her purse and car keys. "I've got to go."

Tate stopped her at the door. "I'm going with you," he demanded.

"Okay," she said. She had a bad feeling about this and didn't really want to go by herself. He lifted his damp hoodie off the couch and slipped it on, then they walked out to the truck parked at the curb. Climbing in, he turned the truck back down the street and they headed out of town.

They didn't talk much as they approached *Cater 2 U.* Tate pulled into the tiny parking lot next to Rebekah's Spider and turned off the engine, then he reached across Zion to open the glove compartment and take out the gun he'd stored there. He tucked it at the small of his back and pulled his hoodie over it to conceal it from sight.

Shifting on the seat, he forced Zion to meet his gaze. "It's probably nothing, but I want you to wait here while I go in first."

"Tate, I have a bad feeling about this."

He clasped her hand. "It's okay, Zion. I'm just going to take a look around, then I'll call you. Just wait here, please."

She nodded. "Be careful."

She watched him walk away, feeling a knot forming in her gut. Taking out her phone, she stared at the display, but there were no more messages from Rebekah. When she looked up, her eyes fell on the gate that led to the little backyard off the master bedroom. She looked toward the front of the building, but Tate had disappeared from view.

Besides Tate's truck and the Spider, there were no other cars anywhere around. This was silly, she told herself. Rebekah was just being dramatic and wanted to run everything by Zion again. Zion was basing her feelings on the fact that Rebekah had called her by her name. That was ridiculous.

She pushed open the truck and climbed out, shutting it again, then she started toward the front of the building, but something stopped her. Tate should have called her by now. It wouldn't have taken thirty seconds to go inside, find Rebekah, and text Zion to let her know everything was okay.

Zion pressed a hand to her belly and fought the wave of anxiety that went through her. Then she turned around and walked to the gate, gently pulling on the latch to open it.

* * *

Tate eased up to the door of *Cater 2 U* and found it slightly ajar. That wasn't good. He pushed it open, reaching behind him to curl his hand around the grip of his gun, then he eased inside. The door opened onto a living room that had been converted into a waiting room. He peered around at the antique furnishings, then his eyes tracked over the beaded curtain leading to another part of the cottage.

He crept across the floor, but as his foot came down on a floorboard, it creaked beneath his weight. He heard someone whimper beyond the beaded curtain, then a male voice spilled out. "Come in already. I know you're out there. I heard the truck pull up."

Poole.

Tate drew the gun and held it at his side as he crossed the room. He parted the curtain and saw Poole standing in the middle of the room, holding Rebekah in front of him. He had his hand wound in her hair and he had a gun pointed at her temple. Directly behind him was a hallway and to his right the kitchen.

Rebekah's dark eyes widened when she saw Tate. Tate eased through the curtain, keeping his gun at his side. "What's going on, Poole?"

"Where's the redhead? Tell her to come out here too."

"I made her stay home. She was suspicious when she read the text, so I came by myself."

"Always the Boy Scout," muttered Poole. "Even when your wife was banging the gardener, you gave her whatever she wanted."

"Why are you doing this?" asked Tate.

"You found the money, didn't you?" Poole said.

Tate nodded. "In the wall. There was only $25,000. Hardly enough for what you're going to face."

Poole laughed. He had dark circles under his eyes and his clothes were dirty and damp. A puddle had formed on the floor beneath him. "Always the Boy Scout," he repeated. "You know what, Tater Tot, I liked Jason so much better. He knew how to have a good time, but you, you were always such a tool."

"What do you think is going to happen now, Keith? The sheriff has a BOLO out on you. You aren't going to get far."

"I need your help. That's all I need."

Tate frowned. "My help? Why would I help you?"

Poole rubbed his face against Rebekah's and she shuddered, trying to pull away. "You don't want me to blow her brains out all over this room, do you?"

Tate's eyes met Rebekah's. She shivered, but she wasn't crying. He admired her strength. "Hasn't there been enough death, Keith? Hasn't there been enough blood shed?"

"You don't know what you're talking about."

"You took more than $25,000 from the Devil's Tongue, didn't you?"

Poole's expression grew cunning. "That's right."

"Where's the money?"

"Off-shore accounts. I just kept enough to get me out when the time came. That's why I need your help. I need you to get me out of the country."

"I can't do that. There's a BOLO out on you."

"You can drive me across the border. That's all I need. Give me a few hundred bucks and drive me into Mexico or Canada, it doesn't matter which one. From there, I'll do the rest."

"Why would I do that?" said Tate, wearily. Even though he'd never liked Poole, it hurt to see what he'd become. "And what makes you think the Devil's Tongue won't follow you wherever you go?"

"Then I'll keep taking them out one at a time. I just need to get out of the country, Tater Tot." He gave him a grim smile. "We were brothers in blue, you and me. You owe me this much."

"I don't owe you a damn thing, Poole."

"But you do. I saved your life."

"You keep saying that, but how? Explain it."

"Later. When you get me out of here. We can go right now. We'll walk out and get in your truck and we'll head for the border. Again, I don't care which one."

"And then I become a hunted man."

"I'll make it worth your time. I promise you."

"How?" Tate shook his head. "How are you going to make it worth my time?" He had to keep Poole talking. When Tate didn't come back or text Zion, she'd realize something was wrong and she'd call Wilson. He just had to buy time.

"I have more than a million in an offshore account. Think about it, Tate. Think about all the hours we put in, the risks we took. Think about Jason's dead body. You deserve better than this. I deserve better than this."

"So you stole from the Devil's Tongue and you think that makes you any better than they are."

"They're criminals. They sold drugs and guns. They held people up for money."

"And you stole from them."

"It's not like that."

"No, how is it, Poole? Explain it to me." He eased around until he was facing Poole directly. "How is it justified what you did?"

"I did it to protect myself. After all the years we put into the force, what do we get? We get a measly little pension and a certificate, then they send us on our way to re-live the shit we've seen again and again and again until we die."

"How did you get in with the Devil's Tongue? How did they give you access to their money?"

"These gangs, they all want the same thing, and if you provide it, they'll help you out."

"They paid you?"

"Some of it. It was so simple. All they wanted to know was what we were doing and when. I invested those payments, but the risks were high. Really high, so I took a little more here and there. I helped myself and now I can help you."

"How?" Tate realized Poole was serious. He believed what he was saying. And to be honest, he had a point. It wasn't a strong point, it wasn't an ethical point, but it was a point.

Poole nodded. "Finally. Now we're getting somewhere."

Rebekah's eyes bore into Tate's. He deliberately looked away from her.

"What are you offering?" Tate asked, genuinely intrigued. Poole couldn't possibly think this would end well, unless…unless he convinced Tate to help him.

"Help me get across the border and I'll give you a quarter of a million. It's enough to let you start over fresh. It can't be traced, I made sure of that. We'll set up an offshore account of your own and I'll wire the money to you. You can still play shopkeeper for a while if you want, but when you need it, the money will be there."

Tate narrowed his eyes. Clever. Poole had made the one offer that most people would have to consider no matter what their loyalties or morals were – a no strings attached way to get financial security for himself. When he hesitated longer than he should have, Rebekah's expression grew stunned.

* * *

Zion found the French door to the master bedroom open. She eased up to it and pushed it in, then she stepped inside and hugged the wall. She could hear two male voices in the other part of the cottage and she hurried to the bedroom door, peering through the crack into the hallway.

A man stood with his back to the hallway, another person in front of him. He held something in his hand against the other person's temple. Zion looked around for a weapon, spotted a brass lamp on the floor, and picked it up. Thankfully, it wasn't plugged in.

She came back to the door and peered out. She couldn't see who the man was holding in front of him, but looking through his legs she noticed the Ferragamo pumps. *Rebekah.* Then she went still, listening to the voices.

"What are you offering?" came Tate's voice.

Zion caught her breath. Holy hell, what was he saying? She felt her heart hammering and she was suddenly sick to her stomach. He couldn't mean what that sounded like. He had to be planning something. Didn't he? But she realized she didn't know him that well. They'd been friends for the last six months, and they'd been dating for a few weeks, but what did she really know about him? She'd only just recently found out about his partner's death and she'd known all along that he had secrets. Dark secrets.

She remembered the phone in her pocket. She took it out and sent a text to Sheriff Wilson. Then she pressed her ear back to the door, straining to hear over the rain pounding on the roof.

"Help me get across the border and I'll give you a quarter of a million. It's enough to let you start over fresh. It can't be traced, I made sure of that. We'll set up an offshore account of your own and I'll wire the money to you. You can still play shopkeeper for a while if you want, but when you need it, the money will be there."

"I'm listening."

"What?" sputtered Rebekah. "This maniac murdered people!"

"Shut up!" Poole shouted, shaking her.

Rebekah whimpered and Tate moved into sight, holding up one of his hands. "Don't hurt her, Poole. Look at me. Talk to me. I want to know what you have planned."

Poole stopped shaking Rebekah. Zion tightened her hold on the lamp. She knew Poole had a gun and Tate had a gun, while she had a lamp. What the hell was she going to do now?

"We head for Mexico. It's quicker. They're less likely to question us going in. Once we're on the other side, we'll get plane tickets to the Caymans. That's where my money is. We'll set up an account and I'll have them wire the quarter million to you."

"How will we get plane tickets? They'll be monitoring your accounts," said Tate in a reasonable voice.

Zion felt as if her heart were breaking. This couldn't be true. She couldn't be such a bad judge of character.

"You'll have to buy them."

"Which makes me an accomplice?"

"What's here for you, Tate? Seriously? The sad hardware store or the cute redhead? You can have a million of them somewhere else. This is a chance to leave it all behind. Start over fresh. No more nightmares."

Zion's heart raced. What if he took it? What if he walked out with Poole? How could this be happening?

"Okay," Tate said, his voice strange, foreign to Zion.

She felt her legs weaken. Okay? How could one word cut her so deeply? She realized that some part of her, some silly, foolish part had actually invested in this relationship, had believed they were building something together.

"But I'm gonna need something from you first, Poole. A show of good faith."

Zion forced herself to continue listening.

"We're wasting time. We need to get out of here. I'm sure the redhead's waiting to hear from you, isn't she?"

"She does whatever I tell her," Tate said levelly. "Don't worry about her."

Rebekah struggled, but Poole shook her again. Tate took a step closer to him.

"Stop!" he said. "Look at me, Keith. We need to focus right now. One wrong step, one miscalculation, and it's all over."

"Okay. You're right."

"I need a show of faith, Keith. In order for me to trust you, I need you to do something for me."

"I'm going to give you a quarter mill. You don't need anything else."

"I need you to let the girl go."

Poole went still. Zion held her breath, listening to the weighted silence. Finally, Poole made a growl.

"Ah, Tater Tot, I really thought for a moment that we had something. I really did."

"We do," said Tate quickly. "She's a liability. We need to let her go."

"She's not going anywhere. She's seen me. She's heard everything."

"I'm not hurting a woman, Poole. You should know that."

"I really thought we had something here," said Poole. He turned the gun and pointed it at Tate.

Zion knew she had to do something. She lifted the lamp and reached for the knob, ready to charge Poole, but suddenly her cell phone rang.

Zion froze.

* * *

"I really thought we had something here," said Poole. He turned the gun and pointed it at Tate. Tate started to lift his own gun, but suddenly a shrill ringing sounded from the master bedroom.

Poole's gaze whipped behind him, the gun shifting away just the slightest amount. Tate yanked his own gun up and pointed it at Poole's head, but Rebekah burst into action.

She kicked backward and slammed her foot against Poole's shin. He grunted and bent over, then she rammed her elbow into his face, snapping his head back. Blood sprayed from his nose and he staggered, but before he could right himself, she swung her leg around and caught him in the throat, dropping him to his back like a sack of cement. The gun skittered out of his hand and before Tate could move to grab it, Zion tore out of the bedroom, brandishing a lamp.

Tate winced as Rebekah kicked Poole between the legs and Zion threw the lamp at him, then she grabbed the gun and pointed it at him, bracing it with both hands. Poole writhed, trying to get away, but Rebekah stamped on his stomach, then when he doubled over, she kicked him in the head again.

Tate shoved the gun behind his back and caught Rebekah around the waist, lifting her up and swinging her around. She kicked and struggled in his grasp as he set her down behind him, but she stopped when the deputies streamed into the room, pointing their weapons at Poole.

* * *

Zion stood beside Tate and Sheriff Wilson, watching through the two-way glass as Murphy took a seat across from Poole. They hadn't said much to each other after the sheriff arrived, in fact Zion didn't know what to say. Poole had been taken into custody and Rebekah had thrown her arms around Zion, hugging her frantically.

When Sheriff Wilson asked them all to come back to the sheriff's office, Rebekah had insisted Zion ride with her in the Spider. Rebekah had gone off to let a medic check her over, but when Zion had last seen her, she'd been bubbling over with adrenaline.

"This is your one chance to tell us what happened," said Murphy.

Poole's face was swollen, one eye shut, pieces of tissue shoved up his nose to stop the bleeding. He had a bag of ice that he held between his legs. "I have nothing to say. I want a lawyer."

Murphy clenched her jaw. "Okay, but he's gonna take awhile to get here and you probably need to get to the hospital. Why don't we talk a little bit, then I can have you transported. They have some nice painkillers there." She chuckled. "Man, you got your ass handed to you by a girl."

"I'm not saying anything," repeated Poole.

Beside Zion, Tate's hands curled into fists.

"Prison isn't kind to cops, especially cops that cross a gang. How long do you think you're going to last in there?"

Poole bent over and spit blood onto the floor. Zion shuddered. No matter what she thought of him, he needed a doctor. Rebekah had beaten the hell out of him. Zion couldn't believe she'd been holding all of that inside.

"I say you last a week at most. Then one of them is gonna shank you. I could get you protective custody. I could make it easier on you."

"I'm not saying anything," said Poole.

Wilson blew out air, then he rapped his knuckles on the glass.

Murphy shook her head, but she motioned to a uniform standing off to the side and they pulled Poole to his feet, moving him toward the door. Zion felt disappointment. She knew Tate wanted more closure than this. She knew he wanted to understand the role Poole had played in the raid that cost Jason his life.

As they left the interrogation room, Tate suddenly moved. He burst into the hallway and slammed into Poole, taking him back into the wall, his forearm pressed against Poole's windpipe. With his arms cuffed behind him, Poole couldn't defend himself.

Murphy and the deputy tried to pull Tate away, but Tate slammed Poole back into the wall. "What did you do? Was it you?"

"Tate!" shouted Wilson, pushing past Zion.

Tate threw Murphy and the deputy off and rammed Poole's head against the wall. "Did you tell them for us to raid the tenement that night? Were you the one that gave them the information?" He took out his gun and pointed it at Poole's head. Poole closed his eyes and turned his head away.

Everyone went still. Murphy and the deputy each had their hands on their guns and Wilson had moved between them, his back to Poole. Blood and spittle ran off Poole's chin.

"Tate, don't do this!" said Wilson.

"I want answers! I deserve answers!"

"Yes!" spat Poole. "Yes! I had to cover it up. The Devil's Tongue knew I stole from them and I had to end them!"

"You told the commissioner we should go in?"

"I told him they had children in there. That they were human trafficking. I didn't have a choice. I had to destroy them. They put a hit out on me."

"What about the kid you shot? Davonte Walsh?"

"He came after me. He wanted the bounty they put out on my head. I didn't have a choice."

"He was fourteen!"

"He wanted to kill me."

Tate shook his head. "You got Jason killed!"

"But I saved your life! I saved you!"

"You keep saying that! How? How did you save my life!"

Poole looked at him through his one good eye. "I blew up the meth lab."

Tate's hand dropped. Wilson grabbed the gun from him and shoved him back.

"Get him out of here!" he shouted at Murphy.

Murphy nodded, then they turned Poole toward the exit. Poole looked back over his shoulder at Tate, but a moment later, he was lost to sight. Zion didn't know what to do. Tears filled her eyes.

Wilson shoved Tate into the viewing room and pushed him into a chair. "What the hell were you thinking?"

Tate stared at the floor. "Thirteen people died in that explosion. Women and children."

Wilson hunkered down in front of him. "I know, son, but you can't go pulling guns on people. You need help. You need to see someone. I can't have you back here, working with us until you do."

Tate looked up at him, then he nodded. "I understand. What about Logan? Are you going to have Logan taken away from me?"

"I'm taking the gun you have at the house too, but I'm not going to say anything to the social worker. You need Logan as much as he needs you."

Tate swallowed hard. "Thank you. Thank you for that."

Wilson patted Tate's knee. "After what you've been through, I get it. I can't have it happen in my precinct, but I get it." He pushed himself to his feet and tipped his hat to Zion. "Let me know when you get a counselor, you hear?"

Tate nodded, staring at the floor.

Wilson gave Zion a weary smile, then he walked from the room.

Zion didn't know what to do. This was the very thing she'd feared. The very reason she'd avoided Tate all these months. He had demons. Desperate, dark, and violent demons and they were eating him alive.

She knew she should run. She knew she should walk away from this while she could. It would be safer that way. It would be better for her. Instead, she walked over to him and touched his shoulder.

He looked up at her and his eyes were anguished, the demons lurking there just under the surface. Without hesitation, Zion sank onto his lap and wrapped her arms around him, then she pulled his head down to her breast and she held on because…well, because there was nothing else she could do.

EPILOGUE

The weather was perfect for the first annual Sequoia Fangtastic Howl-o-ween Monster Bash. Zion laughed as Dee dunked his whole head into the barrel and came up triumphantly with an apple in his teeth. He danced around, shaking water off like a dog. Dottie swatted him.

Dee wore a knit cap over his unruly blond hair and a red and white striped t-shirt. Dottie swatted him again. "I'm gonna make it impossible to find Waldo, if you don't stop it?"

Zion laughed again. Dottie was dressed as a cupcake. As they walked down the street to the concert area, she cut a path through the crowd with her costume. Zion had opted for a witch, but when she'd tried to put the fake nose on, Rebekah had thrown a fit. She snatched it away and flushed it down the toilet, saying no friend of hers was wearing warts. Of course, Rebekah had gone as a fairy princess, wings, wand and all.

Zion stopped on the edge of the makeshift dance floor beside Dottie and Dee, watching everyone boogying down to *Anaconda Glee Club*. Of course, Jaguar was dressed as a pirate. Zion had to admit he made a gorgeous pirate and the costume seemed made for him. Betty and Barney Brown shimmied past, wearing Tweedle Dee and Tweedle Dumb costumes.

"Wanna dance?" Dee asked Dottie.

"You betcha," she said, taking his hand and letting him lead her out into the crowd.

Daryl appeared beside her. He looked dashing dressed as Batman. "Come on, you can't just stand on the sidelines."

She let him lead her onto the street and they found Rebekah in the middle of the crowd, shimmering sexily to the music across from David Bennett. David was dressed as

Dracula and he wasn't dancing as much as he was bopping up and down in place.

Zion laughed and let Daryl swing her around. Across from them were Jim Dawson and his wife Minnie. Zion couldn't help but giggle when she realized they were dressed aptly as Mickey and Minnie Mouse. Beatrice and Carmen were dancing together right in front of the stage, wearing Raggedy Ann and Andy costumes that Zion suspected they'd sewn themselves.

Trixie shimmied past with her husband. The sexy middle aged woman was dressed as a cat and she made a hissing noise at Zion, showing her claws. Zion gave her a witch's laugh. When the song ended, she eased her way back through the crowd and found Dwayne and Cheryl Ford by the reception table, pouring themselves a glass of wine.

Dwayne was Frankenstein and Cheryl was his bride. Zion kissed Cheryl's cheek. Cheryl could make the Bride of Frankenstein look sexy. "Are you having fun?" she asked them.

"How do you women wear heels?" said Dwayne, holding up his huge stacked heel boot. "These are killing me."

Cheryl patted his chest and shook her head at Zion. "Always complaining."

Zion laughed and poured her own wine.

"Sliders!" said Dwayne, looking over to the booth his busboy Pedro had set up across the square. "I'm getting me some of those."

Cheryl and Zion watched him heaping his plate full of the tiny burgers. "Pedro wants to open a restaurant. Thank you for suggesting that some of the vendors offer food samples."

"No problem. If he wants to open a restaurant, why's he working as a busboy?"

"He asked Dwayne to show him how to run the business while he gets a stake up."

"That was smart. Maybe Rebekah can help him set things up."

"That's a great idea," said Cheryl. "How are things with her business? Has she moved out yet?"

"Not yet. She wants to do the updates on the cottage before she moves in."

"I wondered if she might back out after what happened in there."

"Are you kidding?" said Zion, sipping her wine. "She says the memories remind her she can do anything."

Cheryl laughed. "Where's Tate? I didn't see him out here."

"He went to LA to talk to his partner's widow. He said he might make it back in time, but I think his flight was delayed."

Cheryl gave Zion a serious look. "How's he doing? He hasn't been by the barbecue lately."

"He's better, Cheryl. He agreed to start seeing Dr. Martin for therapy. I think it's been good."

Cheryl nodded, then she slipped her arm through Zion's. "How about the two of you?"

"We're good. I mean, we haven't gotten any privacy…" Zion blushed and looked down, making Cheryl smile. "…but I care about him a lot."

"Who do you care about?" came a voice behind her.

Zion turned and blinked in surprise, then she and Cheryl both burst into laughter. Throwing her arms around the man dressed in the blue overalls and red shirt and red cap, she kissed him on the mouth. His thick black moustache tickled her lip and she made a face.

"Welcome home, Mario," said Cheryl wryly. "I'll just go pull Frankenstein away from the sliders." And she ambled off.

Tate swung Zion around and kissed her again.

"I like you better clean shaven," she said.

He nuzzled her neck with the moustache and she giggled. "You seen Luigi around?"

Zion pointed over her shoulder at the dance floor where Logan was jumping up and down next to Tallah, who'd come dressed as a red crayon. When the two teenagers turned and sang the lyrics in each other's faces, Logan's moustache tilted to the side. Tate and Zion laughed.

Turning back to Tate, Zion straightened his own moustache. "How was the trip?"

"Hard," he said, "but it was good. I should have done it a long time ago."

He looked around at the activity on all sides and sighed. "But I'm not gonna lie, it sure does feel good to be home."

Then he grabbed her hand and dragged her with him into the middle of the crowd in front of the band and twirled her around and around until she was dizzy. When he set her down again, she clung to his shoulders and laughed, happier than she'd been in a long time.

Especially when he spun her away from him, brought her back, and dipped her, kissing her silly.

THE END

Now that you've finished, visit ML Hamilton at her website: authormlhamilton.net and sign up for her newsletter. Receive free offers and discounts once you sign up!

The Complete *Peyton Brooks' Mysteries* Collection:

Murder in the Painted Lady, Volume 0
Murder on Potrero Hill Volume 1
Murder in the Tenderloin Volume 2
Murder on Russian Hill Volume 3
Murder on Alcatraz Volume 4
Murder in Chinatown Volume 5
Murder in the Presidio Volume 6
Murder on Treasure Island Volume 7

***Peyton Brooks FBI* Collection:**

Zombies in the Delta Volume 1
Mermaids in the Pacific Volume 2
Werewolves in London Volume 3
Vampires in Hollywood Volume 4
Mayan Gods in the Yucatan Volume 5
Haunts in Bodie Volume 6

***Zion Sawyer Cozy Mystery* Collection:**

Cappuccino Volume 1
Café Au Lait Volume 2
Espresso Volume 3

The Complete *Avery Nolan Adventure* Collection:

Swift as a Shadow Volume 1
Short as Any Dream Volume 2
Brief as Lightning Volume 3
Momentary as a Sound Volume 4

The *World of Samar* Collection:

The Talisman of Eldon Emerald Volume 1
The Heirs of Eldon Volume 2
The Star of Eldon Volume 3
The Spirit of Eldon Volume 4
The Sanctuary of Eldon Volume 5
The Scions of Eldon Volume 6
The Watchers of Eldon Volume 7

The Followers of Eldon Volume 8
The Apostles of Eldon Volume 9
The Renegade of Eldon Volume 10
The Fugitive of Eldon Volume 11

Stand Alone Novels:

Ravensong
Serenity
Jaguar

Ready for the next *Zion Sawyer Cozy Mystery*?
Coming soon!

As snow begins to fall in Sequoia, things have settled into a routine. Both Jaguar and Rebekah have opened their businesses, the merchants on Main Street are preparing for the Christmas sales season, and Zion has moved forward with her plans to open a second *Caffeinator* location. Her relationship with Tate has progressed, even if they find it difficult to get time alone, and Logan seems to be settling in.

Just when they think everything is nearly perfect, a mysterious man appears and throws everything into chaos, threatening Logan's future and dragging Zion and Tate into a new mystery. With the stakes as high as the snow drifts, Zion must help Tate solve a murder that reminds her of the reason she came to Sequoia in the first place.

Made in the USA
Las Vegas, NV
06 December 2021

36272375R00167